From Spring to Spring

by the same author

A TRAVELLER IN TIME
THE SAM PIG STORYBOOK
ADVENTURES OF SAM PIG
FAIRY TALES
(chosen by Kathleen Lines)
STORIES FOR CHRISTMAS
(chosen by Kathleen Lines)

Some Faber Fanfare titles

FAVOURITE TALES OF HANS ANDERSEN   translated by M. R. James
A TIME TO LAUGH: Funny Stories for Children   edited by Sara and
Stephen Corrin
A WHITE HORSE WITH WINGS   Anthea Davies
PEACOCK PIE: A Book of Rhymes   Walter de la Mare
TALES TOLD AGAIN   Walter de la Mare
TIMI   Barbara C. Freeman
THREE GAY TALES FROM GRIMM   Wanda Gág
GRIMBOLD'S OTHER WORLD   Nicholas Stuart Gray
MAINLY IN MOONLIGHT   Nicholas Stuart Gray
JESSICA ON HER OWN   Mary K. Harris
THE PRIME OF TAMWORTH PIG   Gene Kemp
TAMWORTH PIG SAVES THE TREES   Gene Kemp
TALES OF TROY AND GREECE   Andrew Lang
THE ROUT OF THE OLLAFUBS   K. G. Lethbridge
MELANIE BROWN GOES TO SCHOOL   Pamela Oldfield
MELANIE BROWN CLIMBS A TREE   Pamela Oldfield
TIMOTHY AND TWO WITCHES   Margaret Storey
THE STONE WIZARD   Margaret Storey
THE DRAGON'S SISTER and TIMOTHY TRAVELS   Margaret Storey
FROM SPRING TO SPRING: Stories of the Four Seasons   Alison Uttley

From Spring to Spring

Stories of the Four Seasons

Alison Uttley

CHOSEN BY KATHLEEN LINES

illustrated by Shirley Hughes

Faber Fanfares

First published in 1978
by Faber and Faber Limited
3 Queen Square London WC1
First published in Fanfares edition 1980
Printed in Great Britain by
Jarrold and Sons Ltd, Norwich

British Library Cataloguing in Publication Data

Uttley, Alison
    From spring to spring. – (Faber fanfares).
    I. Title II. Lines, Kathleen
    823'.9'1J   PZ7.U|

    ISBN 0–571–11491–1

Contents

Foreword   *page* 7

Mrs Mimble and Mr Bumble Bee   9
    (from *Mustard, Pepper and Salt*)

The Three Flowers of Fortune   22
    (from *Mustard, Pepper and Salt*)

Green Shoes   28
    (from *Cuckoo Cherry Tree*)

The Rainbow   40
    (from *Mustard, Pepper and Salt*)

The Cornfield   46
    (from *Mustard, Pepper and Salt*)

John Barleycorn   53
    (from *John Barleycorn*)

Country Mice meet Church Mouse   71
    (from *Lavender Shoes*)

Sam Pig's Trousers   79
    (from *Adventures of Sam Pig*)

The Wind in a Frolic   86
    (from *Mustard, Pepper and Salt*)

The Snow Goose   91
    (from *Adventures of Sam Pig*)

Star-shine   102
    (from *Cuckoo Cherry Tree*)

The Seven Sleepers   118
    (from *Moonshine and Magic*)

The Queen Bee   125
    (from *Moonshine and Magic*)

Foreword

Alison Uttley grew up on a steep hill-side farm in Derbyshire. The house, looking like a fortress against the sky, stood on the crest of the crag, half-encircled by a beech-wood, towering above the clustering farm buildings; a fast-flowing river ran over rocky falls in the valley below, and between was the child's world, her own private kingdom.

She knew every corner of the meadows, fields and copses. Individual trees and rocks were friendly or were strange and frightening. "A child left alone as I was, free to wander in the fields, makes her own discoveries in the world in which she lives . . . I spent most of my time seeking, hunting, pursuing the flowers, animals and butterflies, the stones and springs, the shadows and dreams of the countryside which I was making so surely my own possession." That is how, in *Ambush of Young Days*, Mrs Uttley described her own early involvement in the world of nature. And there also, and in *The Country Child*, she wrote about the excitement with which she responded to the rhythm of the year and the coming of each new month and season.

Her memories of childhood remained vivid all her life and in her stories she returned time after time to the experiences and inventions of the child she had been.

Since she felt so at one with nature, it is not surprising that in many of her fairytales the setting is out-of-doors, or that sometimes a manifestation of nature is the chief character.

The stories in *From Spring to Spring* (taken from books published during the long span of her writing life) are happy and childlike; they reveal Alison Uttley's knowledge and intuitive understanding of nature's world, and also the constant, undiminished quality of her creative imagination.

KATHLEEN LINES

Mrs Mimble and Mr Bumble Bee

In nearly the smallest house in the world lived Mrs Mimble, a brown field-mouse. She had bright peeping eyes and soft silky reddish hair, which she brushed and combed each morning when she got out of bed. She was a widow, for her husband went to market one night for some corn, and never returned. Old Mr Toad said he had met Wise Owl on the way. This made Mrs Mimble nervous, and a loud sound would startle her so much she would lock her door and go to bed.

There was only one room in the nearly-smallest house, and that was the kitchen. Here Mrs Mimble did her cooking and sewing, but on wash-day she rubbed her linen in the dew and spread it out on the violet leaves to dry. In a corner of the kitchen was a bed, and above it ticked a dandelion clock. In another corner was a wardrobe, and there hung her best red dress edged with fur, and her bonnet and shawl, and the white bow she wore on her breast.

The house was built under a hedge, among the leaves. Its chimney reached the bottom bell of the tall foxglove, which overshadowed the little dwelling like a great purple tree. Mrs Mimble could put her head out of the kitchen window and listen to the bees' orchestra in the mottled flowers. She dearly loved a tune, and she hummed to the bees as she went about her work. Her house was so cleverly hidden, no one would notice it. Even the tiny spiral of smoke from her chimney disappeared among the foxglove leaves like blue mist, and left only the smell of woodruff in the air.

Farther on, separated from her home by a wild-rose bush, was the very smallest house in the world.

There lived Mr Bumble Bee. He also had only one room, but it was so little, and so crowded with furniture, it was lucky he could fly, for he never could have walked through his very little door at the end of the passage.

Mr Bumble was a stout furry bee, with such a big voice that when he talked his pots rattled, and the little copper warming-pan which hung on the wall often fell down with a clatter. So he usually whispered indoors, and sang loudly when he was out in the open where nothing would be blown down. The trees and bushes were too firmly rooted for that.

He was a merry old bachelor, and it was quite natural that he and gentle Mrs Mimble should be great friends.

All through the winter the little neighbours were very quiet. Mr Bumble Bee felt so drowsy he seldom left his bed. He curled himself up in the blankets, pulled the bracken quilt over his head, and slept. His fire went out, but the door was tightly shut, and he was quite warm. Now and then he awoke and stretched his arms and legs. He fetched a little honey from his store of honey-pots in the passage and had a good meal. He drank a cup of honey-dew, and then got back to bed again.

Mrs Mimble was asleep in her house, too. The wind howled and gusts of hail beat against the door. Snow covered the ground with its deep white eiderdown and Mrs Mimble opened her eyes to look at the unexpected brightness at the small window. She jumped out of bed

and had a dinner of wheaten bread from the cupboard;
but the cold made her shiver, and she crept back under
her blankets and brown silk quilt.

Sometimes, when she felt restless, she sat in her chair,
rocking, rocking, to the scream of the north wind. Sometimes she opened the door and went out to look for holly
berries and seeds, but she never stayed long. Sometimes
she pattered to the Bumble Bee's house, but the smallest
house in the world was tightly shut, and she returned to
bed for another sleep. No smoke came from the neigh-
bouring chimneys; there were no busy marketings in the
wood and orchard, no friendly gossips on the walls. All
the very wee folk, the butterflies, bees and ants, were
resting.

One morning a bright shaft of sunlight shone straight
through the window on to the mouse's bed, and a
powder of hazel pollen blew under the door and settled
on Mrs Mimble's nose. She sneezed, Atishoo! and sprang
up.

"Whatever time is it? Have I overslept? Catkin and
pussy willow out, and I in bed?"

She washed her face in the walnut basin, and brushed
her glossy hair. Then she put on her brown dress with
the fur cuffs, and pinned a white ribbon to her breast.

"I must pop out and look at the world," said she to
herself. "Are the snowdrops over, I wonder?"

She reached down her bonnet and shawl, opened wide
her window, and set off.

Mr Bumble's door was fast shut, and although she
knocked until her knuckles were sore, no sound came
from the smallest house, and no smoke came from the
chimney.

The sun shone down and warmed Mrs Mimble's back,
and she laughed as she ran up the hill.

"Soon he will wake, and won't I tease him!" she chuckled.

She crept under a tall narrow gate into the orchard on the hillside. Over the wall hung clusters of white rock, heavy with scent, and among the flowers sang a chorus of honey-bees.

"Bumble is getting lazy," said Mrs Mimble. "He ought to be up and out now," but the bees took no notice. They were far too busy collecting honey for their hive in the corner of the orchard to listen to a field-mouse.

Under the wall was a bed of snowdrops. They pushed up their green spear-like leaves and held the white drops in veils of green gauze. Mrs Mimble wrinkled her small nose as she ran from one to another, sniffing the piercingly sweet smell of spring. In a corner a company of flowers was out, wearing white petticoats and green embroidered bodices. Mrs Mimble sat up on her hind legs and put out a paw to stroke them. The bells shook at her gentle touch, and rang a peal, "Ting-a-ling-spring-a-ling."

She turned aside and ran up the high wall to the white rock and gathered a bunch for Mr Bumble Bee, to the honey-bees' annoyance.

"Let him get it himself," they grumbled.

Then down she jumped, from stone to stone, and hunted for coltsfoot in the orchard to make herb-beer.

Time had slipped away, and the sun was high when she neared home. A fine smoke, which only her sharp eyes could spy, came from Mr Bumble's chimney. The door was wide open, and a crackly sound and a loud Hum-m-m-m came from within as the Bumble Bee cleaned his boots and chopped the sticks.

There was no doubt Mr Bumble was very wide awake, but whether it was through Mrs Mimble knocking at the door, or spring rapping at the window, nobody knows.

As Mrs Mimble stood hesitating, a three-legged stool, an arm-chair, and a bed came hurtling through the air and fell on the gorse bush, over the way.

"There it goes! Away it goes! And that! And that!" shouted Mr Bumble, and the warming-pan and the kettle followed after.

"Whatever are you doing, Mr Bumble?" exclaimed Mrs. Mimble, now thoroughly alarmed.

"Oh, good day, Mrs Mimble. A Happy New Year to you," said the Bee, popping a whisker round the door. "I'm spring-cleaning. There isn't room to stir in this house until I've emptied it. I am giving it a good turn-out," and a saucepan and fiddle flew over the Mouse's head.

"It's a fine day for your spring-cleaning," called Mrs Mimble, trying to make her high little squeak heard over the Buzz-Buzz, Hum, Hum, Hum-m-m, and the clatter of dishes and furniture.

"Yes, Buzz! Buzz! It is a fine day. I think I slept too long, so I'm making up for lost time."

"Lost thyme, did you say! It isn't out yet, but white rock is, and I have brought you some." She laid her bunch near his door.

But when a table crashed down on her long slender tail, she fled past the gorse bush where the bed lay among the prickles, past the rose bush where the fiddle and warming-pan hung on the thorns, to her own little house. She pushed open the door and sank on a chair.

"Well, I never!" she cried. "I'm thankful to get safely here, and more than thankful that rose bush is between my house and Mr Bumble's! His may be the tiniest house in all the world, it is certainly the noisiest!"

She looked round her kitchen, and for the first time noticed a cobweb hanging from the ceiling, and drifted leaves and soil on her grass-woven carpet.

Up she jumped and seized a broom. Soon she was as busy as Mr Bumble. She hung out the carpet on a low branch of the rose-tree to blow in the wind and she scrubbed her floor. She swept the walls, and hung fresh white curtains at the window, where they fluttered like flower-petals. She festooned her blankets on the bushes, and wound up the dandelion clock, and polished her table and chairs. She made the teapot shine like a moonbeam.

All the time she could hear a loud Hum-Hum-Boom-Boom-Buzz coming from over the rose bush, and a bang and clatter as knives, forks, and spoons flew about.

When she had finished her work, and her house smelled of wild-thyme soap, and lavender polish, Bumble Bee was collecting his possessions from the gorse bush and rose bush where they had fallen.

"Boom! Boom! Buzz! Help me, Mrs Mimble!" he called, and she ran outside and sat with little paws held up, and her bright eyes inquiring what was the matter.

"I've lost a spoon, my honey-spoon. It has a patent handle to keep it from falling in the honey-pot, and now I've lost it," and he buzzed up and down impatiently, seeking among the spiny branches of the rose bush.

Mrs Mimble looked among the brown leaves of the foxglove, but it wasn't there. She turned over the violet leaves, and peeped among the green flowers of the Jack-by-the-hedge, and ran in and out of the gorse bush, but still she could not find it.

It was lost, and Mr Bumble grumbled so loudly that a passer-by exclaimed: "It is really spring! Listen to the bees humming!"

Except for the loss of his spoon Mr Bumble was perfectly happy, and his friend, Mrs Mimble, was so merry it was a joy to be near her. Although she was too large to enter his house, he used to visit hers, and many an evening they spent before her open window, eating honey and wheat biscuits, and sipping nectar as they listened to the song of the bees. Each day was a delight to these little field-people.

One morning the Mouse knocked on Mr Bumble's door and called to him to come out.

"I have some news, Mr Bumble, some news! I've found a nest to let," she cried.

Mr Bumble was resting after a long flight across the Ten-Acre Field, but he put down his newspaper and flew to the door.

"A nest? What do you want with a nest?" he asked.

"It's a chaffinch's nest, a beautiful old one, lined with the very best hair and wool. It will make a summer-house, where I can go for a change of air now and then."

"Shall we both go and see it?" asked the Bee, kindly.

Mrs Mimble ran home and put on her best red dress with fur edging, and her brown bonnet and shawl in honour of the occasion. The Bee combed his hair and brushed his coat with the little comb and brush he carried in his trouser pocket.

They walked down the lane together, but soon Mr Bumble was left behind. He was such a slow walker, and Mrs Mimble was so nimble, she ran backwards and forwards in her excitement, urging him on.

"Come on, Mr Bumble. Hurry up, Mr Bee," she cried.

"It's this dust that gets on my fur," said the Bee. "Besides, you must remember that my legs are shorter than yours."

He puffed and panted and scurried along, but Mrs Mimble was impatient.

"Can't you fly?" she asked.

"Oh, yes, I can fly," he replied, ruffled because he wished to try to walk with her. He shook the dust from his legs, and with a deep Hum-m-m-m he soared up into the air. Higher and higher he flew, into the branches of the beech-tree, where he buzzed among the long golden buds with their tips of green.

"Now he's gone, and I have offended him," said the Mouse, ruefully. She sat sadly on a daisy tuffet, with her tearful eyes searching among the trees for her friend. At length she spied him, swinging on a twig, fluttering like a goldfinch on a thistle.

"Come down, Mr Bumble, come down," she piped in her wee shrill voice. "I will run, and you shall fly just over my head, then we shall arrive together. And I do think you are a splendid pedestrian for your size."

Mrs Mimble looked so pathetic and small down there under the great trees, that he relented and flew down to her. He was flattered too at the long word she had used. So they travelled, great friends again, along the lane, under the hedge of thorn and ash, she running in and out of the golden celandines and green fountains of Jack-by-the-hedge, he buzzing and singing and sipping the honey as he flew near.

When they reached the thickest part of the hedge, she ran up a stout hawthorn bush, and leaped into a small oval nest which had a label "To Let" nailed to it by a large thorn.

"Isn't it a perfect house, with a view, too!" said the Mouse, waving her paw to the hills far away.

The Bee perched near on a bough, and swayed backwards and forwards with admiration. The nest was green and silver with moss and lichen, delicate as a mistletoe bunch. Its roof was open to the stars, but an overhanging mat of twigs and leaves kept out the rain. All that Mrs

Mimble needed was a coverlet, and then she could sleep, lulled by the wind.

"I shall bring my brown silk quilt and keep it here, for no one will take it, it's just like a dead leaf. When I want a change of air, I shall come for a day or two, and live among the may blossom."

They agreed she should take possession at once.

Mr Bumble, whose handwriting was neat, wrote another notice, and pinned it to the tree, for all to read who could.

MRS MIMBLE
HER HOUSE
PRIVATE

The very next day she came with the brown silk quilt, and her toothbrush and comb packed in a little bag. The Bee sat outside his own small house, and waved a red handkerchief to her.

"Good-bye. I will keep the robbers from your home," he called, and he locked her door and put the key in his pocket.

Mrs Mimble climbed up to her summer-house, and leaned from the balcony to watch the life below.

Ants scurried along the grass, dragging loads of wood for their stockades. Sometimes two or three carried a twig, or a bundle of sticks. One little ant dropped his log down a hole, and all his efforts could not move it. As he pulled and tugged a large ant came up and boxed his ears for carelessness. Then he seized the wood and took it away himself to the Ant Town.

"A shame! A shame!" called Mrs Mimble. "It's the little fellow's log. He found it," but no one took any notice, and the small weeping ant dried his tears on the leaves.

Then Mrs Mimble heard a tinkle of small voices, and a lady-bird came by with her five children dressed in red spotted cloaks.

"How many legs has a caterpillar got, Mother?" inquired a tiny voice, but the mother hurried along, and then flew up in the air with the children following, and Mrs Mimble, who nearly fell out of her nest as she watched them, never heard the answer.

"I will ask Mr Bumble," said she. "He knows everything."

Two beetles swaggered up and began to fight. They rose on their hind legs and cuffed and kicked each other. They circled round and round one another, with clenched fists and glaring eyes.

"It's mine. I found it," said one beetle, swinging out his arm.

"Take that, and that!" shouted the other, boxing with both arms at once, and dancing with rage. "I saw it fall, and I had it first."

"I carried it here," said the first beetle, parrying the blows.

Mrs Mimble glanced round, and there, on a wide-open dandelion lay a tiny gleaming spoon—Bumble Bee's honey-spoon with the patent handle.

Softly she ran down the tree, and silently she slipped under the shelter of the jagged dandelion leaves, and put the spoon in her pocket. Then she returned as quietly as she had come, and still the beetles banged and biffed each other, shouting: "It's mine."

At last, tired out, they sat down for a minute's rest, and lo! the treasure was gone! Whereupon they scurried here and there, hunting in the grass, till Mrs Mimble lost sight of them.

She put on her bonnet, intending to run home with the find, when she heard the loud Zoom! Buzz! Buzz! of her friend, and the Bumble Bee came blundering along in a zig-zag path, struggling to carry a long bright object on his back.

"I thought the new house might be damp," he panted, bringing the copper warming-pan from across his wing, "for no one has slept in it since the chaffinches were here last spring."

"Oh, Mr Bumble, how kind you are! How thoughtful!" exclaimed the Mouse. She rubbed the warming-pan, which contained an imprisoned sunbeam, over the downy nest and drove out the little damps.

"Now I have something for you," she continued, and she took from her pocket the honey-spoon, the small spoon as big as a daisy petal with its patent handle and all.

The sun came out from behind a round cloud, the small leaves packed in their sheaths moved and struggled to get out. Mrs Mimble heard the sound of the million buds around her, whispering, uncurling, and flinging away their wraps as they peeped at the sun. She leaned from her balcony and watched the crowds of field creatures, snails and ants, coming and going in the grassy streets below.

But restless Mr Bumble flew away for his fiddle, away across the field and along the lane to his own smallest house. He tuned the little fiddle, and dusted it, and held it under his wide chin. Then he settled himself on a bough near his dear friend, and played the song of the Fairy Etain, who was changed into a bee, in Ireland, a thousand years ago, but has always been remembered in legend and verse by the bees themselves.

The gentle Mouse sat listening to his tiny notes, sweet as honey, golden as the sunlight overhead, and she was glad, for she knew that summer was not far away.

The Three Flowers of Fortune

One fine day in spring, when the orchards were full of apple blossom, and the lambs were playing in the meadows, a little girl named Sally Thorne ran out of her mother's cottage. She skipped between the lavender bushes, and through the wicket gate, to the field at the bottom of the garden. The grass was full of flowers, daisies and primroses, violets and bluebells, but Sally liked the daisies best of all. She gathered a tight little bunch and every flower had a circle of frilly white petals round a yellow face. Among them she found one with two heads. Fancy that! Two heads on one stalk! There never was such a strange happening before in all Sally's life, for everyone knows a daisy has only one head.

Sally raced back to her mother, up the garden, and in at the door. Mrs Thorne was busy with her arms in the wash-tub, washing the clothes for the Big House up on the hill.

"Mother! Mother! Look! I've found a daisy with two heads growing on one stalk! What does that mean, Mother?" cried Sally, holding out her double flower.

Her mother put down the sheet she was washing, wiped the suds from her hands, and took the daisy. She held it up to the sunlight, and twirled it round.

"Well I never!" she exclaimed. "A daisy with two heads! I don't know what it foretells, child, but it must have some meaning. I will show it to the lady's maid at the Big House, for she is very clever."

She put the daisy in water on the window-sill, and went on with her washing, but Sally peered at it and wondered about it all day long.

The next day Sally ran out to the little field to pick a bunch of clover. There was a fine clover bed, humming with bees, and the smell was so sweet she wrinkled her nose and lay on her face to get close to the flowers. As she picked the red and white spiky balls, and tasted the honey which lies deep inside them, she noticed a strange thing. There was a four-leaved clover growing among the others. Everybody knows a clover has only three leaflets, and here was one with four! It was a miracle, Sally thought, and she gathered the leaf and put it in with her bunch of flowers.

She ran back to her mother, across the grass and through the lavender hedge, shouting: "Mother! Mother! Look!" as she waved her four-leaved clover to her mother, who was busy ironing the clothes and hanging them round the fire.

"Mother! I've found a four-leaved clover! What does it mean?"

Mrs Thorne put down the shirt she was ironing, and replaced the iron by the fire. Then she took the clover-leaf to the window, and looked at it.

"Well I never!" she cried. "A four-leaved clover! Three-leaved clover is the sign of the Trinity, I learned at school, but whatever can a four-leaved clover mean? I must take it to the lady's maid when I go up to the Big House with the laundry. Maybe she can tell me the meaning," and she put the clover-leaf in water along-side the daisy.

The next day Sally ran out to the field to pick a bunch of bluebells. They grew close under the wall, so blue that they looked as if a bit of the sky had fallen down, or a pool of water lay there. She snapped the brittle stalks, and filled her small hot hands, and each flower seemed to tinkle its bells at her, and each flower seemed to be larger than the one before. Just as she was going away she found a white bluebell, growing apart from the others, pure and snowy in the deep green grass.

She scampered home, carrying her bunch of sweet-scented bluebells, and among them the flower with its bells like pearls. She hurried through the wicket gate, and up the stony path, to her mother who was baking in the kitchen.

"Mother! Mother! Look what I've found! A white bluebell! What does it mean, Mother?"

Mrs Thorne wiped the dough from her hands, and picked up the bluebell. It really was a wonderful flower!

"Well I never!" cried she. "I'm sure I don't know what it means, but it must have some reason for growing this colour, when it ought to be blue. I'll take it up to the Big House tomorrow, and then I shall find out. The lady's maid is a friend of mine, and she'll tell me."

So she put the white bluebell with the four-leaved clover and the double-headed daisy on the window-sill, and went on with her baking, and Sally had to be content.

The next day Mrs Thorne packed all the washing in a basket and put it on a wheelbarrow. On the top of the cloth lay the three flowers. She wheeled her burden up the drive, and turned aside to the back door, behind the kitchen garden.

"Look what my little girl found in our field!" she said to the lady's maid, as she sipped a cup of tea before going back. "What do you make of these? All three growing in our field. None of them ordinary, you see."

The lady's maid was a clever young woman, who came from a big town. She had been to school in a great red-brick building, with inspectors popping in and out of the doors, and certificates awarded once a year. She knew all kinds of things, but she didn't know the meaning of the double-headed daisy, the four-leaved clover, and the white bluebell.

"I'll show them to the governess," said she. "She is certain to know."

The governess was a high-born young lady who had studied nearly everything. She had been to college, and knew about flowers and their insides, and even about their thoughts. There was nothing she did not know, till she saw the double-headed daisy, the four-leaved clover, and the white bluebell, but she did not know what they meant.

"These are extraordinary botanical specimens," said she. "I do not remember the exact significance of their queerness, but I will ask her ladyship."

Her ladyship was walking in the garden, and the governess took the flowers out to her at once.

But her ladyship did not know either. She had spent her childhood in foreign countries, and she could speak five languages, but she could not tell the meaning of the double-headed daisy, the four-leaved clover, and the white bluebell.

In the garden bed a short distance away a young boy was weeding. He was Tom Thatcher, the fourth gardener's assistant. He heard the conversation between the governess and her ladyship, and he saw the three flowers in their hands, so he upped and spoke.

"Please, your ladyship, and please, miss," said he, pulling his forelock. "Please, I knows what them flowers means. Please, they means: 'Good Luck and God Bless you,' for whosumdever finds them. That's what they mean, your ladyship and miss, if you'll excuse me."

And he blushed for his boldness, pulling his forelock again, and returning to his weeding.

So the governess told the lady's maid, and the lady's maid told Sally's mother, and she told her young daughter.

"Good Luck and God Bless you," whispered Sally to herself, and she hid the words in her heart.

But when Sally was grown up she married the fourth gardener's assistant, for he had become the head-gardener, and he was her luck.

🌿 Green Shoes

Underneath the hedge lay an old pair of shoes. The toes were broken, and the soles nearly parted from the uppers. The laces had long ago decayed, and the tongue was a ragged scrap of wet leather. They had lain there among the dog mercury and Robin-run-in-the-hedge for many a long month. They had been hidden under snow, and rimed with the frost, and soaked with winter storms, and now they were lost in the hedgebottom, as much a part of it as the ferns and velvety moss and young leaves. Soil was washed into the cracks, and moss took root there and grew with feathery tufts and pearly beads. Little ferns of exquisite shape sprang up and waved their green fronds from the soles. Seeds of tiny plants dropped from above and after the sun had shone little red and blue flowers came out where the tongue should have been. Very soon the shoes would have disappeared altogether, and become absorbed in the green mat of Mother Earth, but before they were completely changed they were discovered.

An old man walked down that green lane, and a very ancient man he was. He had a store of knowledge and a power of wisdom remembered from other days. He carried a sack on his bent back, and he stooped so low he almost touched the ground with his beard as he went along the leafy way. His eyes missed nothing, not a pearly-striped snail-shell, or a mailed beetle, not a moth with folded wings, or an ant busy with its citizen's work. He stayed to watch one of these little creatures carrying a log twice its own size, and he nodded his head to it and whispered a word of encouragement. Then he spoke to a butterfly, and the insect flew upon his hand and kissed him with soft kisses. He talked to the booming bumble bee, and touched the warm furry body, and the bee's voice was quiet as it listened. Then away it went, deep in the flowers' honeybags. He gave a greeting to the Lords and Ladies in their green voluminous gowns, and they threw wide their cloaks and bowed their brown heads to his words. Evidently he was somebody whom they all knew very well indeed.

"If only mankind would listen to the talk of the country lanes, they would forget their cares and find that peace of mind which they seem to have lost," murmured the old man, as he stroked the brown sleek head of a robin. The robin flicked its tail and cocked its head aside in a knowing way, and flew straight as an arrow to tell the student at his desk what it had heard. The student went on reading, and although the bird sang with all its might he took no notice at all.

Down in the hedgerow the ancient one had spied the pair of old shoes. He leaned over them and contemplated them for many minutes, and then he made a sign over them. He spoke a word of an old forgotten language, and then he trudged away down the lane, bestowing the kind glances of his brown eyes on the humble creatures of earth, whispering a word of cheer, helping a hurt one, bringing the balm of forgetfulness to another, praising flowers and birds and insects.

From that moment the shoes were enchanted. Ferns
and moss and many coloured flowers were woven into a
living tissue, strong as leather, supple as silk. Immortal
powers were breathed into them. They lay under the
hedgerow a pair of magical shoes. They were found a
few days later by Tom Gratton the farm labourer as he
went home from his ditching and hedging.

He picked them up and examined them in wonder.
He saw a pair of green shoes, made of painted leather,
soft as velvet, with red and yellow flowers on the tongues
and laces made of rainbow gossamer. The lining was of
thistledown fur, silver-white. The soles were made of
growing moss. Never were seen such dainty shoes! He
wrapped them in his red spotted pocket-handkerchief,
which had held his dinner basin, and he carried them
home to his daughter Milly.

They fitted her slim little feet as if they had been made
for her. Milly had only worn heavy nailed boots, iron-
tipped and harsh to her toes, and these were soft and
warm, light as a feather, and a joy to look upon.

"Oh, look at me! I'm a lady! Oh! Can I wear them to go to school to-morrow? I want to show them to the other girls!" she cried, dancing across the kitchen like a kitten at play, and the shoes seemed to spin her round.

"Well, they aren't really suitable for school, but you can wear them to-morrow, my poppet," said her doting mother, smiling at the little girl's happy face.

So Milly went to school in the fairy shoes. At least she started for school, on that fine morning in spring. How the children stared! "Green shoes! Green shoes!" they mocked enviously, but Milly danced down the village street, willy-nilly, where the shoes took her. The school-bell jangled in the little tower, the boys and girls trooped into the classroom, but Milly didn't appear.

"Her's gone off down th' Fox's Hollow," cried a little boy. "Her's playing truant, is Milly Gratton."

"In a pair of lovely shoes, green velvet," added a little girl.

But Milly wasn't playing truant. The shoes were taking her to the places they knew, where the moss was thick and clubbed with golden seeds, and the lichens starred the stones, and little red and yellow flowers sprang from cushions of tiny plants. Her eyes opened wider than ever as she saw all the beauties which had been invisible to her before. There she stayed, listening to the talk of the finches, the whispering chatter of insects, the deep wisdom of the rustling trees, and there her father found her at nightfall when the whole village had been searching for her.

The pretty green shoes were taken off and wiped dry, and Milly was sent to bed with a basin of bread and milk for supper. She told her mother and father she had been by the side of the ditch hearing the talk of the rushes, and the gossip of the little yellow frogs. She had watched

the spider spin its silken web, and heard the creak of the
threads as they rubbed the twigs. Quite plain to her had
been the mumble of flies, and the whir of wings and
feathers, and the swish of the butterfly's wings.

Her poor parents shook their heads at her, and fetched
the wise woman.

"Yes, she must stay a-bed and drink camomile tea,"
said the wise woman.

She picked up the green shoes which lay by the side of
the bed, and turned them over and smelled at their
sweetness.

"Shoes too fine for the child to wear on weekdays,"
said she disapprovingly. "She's got a chill with wearing
them down in that ditch. If you want her to keep sensible,
you must put aside these till Sundays. Let her go to
church in them and nowhere else. Let her go to Holy
Church."

On Sunday Milly was dressed in her Sunday frock, her
Sunday tippet and Sunday gloves, and best hat. On her
feet she wore the green shoes, with their silky laces and
flowery tongues. As she went up the churchyard, under
the yew trees, the shoes gave a tug at her feet. They
twisted her right round, and away they ran with her,
away from the parson and the choir-boys and the pealing
bells. Away they ran, as fast as they could patter, and
they never stopped till they came to the green lane
where the Lords and Ladies stood in their green cloaks.
"Jack-in-the-pulpit" was the Sunday name of the
flowers, and they preached a sermon to Milly in her
green shoes.

So Milly sat down in the hedgebottom, and rested her
little feet, while she listened to the words of the brown
preachers in their green pulpits among the flowers and
leaves. The birds sang the psalms, the chiff-chaff sang a

hymn, and all the tiny creatures of the lane with the trees
above and the flowers below chanted praises to God. Far
away the church bells rang in vain for Milly. The only
bells she could hear were the bluebells swinging their
chimes and the Alleluia flowers shaking their delicate
heads close to the ground.

After a time Milly got drowsy with the music around
her, the singing and the chanting of the wild world.
She leaned over the little brook and listened to the reedy
talk of the fish. She untied the gossamer laces and
stripped off her shoes and stockings and dipped her feet
in the water, intent on hearing the talk down below. The
fish had scales of silver and green, they stared with un-
winking eyes and opened and shut their mouths in
amazement at the tale their brother was telling. It was a
magical tale of a mermaid who lived at the bottom of the
sea. On and on went the story, and some said they didn't
believe it, and others swore it was true. Milly bent her
head low till her dark locks touched the water. The
voices were suddenly hushed, and the fish no longer
talked. She could only hear the murmur of the stream
as it fell over the stones and the singing of the birds in the
overhanging trees. She stepped to the bank, but her
green shoes were gone. They had floated away down that
little stream, and although Milly hunted for many a day
in the meadows and ditches, they had gone for ever.

But they had left a memory behind them, and Milly
never forgot the lessons they taught her when she wore
them that Sunday morning.

In the meantime the shoes were carried by the current
to a small brook that flowed into the millpond. The
green shoes were caught among the water-lily leaves in
the silent pool off the mill-race. Little Jack Peter saw
them and he ran to the shed for his fishing net.

"Here's a fine catch," he cried, as he drew them from the water. "A pair of shoes, quite good ones, and the wet hasn't even got inside them. Lined with fur, and all painted and broidered in colours! Oh my! Perhaps they will fit my mother!"

The miller and his wife rejoiced over the pretty shoes, and when the good woman tried them on they fitted her perfectly. It was part of their magical power to fit anyone who tried them on. They never ran away with her, for she lived in the green lanes. They took her to the orchard drying ground with her linen basket, to the field to feed the hens, to the garden to pick the herbs to stuff the fish for dinner, and they always behaved in the most decorous manner.

Her eyes were brightened, she saw many a thing unseen before, but she was wise enough to say nothing to others. She stored the marvels in her mind, and told the tales of them to little Jack Peter. Every day she told him a new story, and nobody knew where she got them all from.

One day the shoes were set neatly side by side in their usual place underneath the kitchen dresser, when a tramp pushed open the door and saw them. Quickly he picked them up and popped them in his pocket. Then away he sidled before even the dog could bark or the gander give a warning cry.

The poor miller's wife burst into tears for her loss, but her husband tried to console her.

"They came by mystery, and by mystery they've gone away, so don't 'ee take on, my love."

" 'Twas no mystery. 'Twas an old bad tramp as took 'em, I'm sure certain," she exclaimed, but there was no getting the shoes back again.

However, in a few months' time a little daughter was

born to her, and the child shared Jack Peter's delight in
the magical tales the miller's wife told them.

The tramp carried away the dainty shoes. He wandered
along country lanes and slept in ditches and cooked his
dinner and boiled his billy-can under the hedges. He
thought he would never get to the town, for while he had
the green shoes in his pocket every road took him away.
Finally he arrived, and he tossed the shoes on the wooden
counter of a little cobbler's shop.

"How much for these? High-class shoes, come from a
palace, I 'specks," said he.

"I'll give you a shilling for them," said the cobbler
sternly, "and not a penny more, for it's my belief you've
not come by them honestly."

So the tramp had to part with them for a shilling. The
cobbler put them in his window with a fair price on them.
They were strange shoes. They made his fingers tingle
when he held them, and he heard bells ringing and he
smelled meadow-sweet and honeysuckle and he heard
little voices calling in the wainscot where the mice lived.
He was glad to get rid of the green shoes to a young man
who entered the shop and asked about the pair of strange
outlandish shoes with their tongues of flowers and their
gossamer laces.

He wanted them for his sweetheart. He called her his
sweetheart, but she would have nothing to do with him.
She was a dancer at the theatre in the town. He was a
poet, but he had written nothing for weeks. Every night
he sat at the back of the theatre, in the cheapest seat, and
he craned his head to watch those little twinkling feet,
and the sparkling eyes of his beloved. She had danced
away with his heart and left him with an empty space.
He thought that if he gave her the lovely green shoes he
might smile on him and give him her heart in exchange.

So he carried the shoes home to his lodging and put them down by the side of the empty grate while he wrote a letter. Even as the pen scratched the paper he was disturbed by soft movements, rustling whispers. The shoes were feathery with growing ferns, and the flowers embroidered upon them were opening new buds. He stooped down and slipped his hands into them, and the warmth of the growing things seemed to fill his chilled body. His cramped fingers took up the pen again, and he began to write. The pen flew over the paper, as if invisible fingers guided it. The warmth spread through his body. Something had happened to him. He wrote on and on, aware only of the scent of wild flowers, the humming of bees and the song of birds. He seemed to be in a leafy lane again, under the hedgerow, filled with the delight of his native country.

He looked at the shoes, and they were covered with growing flowers and delicate young leaves. He looked at his words, and it wasn't a letter at all that he had written. It was a poem, the outpouring of his soul. The words burned him. He was no longer lonely or sad. He forgot the dancer and the theatre and the poverty of the town. He held the green shoes to his heart, and he went on writing till dawn.

The next day he sent the shoes to the dancer. At night she danced so divinely in the soft flowery shoes that everyone said they had never seen the like. She was a ballerina, a star, a genius. At the back of the theatre sat the poet, and the dancer smiled at him, and kissed her hand to him alone when the house applauded her.

She came dancing through the streets with the green shoes on her dainty feet and the poet took her away to the countryside. There in the lane they told their love, and they hung the shoes in the hedge.

They sat on a cushion of Queen Anne's Lace, violets and rosy campions, and the poet read his poem.

They vowed to love each other for ever, the poet who had written his greatest poem, and the little actress who had danced her finest dance. When they stood up the little shoes had gone. That didn't matter. They went back without them and bought another pair, not so pretty but quite useful. When people are deep in love shoes do not matter.

The little green shoes had fallen in the ditch once more and there they lay, growing even more beautiful in the sun and rain, till they were found by a gypsy with a roving eye and jet black hair.

He held them up aloft and sang with joy, for he knew what he would do with them. He went back to the painted caravan for his piebald pony. He flung himself on its back and rode off to the castle, where the lovely young bride had lately come. He rang the iron bell at the great door, and asked to see the lady.

"My lady is not at home to a gypsy fellow," said the man-servant, and he shut the door.

Out of the window peeped the lady herself, in her blue silk dress and her green silk hood.

"Shoes for sale. Fine shoes for sale," called the gypsy, holding the delicate shoes aloft, and standing up on the pony's back.

She stretched out a white hand and took them and tossed down her purse of gold, but the gypsy threw a flaming kiss to burn her.

She ran back to her room and slipped the shoes on her feet. How beautiful they were! How gay she felt! Never in all her dull, short, married life had she felt such happiness.

She leaned out of the window and the gypsy still waited.

"I'm coming with you!" she whispered. "Will you have me?"

"Most willingly," he laughed back to her.

She tore off her gold ring; she changed her silken dress; she wrapped a scarf round her curls and draped a cloak on her shoulders. "Tell my lord I'm off with the gypsies," said she to her maid, and away she went.

Ah! How the green shoes danced that night! How they flashed in and out of the firelight, as my lady swung round in the arms of the dark gypsy man. And when the fire burned low, and the gypsies slept under the stars, the little green shoes lay tossed in the gorse bush where the lady dropped them with her cloak and dress.

Deep into the yellow gorse they fell, and nobody missed them when the gypsies went away to a new camping-ground the next day. The lady rode on the piebald pony, and the gypsy ran by her side, holding her bridle, whispering to her, enchanting her ears, and no one saw the little green shoes in the gorse bush.

There they lie, waiting for another wearer, for they are immortal shoes, and who knows who will find them next?

The Rainbow

Tom Oliver had been fishing all the morning in the little brook which ran down the fields—the silver shining brook which rattled over the stones, grinding them into pebbles, the stream which seized the meadow grasses and dragged them by their green hair, so that they looked like water-nymphs, swimming in the rapid little torrent.

Tadpoles and minnows and Jack Sharps were the only creatures that lived there, for the brook was so noisy that the big fish preferred to swim in the quiet river lower down the valley. Tom's mother would not allow him to go near the deep pools and hollows of that tranquil water, but when he leaned over the humpbacked bridge, with his face half-buried in the ferns on the edge, he could watch the dark slim shapes mysteriously moving down below, and sometimes he saw a real fisherman in waders standing in the water, and landing a speckled trout.

But the brook was a splendid place for a boy's fishing. The quickest way to catch anything was to dangle an empty jampot in the water, or to dip a brown hand under a stone, although Tom preferred to do it properly, and to use a fishing rod made of a hazel switch, with a bit of string on the end, and almost anything for bait—a holly berry, a cherry, an acorn.

He was fishing like this, sitting cross-legged on a stone under an alder-tree, and the sun was shining brightly, so that spickles and sparkles of light flashed about on the water, and flickering nets of sunshine lay on the bottom of the brook. Suddenly he felt a bite, and the cherry bobbed and dipped as if something very much alive was on the end.

Quickly he pulled in his line, and there, wriggling on the end, was no minnow, or Jack Sharp, or Miller's thumb, but a rainbow, a curving iridescent rainbow, with all the seven lovely colours in its arching back. It leaped and danced on its tail so that Tom had much to do to catch it.

It was quite a little rainbow when Tom carried it home, all writhing and slipping in his fingers, but when he put it in the garden, it grew so large that it stretched across from the lilac bush to the silver birch-tree, in a beautiful curving sweep of misty colours. He could no longer hold it, for it slithered through his hands like dewdrops, but there it hung, in a fine archway, a marvel for all the world to see.

Tom's mother left her wash-tub, and stood at the kitchen door for a moment.

"Yes, it's a rainbow, right enough," said she. "I've never seen a rainbow in our garden before. It cheers one up to see it," and she went back to her work.

Tom spent all day looking at his rainbow, running his fingers through its elusive colour bands, catching the blue and orange in his hands. The chaffinches fluttered through it, and the tom tits swung on the top, as if it were a bough of a celestial tree, so that their wings were flecked with many lights.

A blackbird whistled at the foot where the arch rested on the lilac-tree, and a thrush sang at the other end, on

the silver birch. All the birds saw the rainbow hanging
in the garden, and they called to one another to play in
and out of the great arch.

"It would make a nice clothes' line," said Tom's
mother, thoughtfully, and she carried out the washing-
basket and started to peg the shirts and towels on the
bands of colour. But they slipped through and fell to the
ground, and the rainbow shook itself so that drops of
water sprinkled them like rain. With a sigh Mrs Oliver

gathered them up and took them to the drying-ground. It was a pity she could not make use of such a nice clean rope of colour, for it was a pretty sight.

The curious thing about it was that some other people could not see it. Cross Mr Jenkins, the chimney-sweep next door, saw nothing at all. Mrs Stone, who kept the little grocery store in her front window, saw nothing either, although she put on her spectacles and peered quite close, but little Jemima Stone could see it, and she came into the garden and stood with Tom Oliver, watching the rainbow's twinkling colours, which changed as the children moved.

Night came, but still the rainbow glowed in the garden. Tom's mother said it would disappear when the sun set, and certainly even Tom's sharp eyes couldn't see it in the dark, but when he moved his fingers across it he could feel it like a ripple in the air, and he knew it was there.

The stars came out, and the moon rose above the hill. Tom leaned from his bedroom window, and looked down to the garden. Yes, the bow was still there, with strange pale colours of silver, and on the highest point of the arch a nightingale perched itself and sang its haunting passionate song. That was indeed a sight to remember!

The next morning when Tom sprang from bed and poked his head out of the casement the first thing he saw was the rainbow, all fresh and bright, swinging lightly across the garden. So it hadn't gone! Surely somebody would see it to-day! He wanted to share the good news with all the village.

He ran off to school with his bag flapping on his back, eager to tell his friends about it.

"We've got a rainbow in our back garden," he boasted.

"Don't believe you," said one.

"Rainbows don't belong to gardens," said another.

"You come home with me, and I'll show you," said Tom.

When the boys followed him through the garden gate they said there was nothing there, and mocked at Tom.

"It's hanging in the lilac-tree. Can't you see it? Can't you see it? You must all be blind," said Tom, exasperated, and he put his head on one side and pointed out the lovely colours spanning the trees in the airy filmy archway.

"Oh leave him! It's all nonsense! There's no rainbow! Leave him to his moonshine," they exclaimed, and off they ran to look for birds' nests in the hedges.

Tom hung his head and walked into the house. Only his mother and little Jemima Stone could see the rainbow. What was the good of it if nobody believed in it? Perhaps it wasn't there at all, and he had imagined it. He ran to the door and looked out, and was just in time to see the rainbow rapidly growing smaller. It curled into a little ball and fell in a wreath of colour to the ground.

Although he hunted and hunted he couldn't find it. He searched among the cabbages, the carrots, and onions, but there was no rainbow. He looked among the pansies, the sweet-williams and bachelor's buttons, but there was no sign of a rainbow among the flowers. Where could it have gone? He turned sadly away, unhappy that he had doubted and so lost his treasure, when a sparkle on the rubbish heap caught his eye. He picked up a little prism of glass, and held it to the sun. Bands of coloured light fell from it, and he shouted with joy.

"I've caught the rainbow again, Mother. It's shut up in this glass, like a ship in a bottle!"

He turned it this way and that and let the spectrum of colour fall on his hands.

"Where was it, Tom?" asked Mrs Oliver, running to the door.

"On the rubbish heap. Look at it, all the colours, and not one missing. Violet, indigo, blue, green, yellow, orange, red. All of them, fast in the glass."

"It can't escape me this time," he continued, twirling the prism. "I can take it to school, and the boys must believe me."

He put the prism from the chandelier in his pocket and ran laughing down the lane, and when he showed it to the other boys they all agreed they could see the rainbow now.

But his mother returned to her wash-tub, and bent over the clothes. There, dancing over the soap-suds, glimmering in the bubbles, were a thousand little rainbows of light.

"I've got a bit of that rainbow, too," she told herself. "Once I thought it lived in the sky, and now I've seen it even in my old wash-tub. Who would believe it?" She took up her soap and rubbed the clothes, and then she began to sing with happiness.

🌿 The Cornfield

It was a warm, sweet-scented summer evening, and the moon and a few stars shone down on the fields, which lay like sheets of pale silver on the hillside. A hedgehog jogged along the country lane between the hedges, singing to himself his own little song of happiness.

> *My lantern's the moon,*
> *My candle's a star,*
> *I travel by night,*
> *I wander afar.*

He stamped his small feet in the dust in time to his thin high voice, and he felt the cool air in his prickles. A nightingale sang in the wood, but the hedgehog took no notice of its passionate music. He went on with his own song, singing so softly nobody but himself could hear it.

> *My carpet's the moss,*
> *My firelight the sun,*
> *My house-roof the hedge,*
> *When work is all done.*

It was a good song, he told himself, a traveller's song, and he was a hedgehog who couldn't abide staying at home. All day he had slept in his little bed of leaves, under the hedge, warmed by the hot sun, sheltered by tall ferns and velvety moss. Now night had come, and, in common with many small animals, he was wide awake, and off for a moonlight adventure.

He padded along the grassy verge of the lane, humming to himself, well content with life. Not far away stretched the broad smooth highway, the great road to London. Motor-cars and lorries whirled along with bright lights illuminating the hedges, spinning like gigantic golden-eyed animals, devouring all before them, and the hedgehog kept away from their roaring speed. They wouldn't follow him down the narrow rough lanes and the tiny green highways, under the arching meadowsweet with its white, sweet flowers dipping to touch his back, and the forests of soft willow-herb. They couldn't hear the rustles among the leaves, or smell the flowers which attracted the white night-moths. He plodded cheerfully on, aware of every movement and smell around him.

He came at last to a gate, and against its bottom bar leaned an old Jack Hare.

"Hello, Jack," said Hedgehog in his friendly way. "How's the world treating you?"

"Pretty middling," replied the hare, taking a straw from his mouth and turning round to the hedgehog. "How's yourself?"

"Oh, pretty fairish," said Hedgehog. "It's a grand night."

" 'Tis indeed! Where might you be going, Hedgehog?"

"Just over the fields to look at the corn a-growing. I allus likes to watch it grow. On a moonlight night it comes on a bit, and there's nothing like a cornfield to my thinking."

"I'll come along with you," said Jack Hare. "I don't mind a bit of adventure. I've seen nobody all day but a couple of magpies, and a few rabbits, and a lost hen. I should like to see the corn a-growing."

"There's a bright lantern hung in the sky to-night," said Hedgehog as they ambled along together, the hare suiting his long steps to the short legs of the hedgehog. "It gives a kind yellow light, that lantern aloft, not trying to the eyes like those twinkly lamps the farm men carry, or those tarrible dazzlers on the motors."

"I can't understand why they bother with those flashing lights when they've got a good lamp in the sky, that costs nothing and is held up for all the world to see," said the hare. "The ways of man are beyond me."

"And me." Hedgehog shook his little head and rattled his prickles in disdain, and very softly under his breath he sang his song.

> *My lantern's the moon,*
> *My candle's a star,*
> *I travel by night,*
> *I wander afar.*

The two crossed a stream, the hare leaping it, the hedgehog paddling in the shallow water, and scrambling on the stones and twigs. By the water's edge, dipping his toes in the dark stream, sat a water-rat.

"How d'ye do?" said Hedgehog. "How's life treating you?"

"Not so bad," replied the water-rat. "Where are you off to? Won't you stay here a while and cool yourselves in my brook? Come and look at the ripples I can make, and the waves all running away from my toes, one chasing another, like swallows in the air."

"We're going over the fields to see the corn a-growing," said Hedgehog, and the hare nodded and echoed: "The green corn a-growing."

"That's a pretty sight, and worth a journey," agreed the water-rat. "It does my heart good to see the corn

a-sprouting and a-springing out of the ground, and waving its head. I'll come too if you don't mind. I've seen nothing all day but a couple of dilly-ducks, and a young frog. I'd like to see something sensible."

They went along together, the hedgehog with his pointed snout and little bright eyes, humming his song, the hare with his great brown eyes glancing to left and right and behind him, and the water-rat with his sleek soft skin and little blunt nose. All the time the moon shone down with a bright silvery light, so that three little dusky shadows ran alongside the three animals.

They made a tiny track in the dewy grass, and they sipped the drops of pearly moisture from the leaves to quench their thirst. They passed a company of cows, lying near the path, and they saw a couple of farm horses cropping close to one another for company. Sweet scents of honeysuckle and briar came to them, and Hedgehog sang his little song once more.

A young hare was racing up and down in the moonlight, and Hedgehog called to him.

"Hello! young Hare," said he. "Why are you in such a hurry?"

The hare sat up, with his long ears twitching as he listened to the little sounds of night.

"I'm a bit mad," said he. "It's the moon. It makes me want to leap when I see that bright light. Can't stop, sorry!" and away he went, galloping over the pasture till he was out of sight.

"Poor fellow! I was just like that once," said Jack Hare, "but I've got a bone in my leg now."

They reached a little knoll, and there they stopped, for in front of them stretched a field of golden wheat. It swayed gently as if an invisible hand stroked it, and even in the silence of the night a murmuring musical sound came from those million million ears of rustling corn.

The moon seemed to stand still in the sky, and look down at the wide cornfield, and the Great Bear blinked his eye and stared.

"Can you hear it muttering?" whispered the hedgehog. "Can you hear the corn talking?"

"Is it alive like us?" asked the little water-rat.

"I can see it breathing, all moving as it takes a big breath," said the hare. "It's a wunnerful sight, a field of corn."

"It's like water," said the water-rat. "It ripples and sighs and murmurs like the water in my brook at home."

The great field with the tall slender stems of wheat growing thick and close, covering fifty acres, seemed to whisper, and the wheat-ears rubbed together as they swayed in the night air, and the sound was that of the sea, a low soft talk of myriad voices.

"This is my adventure," said Hedgehog. "I come here nearly every night, just to see the corn a-growing and a-blowing, and to listen to what it says."

"It's a comforting homely talk," said the hare, "but I can't understand the language. I was never very good at languages. What does it say, Hedgehog?"

"Nay, I c-can't tell you exactly," replied Hedgehog, hesitating, with his head aside, as he listened. "I don't know the words, but they seem to me to be like a song. Listen. Now it's plainer."

He held up his tiny fingered hand, and a myriad rustling voices sang:

> *We are growing, growing, growing,*
> *The corn for the children's bread.*
> *The sap is flowing, flowing, flowing,*
> *From the roots unto the head.*
> *We are the corn,*
> *New-born,*
> *We make the bread.*

The three animals sat breathless, listening to the little sounds and murmurs of the corn's voice. From the wood-side came the song of the nightingale, and overhead the moon and stars looked down.

"Aye, that's it!" said Hedgehog. "That's what it tells you. It's growing, ripening, preparing for harvest. It's living, like us."

They turned round and started off home again.

"Good night! Good night!" they said as they parted company. "It was a grand sight. Something to remember. We'll go again, all three of us, when the Harvest moon comes along. Good night."

Hedgehog trundled home to his house-roof under the hedge, and Hare went back to the gate, but the little water-rat sat for a long time on the bank of his stream listening to the murmur of the water, and dreaming of the rustle of the corn.

John Barleycorn

There once lived an old woman who was poor and lonely, for her husband was dead and she had never had any children. She had no one in all the world to care for her except the creatures of the woodland, and these she loved. There was the robin which hopped in at the open door every morning to wish her good-day. She fed him with crumbs and he sang a merry song for her. He flew to the back of her Windsor chair, bobbing up and down as if he were making curtseys to the quality.

"I believe you love me," said she, "or is it cupboard love?"

The robin held his little head on one side, listening to her soft voice, and then he sang again with all his might and main.

In a corner of the garden the old woman kept a few hens. They always ran to welcome her. Even when they were busy scratching the soil and murmuring to each other they rushed off when they saw her bonnet coming down the path among the bushes. She looked at their bright eyes, and she longed for a word from one of them. They laid large white eggs and she never forgot to thank them for their trouble.

"Thank you kindly, my chucky hens," said she, as she gathered up the eggs in her wrinkled hand, and cupped them in her shawl. "Thank you kindly."

"Cluck! Cluck! Cluck!" went the hens, turning their backs and hurrying to eat the scraps she had given them.

"I hope you love me," said she doubtfully. "It may be cupboard love, too, I shouldn't wonder."

Every autumn she went gleaning in the cornfields to gather the ears of corn left by the reapers. Of course she called it "leasing", in the old manner of talk.

She went off at daybreak and stayed in the fields till night, eating her dinner of bread and cheese under the hedge, stooping all day to the stubble. To be out in the warm sunshine, close to the good earth, gathering up the crumbs left from the rich man's table, was a grand life, she thought. She searched among the scarlet pimpernel, and the field pansies growing there in the roots of the wheat and barley. She got so much corn there was a good-sized bag filled to the brim. She picked up the wheat and barley, tasselled and plumed with golden awns, till she had a sheaf. She put it under a tree, bound it with a wisp of straw, and went back for more. At night she stripped the corn from the ears, fanned away the chaff, and sorted the golden grain into a sack.

When gleaning was over, she took the corn to the miller to be ground into flour to make her bread. She kept some grain for her hens. So the gleaning brought her riches and comfort and the farmer always left some extra ears of wheat and barley in the fields for her sake.

One day when the cornfields had been ploughed and prepared for sowing the spring wheat, the old woman went off to the village. She carried a basket of eggs for the market, where she had a seat for selling her wares. She went as usual by the field path which passed through the cornfields. Suddenly she noticed a little green-yellow parcel lying in the middle of the way. It was tied up with green grasses instead of string. It was exactly the colour of the fields and she nearly stumbled over it.

She put down her basket of eggs and sat on the low wall to rest for a while as she examined the packet.

"Whatever can there be inside it?" she asked herself. "Has a little 'un dropped his dinner packet on the way to school? But no childer goes this road. I'm about the only one as ever walks on this forgotten path."

Carefully she untied the knotted grasses, which were twisted into a fine cord, and fastened in an intricate bow. It wouldn't do to cut it, even if she had a knife. Careful folk do not cut string.

She removed the wrapper and saw that it was made of green leaves stitched together with the tiniest little stitches to make a cloth.

"Nay, did you ever see the like!" she questioned the sky and the clouds. She held up the minute cloth in admiration, and the birds in the trees twittered back to her in surprise.

She turned again to the parcel. There was another wrapper, and this one was golden yellow. It was veined all over like autumn leaves, and it crackled like dry leaves. It had the sweet smell of the end-of-the-year. This stuff was stitched with large irregular stitches, and the thread was brown as earth. She slipped off the yellow string made of corn stalks, with its tassels of rushes, and held up the wrappering. It crumbled to pieces under her fingers, for it was brittle. Underneath was another parcel.

This was wrapped in a cloth of straw, and there was no string around it. Her old fingers trembled with excitement. She hoped it wasn't a trick played by somebody, a naughty boy or a fairy man, but it wasn't April Fool's Day, so who would tease an old poor woman?

She removed the woven straw cover, and inside there

was an egg. It was covered with barley whiskers, and the colour of it was gold.

She was so surprised she cried out in astonishment, "Eh, my goodness! Deary me! Whatever in the world is this?"

She looked around, for she felt in her bones that somebody was watching her. There was nobody to be seen, except the pony in the next field, and a robin hopping along the wall, regarding her with his beady eye. He was as interested as she, but when he saw the egg he flew off to tell his neighbours.

It was not a robin's egg, or thrush's egg, or a plover's egg, or a pheasant's. This gold egg had little pictures painted on it, just as if it were an Easter egg. Perhaps it was an Easter egg, for Easter Sunday was coming in a few weeks, and somebody had sent it in plenty of time. But who had dropped it there?

She turned it over and fumbled for her spectacles, but she hadn't them with her. People don't take their spectacles when they are going to market with eggs to sell. So she peered at the little pictures, and tried to make them out. There was no doubt, one was a growing wheat-ear, another was barley, a third was oats and the fourth was rye.

"A pretty thing and no mistake," she murmured, and again she felt a pair of eyes watching her, and she thought she heard a sound of laughter and a ripple in the ground at her feet.

She wrapped the golden egg in its coverings, and tied it with the string. She lifted her skirts and hid it safely away in her pocket, deep among her many petticoats. Then she picked up her market-basket, and went on to the village.

She sold her eggs very quickly that day, and with the money she bought some sausages, and tea and sugar, and a piece of red flannel for a cloak-lining. Her fingers patted her pocket where the golden egg lay, but she was too shy to show it to the man who sold cups and mugs at the next stall, or to the woman who had black puddings and chitterlings on the other side. They might have cracked the frail shell, or laughed at her tale.

When she got home it was dusk, but no light shone from the cottage to welcome her. Only the robin sang his good-night song in the apple-tree as she looked under the shell in her rockery for the house-key.

"Aye, my dear Bobby," she called. "Do you know what thing I've found? Had ye summut to do wi' it?"

The robin shook his little head and flew off.

She unlocked her door and poked up the kitchen fire, and threw a handful of sticks on it, so that a blaze shot out and a pleasant glow shone on the dresser with its row of jugs and plates. She cooked the sausages and made the tea. The golden egg lay on the dresser-end, and she kept stopping to touch it, and to peep at it, and to hold it in her hands.

"A double-yoked goose egg, maybe," said she to herself. "But I daresn't crack it, for the shell's so pretty. It would be a sin and a shame to spoil it."

Whether it was the heat of the branches blazing in the hearth, or the warmth of the old woman's fingers that continually caressed it, I do not know, but something moved within the egg. The shell went Crick-cr-cr-crack! Crack! It fell apart, and a little face grinned up at her.

"Mercy me! Whatever's this?" she cried aloud.

A voice as shrill as a cricket's and as sweet as a wren's piped back to her.

"John Barleycorn. John Barleycorn," it said, but the words were uttered with such shrill intensity they sounded like utter gibberish to the old woman.

A tiny child lay there, nestling in the broken egg-shell, stretching its legs, which had been cramped in the egg, holding out its skinny arms to the firelight, smiling with a crinkled little smile on its small pointed face.

She brought the candle near, and fetched her spectacles to look at the child. She wasn't quite sure whether he was a bird of some kind, for on his head grew fluffy yellow feathers instead of hair, and he seemed to have a pair of wings on his back. His eyes were blue as the speedwell, that little bird's-eye flower that covers the banks in spring, and his mouth was curved in a cupid's bow. He was a beautiful little boy, or perhaps a fairy child. She couldn't make him out at all. One doesn't find a baby in an egg-shell every day of the week.

She put her old puckered hand under him, and gingerly carried him to the fire. How he kicked and laughed! A thrill of joy ran through her as she felt his warm flesh and his tiny pulsing heart beating on her hand. They weren't wings either, and she was glad of that, for, when she looked more closely, she saw they were gold hairs as thick as the awns of barley, and they dropped off in her

hands. She was pleased he hadn't got wings and couldn't fly away. His tiny ears were pointed, silky, and hairy, but that didn't matter. He was a darling little creature, whatever he was, and she loved him.

"Oh, the tiny wee bairn," she cried, laughing at his funny little face, and she gave him a spoonful of milk.

"Here, sup this up," said she. "It'll warm ye."

He drank greedily, and opened his mouth for more and more. Already he seemed to be growing. His little arms lost their wrinkles, his face became smooth and sweet to look upon.

She cut off a morsel of her red flannel and made him a cloak, and she wrapped him up like a little doll to keep him warm.

She made a bed in the pie-dish, and lined it with sheep's wool, from her store of pickings from the hedges. There she laid him while she heated up her sausages and drank her cold tea. It wasn't long before he struggled to his feet and climbed over the edge of the dish. He carried the red flannel on his shoulders like a lady's train, and walked across the table. He peeped into the glass salt-cellar, and tasted the salt. He liked that, and he nibbled the hard grains. Then he found the sugar basin, and there he sat, licking his fingers as he dipped them in the bowl.

"You funny little boy," said the old woman. "What shall I call you? Thumbkin? Fingertip? Bittikins?"

"John Barleycorn," said the child, and now his voice was so clear the old woman was quite startled.

"So you can speak, you wee thing. John Barleycorn, is it? I'll take ye to church soon to be christened by the parson, all good and proper, John Barleycorn."

The little creature yawned, stretched his arms, and suddenly fell fast asleep on the tablecloth among the spoons. She lifted him up, and spoke tenderly to him as she placed him in the pie-dish bed for the night. Then, when she had sewn a little red coat and a nightgown from the flannel and fashioned a small vest of wool she went to her own bed in the corner of the room.

Never had she spent such an exciting day in all her long life, she thought, as she lay watching the darting shadows on the wall, and the flickering firelight which glanced on the tiny figure in the dish. The light made his skin glow like molten gold; his feathery hair shone like rubies. He tossed in his sleep and stretched his arms to the shadows that seemed to be hovering around him, bending to watch him.

Once, when the old woman had been fast asleep, she awoke suddenly, thinking there was somebody in the room. The tiny boy slept there, but a field of tall ripe corn was growing around him, higher than the table, waving like a fire, and the sound of the rustling ears made strange music. She was frightened, as she watched the corn sway to and fro.

Then a lady of wonderful beauty rose from the stalks. A benign face leaned over the child, and golden fingers touched his cheeks. The corn was swept up in her arms and she faded away.

The room was bright with firelight. It must have been a dream. The flashes of fire from a fallen log had made the effect of golden corn filling the room. Yes, it must have been a dream, but she thought of tales she had heard in her childhood of a corn goddess who looked after the harvests throughout the land. She hoped the little boy would still be there at day-break.

He awoke before she did and lay kicking his legs, laughing and singing a wild little song like a bird's.

"You sing as bonny as the sky-lark," she cried, smiling at his antics. She blew up the fire while he sprang to his feet and watched her with intent gaze. He puffed out his little cheeks and blew too, and didn't the fire go well that morning! It was the same all through the day. He imitated everything she did, and kept her laughing like a young girl. Her years seemed to fall away from her with such a merry elf in the house.

"I must take you to church to be baptized," she told him. "I must have a christened child. You may be pagan, or summut."

How he laughed at her! He said the words after her, speaking in a tiny clear voice which did her heart good to hear.

"White for Christians," said she. "I mun make ye a white robe, though I doubt if you're the kind to wear a christening robe. Coat and trousers for you, I think. You can't wear that red flannel coat at your christening, can you?"

She hunted in an old leather trunk and brought out a piece of white embroidered lawn, which had been her wedding veil. She cut it into a christening gown for him. It took all day to make it, but she was a neat seamstress, for she had been a lady's maid in her youth.

"It's like making a dress for a dolly," said she.

"A Corn dolly," said he. "John Barleycorn and a Corn dolly."

"Nay, don't chatter so much," she admonished him, wagging her finger at him. "If ye talks as much as this at one day old, how much will ye talk at a year old?"

He grabbed her brass thimble and stuck it on his head. Then he pranced up and down the table, like a little king wearing a crown. He was up to tricks all that livelong day, but at night he slept soundly in the pie-dish, as good as a human child.

Again came the waving corn, and the old woman awoke to see the radiant vision leaning over him, touching his golden cheek. The beauty faded, the corn sank into the earth, and only the flashing firelight remained to gild the tiny figure lying there.

The next day the old woman carried him to the rectory. The good rector was much astonished, you may be sure, to see such a wee fellow in a market basket. However, he was a countryman himself, so he didn't ask too many questions.

"What name do you wish this child to have?" he asked.

"John Barleycorn," said the old woman. "You see, sir, I found him, at least I kind of found him, in Farmer Taylor's barleyfield, where I goes a-leasing. It's a good field, and I've got many a peck of barleycorns from it, so if you don't mind, sir, I would like John Barleycorn to be his name."

"Well," hummed the rector. "It's a queer name, an outlandish name. Why not call him Moses? He was found out of doors, and although he wasn't in the bulrushes, he was in the barleyfield, not far from the pond."

"Moses. Yes. That's nice," said the old woman.

"Then you could give him your own surname of Winkle. Moses Winkle. How do you like that?"

The old woman liked it very much, for she was partial to Bible names, and it would be very nice, she thought, to have a child called Winkle after her. So she nodded her head in agreement. She didn't notice the little fellow, shaking his yellow feathery curls, frowning with all his wee might.

They entered the ancient church, and at once all the stone faces on the walls looked down and began to smile when they saw who was in the basket. The tiny child smiled back at bishop and king and queer wide-mouthed men carved on those old walls. His quick eyes darted round as he lay in the old woman's arms, up to the arching roof with its king-posts, away to the altar. He was carried to the beautiful old font, to be baptized where generations of children had been christened since Norman days, but in all the centuries never a baby like this had been dipped in holy water.

There was a stir among the tall wooden angels carved under the great roof, and a flutter of their outspread wings. There was a movement among all the queer grimacing stone faces on the chancel arches, and sleepy eyes goggled and mouths opened and shut.

"John Barleycorn! John Barleycorn!" The whisper seemed to go round the walls, circling high in the timbered roof, echoing to the tower, floating to the bells.

"Where are the godparents?" asked the rector, looking about for the village people who should have been present.

From out of the shadows of the church came two majestic figures, moving serenely, gliding down the aisle with a rustle like the wind in the corn. One was a fair-haired man, tall and golden-skinned like a god. His strong arms were bare and he carried a sickle of shining light. The other was a woman, young and beautiful, draped in a green shawl, carrying a sheaf of ripe corn in her arms as if she had just returned from gleaning.

They took the baby without speaking, but the old woman was so surprised she stood open-mouthed, for she recognized the godmother as the one who leaned over the tiny child in the field of growing corn during the night-time.

When the rector asked the child's name the words "John Barleycorn, John Barleycorn" came ringing out like bells. Everything in the church answered, every angel

and carved figure spoke. There was no question of Moses
Winkle, and John Barleycorn was the name given to the
baby. The godparents turned to the old woman standing
so meekly there. One dropped a little gold spoon in her
wrinkled hand, and its shape was a wheat-ear. The other
gave her a little gold bowl with barley ears engraved upon
its side, and John Barleycorn's name upon it.

Then they walked away out of the church door, into
the sunshine. When the startled rector hurried after them
to the door, they had vanished, and nobody saw them any
more.

Now John Barleycorn grew very fast, and in a few
months he was full-grown. He stood tall and slim and
straight as an arrow, about three feet high. His feathery
hair was like a gold mop that waved on his head in the
wind. His feet were long and narrow, and he ran very
swiftly. His hands were beautiful and his fingers could
make anything he set about. He could weave baskets from
osiers and rushes, so delicate and well-made that the
people at the market bought every one. He could cut
musical pipes from elder and ash, and produce such sweet
tunes from them that even the birds stopped singing to
listen to him. He carved little people from pieces of wood,
but they were strange queer men he made, such as live
underground, and the old woman put them out of sight.
Sometimes he carved wheat-ears and barley-ears so
exquisitely, they would rustle as he held them up in the
wind, and these the old woman sold to the shops. To
amuse himself he took a burnt stick from the fire and with
the charcoal he drew flowers and birds and animals with
startling exactness. All these were his games, his pleasures.
He worked hard too.

The garden flourished in an astonishing manner when
he planted roots or scattered seeds.

The fruit trees were laden with apples and plums, although he only touched the branches and spoke to the buds, or leaned his golden cheek against the trunks. It was as if everything loved John Barleycorn, and he loved everything in return.

He went with the old woman to market, and carried a small basket of eggs while she carried the large basket in which he had been taken to his christening. At first people stopped to stare at his bright gold hair, which they said was the colour of corn, but they soon got used to him. He held their horses for a penny and he ran their errands. He was willing to work for all.

Sometimes he went alone to the church, and gazed up at the stone figures and the wooden angels under the roof. The gargoyles and saints seemed to delight in his company, and they blinked their eyes, and screwed up their mouths and spoke in muffled voices.

"John Barleycorn. We remember you, John Barleycorn, our friend. Long ago we played with you, John Barleycorn."

Then he ran out to the churchyard and danced among the tombstones, and planted flowers on the graves.

"Thank you, John Barleycorn. Thank you. We remember you, John Barleycorn," whispered the voices of the dead.

His greatest joy was to go into the cornfield, to walk along the verges, and seek for the small flowers that grew there, to laugh at the hares and tease the hedgehogs and scare the cock pheasant from trampling the corn. He came home decked with garlands of cornflowers, and purple corncockle, and scarlet poppies.

"I can see where you've been, John," said his mother, for the old woman thought of the child as her very own bairn. "You've been to watch the barley growing. You shall come with me a-leasing when the corn's cut."

"I want to earn my living, Mother," said he one day. "I want to help at the farm for harvest."

"Nay, you are too little, my wee son," she replied. "Wait till you grow bigger."

"I'm grown up, Mother. I'm as tall as the corn now," he pouted. "I'm full-grown."

"You would get lost in the great field, lost in the forest of barley stalks," said she. "You would be cut by the reapers."

However, when the men began to reap the harvest, little John Barleycorn went to the farmer and got the

job of making the shocks of corn. They were as big as himself, and the men laughed to see him, but they were filled with admiration for the way the small boy worked. There was a magic in his touch, for with little trouble he shocked the corn and kept pace with the harvesters. Sometimes it was difficult to distinguish the boy from the barley sheaves, they were the same height, and the same golden colour, and they seemed to move together, corn swaying to boy, and boy binding the sheaves and caressing them as if he loved them.

At the Harvest Home the farmer put little John Barleycorn on the last wagon, on the great load of sheaves. The white horses drew the load, and there sat little John Barleycorn, wreathed in scarlet poppies and blue cornflowers and honeysuckle, like a king of the cornfield.

On the cart was the harvest doll, called the Kern Baby, which the oldest worker had made from some good ears of corn.

She was the symbol of good luck to the harvest. Little John Barleycorn sat by her side, his golden hair like the barley blowing in the wind, his face smiling, his blue eyes the colour of the cornflowers.

The harvest men sang a song as the great swaying wain laden with corn went through the fields to the rick yard and barns.

> *We have ploughed, we have sowed,*
> *We have reaped, and we have mowed.*
> *We have brought home every load.*
> *Hip! Hip! Hip! Harvest Home!*

They had the harvest supper in the farmyard and John Barleycorn danced on the table among the tankards of ale and the boiled beef and suet dumpling.

"It's been a bumper crop this year," said the farmer, "and I do believe it's all along of John Barleycorn here. I shall send your mother a sack of corn in payment, John, for she's getting old to go a-leasing."

"Thank you, sir," said little John. "She can't stoop very well, but can I go, sir? I want to go a-leasing. I've been looking forward to it all my life."

"All your short life," laughed the farmer. "All right."

So little John Barleycorn went a-leasing by himself, and the old woman insisted on coming to the gate of the cornfield with him, and bringing his dinner and tea in a basin with a cloth over it.

She could see the small figure walking the fields, stooping close to the earth, and talking to somebody who was invisible. He was laughing and nodding, and now and then he took someone's hand in his. Then he gathered up the scattered corn, and clasped it to him. He gathered as much in a day as his mother had done in a week. He seemed to have grown older in that one day leasing, alone with the cornfield.

At the Harvest Festival he went to church with his mother. A tiny little person, his head scarcely reached the top of the pew, and he was put on a hassock. All went well, till the harvest hymn was sung. Then John Barleycorn piped up in such a shrill treble that the sound of it rang through the church and startled the congregation. They looked round to see who was warbling so loudly. They gazed up and about them, for somebody else was singing too. Every carved face on the old church walls, every wooden angel with outstretched wings on that grand roof, every beam and stone in the ancient building gave thanks to God Almighty for the splendid harvest. Never was such singing heard in a church!

The hymn came to an end, the organ tones died away, the voices were quiet and there was an astonished silence. Then there was a scamper of little boots and little John Barleycorn ran down the nave to the chancel, where he sat among the sheaves of corn and the miniature thatched rick and the long loaf of bread brought in from the farm for the festival.

The rector hesitated a moment, and the little choir-boys gasped, and the churchwarden stepped forward. Something restrained them all, and the service went on. Little John Barleycorn looked like a cherub as he sat there with one arm around a sheaf of corn, his gold hair sweeping into the barley, his cheek resting against it. His golden skin was exactly the same colour as the ripe corn. He *was* the corn and nobody could turn him away.

"Eh, John. You shouldn't have done it," said his mother afterwards as they walked home. "I couldn't believe my own eyes. It's not proper. Eh, I was shocked."

"But, Mother, I was thanking God. I had to go there. I had to be with the barley sheaves. They are my brothers, Mother."

When the corn ricks were thatched, and the thatcher made the little crown of corn to decorate the top of the rick, John Barleycorn watched him. The labourer tied some ears together in a tassel, and twisted a straw band round it, to form a crown, with the ears poking through the little archway of straw. John Barleycorn followed him up the ladder with it, and there he stayed, night and day, only coming down now and then to visit his mother.

He disappeared after that, but each spring when the barley came up in the fields, little John Barleycorn came to stay with his foster mother, to help the corn to grow, and to be the guest of honour at the Harvest Home.

They all sang around him the harvest song:

> *We have ploughed, we have sowed,*
> *We have reaped, and we have mowed.*
> *We have brought home every load.*
> *Hip! Hip! Hip! Harvest Home!*

And as long as John Barleycorn came to the fields the corn grew tall and strong and the ears were large and well filled.

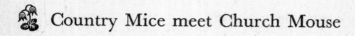 Country Mice meet Church Mouse

Jemima and Jeremy were two little field-mice who lived in a house under the hawthorn tree on the common, and they had a strange adventure one fine autumn day. It was a morning of sunshine, and golden light filled the fields of ripened corn, and scarlet poppies grew in the hedgerows.

The little mice ran along the edge of the big cornfield, through the tall stalks of the wheat, on a tiny track invisible to the eyes of people, but clear to the bright eyes of the mice. The track led to the village, but it seemed a long way to the mice. The harvest mouse peeped from the doorway of her round house high in the cornstalks, and the mice stopped for a talk.

"Please, Mrs Harvest, are we on the right path to the village?" asked Jeremy Mouse.

"Yes, my children," said the comfortable harvest mouse. "Go straight on, and under the gate, and turn to your right."

"Thank you, Mrs Harvest Mouse," replied Jeremy politely, and he took Jemima's hand and led her through the forest of cornstalks to the gate and the village green.

Children were running about, and there was an excitement in the air. So the two mice hurried under a small gate which had a wooden roof over it, into a large garden,

with upright stones. They thought it was a garden, for there
were many flowers lying in the grass, garlands of flowers,
but it was a churchyard, with old graves and crosses.

The two ran lightly over a gravestone, where some
flowers lay, but a dark head appeared near them and Mr
Mole stood there, waiting.

He shook his fist at the two strangers, who leapt down
and bowed to him.

"Go away," said he sternly. "This is not a place for
field-mice, not for bad little mice like you. This is the
quiet garden for good mice who always behave themselves."

"We are good mice, sir," said Jeremy quickly. He
danced back on the gravestone and wiped a dark stain
from the stone with a dock-leaf. "We are very good mice.
We won't harm anything, sir," said he to the mole.

Jemima stroked a butterfly which settled near her and
the butterfly waved its wings up and down with pleasure
at her soft touch. Jeremy waved his paw to a jackdaw who
sat listening, and he let a ladybird settle on his fur. "My
mother says we are good," said Jeremy. "Do let us stay.
We like this garden and no children are playing here. It is
safe and quiet."

"It is Sunday," said the mole sternly. "People are
coming to church. Go away. You are not wanted."

The mole dug a hole near the grave, and disappeared.

"Where has he gone?" asked Jemima.

"He's looking for bones," jeered the jackdaw. "Bones
like yours," he added, and he flew off with a cackle.

The church door was open and there was a trail of
leaves and berries and broken stalks of flowers, with here
and there a poppy and a rose head. Jeremy and Jemima
Mouse entered the porch, and leapt down a step into the
great empty church.

There were flowers everywhere, for it was the Harvest Festival and the decorators had finished their work. "How pretty it is," whispered Jemima, looking round at the chrysanthemums on the font, and the dahlias decorating a little wooden house which had a flight of wooden stairs. "A house of flowers!"

Jeremy ran up the stairs to the pulpit and gazed over the edge at the church below. There was a big sheaf of corn on the ledge and he ate some ears of wheat and tossed a few down to Jemima below.

"What a nice little house," said he, "I could go to sleep here," and he ran back to his sister. She had found a long loaf of crusty bread, freshly baked, resting against a stone figure of a sleeping man. She nibbled a little and found it very good. Then she climbed up to look at the statue. The stone man's feet rested on the back of a little dog, and the dog seemed to lick its lips when it saw Jemima perched there. "Poor little dog," said Jemima. She ate more of the wheat-ears which hung in tassels from each wooden pew. There was a sweet smell everywhere, and plenty of food for a hundred mice.

"This is like a storehouse of food," said Jeremy, as he nibbled some red berries and swung on the cornstalks. They bit the edges of a prayer-book and tasted the wool of an embroidered kneeler. They skated on a brass tablet let into the floor and admired their own faces reflected there.

"It could be brighter," said Jemima. "Let us polish it."

She took out her tiny leafy handkerchief and rubbed the brass, and Jeremy removed his scarf and polished too. Soon the brass was bright as gold, and the words on it shone as never before. They were so busy that they did not notice someone was watching them.

"What are you doing here?" asked a cross voice, with a squeak in it. "What do you think you are doing in our church, you bold little field-mice?"

A black mouse, thin and tall, in a black coat and black leather boots, came down the aisle and stood over them.

"Why do you come to our church, to bring your untidy ways? Why do you come here and eat our feast, that we have only once a year, when there are many poor thin church mice waiting to come and feast?"

"Please, sir, please, sir, we are very sorry, sir. We didn't know," stammered Jemima. "We saw the door open and here are the grains of corn from our cornfields, where we live."

"This is our special day," growled the church mouse. "No food on ordinary days, no wheat-sheaves, or loaves of bread. We starve and we have to nibble the hymn-books and hassocks, the floor polish and the fringes on the cloths, and the crumbs the choirboys drop for us," said the old weary church mouse.

Jemima felt so sorry that tears came into her eyes.

"You have polished that brass plate very well," said the church mouse, relenting as he saw her sorrow. "If you polish the candlesticks over yonder, the Vicar will be pleased."

"Yes, sir," said Jeremy and Jemima, and they pattered quickly down the aisle to the chancel and ran up the big brass candlesticks to polish them.

They were busily working on these when the church bells rang out a merry peal, and the doors were opened wide. Into the church came people, all smiling with happiness to see the flowers and wheat sheaves. Jeremy

and Jemima polished as quickly as they could, scurrying up and down, and nobody saw them. Now and then they took a nibble of the wax candle, but a man came across to light the candles and the two mice ran swiftly to the ground and hid in corners.

Down in the chancel they saw a tiny black flag waving on the church floor, a little black wing which fluttered piteously, and they heard a faint squeak. "Help! Help! Help!" was the cry.

Jemima went to look and she saw a baby bat which had hurt its wing and could not fly.

Quickly she climbed into a dark corner behind the altar and gathered up a thick spider's web which hung to the wall.

"Excuse me, Mrs Spider," said she to a large angry spider which came forward to stop her. "Excuse me, but a spider's web is the best cure for a torn wing or a cut leg," said she.

"It is the ancient cure," agreed the spider, "but nobody bothers nowadays. Who is hurt? Not a choirboy, surely? They have no wings." She laughed hoarsely.

"No, a little bitbat," said Jemima, and she hurried across the floor with the web. She laid it over the cut wing and bound a piece of web to keep the wing in shape. Then she lifted up the little creature and placed it on a flower petal. It fluttered its wing slowly, waveringly, it rose in the air, sailed across the church and up into the oak beams where its mother was anxiously watching.

"That was a good little mouse," said the bat as she embraced her child.

A choirboy had seen Jemima and he threw a hymn-book at her, but she only smiled and sat down on it.

The boys began to sing. The organ poured out rich music and all the people stood and joined in. Jemima also

stood and sang and her little voice squeaked an octave
above the voices of the choir, so that it made a harmonious
cadence.

> *All things bright and beautiful,*
> *All creatures great and small,*
> *All things wise and wonderful,*
> *The Lord God made them all*

sang the people, and Jemima crept near Jeremy and said,
"We are creatures small, aren't we, Jeremy?"

"Yes, very small, but they know about us," whispered
Jeremy.

The choirboy was watching them and the mice felt
nervous. Quietly they stepped down the chancel and
walked one behind the other down the aisle. People's eyes
were on the flowers, on the lights and on the stained glass
windows. They did not notice two little strangers who
moved quietly like two small shadows, but the church
mouse watched them go.

"Goodbye, my cousins," he squeaked. "Goodbye. You
are good little creatures after all."

The bats in the belfry flew out over the roof of the
church, singing with the people. "All creatures great and
small," they squeaked.

Jeremy and Jemima crept through a hole in the door
and went out to the graveyard and to the bright sun.

"Safe," murmured Jeremy. "I thought that boy would
try to catch us."

"We are creatures small," said Jemima. "They said
so. Let's go home and tell our mother."

So off they went, back through the cornfield, under the
nest of the sleeping harvest mouse, among the butterflies
and beetles, the frogs and the field-mice, the hedgehogs
and the spiders, all the way home to their mother.

"Welcome in, my dears," said Mrs Mouse. "Where have you been? I've been listening to the church bells. It must be a special day, for they rang so loudly."

"We've been to Church, Mother, and it was nice," said Jemima, hugging her mother.

"And it was all full of flowers and food, so we had our dinner there," added Jeremy.

"And we are all creatures great and small," said Jemima.

"Are you, my dears?" asked Mrs Mouse.

"The Lord God made us all," added Jeremy. "They said so, all singing with choirboys."

"It must be true," said Mrs Mouse, and she smiled in happiness.

Sam Pig's Trousers

Sam Pig was always hard on his trousers. He tore them on the brambles and hooked them in the gorse bushes. He lost little pieces of them in the hawthorns, and he left shreds among the spiky thistles. He rubbed them threadbare with sliding down the rocks of the high pastures, and he wore them into holes when he scrambled through hedges. One always knew where Sam Pig had been by the fragments of check trousers which clung to thorn and crooked twig. The birds were very glad, and they took bits to make their nests. The rooks had little snippets like gay pennons dangling from their rookery in the elms, and the chaffinches and yellow-hammers mixed the thread with sheep's wool to line their beds. It seemed as if Sam Pig would provide material for everybody's home in the trees and hedgerows, but trousers won't last for ever, and Sam's were nearly done.

Sister Ann patched the seats and put pieces into the front. She stitched panels in the two sides, and then she patched and repatched the patches until there was none of the original trousers left. They were a conglomeration of stripes and plaids and spotted scraps, all herring-boned and cross-stitched with green thread.

"Sam's trousers are like a patchwork quilt," remarked Tom, when Ann held up the queer little garments one evening after she had mended them.

"Pied and speckled like a magpie," said Bill.

Sam Pig leaned out of the truckle bed where he lay wrapped in a blanket, waiting for Ann to finish the mending. They were the only trousers the little pig possessed, and he had to go to bed early on mending nights.

"I like them patched," said he indignantly. "Don't mock at them. I love my old trousers and their nice patches. It's always a surprise when Ann finishes them. Look now! There's a green patch on top of a black patch, on top of a yellow patch, on top of a blue one. And there's lots of pockets hidden among the patches, spaces where I can keep things. When Ann's stitches burst I stuff things in between."

"Yes," frowned Ann. "I've already taken out a lady-bird, and a piece of honeycomb, and some bees and a frog that was leaping up and down, and a stag-beetle that was fighting, not to mention sundry pebbles and oak-apples and snail shells! No wonder you look a clumsy shape with all those things hidden in your patches, Sam! All corners and lumps, you are!"

Sam curled himself under the blanket and laughed till he made the bed shake. She hadn't found the most important thing of all, something that was hidden under the largest patch! If she did——!

Just then Ann gave a shrill cry and dropped the trousers.

"Oh! They've bitten me! Your trousers bit my finger!" she exclaimed, and she put her hand in her mouth and sucked it.

"Trousers can't bite," said Tom, but Sam dived deeper under the blanket, and laughed all the more.

"What is it, Sam?" asked Tom sternly. "Confess! What is hidden there in your trousers?"

There was no answer, but from the patch came a pair of ears and two bright eyes. A white mouse poked out its little head. It stared at Ann, it peeped at Sam, and then it bolted down the table leg and into a hole in the floor.

"Now you've lost her! You've lost Jemima!" said Sam crossly, coming up from the blankets. "She was my pet mouse, and you've lost her. She was a most endearing creature. I kept her in that patch and fed her on crumbs. Is her family safe?"

"Family?" cried Ann, shrilly.

"Family?" echoed Bill and Tom.

"Yes. She has four children. They all live in the patch. They have a nest there. I helped Jemima to make it. I'm the godfather to the children. They know me very well."

Ann hurriedly unpicked the stitches and brought out a small round nest with four pink mice inside it.

"There they are! Aren't they charming creatures?" cried Sam. "But they will be lonely without their mother. You must put them by the hole in the floor, Ann, and Jemima will come for them. She'll miss her warm home in my trousers, and the food I gave her."

Ann carried the nest and placed it close to the hole. In a minute the mother appeared and enticed her brood away.

"Good-bye, Sam," she squealed in a shrill voice, thin as a grasshopper's chirp. "Good-bye, Sam, and thank you for your hospitality. We are going to travel. It is time my children saw something of the world."

"Good-bye," called Sam, leaning out of bed. "I shall miss you terribly, but we may meet again some day. The world is small."

"Hm!" sniffed Ann Pig. "The world may be small, but surely there is room in it for a family of white mice without their coming to live in a patch in your trousers, Sam."

She threaded her needle and took up a bodkin and cleared away all the odds and ends the mice had left, their pots and frying-pan and toasting fork. She tossed the bits of cheese in the fire and frowned as she brought out bacon rind.

"Bacon in the house of the four pigs is an insult," said she sternly.

"It came from the grocer's shop, Ann. Really it did! Jemima's husband brought it for the family," protested Sam.

"Then it's quite time you had a new pair of trousers, Sam. Jemima's husband bringing bacon rinds! I won't have it! These mice are the last straw!" cried Ann, and she banged the trousers and shook them and threw them back to Sam.

"Yes," agreed Bill. "It is time you had new breeks. We can't have a menagerie in our house. You'll keep ants and antelopes hidden in your patches, Sam, if you go on like this."

"Bears and bisons," said Tom, shaking his head at Sam.

"Crocodiles and cassowaries," whispered Sam, quivering with laughter.

"It's no laughing matter. Trousers don't grow on gooseberry bushes."

"I don't want a new pair," pouted Sam. "I know this pair, and they are very comfortable. I know every stitch and cranny, and every ridge and crease and crumple." He pulled the trousers on and shook himself.

"These will soon be quite worn out. One more tear and they will be done," said Ann. "We must get another pair, and where the stuff is to come from in these hard times I don't know. You'd better go collecting, all of you."

"Collecting what? Trousers? From the scarecrows?" asked Sam.

"No. Sheep's wool. Get it off the hedges and bushes and fences. Everywhere you go you must gather the wool left by the sheep when they scramble through gaps and rub their backs on posts. Then I'll dye the wool and spin it, and make a new pair for you."

Each day the pigs gathered sheep's wool. They picked it off the wild-rose trees, where it was twisted among the thorns. They got it from low fences under which the sheep had squeezed, and from the rough trunks of haw-thorns and oaks where they had rubbed their backs. Sam found a fine bunch of fleecy wool where the flock had pushed under the crooked boughs of an ancient tree to sleep in the hollow beneath. It was surprising what a quantity of wool there was lying about in the country lanes, and each day they brought back their small sacks filled to the brim.

Ann washed the little fleeces and hung them up to dry. The wool was white as snow when she had finished dip-ping it in the stream. She tied it to a stout stick and swung it in the sunshine till it was dry and light as a feather.

Bill filled a bowl with lichens and mosses and pieces of bark, and Ann dyed the wool.

"What colour will it be?" asked Sam, anxiously peer-ing at it. "I don't want brown or grey or anything dull."

"It looks like drab," confessed Ann.

"Oh dear! What a dingy shade!" sighed Sam. "I don't want miserable gloomy trousers, or I shall be a gloomy little pig."

"I'm afraid they *are* going to be sad trousers, Sam," said Ann, stirring them with a stick. "I'm sorry, but this is the colour, and there's one good thing, it is the colour of dirt."

"Gloomy and black as a pitchy night in winter," said Sam.

So off he went to the woods. He picked some crimson bryony berries, and scarlet rose-hips, and bright red toadstools. He brought them back and dropped them into the dye.

"Ann! Ann! Come and look," he called, and he held up the fleece on the end of the stirring stick.

"Oh Sam! Bright red! A glorious colour," cried Ann.

"Like a sunset," exclaimed Tom, admiringly.

"Like a house on fire," said Bill.

Out rushed Sam again, for blueberries and blue geranium and borage. He dipped another wisp of sheep's wool into the juices and brought it out blue as a wood in bluebell time.

They dried the wool, and Ann fastened it to her little spinning-wheel. She spun a length of red yarn and then a length of blue. Then she knitted a new pair of trousers, in blue and red checks, bright and bold, with plenty of real pockets.

When Sam Pig walked out in his new trousers all the animals and birds came to admire him. Even the Fox stopped to stare at Sam.

"As red as my brush," he murmured, and the Hedge-hog said, "As pretty a pair of trousers as ever I seed in all my prickly life."

When Sam met the white mouse and her family they refused to visit his new pockets.

"We like something quieter," whispered the mouse. "You are too dazzling for us nowadays, Sam. Besides, we have found a lodging in an old boot. It suits us better."

"As you will, Jemima," shrugged Sam. He sauntered off to show himself to acquaintances in the fields, to visit his old haunts in wood and lane.

Soon his trousers lost their brightness, as they took on the hues of the woodland. They were striped green from the beech trunks, smeared with the juices of blackberry and spindle, parched by the brown earth herself. The sun faded them, the rain shrank them, and the colours were softened by the moist airs.

"I declare! There is no difference in Sam's trousers," Ann remarked one day. "These might be the old check trousers; they are marked and stained in just the same way. I haven't patched them yet, but I can see a hole."

"Yes," said Sam, slyly, and he brought a dormouse from his pocket. "Here is a little friend who lives with me, and he's waiting for a patch to make his winter sleeping-quarters, Ann."

"Get along with you," cried Ann, and she chased him out with a besom. But her eyes were twinkling as she watched her young brother dance down the garden path with his dormouse perched on his arm.

The white mouse Jemima in this story is of course not the same character as the field-mouse Jemima in *Country Mice meet Church Mouse*.

🌸 The Wind in a Frolic

One day the Wind awoke from a little nap under the quiet trees. He stretched himself lazily, and yawned with wide-open mouth, so that the bees and butterflies resting on the flowers were blown away by the tiny gust.

"Oh! Ho-o-o!" he yawned, again. "I'll go for a stroll, and say how-do-ye-do to the village folk. I'm sure they've missed me lately. I'll go and cheer them up, play with them, amuse them. Yes, that's what I'll do to-day."

He picked up his long length from the mossy ground, and stalked off down the path, snapping twigs from the trees with his slender fingers, blowing the leaves with his breath.

Now he hadn't gone far when he met a little boy going to school. Such a neat little, nice little, clean little boy, with his cap on his head, and his school-bag on his back!

"How d'ye do?" said the Wind, and he put out one thin finger, twitched the cap and flung it up in a sycamore-tree. There it hung till the nice little boy climbed up and got it down, but his hands were dirty, and his hair was awry. The Wind sat on the ground watching, waiting for the little boy to laugh.

"Bother the wind!" exclaimed the little boy, and he stuffed his cap in his pocket and went whistling to school.

"That was clever of me," said the Wind, "but he wasn't amused. I must do something better next time."

He went a bit farther, and overtook a little girl. A few drops of rain were falling by this time, and she put up her umbrella.

"I always think umbrellas are such comical things," said the Wind, "don't you?" The little girl answered never a word, but held tight to the handle when she felt the Wind's presence.

"Away it goes!" cried the Wind, putting his face under it, and giving a small puff. Away it went, inside out, and the Wind laughed and laughed at the funny sight. But the little girl didn't laugh. She ran after her umbrella, and picked it up sadly. It was her birthday umbrella the Wind had spoilt, but of course the Wind didn't know that.

"Dear-a-me," said the Wind. "I thought that was amusing. I must find some one else to tease."

He went rollicking along the road, and the cows and horses turned their backs or stood close to the hedges for shelter. Then he saw a farm man carrying a load of hay on his back. The Wind blew and blew, till the man staggered against a wall and the hay went floating off in the air.

The Wind laughed to see the sight, but the man grumbled and groaned as he collected it together again, and tied it with a rope.

"The wind's something awful!" said he crossly, and the Wind, very much surprised, skipped away to find someone with a sense of humour.

Along came a woman with a basket of eggs, and the Wind hurried up to her.

"Madam," said he politely, taking off his pointed hat. "Madam, may I carry your basket for you?" He put a hand on the basket, but the woman felt the strong gale around her, and held on with all her might. What was happening to the weather, for the wind to blow like that all of a sudden? she wondered. Her skirts flew out behind her, her hat blew off, but she wouldn't let the basket go.

Then the Wind tossed an egg in the air, and it fell with a splash of yellow.

"Isn't that a joke! Ha! Ha! If only you would give me your basket, I would show you even funnier things. Eggs sailing in the air, and dropping like raindrops!"

"Goodness!" cried the woman. "There's one of my eggs! Twopence gone. This wind's a regular nuisance." She held the basket close to her side to protect it, but the Wind had flown away to find someone else.

He blew the hens in the farmyard, so that they ran squawking to the barn, and he drove the dog to the kennel. He shook the sign outside the village inn, and rattled the shutters on the wall. He threw a slate off the roof, and dropped a chimney-pot. The Wind chuckled at all these pranks, but the people frowned and shut their doors.

Then away went the Wind, away, away, over the fields and woods. He felt very unhappy, for nobody laughed, nobody wanted the Wind's frolic. He felt so dejected that he began to walk, and then to crawl, with his head bent, and his arms hanging limp.

"There isn't a laugh left in the world! It's a sad, sad place, and I shall go away and play with the Polar bears and penguins. They will welcome me." He didn't really want to go to such cold places, and he glanced round to see if there was still a chance of a laugh.

On top of the hill was a windmill, with great sails lying idle. In the orchard near was a clothes-line full of washing, and a little boy ran up and down, trying to fly a kite.

The Wind tripped lightly to the house, and blew, just a little. The clothes flapped and sank and flapped again. He blew harder, and the clothes began to dance. Sheets cracked with a delicious sound, pyjamas seemed to have invisible legs, coats and petticoats were full of fat windy people who swung up and down on the line. The little boy's kite flew up in the air, and soared on the end of the string like a blue bird. The great sails of the windmill with many a creak and groan began to turn, and then went rapidly round and round.

The miller and his wife came running to the door.

"Here's the wind at last," said they, laughing to one another. "It will grind my corn," said the miller, joyfully.

"It will dry my washing," said his wife, as she watched the clothes swinging in the wind.

"Look at my kite!" said the little boy. "Isn't it going well! Like an eagle! I do like this wind," and he ran round and round with the Wind tugging at the little blue kite.

"Thank goodness, I've found people who like me! I shall often come and see this laughing family. The world's not so bad after all," said the Wind, and he danced round and round the windmill, puffing out his cheeks, and whistling a merry tune.

🌿 The Snow Goose

Winter was coming and the wind tore the leaves from the trees and threw them down to the ground in showers.

"The wind's in a frolic to-day. He's stripping the trees and the poor things will be cold," remarked Ann Pig. She took her little birch-besom to sweep up the leaves, but they lay so thick in the woods she had to let the wind have his own way.

Then wild gales raged from the north, and the trees were rocked and shaken.

"Let us gather firewood for the winter," said Ann, and they all ran out to collect the fallen branches, to store in the wood-shed.

Next came snow, and the soft flakes fell like feathers fluttering from the heavy clouds.

"The Old Grey Woman is plucking the white geese up yonder," said Ann, pointing to the sky. She shivered and went indoors to the fireside, but Sam Pig stood looking up, trying to see the great white birds whose feathers were falling so fast they covered the fields and woods. It was very cold and the wind cut his cheeks like a knife, so he followed Ann and sat with his brothers in the warm kitchen.

No outside work could be done. The stream was frozen, and Bill had to break a hole in the ice with a stone

to fill the kettle. There was plenty to eat, and the snow
didn't matter, for it was very cosy in the house of the four
pigs. There were strings of onions hanging in ropes from
the beams of the ceiling, and a heap of carrots under
straw in the larder. The wood-shed was piled with
potatoes and logs of wood to roast them. Tom Pig made
good warm soup every day, and Sam shook the pepper
pot over it. It was as hot as a fire, and it kept their
innards comfortable.

Away in the Fox's house it was dismal and cold, for
Mr Fox hadn't had a good meal for weeks. He had been
out every night to the rabbit warren, but the rabbits kept
close to their homes and wrapped themselves in fur
blankets and curled up in bed to keep warm. The Fox
kept watch on the pond where the water-hens and ducks
lived, but the water was frozen and the birds were wary.
They saw the tracks of the Fox in the snow, and they hid
themselves. Then the Fox went to the farm, hoping to
catch a hen for supper. The dog was loose and he
frightened the Fox away.

So the Fox got very thin with hunger, and when he
met fat little Sam Pig, who had just eaten a plateful of
hot vegetable soup, he was really angry. Sam Pig was
going to make a slide, but he stopped when he saw the Fox.

"Have you seen any geese about?" asked the Fox with
a sneer.

Sam opened wide his little blue eyes. "Geese? No,"
said he.

"I thought you might know of a few ganders, as you
know everything," scoffed the Fox, hungrily.

"The Old Grey Woman is plucking the white geese up
in the sky," said Sam, catching a snowflake and eating it.

"How do you know that?" asked the Fox with a sharp
bark.

"Here are the feathers," said Sam, innocently. "Look at them. There's a big flock of geese up there in the fields of the sky, and the Woman is plucking the feathers off and throwing them down to the earth. Ann says so, and it must be true."

The Fox was impressed.

"I could do with one of those fat geese," said he. "Where do you think they live, Sam Pig?"

"In the sky somewhere," said Sam, hesitating and looking up. "There's maybe great fields up there, and ponds and streams where the geese can swim. That's what the rain is, I 'specks. It's a pond running over and coming down on us."

"Yes," said the Fox. "That's it."

"I don't know how you will catch a goose from up there," said Sam, and he ate a few feathers thoughtfully. "Not unless the Old Grey Woman lets one slip from her knees."

"I wish she would," said the Fox fervently.

"They'll be cold if they are like this feather," said Sam, shivering.

"I don't care if they are cold as ice as long as I can get my teeth into them," said the Fox. "When they are alive they are warm. It's because the feathers have dropped such a long way on a winter's morning that they are so cold."

Sam agreed that it might be so.

"I will wait here till a goose falls from the Old Grey Woman's knee," said the Fox, and he sat down in the snow with his head raised to the sky, waiting.

Sam didn't bother to make his slide. He went home to ask all about snow geese.

When he told his brothers that the Fox was waiting for a snow goose to drop from the sky they laughed.

"Let's make one for him," they said. "It would be a pity if he waited for nothing, poor old Fox."

They ran to the back of the house and worked quickly, with handfuls of snow. They made a beautiful snow goose. It had a large smooth body, and a long neck and a neat head. They fixed a pair of feathery wings, ruffled and cut from the snow. Then Sam put a pair of little shiny pebbles for the eyes, and they all stood back to admire their work.

"Did you ever see such a big goose?" they whispered. "It is much more fun than making a snow pig, or even a snow man. A snow goose is a fine bird, and this is as real as life."

Sam carried it out to the field and placed it under a tree. Then he ran off to find the Fox, who was still waiting.

"Mr Fox! There's a snow goose under yonder tree. He must have flown down from the sky. Come quickly before he goes off. Oh, he is such a big one!"

The Fox shook the snow from his back and ran after
Sam Pig.

"What a beautiful goose!" he cried. "Thank you,
Sam Pig. It will feed us all. Thank you."

He hauled the goose on to his back and walked away.
The goose was very large and the Fox was nearly covered
with the snowy body. As he went through the woods the
heat of his fur began to melt the snow goose, and the
weight of it pressed upon him. The water turned to ice
again, and stuck to his back.

"Whatever have you got there?" asked his wife as he
staggered in at the door.

"A snow goose, fallen from the sky," said the Fox
triumphantly. "Come, wife, and take it off my back, for
it seems to have frozen on me."

So she pulled and pulled and the Fox shook himself
and at last the snow goose fell to the ground.

"Why, it's only a heap of snow," cried Mrs Fox. "How
foolish you are, Reynard."

"It's a snow goose from the sky, one of the geese
which drop their feathers when it snows, my dear," the
Fox assured her, and he pulled the goose to pieces. "Sam
Pig helped me to catch it," he added.

"You are a snow goose yourself," snapped Mrs Fox.
"Young Sam Pig has tricked you again."

"You are right as usual," said the Fox ruefully, looking
up from the snowy heap. They both vowed vengeance on
little Sam Pig as they watched the wings and the long
smooth neck and the stiff little legs fall to the floor and
run away like water.

Now a few days later Sam was coming back from the
hen-place with a few eggs he had collected. Eggs are
scarce in cold weather, and the hens had not been laying.
Brother Bill fed them on warm scraps and they were so

pleased they decided to give him some eggs. They
clucked loudly to tell Sam all about it, and he ran
through the snow calling back to them.

"Sam Pig, Sam Pig. We've laid some eggs," they
shouted in their clucking voices, and Sam Pig answered,
"Thank you. Thank you, dear Fluff and Bluff, and Snow-
white and Rose-red and the rest of you."

He gathered the eggs from the warm nests, patted the
hens' soft feathers, and started back home. But to his
surprise he saw the Fox waiting for him. At first Sam
was rather frightened, remembering the snow goose, but
the Fox came smiling up to him and held out a paw.

"Shake, Sam Pig! Shake!" cried the Fox. "I want to
thank you, Sam Pig. You saved me from starvation, Sam.
Shake a paw!"

Sam put down the basket and held out his little fist,
and the Fox shook it up and down so hard that Sam was
nearly thrown off his balance. Perhaps the Fox didn't
know how much it hurt, for he kept smiling, so Sam
smiled back, although it was only a little wry smile he
gave the Fox.

"You remember that snow goose you found, Sam
Pig," said the Fox, and Sam, trembling a little, said that
he remembered.

"It was a wonderful goose, so fat, so luscious, so tender
that it melted in my mouth," said the Fox.

Sam listened, uneasily.

"Yes, Sam Pig, I shall always be grateful to you for
your kindness in telling me of the geese which the Old
Grey Woman is plucking up in the sky, and for giving
me such a fat one."

Sam's eyes widened. He could scarcely believe his ears.

"And that was not the end," continued the Fox, "for
the next day I found another snow goose, and this one

was alive. It had flown down from the sky and there it was a-sitting in the wood as tame as a hen."

"Oh my!" cried Sam Pig. "I wish I had seen it."

"It's in my wood-shed," said the Fox. "It's so tame I haven't the heart to eat it. Besides, it is laying eggs for me. Each day it lays two dozen eggs. You never saw anything like them for size. As for flavour! And shape! And goodness! Words can't tell their excellence."

The Fox spoke slowly and Sam's eyes were popping out of his head. His breath came panting in excitement, and his red tongue licked his lips. Marvels would never cease!

The Fox continued, "Those eggs are the best-tasting I ever had, with yolks all rich and whites as pure as the driven snow. We poach them, and scramble them, and make omelettes with them, and boil them, but we can't use them all up. Think of it! Two dozen eggs a day from one goose! I'm looking for another goose, Sam Pig."

Another goose! Sam Pig gasped and gazed round, also looking for another goose.

"If I can find another I shall have four dozen eggs a day, and I can give plenty away. I can give some to your family, for I don't think you get enough eggs, do you? You look very hungry, poor Sam."

"Our hens don't lay in snowy weather," said Sam. "I've got some eggs to-day, but these are the first we've had, and I am just taking them home."

The Fox picked up the basket and looked contemptuously at the brown eggs, warm from the nest.

"You should see my eggs, Sam. Four times as big as these, and full of meat. Why, one of my eggs would make an omelette for all your family, including Badger. Yes, with Badger too! These are miserable eggs, Sam. I wouldn't give a handful of snow for eggs like these. Are they from pigeons or wrens?"

"They are hen eggs," Sam reassured the Fox, and he peeped at the eggs lying in the basket. It was true, they were not as large as he had thought.

"Mr Fox," said he. "Could you—do you think you could—er—may I see some of the eggs from the snow goose? I've never seen a snow goose's eggs."

The Fox didn't speak for a moment. He frowned as if he were making up his mind on some difficult matter.

"Well, as you are a friend of mine, Sam Pig, and as you were so kind, so very kind to me, showing me the snow goose and saving my life, I will let you have a sight of the eggs. But mind, don't tell everybody about them, or others will be going after the snow geese."

The Fox picked up the basket of eggs and told Sam to follow him. They went into the wood, and the Fox stopped by an oak-tree.

"There they are," he whispered. "She's been laying astray again. That's another dozen. Goodness me! Three dozen in one day! We simply can't get through them."

Sam saw a snowy nest under the tree, and in it a dozen great oval eggs, white as snow, gleamed in the sun.

The Fox stooped and picked one up and stroked it lovingly.

"A beautiful egg! A marvel! Cold because it was laid by my lovely snow goose, but when I put it by the fire it will get warm. This will make a good dinner for a family! How lucky I am! A nest full of new-laid eggs."

He turned to Sam quickly. Sam was stooping over the eggs. It was amazing. They were smooth and beautiful, and white as snow. He had never imagined such big eggs, and all laid by one snow goose!

"Sam," said the Fox softly. "Little Sam Pig. I tell you

what I will do. I will give you these eggs. Yes, I will. I will give you these eggs to take home for your brothers and Ann and Badger. Badger will be delighted. His mouth will water when he sees them! Tom will cook them and you will all have a treat."

"Oh thank you," cried Sam. "Thank you, Mr Fox. It *is* kind of you."

"Not at all," said the Fox. "You deserve them, Sam." He took the hen eggs out of the basket and dropped them casually in the snow.

"You won't want these, Sam. You won't ever want to taste hen eggs when once you've had eggs from a snow goose. There's a different flavour, an aroma, in a snow-goose egg. Your appetites will be whetted, yes, that's the word, whetted, when you get these eggs."

Sam nodded and glanced disdainfully at the little brown eggs which lay rejected in the snow. The Fox was already filling the basket with the snow-goose eggs. The basket was piled high with the glittering frosty ovals.

"If I were you, Sam," advised the Fox, as Sam lifted

the heavy basket, "if I were you I should see if you can hatch one of those eggs, because a gosling might come out of it. Then you would have a goose of your own. What do you think of that?"

Sam beamed joyfully. A snow gosling! A little bird all glittering white which would soon lay two dozen eggs.

"I will, Mr Fox," he cried. "I love goslings."

"So do I, Sam," agreed the Fox. "I see that you and I are birds of a feather, as the old saying is. Birds of a feather flock together. We must flock together, Sam."

Sam looked shyly at the Fox, not understanding his words, but secretly flattered. He had always misjudged the Fox, and really he was a kind friend.

"Put it in your bed, Sam, and it may hatch out to-night if the bed is warm enough," said the Fox.

So Sam went home with the basket of eggs from the snow goose, and the Fox stooped and picked up the hen eggs and filled his pockets.

"Thank you, Sam Pig," said he softly, and he galloped away with a smile on his face.

"Where have you been, Sam?" asked Bill, as Sam came up the garden path with his heavy basket dragging his arm. "You've been a long time gathering a few eggs."

Sam didn't speak, but he walked into the house and put the basket on the table.

"Look!" he cried triumphantly. "Look, all of you. Bill, Tom, Ann! Come here and look! Eggs from a snow goose. Eggs laid by a snow goose."

The pigs picked up the eggs and turned them over and sniffed at them. "Eggs from a snow goose? What do you mean, Sam? Where are the real eggs?"

"Oh, I threw them away. These are much better. Look at the size! One egg will be enough for all of us, Badger too."

"Who's talking about Badger?" asked a gruff voice, and old Brock came lumbering in. "What's that you've got, Sam?"

"A dozen eggs laid by the snow goose, Brock," cried Sam, turning eagerly to the Badger. "And I'm going to put one of them in my bed to hatch into a snow gosling."

Badger picked up an egg and squeezed it in his strong paw, but it was as hard as ice.

"Eggs laid by a snow goose," he said slowly, "and brought home by the biggest goose of all."

He tossed the egg in the fire, and, with a sizzle and hiss, a stream of water ran out upon the hearth.

"Snow goose! Snow gosling!" said Badger again.

Poor Sam Pig never heard the end of that. The tale ran through the woods, so that the squirrels laughed in the tree tops and the moles chuckled under the earth. Little Sam Pig had carried a basket of snowballs home and given his hen eggs to the Fox in exchange. Snow goose! Snow goose!

🌸 Star-shine

It was winter and the snow lay thick on the fields. The trees wore white scarves on their long arms, and every twig had its spangled trimming. The roofs of the cottages were draped in smooth blankets of snow, and sharp icicles hung down from the eaves. Everybody walked softly, and even the cart-horses made no sound when they came back from work, except for the tinkling of the bells on their collars, and the jingling of their harness brasses.

At the end of the village, perched up on the side of a hill, was the shepherd's cottage, and there lived little Polly Shaw and her father. Tom Shaw was the shepherd at the farm across the valley on the opposite hill. From the cottage door there was a view of the farmstead with its fields and sheepfold and cowhouses, and Polly could stand in the porch and wave to her father minding the sheep across the stream.

Polly's mother was dead, and neighbours came in to help the shepherd to tidy the house, but when the little girl came home from school she was the small mistress who mended and darned and looked after her father. The village school was only half a mile away, up the straggling village street, and Polly never started from home until the bell which hung in the gable of the school-house was ringing and jangling. Then off she ran, leaving the cares of the little household behind. All day she did her lessons, she said her multiplication tables and her weights and measures, she read from her school book and did her sums, and sang songs with the other boys and girls. When school was over she left the merry throng who threw snowballs and slid along the black ice paths. A long row of children swooped down the slides, one following another with arms outstretched to balance, and cries of delight as their feet ground the ice. Little Polly too went down the long black slide, but when she reached the bottom of the hill she said good-bye, for she was grown-up, a child who was a home-maker, and she was proud of her trust.

So away she went to light the lamp and make up the fire and boil the kettle for tea. When her father came in he was tired, and he flung himself down in utter weariness while his little daughter cooked and washed up, as if she were a grown-up woman. But her reward came when the teacups were put in the high oak cupboard and the cloth was folded in the dresser drawer. Then Tom Shaw read aloud to her, and played on his shepherd's pipe and answered her questions and told her tales of his own childhood and her mother's, for they had been playmates at the same school in the village.

Sometimes they went to the kitchen door and waited for a signal from the farm opposite. If a lantern swung on the gate it meant that Tom Shaw was wanted that night, but when the only earthly star was the glimmer in the farmhouse the shepherd knew he could stay at home with his daughter. Then they gazed at the sky, and Tom pointed out the constellations, and told her their names.

The shepherd knew the stars, for they were his friends and companions while he guarded the sheep. They seemed to twinkle and talk to him and share his burdens. Through long winter nights he was out with the woolly beasts, tending the ewes, caring for the new-born lambs. He had a small oil stove in the lambing-hut and there he carried the little creatures and fed them when their mothers were weak, and as he went about his work the bright stars looked down. High in the deep blue of the wintry skies shone those little lamps, his own friendly lights, and when his young daughter asked their names he was glad to talk of them.

He pointed out the Square of Pegasus, the bold form of Orion the Hunter, the seven stars which make the Great Bear, and the lovely little group called the Pleiades. There was the Little Bear which prowled round the tree-tops, and the Lady Cassiopeia in her golden chair, and the fierce Dog Stars and many another. He told her how the stars revolve, and the colours change. Sometimes as they stood watching the stars, looking through an ancient telescope at the moon or the rings of Saturn, they saw other wonders. The Northern Lights lighted up the sky in flaming points. Stars shot down the great blue firmament, with a rope of gold behind them, and once they saw a comet with its long tail. Every time a shooting star fell across the sky the little girl made a wish, and since many meteorites fall in a short time for the close observer to see, she had many a wish. As the meteorites resemble each other in their long gold curves among the stars, so the wishes were the same. Polly's wish was to see her mother, who was somewhere among the stars.

One night she got out of bed and drew back the thick winter curtains. Down below was the lane and ice-covered stream, but reaching to the sky were the white hills. A glimmer of light on the distant slope showed where her father was out with the sheep. She could see the lantern moving as the shepherd carried it to the fold. Then it disappeared and she knew her father had gone into the lambing-hut, to stay for a while before he came out to his flock. He was making warm drinks for the ewes, and perhaps he would bring a small woolly black-legged lamb back to the cottage with him when he returned. He had tucked her up as usual that night, and pulled the warm blankets round her, and drawn the curtains closely across the windows. Then he had gone off to the sheep-fold and left her alone. Usually she fell asleep at once, for downstairs lay one of the dogs on guard, but this night she couldn't sleep. She stood by the window and watched the stars.

A great gold star came shooting down the sky as she stood there, and surely it was the largest meteorite ever seen. The golden rope, instead of vanishing in a second or two, hung so close to the window she felt she had only to put out a hand to catch it.

She opened the casement, and grasped it, and the rope was warm and rough with fibre, like a cart-rope at the stackyard of the farm. She shivered a moment as she climbed on the window-sill. Then out she swung, holding tight to the rope. It was just as easy as swinging on the school trapeze, out in the playground. She laughed as she leapt into the cold air. She wriggled her toes into her nightgown, and clung with her hot fists, thinking she would swing over the snowy fields and drop down upon her father at the lambing-hut.

"He'll think I'm an angel or a new-born lamb," she chuckled to herself as the golden rope swayed gently over the apple trees.

"I'll let go just as we pass over the hill," she decided. "Won't he be surprised!"

She was swept up into the air, far away from the hill-side, and the flock of ewes and the lambing-hut. Higher and higher she went towards the stars. She wasn't frightened, for the rope was comforting under her fingers, like her mother's warm clasped hand. She was carried up as easily as if she were in a basket.

At last her feet rested on a ladder, a Jacob's ladder of narrow silvery bars which went into a roof. The rope slipped from her grasp and swung in space, dangling from a ladder rung. She stepped through the door above her head and entered the starry land.

In front of her she saw a vast golden palace, with walls and turrets gleaming with light. All about were winged children playing at ball, flying and leaping, and swimming in a river of silver water.

They ran to welcome her and clustered round as if she were a new girl in the school playground.

"We've caught her, caught her," they cried, jumping round her.

"Who lives there?" she asked. "Is it the king?"

"That's the Sun's house," replied the cherub who held her hand. It fluttered its rosy wings and danced on one toe. "That's where the Sun lives! Surely you know the Sun?"

"Yes. The Sun shines all day at home, except when it rains," said Polly.

The cherub was looking curiously at her, and fat little fingers poked her shoulders and touched her nightdress.

"Where are your wings?" asked other little angels.

"I've never had any wings," replied Polly, apologetically. "I came on a golden rope."

She pointed to the door in the floor, where the ladder pushed its thin beams through, and the dangling rope was visible.

"That's the string of one of our kites," laughed the cherub. "We fly them every night. We've never caught anything before, although we have often tried to get an earth child."

"We've caught you! caught you!" echoed the others, singing like cuckoos in a wood.

"Have you really come from the earth?" they asked.

"Of course I have. I came from home, Robin Cottage, near Greeny-gate Farm. My father is shepherd there. He is out at night looking after the lambs. It's lambing-time, you know. I had a cade lamb of my own, and I fed it with a bottle of milk. There may be another for me soon. Have you sheep and lambs here?"

"No," piped the smallest cherub, and it pursed its red lips and tossed back its hair. "We've got a goat called Capella, and we've other animals whom we love. Look! Here comes one of them!"

A Great Bear came lumbering on furry feet down the slopes, and the cherub hailed him.

"Great Bear! Great Bear! Take this earth-child on your back and give her a ride round the heavens. Mind she doesn't fall off. She has no wings, poor little creature!"

"We caught her with one of the strings from our kites. Take care of her, Great Bear," said another cherub.

The shaggy animal lowered his head, and stooped his broad back. Polly grasped the long bright hair which covered him and settled herself on the thick pelt, with her feet tucked away in the warmth. Away they went, careering smoothly over the sky, with the brightly-coloured meadows under the bear's paws.

Out of the mists leapt a snowy Goat, with long twisted horns and white beard glistening with hoar frost, and golden eyes shining.

"That's Capella, our Goat star," said the Great Bear.

"I know her. She shines over the stackyard at home," said Polly. "My father showed me where she was."

"She feeds on the snow mountains. She has just come down ready for the night, when she will watch over the earth with her bright eye. Auriga, the charioteer, carries her in his arms when she is tired," said the Great Bear in his deep rumbling voice which was like thunder.

"That's like my father. He carries the tired lambs," said Polly.

"We all watch over the sleeping earth when the King Sun goes into his castle," continued the Bear. "There is no need when the Sun is driving over the broad highway which crosses the sky. He sees everything that happens down below, but when he comes home tired at night and his horses are stabled we take our turn."

There was a roar in the rocky heights, and a Lion came rushing forth with flaming jaws gaping, and eyes flashing lightnings. The wild beast ran across the heavens and then went back to its cave.

"That's only Leo," said the Great Bear reassuringly, as Polly clung to his fur. "He isn't fierce although he looks so savage. Nobody minds him. He shoots his fiery arrows to earth. Have you seen them? They are called the Leonids."

"Yes. The shooting stars that come in November, from the Lion. I remember," said Polly.

"Old Leo tries to frighten the horses of the Sun, but they take no notice, and gallop along their way pulling the chariot."

"The horses of the Sun?" asked the little girl.

"Yes. The chariot is drawn by a team of the finest horses in the universe, fiery steeds with flashing eyes and tossing manes of flame. Haven't you seen them cross the sky?"

"Not horses. Only the Sun by himself," said Polly.

"The horses are there, four of them, galloping through space, but your earth eyes are perhaps too dazzled to see them. Some of us help to harness them at dawn, and the Great Charioteer cracks his whip, and the doors of heaven fly open. The grand procession rushes away at a great speed, for it has a long way to go before it returns to the Western door of the castle, and only a few hours for the journey."

"We have cart-horses on the farm where my father is shepherd," said Polly confidentially. She leaned close to the Great Bear's ear, for there was such a rush of wind she could hardly hear herself speak. "Are the Sun's horses cart-horses, or racers? Can I see them up here?"

"They are race-horses, but you cannot look at them. They are in their stables, and so fierce are they that they would burn you up. I can't show you the horses, but you can see the stable doors yonder."

The Great Bear stopped near the castle, and nodded his head towards a monstrous doorway with points of fire running up from the archway which spanned it. There was a stamping of hooves and the shrill whinny of the sun-horses, but the grooms of the stable came to the door and shook their fists, and away went the Great Bear with his small burden.

They came to a starry field, where meteorites flickered like fireflies and the cherubs flew on their short curly wings. In the midst was a chair of gold and in it sat a Lady. Her eyes were soft and kind, and her voice low as she talked to the cherubs. She lifted her head when she saw the Great Bear, and the girl thought she was like her mother.

"There she is! There's the earth-child we were telling you about. She has no wings at all," cried the cherubs, and their voices were like the chattering of little birds at dawn. They rushed up to the Great Bear, and circled round his small rider.

"Be off!" growled the Bear. "Away you go!" and he shook them away as if they were pestering flies, but the Lady stretched out her arms and called to Polly.

"Come to me, earth-child. I have often heard you calling me. Come to me."

Polly dropped from the Bear's back and ran across the starry meadow. Every star was a daisy, soft under her bare feet. She climbed on the lap of the seated Lady and looked up into the beautiful face which bent towards her.

Round the Lady's neck hung a necklace of jewels, like crystals of water. Her dress was a mist of rainbow.

"You are in Cassiopeia's arms," murmured a voice, "You are safe from all evil for ever when you are here, and when you return you will look up at me and remember."

"Tell her a story. Tell her about the Moon and its lakes and mountains. Tell her about the Sun chariot. Tell her about the golden Nebulae, and all the wonderful things of heaven," cried the cherubs, circling round. They crouched at the feet of the Lady in the Chair, and the little girl stared up into the kind eyes and listened with them. Cassiopeia told one tale after another, legends of sun, earth and sky, and each was more exciting than the last.

Then the Great Bear stamped his feet and called to them.

"It's time to move on," said he. "The sun-horses are whinnying and the Grey Wolves of night are howling in the darkness. We mustn't dally here in this starry meadow. We must return."

"Good-bye, dear child," said Cassiopeia, and she took one of the gems from her necklet and hung it on Polly's breast.

"Remember what you have heard and tell the tales to the children of earth, for I love all children and would like to have them in my arms and talk to them."

She kissed her and lifted her to the high back of the Great Bear. Then she took up a harp and played music which filled the sky and echoed in all the windy places of earth, so that the poets looked up at the Chair of Cassiopeia and said, "The stars are singing to-night."

From out of the misty blue leaped a Hare, a slender animal with gilded fur and long pointed ears. After him came two dogs with their mouths open and long jaws gleaming.

"Oh run, Hare!" cried Polly. "Oh, they'll catch him and kill him. Save him, Great Bear!"

"No. He is quite safe," said the Bear reassuringly. "They will run like that for ever. The Dog Stars belong to Orion the Hunter, and the little Hare goes across the fields of night with the Dogs chasing him, but he knows he cannot be caught, for that is the heavenly law. He enjoys himself, racing over the night sky, looking down at the quiet sleepy earth as he flees, peering at the countries and oceans, at the lighted ships and the long white roads, at the villages with children asleep in their beds and the nightlights burning low. All things Lepus, the little Hare of the sky, sees when the two dogs, Procyon and Sirius, chase him."

"The Dog Stars," whispered Polly to herself. "Yes, I know them well."

The Bear ambled along, and he nodded his head to the Little Bear with the Pole Star on its head, which came out of the wood and amiably licked Polly's foot. Then he growled at the Dragon that lay curled in the blue fields. The Dragon's eyes were stars which blazed like green fires, but the Bear marched slowly onward and Polly clung to his thick fur and looked around at the wonderful creatures. A Swan sailed on the silver river of the Milky Way. A Ram shook his gilded curly horns and bent his great head to feed on the pastures. A great Bull walked through the fields. His red eye, Aldebaran, stared at Polly, his dewlap nearly touched the flowers, his flanks were like molten gold. On the back of Taurus the Bull rode one of the cherubs with a whip in its hands. It lashed the Bull, and the whip was like the rope of a meteorite, falling in the sky.

"It's only star-shine," cried the cherub to Polly.

Then a Giant came striding over the mountains, with feet spurning the mists and shoulders heaving the gold dust of the Nebulae. Round his waist was a jewelled belt and a short sword, and in his upheld hands a club. Even the Great Bear treated him with respect and stood aside to let him pass, but the Bull roared defiantly at Orion.

"That's Orion, the mighty Hunter," said the Bear. "He throws his club and never misses his aim. When he does this you see a star fall and one of the dark stars is driven out of heaven. The Bull tries to attack him, but Orion keeps the fierce one at bay. He waves his club on high, he raises his foot with that bright white star Rigel on the toe. Look at his belt. It is one of the marvels of the sky."

The belt glittered like gold bees, and a great jewel of a Nebula hung from it.

Orion glanced at the Great Bear, and then strode away with his hunting Dogs and the little Hare racing near him.

"He only hunts in these parts of the sky during winter months," said the Great Bear. "He visits other parts of the heavens. He travels vast distances."

As the Bear spoke there was a sound of singing, which did not come from the Harp, which played by itself in one part of the sky, nor from the Lady Cassiopeia. Polly looked round to find its source, and she spied the seven little sisters dancing in a ring.

"Those are the Seven Sisters, called the Pleiades," said the Great Bear. "They are everybody's favourites, both in heaven and earth. On the sea the sailors look out for them and call them the sailing stars, and in the fields the shepherds watch for them and call them the shepherd's stars."

"My father told me that," said Polly eagerly. "He says that once one of the stars was a lost girl, but now she has come back again."

"That's true," said the Bear. "One little sister covered her face and refused to shine, but now she is dancing as gaily as ever."

They stayed for a time to watch the dancing little Pleiades, and they listened to the sweet song.

"Would you like to join them?" asked the Great Bear. "Would you like to become a star and remain here for ever in these blue fields, dancing with our little sisters? Then your father would look up from his sheep and he would see eight little stars glittering in a bunch."

"But he would miss me," cried Polly. "Who would carry the lamb-can for feeding the young lambs? Who would light his lantern at night and welcome him home after his work in the fields? Oh no, I couldn't stay for ever up here."

There was a loud neighing from the stables of the sun-horses, and the Charioteer rolled back the doors so that the pointed flames rose high. Brilliant flashes of light came out, so dazzling that they dimmed the colour of the stars. The little Pleiades drew veils over their heads and disappeared. Orion the Hunter was already climbing the last hill with his Dogs and the little Hare. His sword gleamed, and he tossed his great head, so that the stars on his shoulders shone white in the rays that were coming from the stable doors. The sun palace was opening all its windows, and soon the Great Sun himself would step into his chariot and drive over the sky to bring light to the earth and a new day to mankind.

"Be quick!" cried the Great Bear. "You must go at once. Have you got the rope? Hold it tightly. Now away you go back to earth."

Polly slipped from his back and grasped the rope with her hands. The Great Bear held the ladder firmly and gave her a gentle push. She drifted down, down, down, with the golden light of dawn appearing above the horizon.

"Good-bye, stars," she called. "Good-bye, Great Bear, and Orion the Hunter, and the Lady Cassiopeia, and the Seven Little Sisters. I won't forget you."

"Good-bye, little earth-child," sang the stars, and their voices grew faint and they faded with the coming of the sun.

Through the open window swung Polly, and she loosed the gold rope. She climbed into bed and drew the blankets over her head. She slept so soundly she didn't hear the bleating of the newborn lamb which her father had brought home with him.

"Oh Father!" she cried, when the shepherd came up-stairs to see why she slept so long. "Oh Father! I've been among the stars. I've seen them all dancing and hunting and playing up there. I've ridden on the Great Bear's back, and seen the castle of the Sun, and I've been on the Lady Cassiopeia's knee. She was like Mother, just as I remember her."

"You've been dreaming, surely," laughed her father. "You've heard my tales of the stars so often you've gone in your dreams to visit them. Now get dressed quickly and come downstairs, for I've got a weakly cade lamb I want you to look after. It's on the hearthrug before the kitchen fire."

"Oh Father! But it wasn't a dream, really!" she cried. "Look what they gave me. Look!"

Around Polly's neck hung a thin chain of spun gold like a web, and from it dropped a glittering stone which shone blue and yellow and orange, a fire-opal.

"It was a present from the Lady Cassiopeia when she told me her stories."

The shepherd took the jewel in his brown hand, and turned it to the light. It was very beautiful, a strange gem which flashed like fire, unlike anything he had ever seen.

"You must keep it in the little walnut box that was your mother's. Keep it along with her treasures," said the shepherd quietly. "It's something precious, not of this world at all. I wonder——"

He looked at his little daughter curiously.

"I wonder you didn't want to stay if they treated you so well. Didn't you want to stay there for always?" His tone was wistful, he seemed half afraid.

"No." She flung her arms round his neck and held him close, smelling the rough familiar smell of sheep and earth and straw.

"No, I wanted to come back to earth, to look after you and the lambs and the sheep dogs," she whispered, burying her nose in his black hair.

She lifted her head and looked deep in his searching eyes.

"I shall never forget the tales I heard, nor the sights I saw. No, never."

"I'm glad you didn't forget me, alone down here, Polly," said the shepherd and he went downstairs, clumping slowly in his heavy boots. The sound of the bleating lamb came through the floor to the girl. She dressed quickly and ran down to join the little company, her father, the sheep dogs, and the new-born lamb. To these she told all I have told you, and more besides.

The Seven Sleepers

Snow fell softly on the world, covering the fields and hedges with a big white blanket. In the sky the Moon peered this way and that to find the house of the Seven Sleepers. At last she saw a little green cottage under the holly tree in Big Wood, nestling so close to the dark trunk that its thatched roof touched the low, shining branches, and its small chimney pressed against the prickly leaves.

She gazed curiously at its tightly shut windows, and the door with its brass knocker, all dull with the rain and snow. Then she flashed her lantern through the end window, and saw the nose of a red squirrel who lay curled up in bed. Squirrel started slightly when the light fell on her and pulled the sheet over her face.

"Safe as moonshine," said the Moon, and she peeped through all the little windows in a row under the eaves. In each room somebody lay asleep, and the Moon laughed to herself.

As she stared in at the tiny room with delicate blue curtains, the room which was so small she could scarcely get her moonbeam inside, she heard a slight sound, and a strange being came through the wood.

His face was glowing with light, and his kind brown eyes were like the eyes of a young fawn. On his shaggy back he carried a sack, and twisted round his short horns

was a wreath of mistletoe. He danced along on his cloven
hoofs, and played on thin reed pipes the sweetest music
the Moon had ever heard.

The Moon bowed when she saw him, and shielded her
lantern, for no light was needed when Pan the friend of
animals was there.

"You are first," said Pan, resting the sack on the snow.
"Are they all asleep in there?" and he pointed to the
windows.

"Yes, Your Majesty," replied the Moon, "but Squirrel
is restless."

"She always is," laughed Pan, straightening out his
broad shoulders, and stamping his hoofs on the ground.
"She always is. The least sound, and out of bed she hops.
She is the only wakeful one of the Seven Sleepers, and
when she comes out in the Winter, woe betide her if I
am not near!"

"Is Your Majesty honouring them with a visit?" asked
the Moon.

"Of course," answered Pan. "It's Christmas Eve, you
know. Animals as well as men must have their joy. I
cannot do much nowadays, but this is one of the
privileges left to me."

"It's cold for Your Majesty," said the Moon, flashing
her lantern up and down, on the trees and hills and
distant villages, where the dogs howled when they saw
her. "Shall I ask the Sun to hurry up and warm things a
little?"

"Ah! no," cried Pan quickly. "I must work at night
now, there are too many eyes when the Sun awakes."

He slung his pipes round his hairy neck, pushed open
the door and entered the cottage.

"It was a piece of luck to see him," cried the Moon
to herself. "He slides along in the shadows so softly

no one knows he is there, except for the sound of his pipes. I'll wait till he comes out again." And she pulled a cloud over her face and had a nap.

Pan busied himself in the kitchen for a few moments, and then ran noiselessly upstairs.

On the landing were seven little doors.

He listened, and a smile of contentment spread over his wise old face.

Little grunts and squeaks, sighs and shuffles, came from all the bedrooms, as the sleepers dreamed of summer days, of green hills, and shallow streams, of flowery meadows and soft wet bogs. A hundred visions ran through their heads, and each one lived again in the country of his heart's desire, whilst Pan stood outside in the passage breathing happiness into all the little hearts beating within.

But there was no time to lose. He gently turned a door knob and walked into Squirrel's room. There she lay, curled up with her bushy tail over her feet, smiling in her sleep, and at the foot of the bed hung her red stocking.

Pan dipped into his bag and pulled out a pair of curly-wool slippers, white and soft, woven from the fleece of a mountain lamb. He pushed them deep in the stocking, and then skipped lightly out of the room. Squirrel dreamed of waving beech trees, and great oaks, and little nut trees laden with brown nuts, but she did not know who had brought her the dream.

Then the god went into the next room, where, on a round, soft, leafy bed lay Snake, coiled in a ring, with her head on a pillow of grass. From a hook in the ceiling hung her long black stocking, for although she had no feet, she possessed a useful stocking, which she kept for sore throats, or Christmas Eve, or for a portmanteau when she was going on a long journey.

Into it Pan slipped a green silk dress, all frills and spickles and speckles.

"She'll want a new dress next Spring," said he, as he tiptoed out of the room on his pointed hoofs, and left the Snake dreaming of shadowy green glades, and thick wet grass, with deep hiding-places.

Dormouse slept in the next room. He was such a jolly chubby little fellow that Pan stood watching him for a precious minute. He lay in his cot with the eiderdown pulled up to his chin, grunting softly as he dreamed of a round nest under the hedge, with seven tiny babies in it.

At the foot of the cot hung a brown sock, and Pan put a little fur waistcoat inside it.

"Keep him warm when he wakes up, the young fellow," said he, and he touched the small head lovingly, and gently closed the door.

Hedgehog's room was next. He lay in a ball at the top of the blankets, with a pink stocking tied to one of his prickles.

"He doesn't mean to lose it," laughed Pan, as he untied it and dropped inside a pearly knife with two blades and a corkscrew. Then he tied it up again and looked at the gently breathing animal.

"That's a fine present for a Hedgehog, for life will be none too easy for him," and Hedgehog dreamed of a hawthorn hedge, thick and leafy, with wood sorrel and sweet-smelling ferns growing at its roots, and big white eggs laid by some stray hen in a hollow.

"That's four," sighed Pan, as he stepped into the next room.

Frog slept there, in a bed woven of reeds, with a wet sheet tied round his chin. He snored and snored and kicked his little legs about, but when Pan came near he lay very still, as if he felt the presence of the Animals' Friend.

Pan took a pair of skates from his sack and put them in the green stocking which lay on the floor where Frog had kicked it.

"You can skate on dry land if there isn't any ice," he whispered, "and some time you will be saved from an enemy."

And the Frog smiled as he dreamed of murmuring streams, and lily ponds, of hard round pebbles, and soft silky mud.

"Now for Snail," said Pan, as he opened the door next to Frog's. There, on a little white sheet, lay a shell, and inside it was Snail, fast asleep. But she had not forgotten to hang out her tiny grey stocking when she went to bed three months ago.

Pan brought out of his sack a necklace, made of dewdrops, the colour of rainbows.

"Ha!" he chuckled. "Won't little Snail startle them when she wears her jewels!"

There was only one room left, but that was his favourite, and Pan loved to see the neat beauty of that room. He opened the very small door at the end of the passage, and crept in on his shaggy knees, bending his horns to the ground to get through the doorway.

Such a warm cosy room was Bee's! Its walls were hung with blue silk, and its blue velvet carpet was rich as a pansy petal. On the smallest bed in the world slept Bee, with a patchwork quilt over her furry body, and her head on a feather pillow as big as a pea. Tiny, tiny snores came from the bed, and her wings moved up and down as she breathed. But as Pan entered she dreamed of the wide moors with purple heather, of the great lime-trees with golden flowers, of hedges with wild roses and honey-suckle, and a flicker of a smile crossed her face.

Pan searched for her stocking, but it was so small that even his quick bright eyes nearly missed it. There it hung, all feathery and fluffy, on one of the bed knobs. He could only just get a wee pot of honey into it.

"Good Luck to you, little Bee," he cried, as he crept back into the passage and shut the small door.

Downstairs he went, carrying his sack on his shoulder, and out into Big Wood, where the Moon was waiting to see him again. He put his pipes to his lips and played a tune, and the stars leaned down to watch him, and the trees bent their heads to listen.

"Good-bye, Seven Sleepers," he cried. "A Happy Christmas, and Good Hunting in the Spring."

Then away he went, to carry bundles of hay to the cows in their stalls, sieves of corn to the horses in the stables, and comfort and cheer to all the animals who were waiting for him in the byres.

The Moon leaned through the branches of the holly-tree, and peered at the sleeping animals.

"Good night, Seven Sleepers. Sleep well until Spring comes to waken you," she called, and then she sailed away to meet Orion the Hunter with his two dogs, who waited for her in the starry spaces.

🌸 The Queen Bee

The Queen Bee, with her little gold crown on her head, buzzed through the open window of the dining-room to the sugar-bowl on the table. She tasted a bit, and nodded approvingly. Then she broke off a small piece and carried it out into the sunshine, to the palace on the patch of grass under the rose bushes.

She summoned her Prime Minister.

"Taste this," she commanded, holding out the sugar.

He bent his proud head, and gently licked the glistening morsel.

"Your Majesty!" he exclaimed. "It is frozen sweetness. It is crystal honey. May I ask where Your Majesty found it?"

The ladies-in-waiting crowded round, peeping over each other's shoulders, their soft eyes bright, and their delicate wings neatly folded at their sides. They listened breathlessly to the Queen's reply.

"I found it in a dark cave across the garden," said she. "There is a store, nuggets as large as flowers, piled in a silver bowl, on a stretch of grass as white as snow."

The youngest lady-in-waiting pressed forward, and eagerly cried:

"Couldn't we all go, Your Majesty, and bring back a supply for the needs of the people in winter?"

"Wisely spoken," said the Queen, smiling.

She rang a little bell to call her subjects. From clover field and lime-tree, from rose bush and hedgerow, they flew in and surged round her in a black mass.

"Go to the dark cave, my people," she commanded, "and bring the white sweetness to the palace. Fear nothing, your swords will not be needed, for the giants who live there will flee from you."

They each took a little bag from the palace walls, and fastened it to their legs. Then they went out of the big front door, and down the sloping drive, pushing and jostling with their tiny soft feet, rubbing their wings against each other, nudging, whispering, laughing and talking.

They rose in the air and flew in a straight line across the sunny garden, over the sweet peas and poppies, past the mignonette and marigolds, to the open window of the house.

The sugar-bowl lay on the table, and a maid stood near with a tray.

"Mercy on us!" she cried, running to the door. "The bees are swarming in the house," and she ran out of the room into the study where her master sat writing.

"What is it?" he asked, frowning.

"Please sir, the dining-room is full of a swarm of bees," she exclaimed.

"Don't bother me! Just leave them alone, and they'll go away," he said impatiently banging on his desk.

But when she timidly put her nose round the door, there was nothing left, not even a lump of sugar. The bowl was quite empty!

The Queen sat in her parlour, combing and brushing her hair. She put on her crown when she heard the rush of wings outside, and went down to meet her subjects.

She climbed on her throne, and her ladies-in-waiting stood round her. Each bee brought a load of sugar and emptied it out before her.

Soon a great white heap lay on the floor of the throne room.

The Queen clapped her hands, and a party of white-capped little cooks ran in. They stored the sugar in the pantry, and sealed it in the hexagonal cupboards with the royal wax.

But still the bees surged up and down the floor, and the Prime Minister whispered to the Queen: "Your loyal subjects want a speech, Your Majesty."

"Speech! Speech!" buzzed the bees.

The Queen rose, towering above them.

"My good people," she began. "We thank you for this supply of sweetness for the cold months of winter which are before us. If now some of you will get the juices of fruits, we will make the honey beloved of our ancestors, the bees who lived in the Golden Age."

"Hip, hip, hurrah! Long live the Queen!" shouted the bees.

A party of them went off with little vessels under their wings, to rifle the fruit-trees. They sucked the juices from the purple plums and squeezed the richness from the blackberries. They took the sweetness from the yellow pears and the ripe apples. Only the scarlet crab-apples and the little hard sloes they left untouched.

The Queen donned a white apron and went into the big kitchen, where the kitchen-maids stood ready with silver pans. She emptied the juice into the pans, and the busy workers carried sugar from the stores and poured it over the juice. Then the cooks ran out of doors with all the pans, and left them in the sunshine for an hour, whilst a bodyguard marched round and round, to keep off the enemy earwigs and ants, who tried to dip their fingers in the sweet-smelling syrup.

When the air was filled with fragrance, and the tiny silken bubbles burst in the pans, the Queen came to look.

"Take it in and store it in the cupboards," she said, and a hundred cooks emptied it in the cells.

The Queen watched them seal it all up before she took off her apron and returned to affairs of State.

One day, when the cold winds of winter blew, and the flowers had long since disappeared from the garden, the Queen sent the youngest lady-in-waiting to the store-room with a crystal cup and a tiny gold knife. She cut the wax from one of the cells and drew out a rich red liquid.

The Queen drank first, and passed the cup round among her Court. As each bee drank, she smiled and cried, "Wonderful! A miracle!" and passed on the cup to the next eager neighbour.

"What is the name of this marvellous food, please, Your Majesty?" asked the Prime Minister.

"It is the Syrup of the Bees," answered the Queen, proudly, "and it has not been made for a thousand years. But it is a food which must only be used in a time of necessity, for it will not change with age." So she sealed up the syrup again, and returned to her bedroom.

Now that year the Snow Queen decided to reign in England. She brought her ice-maidens with her, and her courtiers with their long spear-like icicles. They locked up the earth for many months, so that nothing could come forth. With strong ice bands, stronger than steel, they bound the trees so that no leaf could get out, and they fastened up the earth, so that flowers and plants were imprisoned.

The Queen Bee looked from her window at the white garden, and waited for that feeling and scent in the air which would tell her spring had come. But spring hammered in vain at the doors of the woods and fields.

A few scouts left the palace and flew over the meadows, seeking for flowers; but they never returned, they were frozen to death.

Then the Prime Minister visited the Queen.

"Your Majesty," said he, "there is no food for the people. They have eaten up all the honey, and the pieces of sweetness we stored for them when the days were sunny. They are clamouring for bread. But the cold winds blow, and the ice binds the flowers, and famine faces us."

Then the Queen knew the time had come to unseal the precious Syrup of the Bees. She gave the rich crimson food to her ladies-in-waiting, and they carried it to the swarms of impatient hungry bees, who surged over the palace floors.

Their strength returned, their eyes sparkled. Every day they were fed, for a little of the syrup went a long way, and every day their wings grew firmer, ready for their long flights when they could escape from the hive.

At last the Sun conquered the Snow Queen, and she fled back to her kingdom at the North Pole.

Then the Queen Bee ordered the porters to open wide the palace door. Out flew the swarm of bees, strong and well, with their baskets on their thighs, to seek the fresh honey from the young flowers which had feebly pushed their way through the earth.

But the Queen went to her parlour with her youngest lady-in-waiting, and there she played a little secret tune on her virginal, to welcome the arrival of the poor late spring.

Elizabeth broke into a run. The car was coming. The engine noise grew stronger, and she imagined she could feel the heat of the motor. It approached in darkness, no headlights.

No longer caring how it would look, Elizabeth punched 911 on her cell phone and continued to run while holding it to her ear. Only it didn't ring. She looked at the screen and saw zero coverage. She was in a dead zone.

The car rumbled closer. The edge of the park was coming. All she had to do was get past it and there'd probably be reception.

The car was at her back; then it pulled alongside her, moving so slowly that she knew the driver wanted her to know that she was being watched. She kept her focus ahead of her, blinking back tears and clutching the phone like a lifeline.

The car moved past, pausing at the corner before turning left and slipping away into the night. A half block. A quarter. The perimeter of the park was a stand of soaring pine trees. All she had to do was get past them and she'd probably have coverage. But getting past them meant landing on the street where the car had turned.

Something was wrong with the streetlight on that corner. It flickered on and off, on and off. As she approached it, the light went out again. She glanced at her phone. No coverage yet.

She didn't see the gloved hand come out of the darkness until it settled on her wrist. The phone dropped, forgotten, onto the street. She screamed once before the other hand closed over her mouth . . .

DON'T BE AFRAID

THE NEXT KILLING

THE DEAD PLACE

Published by Pinnacle Books

THE DEAD PLACE

REBECCA DRAKE

PINNACLE BOOKS
Kensington Publishing Corp.
www.kensingtonbooks.com

PINNACLE BOOKS are published by

Kensington Publishing Corp.
850 Third Avenue
New York, NY 10022

All Kensington titles, imprints, and distributed lines are available at special quantity discounts for bulk purchases for sales promotions, premiums, fund-raising, educational, or institutional use. Special book excerpts or customized printings can also be created to fit specific needs. For details, write or phone the office of the Kensington special sales manager: Kensington Publishing Corp., 850 Third Avenue, New York, NY 10022, attn: Special Sales Department; phone 1-800-221-2647.

ISBN-13: 978-0-7860-1807-0
ISBN-10: 0-7860-1807-9

First printing: September 2008

10 9 8 7 6 5 4 3 2 1

Printed in the United States of America

For Margaret and Joseph
My ever-fixed mark

ACKNOWLEDGMENTS

I'm indebted to Sandy Stephen and Meryl Neiman, who helped plot this novel, and to Amy Moore-Benson, who helped put it to bed. Special thanks to Mary Weidner, Jane Lucchino, and Shelley Blumenfeld, for helping me understand the world of visual artists, and to Nathaniel Drake, for helping me understand the world of musicians. Wickfield is a fictional town, but influenced by places I've lived or visited, including the charming college towns of Bloomington, Indiana, and Swarthmore, Pennsylvania. My own interpretation of the funeral industry was influenced by the writing of Jessica Mitford and Thomas Lynch. Special thanks to The Six; you know who you are! Finally, always and forever, thanks to Joe.

Prologue

No one thinks of death on a sunny day. The sky was the rich, translucent blue of the Caribbean Sea, and Lily Slocum looked up into its warmth and closed her eyes for a moment, thinking how great it would be to go to the beach. She was four blocks from the university and six blocks from home and the messenger bag filled with textbooks was digging into her shoulder and rubbing against her hip.

She didn't notice the car idling at the stop sign up ahead. She couldn't see the driver looking in the rear-view mirror and even if she could, she wouldn't have thought it meant anything more than an admiring glance from a stranger.

Lily Slocum will be described as pretty. Reporters will list the description her roommate gave the police: white, medium height, wheat-blond hair worn long and pulled back in a ponytail, brown eyes. Last seen walking just past midday on Bates Street, brown T-shirt and tan shorts, orange messenger bag slung over her right shoulder, green flip-flops slapping the concrete under her feet.

No one will mention the car that drove slowly past before circling back to follow her. No one will be able to give a description of its make or model or speculate as to the identity of the driver. No one will notice.

Certainly not Lily, who thought she might actually tan on such a sunny day and checked her arms to see if they were getting any color, the tiny bells on her silver bracelet tinkling. A bracelet will be mentioned and her roommate will say, yes, yes, she always wore a silver bracelet. She will also provide a description of her earrings and the small turquoise ring Lily wears on the third finger of her right hand.

A cell phone will also be mentioned. This one small detail will make it all the more remarkable. She had a cell phone. She was talking on a cell phone. So how did she disappear somewhere between Bates and McPherson, the street with the rundown student apartments where her boyfriend waited to celebrate an end-of-year lunch?

He called her as she traipsed along and she had to pause to dig the cell phone out of her bag. "Hey," she said. "I'm on my way. You got lunch ready?" She walked a little more slowly as she talked and if she felt something at her back, she didn't mention it. They were living together and their parents didn't know.

He will rerun their conversation many times in his head. He will be forced to replay it for their parents and the police. He will repeat her last words to hundreds of strangers watching on TV, the camera zooming in so they can see tears overwhelming him: "See you in a minute, babe."

He will describe her as a sweet, friendly girl. Her parents will add kind. Lily was so kind. When the car pulled up to the curb, Lily smiled at the man who asked for her help. "Sure," she said, stepping closer to the car, shielding her eyes so she could see the map he was holding.

The weather will be talked about. It was a hot day. Unseasonably warm for May, the town overflowing with people because graduation was only a few days away. Lily had told her roommate she wished she were graduating now instead of a year from now. She wanted to be free of this small town. She didn't know that the man smiling up at her from the car lived to grant her wish.

People don't just vanish. They aren't there one minute, walking along a sidewalk in the sunshine, whole and sentient, only to disappear the next. Only sometimes they do. Ask Lily.

August

Chapter One

The irony was that the people at the party probably thought the Corbins were the perfect family. Kate Corbin turned her attention from the speech being made by the head of the music department and glanced surreptitiously around the room, watching the large crowd gathered to welcome the new dean and his family to Wickfield.

A sea full of smiling faces in the wide, comfortable living room of Laurence Beetleman's house. They were university folk mainly, but a few local business owners had been invited as well. "I guess I passed muster," a bluff man with white hair and a booming voice had said to her earlier. A banker or lawyer, she couldn't remember which, just that he wasn't a professor. "Town and gown, you know," he'd said with a hearty laugh. "Always that division between town and gown."

Only she didn't know. She didn't know at all. They were Manhattan transplants and that division didn't exist at New York University.

Laurence Beetleman rambled on about the lovely town of Wickfield and how the university community was like a family to him and would now welcome the Corbins into the family.

"We're so happy we finally snared you," he'd said to Ian when he opened the door to them, including Kate with his broad smile, shaking even fourteen-year-old Grace's hand before ushering them inside his gracious, porticoed home, his plump and pretty wife standing radiant at his side.

Helpmeet, Kate thought. Wasn't that what they called such a woman in Victorian novels? Was she the one responsible for the gleaming hardwood floors and well-dusted bookcases? There was a faint scent of furniture polish in the rooms, and Kate pictured Clara Beetleman lovingly rubbing the oval surface of the dark oak table and running her cloth up the curving feet of upholstered armchairs.

She thought of their own home—old home—in the East Village and how every surface carried a thin sheen of dust like the faintest sprinkling of powdered sugar, except when they gave the loft a hasty wipe-down before parties.

She glanced through the open door left of the crowded living room, and noticed with some satisfaction that a catering firm hovered in the Beetlemans' kitchen, and then felt ashamed for feeling any animosity toward the older professor's wife. Clara Beetleman seemed perfectly happy tending to her husband, and Kate had a sudden vision of her watering and pruning him just as she must the numerous glossy-leafed plants lining the windowsills, and had to stifle a giggle.

Ian glanced at her, a question in his blue-gray eyes, and she gave an imperceptible shake of her head. Behave, Kate. Now was not the time or place. Maybe they'd laugh about it later. At one point she would have been sure of their shared humor, but that was before. Things were different now.

"It's been eight months!" he'd yelled at her that last night in their home. "Eight long months, Kate!"

And because she had no good answer to that, no way to pretend that she hadn't recoiled when he'd reached for her, she'd resorted to the role of mother, saying, "Ssh, Grace will hear."

As if Grace, a hallway away, cared about anything but how her life was being ruined by this move. Kate knew if they'd checked on her they would have found her hunched in a corner of her bed, her long, dark hair, so like her father's, hanging like a curtain to block her sullen face from view, and plugged into her iPod so she could unplug from her parents.

If Grace slept that last night, Kate didn't know. She only knew that she herself couldn't sleep, watching Ian instead, his long lean body turned away from her. She'd wanted to touch him, but not in the way that he desired. She'd studied his back with its familiar constellation of moles, a smattering of dark spots scattered across the pale skin, grateful for the reassuring solidness in that long, lean muscled frame.

Yet when he breathed deeply, she spied the faintest out-line of his rib cage and felt the immense fragility of the bones within that skin, knowing they could shatter, that the organs sheltered by them could rupture, that the machinelike working of his body could stall or stop.

This sense of his vulnerability was another frighten-ing result of what had happened to her. Strange that something that had taken place so quickly—she'd been shocked to see on the police report that the span was at most a half hour—could completely alter her life. Their lives. It might have happened just to her, but it had af-fected all of them.

Hearing her own name pulled her out of her reverie. Dr. Beetleman was directing his smile at her now, saying, "—Kate will be sure to paint some lovely portraits of the good citizens of Wickfield."

A ripple of polite laughter, followed by an undercurrent of conversation. People focusing those expectant looks on her now, not Ian, and some of them asking others what Dr. Beetleman was saying about the new dean's wife? *The* Kate Corbin? Yes, of course, they thought the name sounded familiar, but they hadn't realized the connection. She was the painter. Portraitist. Artist. Oh, but hadn't they heard that she'd been attacked? Yes, but maybe it was just a rumor. She certainly looked fine.

Kate met their gaze, smiled wide enough to bare her teeth, catching the anxious glance that Ian threw her way. "Don't worry, I'll be the perfect wife," she'd said with some bitterness when he'd asked for the fifth time if she was sure she'd be all right at the party.

"I can go by myself," he'd suggested. "Or take Grace."

"And wouldn't people wonder where I was? What would you say?"

"I could tell them that you were painting."

"But we both know that would be a lie."

It was the same thing he'd said to her six months earlier, when she'd begged off the latest NYU faculty dinner party and suggested he tell people she was busy painting. "We both know that would be a lie, Kate," he'd said, the first time they'd spoken about the fact that she wasn't painting and hadn't painted since it happened.

The reference hadn't been lost on him. He understood perfectly what she was saying and responded angrily by demanding that she be ready to leave on time since he couldn't afford to be late to his first official function in his capacity as new dean of the College of Arts and Sciences at Wickfield University.

So the three of them got dressed in more or less sullen silence, unearthing clothes from the boxes and garment bags still lining the halls of their new house on one of Wickfield's tree-lined streets.

And here they all were, Ian in a pale linen suit and dashing blue silk tie, looking handsome and arty, and Grace with her long hair pulled back for a change, wearing a batik sundress instead of her usual black T-shirt and jeans, and Kate herself in a navy blue wrap dress and high-heeled strappy sandals that Ian had called sexy when she'd bought them a year ago.

They looked like the perfect family. Smile pretty for the nice people. She could feel the corners of her jaw aching with the effort.

Clara Beetleman touched her husband's elbow, a tiny nudge that hardly anyone but Kate noticed, the unspoken signal between husband and wife that he'd talked long enough and needed to let their guests mingle.

Ian was pulled into conversation by a tall, stoop-shouldered architecture professor with a rope of beautiful African shells hung around her neck. Grace wove through the crowd, unconscious of her lithe beauty, exiting through French doors into the summer evening. Kate started to follow, but caught herself, and stopped by the window instead, looking out on the deck and the manicured lawn beyond it with its tiny iron lanterns winking among the hostas.

The windowsill was lined with immaculate pots of African violets. She stroked one fuzzy leaf, watching her daughter standing on the lawn looking at something out of Kate's view, a drink clutched in one small hand. Grace's hands remained a young girl's, small and rounded, with short, bitten nails that she liked to paint black, green, or purple. Grace was changing in so many other ways— her figure maturing, her mood mercurial—that it was pleasing to Kate to see this last glimmer of her little girl.

"They grow up so fast." Clara Beetleman stood at her

side, beatific smile in place, hands folded serenely over her ample stomach. The aging Madonna, Kate thought, and saw the portrait in various shades of pale brown and gold. "Is she your only one?"

"Yes."

"Not that there is such a thing as an only. One is plenty." Her laugh was light and easy, but her eyes watched Kate with a birdlike intensity.

"How many children do you have?" Kate asked automatically because it was polite. She didn't want to talk with this woman who looked as if she could worm her way to the heart of Kate's insecurities. Did she know that they'd tried unsuccessfully for years to give Grace a sibling? She felt trapped against the windowsill, looking past the woman's shoulder to try and catch Ian's eye, but he was deep in conversation and didn't see her.

"Three boys. All of them raised right here and educated at Wickfield." Clara Beetleman laughed again. "I understand Grace will be studying in the music department?"

"Yes, she was accepted into Dr. Beetleman's program."

"She must be very talented if Laurence has taken her on. A piano prodigy?"

"Yes, I guess." Kate tried to smile. She hated that term because it carried with it so much expectation. Weren't prodigies the ones who burned out early, walking away from that which had once consumed them? She didn't want Grace to experience her talent as a burden or a liability.

Her own parents had been good about that, their ignorance of an artist's life keeping them from any expectations about her future. They'd been older than her friends' parents and having given up on conceiving, were eager to help their only child follow her dreams even if hers was a passion they didn't understand.

All they knew was that as soon as Kate could talk she'd spoken of color, that each and every Christmas letter to Santa had begged for crayons, paints, palettes, and easels. And as grateful as she was for the teachers who'd recognized her talent and helped steer her toward an education appropriate for it, she was still more thankful for those years when she'd enjoyed the gift she'd been given without being defined by it.

She'd tried to give this same freedom to Grace, but the truth was that she and Ian had the education their parents lacked. They could identify what they were seeing almost from the first moment, when Grace reached a chubby toddler's hand above her head to carefully tap, not pound, the ivory keys of a friend's piano.

A man wearing a dress shirt striped like stick candy joined them near the window. He had dark curly hair and large, square-framed black glasses. "Clara, you'll have to scold Laurence for me—he completely forgot to tell us that Kate Corbin came along with the new dean."

Before Clara could respond, the man extended his hand for Kate to shake. "Jerry Virgoli." He smiled at her and took a sip from a balloon glass of deep red wine. It swirled in the glass, and she thought of carmine spilling onto a canvas, and had to pull her eyes back to his face. "I'm a big fan of your work."

"Thank you."

"I saw your show in Brooklyn—when was that?"

"A year and a half ago."

"It was superb."

"Thank you." Her last show. For a while she'd wondered if it really would be her last. The months when she'd stared at the same blank canvas and been unable to pick up a brush. The months when all she saw when she looked at the pots of paint was how they'd been knocked to the floor of her studio when he'd slammed her back onto the table, and how she'd seen them swirling on the floor as she struggled, the colors rushing together, muddying the stained concrete floor.

She took a quick swallow from her glass of white wine. Therapy hadn't chased those images away, but at least she could paint again. Halting progress, but still progress.

"Did you read the article about Lily Slocum?" Jerry's voice lowered. Clara Beetleman nodded, but Kate asked, "Who?"

"She was a student at Wickfield," Jerry began, but Clara corrected him.

"She *is* a student."

"You don't seriously think that she's still alive?"

Clara shuddered. "I don't know, but I hope so."

"She disappeared in May," Jerry Virgoli said to Kate. "Broad daylight, walking back to her apartment from campus, and she just vanished."

Clara shook her head, whether in disagreement or regret Kate couldn't tell. "Someone must have seen something."

"The police would have found them by now." Jerry Virgoli twirled his wineglass lightly in his hands. The nails were manicured and he wore a signet ring on his fourth finger. Light sparkled in the turning glass, glinted against the burnished gold of the ring.

"It's been three months and they still have no leads," Clara said. "It's just horrible."

"I'm sure things like this happen every day in the city," Jerry said to Kate.

"I don't think so." His eyes seemed larger because of those boxy glasses and she felt exposed by them, wondering again how many of those at the party knew about what had happened to her. It had made the news, her identity revealed by a tabloid reporter. Once they knew the name of the artist who'd been assaulted, the other media decided they had free reign, and Kate had fifteen minutes of unwanted fame.

"Her poor mother," Clara said, and Kate remembered the voracious reporters calling and visiting, their false sympathy and strident pleas to tell her story, some of them arguing that the public had a "right to know" and others that she should "warn others." Warn them about what? That their lives could be interrupted by tragedy?

"I just keep hoping to open the paper and read that she's been found alive and well in another state. Like that runaway bride."

Jerry Virgoli smiled, but it didn't reach his eyes. He said to Kate, "Wickfield must seem very provincial to you."

"We were hoping so." Kate gulped at her wine and it burned in her throat. She looked out the window again, anxious. Grace was gone. Kate's eyes flicked over the clusters of partygoers, but she couldn't find her.

Jerry Virgoli talked on, but the words flowed over her like water, a rush of sound she couldn't process because her entire focus was on her daughter.

"I think mothers worry wherever they are," Clara Beetleman murmured. She'd followed Kate's gaze and was searching the lawn, too.

"Even with these missing girls, the crime rate is still lower than Manhattan's," Jerry Virgoli said.

"Excuse me." Kate moved past them and out the French doors. Anxiety propelled her through the people milling about on the deck. A group on the lawn shifted, and suddenly she spotted Grace leaning against the wall of what looked like a cottage tucked in a back corner of the yard.

Kate felt relieved just to have her in sight, though she could see the boredom clearly visible on her pretty face. As she watched, Grace dug into the small knit bag hanging from one shoulder and brought out her cell phone.

Kate's body responded before her brain, tension tightening the muscles in her back, knotting at the top of her spine. She knew what number was being tapped into Grace's phone.

"If I find out you've called him again, I'm taking away your cell phone." Ian's declaration had been backed up by Kate, even though she knew that by drawing that line Ian was practically daring Grace to cross it.

Kate's heels sunk in the soft grass as she stepped off the deck. Grace didn't hear her approach across the soft curve of lawn. She had her back to her mother, phone held against her ear like a talisman. Her voice, high-pitched and sulky, said, "It's just some stupid party they made me attend."

Then Kate's hand was over hers, pulling the phone away from her daughter's ear.

"Hey!" Grace cried. "What are you doing?" She tried to hold on, but Kate pried the phone from her, held it to her own ear.

"Who is this?" she demanded, knowing she sounded shrill and not caring.

"Hi, Mrs. Corbin." A high-pitched voice, amused. "It's Madison."

A female school friend, not that boy. Not Damien. Stunned, Kate let the phone slip from her ear.

"Jesus, Mom." Grace easily plucked it out of Kate's hand and pressed it back to her own ear before turning away. "Sorry, Mad, my mom's just having some freak-out."

She was gone before Kate could apologize, striding away from her mother back across the lawn, heading in the direction of the house. She disappeared inside.

Four hours had to be endured before Ian was ready to leave and Kate could stop smiling. Every hour counted, each minute taking an eternity to pass.

There was silence in the car as Ian drove the second-hand Volvo through Wickfield's quiet streets. The new house was only a few blocks from the center of town, an older residential street with sidewalks in front of frame homes, most with front porches, built in the early years of the twentieth century. Sycamore trees lined both sides of the street, branches stretched to form a canopy high above the road. Street lamps spaced at equally measured intervals cast soft yellow puddles onto the asphalt.

It was too quiet here. There were no sirens, no trucks, no sound of rushing cabs or the subterranean rumble of trains to help lull her to sleep. She found the silence unnerving.

Their house was two-story with a wide front porch. Four bedrooms, two full baths, an updated kitchen, but original hardwood floors and beautiful molding. The selling point, though, was in the back of the house, at the end of a pavered driveway. A previous owner, a furniture maker who liked light, had turned the detached garage into a workroom complete with lots of large windows. It was a perfect studio.

Yet Kate's canvases and easels were still wrapped, sitting in the center of the room with the crates of supplies she'd cleared out of her studio in Brooklyn. Every time she went to unpack them, something else needed to be done in the house. It wasn't that she was avoiding it, or at least that's what she tried to tell herself.

Ian parked on the driveway and they made their way, still in silence, up the path to the front door. Once they were all inside, Kate turned back to check that it was locked.

Ian's soft chuckle surprised her.

"What?"

"You don't have to check here. I'm sure that even if we left the door unlocked nothing would happen."

"There's still crime even in small towns."

"Sure, but c'mon. This isn't like the city."

Grace spoke from the stairs. "Yeah, it isn't nearly as cool."

Ian sighed. "It's late. You need to get to bed, Grace."

"Whatever." The tone was pure teenage disdain. She ran up the stairs before either parent could respond.

Ian scowled and started after her, but Kate stopped him with a touch on his arm. "Let her go."

"And let her get away with talking to us like that?"

"Pick your battles—she's tired and angry about the move."

"She's spoiled is what she is." He ushered Kate ahead of him up the stairs and switched off the hall lights before following. "When I was her age, I held down two jobs to help support my family."

Kate stifled a yawn. Not this story again. She knew it so well that sometimes she felt as if she had been Ian's sibling and had lived through the death of his father and watched Ian deliver newspapers every morning and bag groceries every evening to help his widowed mother make ends meet.

She'd seen Grace roll her eyes when Ian told this story, and knew that she thought it was at best an exaggeration. Not because she doubted the truth of what her father said, but because she couldn't relate at all to the story. Grace's life was too far removed from that kind of suffering to be able to relate. Kate's life had been like that, too. Raised by two doting parents with enough time and money to lavish on her, she'd been protected from grief.

"I can remember being so tired and depressed at night that I literally fell into bed," Ian said behind her as she walked into their new master bedroom. She nodded, understanding. She wasn't protected anymore. She knew what it was like to be so worn down that sleep seemed like her only refuge.

Except it wasn't. Deep sleep evaded her here just as it had in the city. Ever since that awful day in her studio, she hadn't been able to sleep continuously for more than a few hours at a time. Knowing that she'd dream about the assault undoubtedly caused anxiety, but all the relaxation tips she'd tried did little to help.

Ian fell asleep quickly just like always. She watched the slow rise and fall of his chest, envying it, before reaching up to switch off her bedside light. She waited for the darkness to settle, for the various shades of black to emerge. Everything was new here, even their bed. Ian had been excited that the space was finally big enough to get the king-size bed he'd always wanted, but now the emotional gulf separating them had become a physical gulf as well. She could reach him only if she stretched her arm to its farthest point. She didn't.

Rolling onto her side, she stared at the faint stripe of moonlight coming through the filmy curtains, a perfect line of ivory across charcoal. Chiaroscuro. Light and shadow. It wasn't only art that could be explained with this concept. And if her life before had been tipped further toward light, then she'd just been lucky.

She thought again of the student they'd been discussing at the party, Lily Slocum. She tried to imagine someone simply walking down a street and vanishing. Light and shadow. Shadow and light.

She drifted into half sleep with the image of Lily Slocum in her head, picturing her as a line of moving light receding into darkness.

Chapter Two

Ian Corbin stood in front of the mirror adjusting his tie and ran the new job title through his mind. Dean Corbin. Ian Corbin, Dean of the College of Arts and Sciences. He'd been Professor Corbin or Dr. Corbin for so long, it was going to take time to make the switch.

Red silk tie in place, he dropped his arms and looked at himself. Pressed white shirt, new charcoal suit, and a tie Kate had picked for him. It was going to be hot today. He'd probably ditch the jacket as soon as he got to the office.

He had a sudden memory of that late summer day, all those years ago, when he'd taught his first class. Only two years into his doctoral program, he'd been completely green and barely older than the undergrads he was being asked to teach. It had been a hot, sultry morning just like this one and the sense of excitement just the same.

He smiled at his reflection. Except for a slight blurring of his jawline and the silvering of his temples, he looked essentially the same. It was only if he looked closer, stared deep into his eyes and counted the fine lines creasing the skin around them, that he saw the profound change.

He'd been single back then, a small-town boy made good, his own savings and a handful of scholarships making it possible to get his undergraduate degree. It was still some years before he became a husband and a father, a time in his life when he worried he didn't fit in with the other students, the ones who traveled from wealthy suburban towns followed by an endless supply of money from parents who were alumni. He'd rented what was virtually a cold-water flat near the train station, the hot water a trickle when it deigned to appear. The walls of the building were so thin that he could hear every word of recrimination between the couple next door and sometimes startled awake fearing that a whistling engine was about to run over him.

He'd been so strapped for cash that he donated plasma for a couple of bucks each week and pulled discarded newspapers out of waste bins to look for coupons. Cans of crushed tomatoes made barely edible soup. Cheap white bread and ramen noodles. A box of eggs made to last a month and the cheapest cuts of stew meat. A diet of bad food and not enough of it.

He was constantly hungry, his dreams filled with visions of tables groaning under the weight of holiday meals, the gnawing of his empty belly ever present, along with the guilt that he'd left behind his mother.

The sound of the piano broke his reverie. Ian shook his head to clear it, moving toward his dresser and scooping up the gold wristwatch that had been his father's, the last vestige of that time. He slipped his calfskin wallet into his back pocket.

The swell of Chopin's Prelude in E Minor grew stronger as he headed out of the bedroom and down the stairs. Grace was sitting at the Baldwin upright that had survived the move from Manhattan. It had been a lot easier getting it into this house than into the loft eleven years ago. Intent on the music, the sound loud enough that she couldn't hear his footsteps, Grace kept playing as her father entered the room.

One tiny strap of her black tank top had slipped down her tanned shoulder, and with her hair pulled back in a ponytail, and wearing khaki shorts and sandals, she looked younger. For one brief moment he thought she was ten again, happy to see him, eager to have him listen to a new piece she'd learned, her smile radiant as she'd barrel across the loft to hug him as he came in the door.

Grace saw him and the music stopped abruptly, the face turned toward his scowling. "Stop staring at me!"

"I wasn't staring, I was watching." Ian dared to rest a hand lightly on her dark head, but she jerked it off.

"I'm trying to play."

"So pretend I'm your audience." He tried to coax a smile out of her by making a goofy face. "Look, I'm dressed for it. Just pretend."

They'd done this when she was little, calling it Carnegie Hall, and sometimes she'd made her own tickets and issued them to her parents and their friends.

Now the scowl remained firmly in place. "It isn't ready."

Yet she was already a better pianist than he'd ever be. Ian had made peace with his own middling talent years ago, choosing to go into teaching because he'd never be able to support himself as a performer, but there were moments when he felt almost envy for his daughter's talent and annoyance at her lack of awareness of it.

He resisted the urge to force some point of connection with her, and said instead, "Where's your mother?"

Grace shrugged, her attention already back on the sheet music. "The studio, I think."

The music began again, haunting and lilting, as he walked from the living room down the hall to the kitchen where he grabbed a cup of coffee before heading out the back door.

He saw Kate before she saw him. She was bending over a box, her brow furrowed in concentration. It was a relief to see her out here. A relief to think that she was moving forward. Maybe everything would be okay.

He tapped lightly on the door and her head flew up, eyes wide with fear.

"It's okay, it's just me." He hurried to reassure her, chest tightening with sympathy. Her eyes narrowed, the deep blue turning black.

"Don't sneak up on me!"

"I didn't think I was. It's okay, Kate."

He meant to calm her down, but it seemed as if everything he said just inflamed her. Between the frown and the thick titian hair made thicker by humidity and fanned about her head like a fiery halo, she looked like some mythical demon.

"I am calm! Or I was before you snuck up on me."

"Fine." He held up his free hand in surrender. "Whatever." The word slipped from his lips effortlessly, and he only realized what he'd said after the fact. He saw it register in Kate's raised eyebrows, followed by a half beat of silence while they stared at each other, and then they both burst out laughing.

"Channeling our daughter?" Kate said lightly.

"I guess so. Her Holiness has informed me that I'm not to sneak up on her or listen to her playing the piano."

Kate laughed again, but with sympathy. "Oh, poor Ian! And I just jumped all over you again." She gave him a quick hug, her small arm reaching out to encircle his waist and give it a gentle squeeze, her touch startling and electric. He brought his own arm around hers to try and hold it there, but she slipped away, out of reach.

"Too much estrogen in this place," she said, her voice dropping deeper. An old joke between them, something an elderly professor had once said to him in her hearing. She didn't sound like the cantankerous old man, she didn't sound like a man at all, but he smiled anyway.

"I've got to take off, unless you need me?"

Kate's own smile faded, but she shook her head. "I'm fine."

"I was going to take the car."

"Okay."

"You sure you won't need it?"

He was pressing, he knew that even before the crease appeared on her forehead, but he didn't like the idea of her being without transportation.

"I don't know if you can find a cab here," he said out loud, wincing inwardly at the ridiculous cheeriness in his own voice.

"Where would I be going, Ian?"

They both knew she didn't leave the house, that she could barely be coaxed anywhere these days. It had taken a tremendous effort to get her to go to that party the other night, and he'd had the feeling that he'd be paying for the gift of her presence for months to come.

"Okay, I'll take the car then. I'll call you later."

"You don't have to."

"I know. I want to."

She accepted the kiss he offered, their lips pressing briefly together like paper, before Kate stepped back. Ian backed out of her space, noticing that her attention turned immediately back to the canvases at her feet. He heard the door close and the key turn in the lock as he walked away.

His shoes tapped lightly on the old bricks laid out in a herringbone pattern to form a driveway. A few of them looked loose, and he had no idea how they were anchored. Mortar? Years of apartment living hadn't prepared him well for home ownership, but he would learn. When he reached the Volvo, he looked back at the studio and saw Kate standing at the windows looking out, but when he gave a little wave, she didn't see him.

The old car's engine coughed and spluttered, but finally roared to life, resuscitated once again, but soon they'd have to replace it. Or maybe, since they were going to buy a second car, the Volvo could hobble along for another year. It reminded him that he had to find a new mechanic; there was no way he was driving any car back into the city to get it serviced.

As he backed out of the driveway, he caught sight of their next-door neighbor coming out the front door of his weathered-looking frame house, the slap of the screen door catching Ian's ear before the man's striped shirt caught his eye.

He was an average-looking white man, middle-aged and balding, wearing a short-sleeved shirt that strained slightly over the fullness of a belly hanging over the belt of his pants.

Instantly forgettable except that when he saw Ian, the man actually stopped short before reversing and scuttling back up his front steps to hide in his shadowed front porch.

Ian let his hand drop, the friendly wave forgotten, and concentrated on backing onto the street without hitting the dusty white van parked in front of the neighbor's door. Guy was obviously shy. A good thing really. The last thing he wanted was some garrulous country neighbor rushing over at every opportunity to share his expertise with the city folk.

Ian drove down Wickfield's pretty streets feeling a deep sense of satisfaction. This was a good move, a good place to be. Sure, it would take time to get used to the slower pace, but there were lots of advantages to being out of the city, not least getting Grace away from bad influences.

He'd wanted to leave the city earlier, and had received overtures from Wickfield over a year before Kate would seriously discuss it. When he'd first been approached by Laurence Beetleman and others from Wickfield to see if he'd consider becoming dean, he'd mentioned it to Kate, but she'd argued against it. He had tenure in the music department at NYU, she was teaching part-time there, too, and more importantly, there was her whole network of artists and galleries. She'd always talked about her studio when they discussed it, mourning in advance the thought of leaving a space that she'd had for so long, which was entirely hers. It predated their relationship by a year, a loft space in an old industrial building on the edge of Williamsburg that she'd found right before that neighborhood skyrocketed.

She'd extol the light if he suggested that she could find another studio, but he knew that most of her attachment had to do with having been in the space for so long and having so many memories attached to it. She'd taken him there when they were dating, running ahead of him up the dangerously narrow flight of stairs, sliding back the battered metal door with a great flourish, looking for his reaction.

While he'd noticed the concrete floor flecked with paint and the long, battered worktable crowded with pots and brushes, and the three easels holding canvases in various states of completion, his eyes had been drawn relentlessly back to her. Beautiful in her strange hodgepodge of skirts and peasant blouse, an auburn-haired gypsy with clacking metal bracelets that she tossed on the table so they wouldn't get in the way of her work.

She'd insisted on painting him, making him perch on a chair near the window and hold his face just so, tilted toward the light. Asking him questions and scolding him when he automatically moved his head to look at her as he answered.

"Stop looking at me, I want your profile," she'd instructed, brow furrowed with concentration. She'd been so fierce in her work, so beautiful.

"I'd rather look at you."

"I'd rather you didn't." Her laughter came easily, ringing in the room and making him smile and bringing more scolding. "Stop that. No, no—look away from me! I want you in repose, not staring with a fool's grin like some Sears Portrait."

"I can't help it, you're making me laugh."

Once, after they'd been dating for several months, they'd made love in her studio, moving against each other on an old blanket laid across the stained concrete. He could still recall the sunlight dappling her breasts and the feel of the sable brush they'd taken turns tracing over each other's body.

A sudden honk startled Ian, and he realized he'd fallen thoroughly into memory and was sitting at a green light. He stomped on the accelerator and the old car lurched forward. When the lane changed to two, the SUV behind him roared around his left side, the irate driver communicating his displeasure by leaving the Volvo in a cloud of exhaust.

Annoyed at being lured into unproductive reflection, Ian focused on driving, pulling onto campus in record time. There was a spot assigned for him in the newer parking lot. Just one of the perks of the job and as he parked the car, Ian's feeling of satisfaction returned, heightened when he made the brisk walk across campus to the beautiful Beaux Arts building that housed the offices for the College of Arts and Sciences.

His office was on the fifth and top floor in a suite at the end of a long hallway tiled in squares of ocher and black. The brass nameplate on the solid wood door was new, and Ian felt a peculiar mixture of pride and embarrassment, flashing back to his first day as an undergrad, so glad to be there and yet so self-conscious about being the new guy on campus.

His secretary sat behind a boxy wooden desk that he knew to be a smaller version of the one in the inner office, as if she were in training to be dean.

Mildred Wooden was small, round almost to the point of being cherubic, and of indeterminate middle age. Ian could have been convinced she was forty-five or sixty-five. Her bob of perfectly smooth ash blond hair was cut too short to flatter her round face, and she favored boxy suits in harsh colors like puce and orange. She moved her small, bejeweled hands when she spoke, and reminded Ian of a tropical bird.

"You have fifteen calls already this morning, Dean Corbin," she said in greeting, bobbing up from her seat to wave a handful of papers at him.

Ian took them from her into his office while she flapped along behind him chattering on about a faculty meeting and other commitments. He barely heard her, focused instead on the view out the two large windows that dominated the back wall of the office.

Here was the University of Wickfield depicted on postcards undergrads sent home to their parents. The rolling green lawns and massive brick and stone buildings, the bell tower where generations of students had carved their names, the avenue of stately elm trees that

had been saplings when President McKinley visited
Wickfield, and the gentle curve of the river just visible
at the farthest edge of campus that Ian could see. He
knew that at this very moment more than one pencil-
thin scull was slicing cleanly through its silver surface.

In the far right corner of his window he could see an
edge of the field where the new Performing Arts Center
would be built. This was why he'd been wooed, and allowed himself to be wooed, away from NYU. The chance
to be part of something like this center came once, if it
came at all, in a career. The building would be a design
masterpiece, something that would stand for generations, and he would be part of the creative process.

Of course, it was still in the planning stages. They
wouldn't break ground, wouldn't even be able to name
the place, until funding was secure. Finding the money
and convincing the rest of the university community to
back this project would be his biggest challenges this
year, but just the thought of being able to look out this
window and see the product of his hard work excited
him.

"Would you like me to call Mrs. Corbin to let her
know about the reception?"

The question doused his sense of satisfaction like a
splash of dirty water. Mildred Wooden paused in the
doorway waiting for an answer, fidgeting now with the
chain of multicolored pebbles supporting her reading
glasses.

Ian turned his bark of startled laughter into a cough
just in time. Ask Kate to attend two events in one week?
The old Kate, yes, she'd loved socializing, but not the
new one.

Ever since the assault, she couldn't bear to be around
crowds. She also couldn't bear to be touched. He understood this rationally. It had made complete sense to

him after what happened, and he'd been so careful in those first few months not to so much as brush casually against her.

But that was eight months ago. Eight damn months and he couldn't even move his hand toward Kate, much less touch her, without that shuttered look coming over her face and her body stiffening in a way that told him without words that he wasn't wanted.

It was hard not to take that personally. It was hard not to think that this withdrawal from the world was also a withdrawal from him.

The secretary he'd inherited from his predecessor was still fidgeting in the doorway. "No," he said at last to Mildred Wooden. "I'll call her myself."

Chapter Three

A new semester meant a fresh start. Barbara Terry repeated this like a mantra as she walked along Penton Street, killing time before her class. Last semester was a thing of the past and she couldn't change it, couldn't make those C's into A's, couldn't go back in time and choose to study instead of attending those frat parties.

A new year meant a new beginning. She'd let herself get distracted last year, new to college, new to an independent life. Saturday night parties became Friday and Saturday nights and even Thursdays sometimes. She'd told herself that she'd catch up on studying, that everybody's grades slipped their first semester, that she had time to make things right.

Time had crept up on her along with ten extra pounds. It wasn't "freshman fifteen" no matter what her brothers said. As if it hadn't been bad enough going back home with crappy grades, she'd had to put up with them making fun of her. "Some guys like a girl with a little extra meat," Brad said, poking her in the side, and Jim laughed right along with him.

She tugged self-consciously at the waistband of her jeans, which was digging uncomfortably into her stomach. It was why she was walking through town. Part of her new plan to cram in exercise where she could, which, coupled with ridding her diet of fat, sugar, and anything yummy, would have her shedding pounds so fast that Brad and Jim would just have to eat their words.

They were just jealous because she'd gotten as far as college, and when she had a degree and a good job they'd still be squeezing cow teats and kicking manure off the soles of their boots.

She sighed as she passed Corner Bakery. The smell of freshly made muffins and doughnuts didn't help her resolve. There was already a queue of people in the shop and she hurried past, determined not to indulge. She wouldn't yield to temptation, not this year.

A smiling face looked out at her from a faded poster taped to a lamppost. Rain had washed out the word MISSING printed in caps under the picture. Red ink streaked through the plea for information below.

There were dozens of these posters when Lily Slocum first went missing, but now they had faded or simply vanished, torn from telephone poles or covered up by new signs.

Still, it wasn't as if Lily had been forgotten. There were new security warnings on campus about leaving dorm doors unlocked or walking unescorted late at night, even though everybody knew that Lily disappeared in broad daylight.

It was warm outside, but Barbara shivered anyway just thinking about it. It wasn't as if she'd known Lily well, not really, but they'd taken Geo Sci 146 together. Sitting in the same row of the lecture hall for an entire semester counted as some sort of bond even if they never said more than hello outside of class.

Lily had been friendly during Geo Sci, but she was a junior so naturally she didn't want to hang out with a newbie freshman. That was what Barbara tried to think, but a part of her always suspected that the real reason Lily never suggested getting together outside of class was because she didn't want to hang out with someone below her standards.

Lily was one of the beautiful people, those lucky few who beat the genetic crapshoot. She could sit there mainlining M&Ms in class yet never gain a pound, and even when she showed up for class without makeup and with her long blond hair pulled back in a messy knot, guys would still turn to look at her.

The truth was that Barbara had been sort of jealous of her. She'd felt bad about that after Lily disappeared. It was weird, thinking of someone just vanishing like that, but maybe she'd just taken off with some guy. That's what a lot of people said.

Wickfield's business district wasn't much, just a lot of stores that appealed mainly to old people—they didn't even have a Gap—but there was a decent college bookstore and two pizzerias and even one cheap sit-down restaurant that catered to students. Not that she was going to eat out this semester. This semester she was definitely eating in and saving her money.

Barbara felt a little pang, thinking of all the pizza she'd enjoyed last year, but then she pushed it out of her mind and picked up her pace. Her focus had to be on class work or she was never going to have the grades to get into grad school. Not that she knew what she wanted to do yet, but she knew she wasn't going back to the dairy farm.

She walked briskly past Evers Hardware and its display of old-fashioned bamboo rakes, and past First National Bank where a teller about her age was grabbing a smoke. The young woman gave Barbara the disdainful look affected by townspeople who didn't like college students, and stubbed out the cigarette with the toe of her cheap pump before flouncing through the double glass doors.

When Barbara reached Thorney Antiques Emporium at the end of the street, she unconsciously slowed down. This was the one old store she really loved, though her friends laughed at her when she insisted on stopping. Two stories crammed with several centuries worth of furniture and bric-a-brac, the shop looked as if it had stood there forever.

The owner, Mrs. Thorney, was slightly deaf and in some indeterminate period of old age between seventy and ninety. She dyed her hair shoe-polish black and wore it in a twisted cone, pinned to her head, so that it looked like a knob of polished ebony. She was fond of 1960s boldly patterned caftans and 1940s Bakelite jewelry and she called everybody "hon," though her tone of voice could make that either crotchety or a caress.

She didn't like the "college kids," but made an exception for Barbara, who treated her store and its possessions with respect, and Barbara returned her affection.

There was no sign of Mrs. Thorney through the front window, but she'd obviously been busy over the weekend. There was a new display, Victorian-themed with an emphasis on white. Clusters of lush white flowers and greenery framed the window and curved around silver picture frames and a gilt-edged porcelain tea service on a wide silver tray. There were carved ivory fans and a few sparkling broaches mounted on a velvet pillow, and a wide-brimmed hat with fluffy white feathers curving around its brim.

Barbara stared at the montage, oohing and aahing over the various elements and able, as was Mrs. Thorney, to ignore the fact that the flowers were silk, the broaches made of rhinestones, the velvet pillow moth-eaten on one corner, and the band of the hat stained yellow with some long-ago wearer's perspiration.

Her eyes flitted over everything, but came back to rest on a photograph in one corner. It was fairly small, maybe five by seven, and black and white with a sepia tone. It was in a silver frame that was tarnishing on its edges. This in no way detracted from the beauty of the young woman depicted, lying full-length on a chaise lounge, her body covered by a filmy-looking white dress with a high-neck. Her raised head rested on a pillow and she clasped flowers in hands folded demurely just below her chest.

Barbara looked, then looked again. She pressed her face so close to the window that it fogged up and she rubbed away the steam with an impatient hand. The young woman's eyes were closed, but she knew what color they'd be if they were opened. Watery blue. She'd seen them before. She'd seen them in the halls of her dorm and staring out at her from posters all over campus.

"Lily!" Barbara rapped on the window, staring from the photo to the street and back again. "It's Lily Slocum," she cried to a passing car, but the driver only gave her a strange look and didn't slow.

Barbara rushed to the door, but the knob wouldn't turn. She knocked anyway and repeatedly pushed a grimy buzzer adjacent to the mail slot. "It's Lily," she kept repeating, and when Mrs. Thorney finally came to the door, looking angry, then startled, she fell into her arms repeating the same thing over and over.

"Stop it, girl, take a breath," Mrs. Thorney said, giving the much larger Barbara a firm shake belied by her small stature and voluminous green robe. "Get a hold of yourself!"

But Barbara pushed past her and raced to the front window, knocking over a wicker carriage and a tower of moldering books in the process.

"Hey, stop that!" Mrs. Thorney yelled, but Barbara was already reaching into the display and grabbing the frame. She held it out to Mrs. Thorney with shaking hands, pointing at the young woman.

"It's Lily!" she said. "Lily Slocum."

Mrs. Thorney looked from the photo to Barbara's face and shrugged. "It's an old photo, dear, a Victorian mourning photograph. I don't know the identity of the young woman."

"It's Lily Slocum!" Barbara cried, but Mrs. Thorney continued to stare at her. She felt like shaking the old woman. "The student who went missing in May!"

Mrs. Thorney looked affronted, but then recognition seemed to dawn. She grabbed the frame from Barbara and peered through coke-bottle glasses at the photo. "It can't be," she said. "This is an old photograph. Over a hundred years."

Barbara could barely hold onto the frame she was shaking so hard. "It's Lily," she said. "It's got to be Lily."

"But it's an antique, dear."

"Where did you get it?"

"I don't know," Mrs. Thorney looked helplessly around the crowded store and then up at Barbara. "I've had it for a long time, haven't I?"

The dim and dusty shop seemed far less romantic now to Barbara. She pushed past Mrs. Thorney to hold the frame under a lit reproduction Tiffany lamp. Under the clear light she was even more convinced that it was Lily, but she flipped the frame over anyway.

"What are you doing?" Mrs. Thorney demanded. "You can't do that to my property!"

Barbara ignored her, pushing the brackets out of the

way and taking off the frame back. She removed the
paper backing with shaking hands and carefully lifted
out the photo. There was no writing on the back, but the
photograph didn't look so old close up. She held the
photo under the light and scrutinized the face. It was
definitely Lily Slocum. And there was something else,
something she hadn't noticed when it was behind glass.

Lily Slocum wasn't sleeping, she was dead.

Chapter Four

The man who left his calling card in the antique store window watched from the coffee house across the street as the police arrived. He sat in the sun at a small corner table and sipped iced coffee through a straw, delicate beads of sweat dotting the glass and his upper lip.

Two middle-aged women at the table next to him discussed what was going on, craning their necks to see over the squad cars, one of them actually standing up and shading her eyes to get a clear look. She had a runner's legs, the tendons taut against lightly tanned skin. Well preserved, he thought, and smiled at the irony. The girl in the picture was well preserved. He'd seen to that.

From his father he learned everything about death. The man had been the funeral director in their small West Virginia town, a job title that couldn't begin to convey the messy and intricate work of preparing the dead for their final journey.

Half of the boy's house had been a normal family home, the other half devoted to the business, which his father had inherited from the boy's dour grandfather.

Living around people who regarded any talk about the human body as perverse and where death, especially unexpected death, was talked about in whispers, the boy grew up in a world divided in two: above and below the thin floorboards of the old house.

Downstairs, in the cool basement, were two great porcelain tables suspended on large metal cranks. There were shelves filled with bottles and jars that held embalming fluid, and tubs of putty-colored skin enhancer, and even flat tins of hair crème and thin tubes of vermilion lipstick. There were blue cardboard boxes filled with syringes, and red ones bursting with rubber gloves, and a large glass apothecary jar filled with cotton balls.

The floor had a drain in it, and there were lengths of rubber hosing coiled in a corner, and hanging from metal hooks on the far wall were dark oilskin aprons.

Without the bodies it reminded him somewhat of the drugstore in the main street of town, the same medicinal smells and shelving, the same orderliness, and while the shop had penny candy and magazines for sale, the main business of the place was the care and treatment of the body.

The dead were brought to the basement by his father in the back of the hearse, or dropped off by refrigerated van courtesy of the coroner's office. Sometimes they were wearing the same stained clothes in which they'd died and sometimes they came in naked, their bodies already subject to the various indignities visited upon them by the coroner and his assistants.

They were laid upon those slabs of tables and then the boy's father or his assistant, a single man named Poe who lived on the top floor of a rooming house and owned a basset hound named Lucille, would begin what Poe called "prettifying" the body for the viewing public.

The first body the boy could remember seeing was that of a coal miner who died when the shaft elevator slipped on its journey, dropping the cage more than sixty feet into the darkness, and landing so hard that people said the noise was heard above ground and even a half mile away in the small, dirt-rimmed homes of the miners' wives and children.

The boy was four or five, small and young enough that his mother and other neighborhood women talked around him about how the man died and how two other men were crippled and about the dead man's pregnant wife and their two other children and how shameful it was that the company's policy was that she'd have to vacate the house in just two weeks.

He stayed long enough to hear the story, taking small sips of slightly sour lemonade from an enamel cup his mother set down next to him on the floor where he pretended to play with his toy cars.

As soon as he was able, he escaped through the door to the basement, carrying down a glass of iced tea with pieces of fresh mint floating on top, that sharp smell of spearmint forever associated in his mind with the sight of the body emerging from dirt and blood-crusted clothes.

The miner's face and exposed arms were black with soot, and he could still remember that jerk of surprise he felt when Poe cut neatly through the man's trousers and an icy white length of leg emerged. That powerful contrast between light and dark stayed with him, as did watching Poe carefully wash the man's body once it was fully naked, sluicing the dirt and blood down the drain, washing the dead man's face with a cloth just as the boy's mother did to him at bath time. The assistant's touch had been slower and softer somehow, something he wouldn't understand until much later, until his own life's work began and he experienced firsthand the change to human skin when blood flow ceases.

He felt a frisson of excitement when Poe's gloved hands moved down the body to lift the thick, flaccid penis, washing the nest of reddish gold pubic hair, and dipped lower to swipe once around the scrotum. His own penis twitched against him.

The boy's father moved between the man's body and the shelf beyond him, selecting several vials and mixing various lotions and powders into a small bowl. He paused to take the tea from the boy, holding the glass with a gloved hand and taking a long swallow before smiling at the boy and pronouncing it nicely sweet. All the while the smell of blood and soot and mint mingled in the boy's nostrils.

Music played on a small radio high above the boy's head, a woman's mournful voice skating along a scale from high to low. "Jazz," his father said when he saw the boy listening. "It helps the concentration."

When the buzzer sounded, two sharp, short bursts of noise, he reached up a hand and turned off the voice, moving quickly to strip off his gloves and hang up his apron before walking to the back door concealed from view by a floor-to-ceiling striped curtain.

The boy sidled after his father and watched him open the door to a moon-faced woman with red-rimmed eyes holding a small pile of clothes with a framed photo on top. A grim-faced man wearing a black suit and a gray hat held her elbow.

The boy watched as his father took the clothes from the miner's widow, watched as he took a long look at the photo.

"He was a fine-looking man," he said, and something about these words made red flare across the woman's wide cheeks and new tears tremble in her swollen eyes, though she smiled, too, pleased with the comment all the same.

These were the things he would remember: that woman's smile with her swollen eyes. The way his father carried the clothes carefully back into the other room and showed the picture to Poe, both of them discussing how they'd put that flattened face back into the visage looking out at them from the photo.

After they were finished and the body had been carefully placed in the burnished wood coffin with gleaming handles that the company would pay for, the boy crept into the empty viewing room to take another look. Moving swiftly past the rows of folding chairs, he placed his small hands onto the box and carefully lifted the lid.

The face of the miner looked peaceful, clean, his eyes shut as if he were just resting, his arms folded across the breast of the cheap blue suit that had been his best. A wreath of lilies sent by the company stood on one side of the coffin, a cross of roses on the other. The scent of flowers was powerful in the closed room.

Later, much later, he would find the drawer filled with photos, dozens of snapshots of corpses dressed and made up to look like they were living. "I like to keep a record of my work," Poe said with a little smile when he caught the boy. "Best not to tell your mama." He let the boy play with them, sifting through the dead like they were a set of playing cards.

The man took another sip of coffee and watched a young police officer wearing gloves carry a manila envelope out of the antique store. Did the officer remember the last time they'd found a photo like the one he was carrying, or was he too young? Eight years was a long time to live on memories. It was time to create some new ones.

Chapter Five

When Ian and Grace left each morning, Kate double-checked the lock on the front door before retreating to the kitchen to prepare a pot of tea. While waiting for the water to boil, she flicked aside the curtains on the kitchen window several times to scan the backyard and driveway. A new talisman of sorts. In the months before they'd left New York, she'd taken to checking the peep-hole in their front door multiple times a day. Obsessive. She knew that, knew what spurred it, knew what Ian would say about it if he saw her.

When the tea was ready, she poured it into a thermos and carried it out the kitchen door, pausing to lock the door carefully behind her.

It was no more than ten steps from the back door to the door of the studio, but it often felt like a gulf. She unlocked the studio with a silver key, trying not to hurry it so that it stuck in the lock, and when the door opened she stepped in and slammed it closed behind her, breathing hard as she turned the bolt to lock her-self in.

There were wooden blinds on the windows, and she
turned the rods on them just enough to look out. If Ian
or Grace were home, she would pull up the shades
themselves, but not when she was alone. Too much like
being in a fish bowl, though she realized that there was
no one there to look in at her. Well, except their next-
door neighbor. She had a clear view of the back of his
house, and sometimes saw him sitting out there alone
petting a large yellow cat.

He was odd, that one. Apparently he owned a floral
shop in town, but she found it hard to picture someone
so dumpy-looking creating anything beautiful. He gave
her the creeps, the way he skulked from his house to his
van when he left the house, scuttling along the sidewalk
like some overgrown bug. Ian said he was just shy, and she
could tell from the look on his face that he thought
she was hardly one to talk about someone else's reclu-
sive behavior.

Kate sighed and stepped back from the windows. She
poured some tea from her thermos and wrapped her
hands around the steaming mug, remembering all the
mornings she'd done this at her studio in Brooklyn. It
felt strange to be doing it somewhere else, but it wasn't
just that her space had changed. She'd changed. She
was so different from the Kate Corbin who'd walked the
streets of the city after midnight feeling perfectly safe.

"I don't like you coming home alone that late!" Ian
had yelled at her more than once in the early years of
their relationship.

"I need to work!" she'd shout back at him, frustrated
that he didn't understand that an artist couldn't fit the
workday into nine to five.

"It isn't safe, Kate," he'd said. "Call me if you're going
to be late."

Except if she called, he'd be angry that she was gone

so long. He hadn't understood what it was like to be consumed by something, by the emotional energy necessary to get fully involved in her work. She had to be immersed in order to produce. And she'd been immersed. Too immersed to see that where she worked wasn't safe, that the building wasn't secure, that someone could climb the steps unnoticed, could pick the lock on the battered metal door, could wait in the shadows—

Kate squeezed her eyes shut and shoved the memories to the back of her mind. She wouldn't think about that. No. She was in a new space. This was a new beginning. She took a long, slow deep breath and reached for a can of brushes on a shelf.

The previous owner had done a nice job with this space. The room was large and light and there was ample shelving. Kate had unpacked her boxes, taking care to arrange her brushes and paints and carefully set up her easels where she liked in relation to the windows. The paint-flecked portable CD player she'd used for years found a new spot on one of the broad wooden shelves, and she hung the old men's shirt, worn more for luck than protection from splatter, from a hook on the back of the door.

It was strange to have a kitchen so close by. In her old studio she'd kept a hot plate plugged into an extension cord running from the single outlet, but now she could just walk a few feet back into her house. The thermos was more for old time's sake than necessity. Other things were different, too, like the cleanliness of the space and the fact that the windows didn't look out on the flat, tarred roofs of other industrial buildings, but on tidy green lawn and another house.

The incomplete portrait of a banker sat on a maple easel next to one window. She sank into a chair nearby and stared at it with a critical eye. It wasn't working and she didn't know why. It wasn't as if she hadn't done plenty of these bread-and-butter portraits. This commission, from the prominent man's widow, had come over nine months ago and it still wasn't done. It was work like this that allowed her to pursue more creative projects, but she'd never have the time for them if she didn't finish this up.

Halfheartedly sorting through the photos she'd been given of her stout and ruddy-faced subject, she started at the sound of a door slamming. She stepped to the window and caught a glimpse of the dirty white van pulling away. The shop's name, Bouquet, was painted in fading pink letters on the van's side panel.

Somewhere she'd gotten the idea that small towns like Wickfield sent out welcome wagons and were populated by neighbors bearing homemade cookies to newcomers, but in the two weeks they'd been here they'd had no visitors. Aside from the party thrown by the Beetlemans, they hadn't met or socialized with anybody.

Not that she'd wanted to socialize. In fact, just the night before she'd turned down Ian's suggestion that they walk up to town and try one of the local restaurants. Still, she was surprised that no one had shown up on their doorstep to welcome them.

It was too quiet here. In her old studio she'd played CDs to try and drown out some of the louder traffic noise. Here she played them to create noise and distract her from the disturbing silence. She sifted through her CDs and chose an old recording of Sarah Vaughan before squeezing paint onto her palette. It was the banker's face that needed work. A haunting jazz melody filled the studio as she stirred the paints with her brush.

Sharp rapping on the door interrupted her hours later. Startled, Kate dropped her palette and paint spilled onto the floor. Heart racing, she stepped over to the window and looked through the blinds.

A mailman stood outside the studio door holding a large box.

"Yes?"

"Will you hold a package for your neighbor?"

"Who?"

"Your neighbor." The mailman jerked his head at the house next door before glancing down at the label on the cardboard box he held in his arms. "Terrence Simnic. He's not answering and I got to leave it with somebody."

"Sure, okay."

The package was surprisingly light. She locked the door again and left the box next to it. She cleaned up the paint on the floor with a tiny bit of paint thinner and water and returned to the banker's face. It was wrong, all wrong. She started the CD again, resisting her desire to slash through the canvas with a palette knife. It would have to be completely redone, but she wasn't sure she could do it. With a sigh, she picked up her brush.

The package was completely forgotten until tapping at the window startled Kate. She whirled around and saw Grace peering in the window.

"Don't do that," she said when she opened the door. "You scared me."

"Sorry." Grace didn't sound it. She stepped into the studio and bumped against the box. "What's that?"

"Something for the neighbor." Kate leaned toward Grace for a kiss. "How was your day?"

"Eww! Mom, you've got paint all over you!"

"Have an air kiss then." Kate mimed a kiss near her daughter's face and Grace rolled her eyes.

"Fine. Just don't touch me. I'm hungry—can I have a snack?"

With a last look at the banker, who was becoming less distinct with each stroke of the brush, Kate broke away and followed Grace out of the studio, taking the neighbor's package with her.

"You shouldn't leave this door unlocked," she said when the back door, which led into the kitchen, opened as she tried to put the key in the lock.

"What, like someone's going to break in while we're eight feet away?" Grace snorted. "Get real, Mom."

"Just keep it locked."

"Whatever." Grace buried herself in the fridge and Kate reached around her to pull out an apple.

"Here. These are good."

"I don't want an apple."

"What do you want?"

"I don't know, Mom, that's why I'm looking."

The tone of exaggerated patience would have infuriated Ian, but Kate didn't react. Pick your battles, friends with older children had cautioned when she described the strange metamorphosis affecting her once-sweet daughter. Kate had taken to repeating that to herself like a mantra.

She carried the package out to the entrance hall and cautiously peered out the glass-paneled front door before opening it. The dirty white van had reappeared on the street, but when she stepped out on the porch she couldn't see any movement in the neighbor's house.

She looked down at the box and then back in the house, wondering if she could get Grace to carry it over for her. Only Grace would ask why and probably mention it to Ian and he would want to talk about it. "You're becoming agoraphobic," he'd said angrily when she refused to walk up to town the other night.

As if she didn't know that, as if she didn't realize it was a problem. It wasn't as if she wanted to be this way.

She'd tried once to explain how painful it was to be around other people since the attack, how it made her feel as if she were exposed.

To feel her skin tingling, as if everybody knew, to wonder if every man she saw was the stranger who'd broken into her studio—sometimes it was more than she could bear and she just wanted to hide. It was as if the assault hadn't been a single incident, but a virus infecting her and all parts of her life.

The days when she'd felt safe on the streets of the city seemed so far in the past that it was as if they'd happened to another person. She'd been so naïve about danger, so blasé about her own personal safety. Rape was something that happened to women who lived in dangerous neighborhoods or went out at four in the morning or dressed provocatively. Rape didn't happen to married women, to mothers, to women who always locked their car doors.

She glanced down at the box in her hands and read the address label again. Terrence Simnic. Well, maybe she'd just leave the box on the porch, ring the bell, and walk away.

That decision propelled her off her own porch, over the driveway, and up Mr. Simnic's clipped lawn to his front steps. The house was similar in style to hers, but there was something timeless about this one, as if she'd stepped back into a Victorian novel. Maybe it was only that the old wicker furniture on the porch reminded her of her grandmother's house.

The door had probably once been painted a deep green, but it had faded over time. She rang the bell and heard it echoing faintly through the house.

Nobody came. She shifted the box in her arms and hit the bell again. Something brushed against her leg and Kate screamed and dropped the box.

A yellow, short-haired cat stepped between her legs and leaped soundlessly on top of the box, looking up at her quizzically, its sinuous tail curling like a question mark.

"You scared me," Kate said, crouching down and extending her hand. The cat leaned into her tentative touch, and she stroked his soft fur and wondered what to do about the box. She couldn't just leave it here, not after she'd dropped it. She picked it up again and gave it a slight shake, praying whatever was in it wasn't fragile.

A third try of the doorbell, though she'd given up hope of finding Mr. Simnic. Maybe he was hard of hearing. She knocked on the door anyway and it swung open. Startled, Kate looked into the house. It was gloomy thanks to the heavy curtains drawn over the front windows.

"Mr. Simnic?" She wasn't even sure she was pronouncing his name correctly. There was no answer, but the cat had followed her in and meowed loudly near her feet.

"Hello? Mr. Simnic?" she called louder, and took a few more steps into the house.

"What do you want?"

The voice, deep and flat, came behind her. Kate whirled around and managed to turn a startled cry into, "Hello!" She gestured at the package. "Just dropping this off for you. I rang the bell but nobody answered."

The man standing in the doorway looked down at the box and back up at her. He was anywhere from thirty-five to fifty years of age, just above average height, and with skin that looked pasty white as if he spent no time in the sun. His short, brown hair was wispy and receding, but as if his body were compensating for that, he had thickly haired arms hanging, somewhat chimp-like, down at his sides. He was wearing a short-sleeved

baby blue shirt with sweat stains visible at the under-
arms. More body hair sprouted from the open neck-
line. His khaki pants had an oily-looking stain on one
knee and they looked like they were dependent on his
cracked leather belt to hold them up.

"Who are you?" he said in the same flat voice. His
eyes were large and the muddy brown of river silt. It was
too late to flee. Kate saw no other option and stuck out
her hand.

"I'm Kate Corbin, your new neighbor." She gestured
at her house, but the man's eyes remained focused on
her face. "You're Terrence Simnic, right?"

"Yes." He sounded deeply suspicious.

"Well, I guess you weren't here today when the mailman tried to drop this off, so he asked if I'd hold it for
you."

The man looked at the box again, and this time held
out his arms to take it from her.

"I'm afraid I dropped it," Kate said, adding hastily,
"It was an accident—your cat startled me."

A frown creased the flat face. "I hope you didn't
break it."

"I hope not, too. Just let me know if it's damaged, I'll
reimburse you." She inched toward the door.

He shook his head. "You can't."

"No, really, Mr. Simnic, I'll gladly pay for any repairs
or replacement costs."

"It can't be replaced. It's too valuable."

Oh, great, a potentially litigious neighbor. Ian was
going to love this.

"Whatever it is, Mr. Simnic, I'm sure we can—"

"It's a doll."

That startled her. Kate stared at him, trying to fit doll
and this simian-looking man into the same universe. It
didn't work.

"It's for my collection. Well, Mother's collection."

He reached a hand into his pocket and produced a pocket knife. For one horrible moment, as she watched his blunt fingers pinch forth the biggest blade, Kate thought he meant to use it on her. Instead, he set the box on the floor and squatted beside it, running the tip of the blade through the packing tape.

Pulling back the flaps, he scooped handfuls of Styrofoam peanuts onto the dusty floor, making little grunting noises. Multiple layers of bubble wrap appeared, and through them Kate could make out the hazy shape of something human-looking. Terrence Simnic unwrapped the layers, being careful not to jostle what was inside, reminding Kate of an archaeologist removing gauze from a mummy. Suddenly he stopped.

"She's perfect!" It was a heavy, heartfelt whisper.

Kate stepped closer to look for herself and gasped.

Lying amid the wrapping was a porcelain doll with features fixed in a scream. The red-rimmed mouth was wide open and the glass eyes horrified. It was grotesque, but Terrence Simnic was actually smiling.

He twisted something on the back of the doll and all at once the face turned. A new expression appeared, happy, and then he turned a knob again and a sleeping face appeared.

"German. Late nineteenth century. Mint condition." He mumbled the words, and Kate wasn't sure if he was talking to her or himself. He lumbered to his feet, cradling the doll in his massive arms. It wore a nightgown of yellowed white lace and he stroked the cloth.

"She's my latest. Do you want to see the others?"

Kate hesitated, wanting to issue a polite demurral, but Terrence Simnic was leading the way to another room. "It's in here," he said. "Mother always kept them in the dining room."

Reluctantly, Kate stepped after him. The dining room was papered in deep red with little crescents of gold that had faded over time. It was peeling at the corners of the high ceiling and there was water damage in one spot, spreading in concentric brown circles. A dusty, oval-shaped walnut table and six chairs stood in the center of the room, but the focal point was really the antique curio cabinets lining the wall. They were made of oak or mahogany and didn't all match, and every shelf was literally crammed with antique dolls.

"Mother would have loved you." Terrence crooned to the doll. He carefully unlocked one of the oak cabinets and shifted two frilly dressed baby dolls so that his newest acquisition could sit between them. "There you go, little one, there you go."

It was spooky, the faded room and the shelves filled with dolls. There was dust everywhere but on the curio cabinets, which looked as if they were cleaned every day. They smelled faintly of furniture polish.

"Aren't they beautiful?" This time Terrence Simnic's question was directed at Kate. She struggled to think of something to say, but he seemed to take her silence for awe, nodding with a goofy smile on his face.

"It's something, isn't it?"

"Oh, yes." That she could be honest about it. It was certainly something.

"Mother took such pride in her collection," Terrence said. "She had such a good eye and I've tried to match it. I'm very particular about what I buy. Every doll has a complete history and the most damage I'll accept is a single, hidden, hairline fracture."

A phone rang somewhere in the house, a loud, jangling old-fashioned sound that made both Terrence and Kate start.

"That's for me," he said. "You need to leave now."

She didn't need to be told twice. Kate walked quickly back to the front of the house while the phone continued to ring, fighting the urge to look over her shoulder until she reached the door. When she looked back into the gloomy, dusty house, she could see Terrence Simnic standing in a doorway at the other end of the dining room, an outdated phone, complete with long cord, in one large hand. He stared at her and she fled out the door.

Chapter Six

Kate crossed the yard back to her own house feeling as if she were being watched. Grace was playing the piano. A haunting melody floated out the window, stopping abruptly as Kate came in the door.

"That was lovely," Kate said, pausing at the entrance to the living room. Grace looked up from the keyboard and scowled.

"It sucks. I can't get it right. It's too fast and it lacks feeling."

"It sounded good to me."

"That's because you don't play the piano, Mom." Grace turned her attention back to the score in front of her, and Kate knew she was being dismissed. While this behavior annoyed Ian, Kate chose to ignore it and was even, secretly, amused by it. She saw herself in this devotion to one's passion, and even though Grace's snotty attitude wasn't pleasant, Kate could still understand and respect her daughter's devotion to her music.

Kate made her way to the kitchen to prepare dinner, listening to the music start again. She moved about easily in the large kitchen, so much larger and newer than their old one. So why did she miss it? The kitchen in their apartment had been galley style and they'd re-modeled it, on the cheap, two years before Grace was born. This kitchen was wide and spacious, with solid wood cabinets and granite countertops and stainless-steel appliances. Everything she'd lusted after in magazines, and yet now that it was hers, all she could think about was the edge of the old laminate countertops where they'd marked Grace's height in pencil.

She reached up to take a pot from the rack hanging above the center island, and caught a glimpse of Terrence Simnic's house through the window. The lights were on in the back of his house, and she wondered if he was cooking dinner. It was impossible to tell, because old curtains hung in the windows back there just like in the front of the house.

He was a strange man, but they'd dealt with strange neighbors before. Kate remembered the old woman who'd lived in the apartment below theirs and regularly cooked tripe, the awful smell invariably sliding up and under their door and lingering for days despite their best efforts to shoo it away. Or the shifty-eyed, pock-marked man two floors down, who'd worn a full-length fur coat in the middle of July and had screaming matches in some Slavic language with a string of anemic-looking bottle blondes.

Compared to these neighbors, Terrence Simnic with his doll collection really wasn't that bad. She turned away from the window and concentrated on what to make for dinner, but she couldn't shake the crawly feeling being in his house had given her.

Ian arrived home shortly after six, dumping his brief-case in the hall and coming straight through to the kitchen with a troubled smile on his face.

"God, it's good to be home," he said, pouring a glass of the South African white wine that she'd opened.

"Long day?"

"That doesn't begin to capture it. Did you hear the news about Lily Slocum?"

Kate shook her head, concentrating on chopping tomatoes to add to the salad. "Has she been found?"

"No, but they found a photo of her." Ian took a sip of wine. "Apparently she's dead."

The knife slipped in Kate's hand and she narrowly missed slicing her thumb. "What? That's terrible!"

Ian described the photo found in a local shop, and Kate thought of the poor girl's parents getting the news. She rinsed the cutting board, the red smears from the tomatoes suddenly making her queasy. "Are the police even sure this photo is real?"

"They're not saying much, but since it's not the first time this has happened, everybody seems to think it's real."

"What do you mean it's not the first time?"

Ian put down his wine and pulled a copy of the *Wickfield Gazette* from his briefcase. "Here, you can read about it yourself. Copies were distributed at the emergency meeting I got called to with the university president and provost, as well as another meeting with legal office representatives and public relations folk."

Kate read the story of the discovery of the photograph, but her eyes were drawn over and over again to the haunting photo. A young woman dressed in a flowing white gown reclined on a chaise lounge. It was a beautiful picture, the figure seeming to float within the clusters of delicate flowers arranged about her body. Her eyes were closed, she might have been sleeping.

A recap of the details surrounding Lily Slocum's disappearance was included in the article, along with a smaller headshot. She was a pretty girl with a sweet, very pale face and long, straight blond hair. She wore too much eye makeup, which made her look even younger than her twenty-one years. She looked like a child, a little ghost child, and Kate realized with a start that she was only six years older than Grace.

"She's so young," Kate said out loud.

Ian took a long swallow of wine and rubbed his forehead. "Yes, she was."

His use of the past tense jumped out at her. "You believe she's dead then?"

"I don't know. If she isn't, why hasn't anyone heard from her?"

Kate followed the story to the inside pages of the paper, and was surprised to find three more photos of smiling, attractive young women.

> Police won't speculate whether the disappearance of Lily Slocum is in any way connected with the disappearance eight years ago of Ann Henke or the disappearance of Lisa Myers and Barbara Lutz the year before, though similar photos of all three young women were found in Wickfield after their disappearance. The bodies of Ann Henke and Lisa Myers were recovered in 2000. Barbara Lutz has never been found.

Kate folded the paper, surprised that her hands trembled. "So much for the safe community."

Ian sighed. "This is exactly what the university is afraid of. It *is* safe. Think how many more homicides are committed in New York every year. It just gets more publicity here because it's a small town."

"Tell that to the Slocum family." Kate handed the salad

and dressing over to Ian to toss so she could take the
chicken out of the oven.

"Fortunately, I don't have to. Today's meeting was
bad enough. There's a lot of finger-pointing about campus security, which makes no sense to me since she wasn't
on campus when she was abducted."

It made perfect sense to Kate. People needed to feel
as if something could have been done to prevent Lily
Slocum's disappearance, so they blamed things like lax
security.

"Grace, come set the table!" she called, adding the
paper to the recycling bin and then moving it under
some other papers so their daughter wouldn't see it.
Even as she did it, she realized the futility of the gesture. Grace wasn't much younger than these other girls
and she'd probably already heard the news the way that
kids seemed to hear and know everything.

Ian took plates from the cupboard and handed them
to Kate. "I've got to work late a few evenings this week
because the meeting I had scheduled on the Performing
Arts Center got bumped by today's emergency meetings."

"We'll be here alone?" For some reason Kate had a
sudden image of Terrence Simnic next door in that
gloomy house with his dolls.

"Is that going to be a problem?" Ian gave her a funny
look, and Kate realized she was gripping the counter.
She let go, giving herself a mental shake. There was nothing to be afraid of. The person who'd taken Lily Slocum
wasn't going to break into her house and Terrence
Simnic was just a harmless eccentric.

"No problem," she said. "Grace and I can manage."

"Manage what?" Grace slouched into the room and
looked suspiciously at her parents. "I hope you haven't
signed me up for something like that stupid pottery class."

Her parents laughed and Ian said, "You enjoyed that once you gave it a try and stopped complaining."

"Yeah, who doesn't want to hang out with some freaked-out hippie lady whose place reeks of patchouli and get your clothes covered in gray shit so you can produce one lopsided ashtray."

"Don't use that language," Kate said, handing her a fistful of silverware. "And I loved your lopsided ashtray even if none of us smoke."

"Mom, I could snort into a Kleenex and you'd treasure it."

Ian put his wineglass down. "Don't talk to your mother like that."

Grace rolled her eyes, but only after she'd turned away from her father, Kate noticed. Instead of challenging Grace's statement, she simply said, "Set the table and pour yourself some milk."

"I want a Diet Coke."

"Milk." Kate held up a hand as Grace opened her mouth to argue. "You're growing, you need the calcium, and it's nonnegotiable."

Grace gave a put-upon sigh, but after halfheartedly setting the table, she clumped past her parents to grab a glass from a cupboard and the milk from the fridge.

"Did you practice today?" Ian asked.

"Of course." Grace sounded exasperated, but Ian pressed on.

"How was school today?"

Grace shrugged in reply and slunk over to the table with her glass, which, despite her protests, she immediately began taking sips from.

"C'mon, what happened? What did you learn?"

"Nothing."

"I'm going to ask for my tax money back," Ian said with a smile, nudging her with an elbow. The old, pre-

puberty Grace would have laughed at this, but teenage
Grace, the bad seed, screeched.

"Watch it! You'll spill my milk!"

Kate silently gave her own put-upon sigh as Ian came
to serve the plates.

"Boarding school," he muttered under his breath.

"Are you kidding? Then we wouldn't be able to mon-
itor her at all. I'm sure she'd have Damien as her guest
in under a minute."

Kate had spoken in a whisper, but Grace managed to
pick up on a familiar name. "What are you saying about
Damien? Did he call?"

"We're not talking to you, young lady," Ian said. "Sit
down."

"No! I want to know if Damien called. Did he?"

Ian squared off with her, arms crossed over his broad
chest. "First of all, Damien isn't allowed to call—remember? Secondly, you don't say no to me. Sit. Down."

Grace hesitated, staring at her father with hatred. Ian
took one step toward her and she dropped in her seat.

Kate passed out plates and took her own seat. "Well,
bon appétit, everybody," she said, trying not to imbue it
with sarcasm.

The photographs of Lily Slocum preyed on Kate's
mind, the image of the still girl lying on the chaise con-
trasting with that young, smiling face. After reading the
article, she followed Grace out the door every day, accompanying her down the porch steps and their front
walk and standing on the sidewalk in front of their
house to watch her make her way to the end of the
block to catch the bus.

"I could drive you," Kate had offered. "Now that
we've got a second car you don't need to take the bus."

Ian had spearheaded the purchase of a silver Toyota Prius, and was as thrilled as if he'd built it himself. He'd insisted on discussing all the features, and bored Kate with a detailed description of how hybrid cars work. When he offered to drive the Volvo to campus every day and leave the new car with her, she had to hide a smile at the strain in his voice. When she politely declined, he couldn't hide his own delight.

The purchase of the new car didn't interest Grace once she'd established that Ian wouldn't let her drive it until she was old enough to get a learner's permit. She turned down Kate's offer of a ride claiming that she liked to take the bus.

"I'm not a little kid, you know," Grace complained for the umpteenth time as her mother followed her to the front door. "I don't need an escort."

"Tough," Kate said, catching the screen door that Grace tried to slam and following her daughter out onto the porch. "Do you have your lunch?"

"Yes, Mom." The words were drawn out, exasperated. She wore shades of black as usual, a charcoal T-shirt and dark jeans, her matching hair a tangled curtain blocking her face. She jammed her iPod headphones into her ears and stalked away without a good-bye.

Kate watched her go, peering past the green leaves of the oak trees to see her reach the end of the block. She felt another wave of anxiety as Grace's steps slowed the closer she got to the other kids at the bus stop. Did she have friends? These kids were a preppy-looking bunch. What did they make of Grace and her urban-guerrilla look? Was she happy at her new school? Wick-field High School had a good reputation and high test scores to back it up, but so had the school Grace had gone to last year, and that had turned out to be a disaster.

Kate walked back inside and locked the door behind her, checking it again two seconds after she'd turned the dead bolt. She jumped when the doorbell rang five minutes later.

Switching off the teakettle, she tiptoed back to the front door, pushing aside the curtain to see who was there.

"It's me, silly, open the door." Margaret Newman grinned at her, pressing her face close to the window as if Kate were partially blind.

With a feeling of relief, Kate unlocked the door and stepped into the embrace of one of her oldest friends.

"Good Lord, you've gone *Green Acres* on me already," Margaret said, stepping back and surveying Kate's blue jeans and old T-shirt.

"I'm working," Kate said defensively, self-consciously smoothing her hair.

"So am I," Margaret said, indicating her hand-tailored brown suit, "but us city folk don't slop the hogs."

"I prefer to call it painting," Kate said, but she couldn't keep from laughing. Margaret always made her laugh. "I'm so glad to see you!"

"I promised I'd visit your country retreat and here I am." Margaret hoisted an H&H bag she had resting at her designer-clad feet. "And I came with provisions."

Kate led her to the kitchen, and while Margaret unpacked bagels and chattered about the charm of "the hinterlands," Kate made a pot of strong, black coffee just the way her friend liked it.

"They do sell these here, you know," Kate said, smearing an everything bagel with cream cheese.

"I'm sure they're a poor imitation." Margaret took a large bite out of a sesame bagel and picked a seed delicately off the corner of her lip.

They'd been friends for almost eighteen years,

longer than Kate had been married to Ian. In fact she owed her relationship with Ian to Margaret, since she'd invited them both to one of the wild parties she'd thrown regularly when they were all in their early twenties and new to New York. At least Kate and Ian had been new. Margaret was a born and bred Manhattanite and swore that she'd never live anywhere else, though she complained often enough about the high cost of living. It was the one area of her life where emotion overcame pragmatism.

"How's Ian?"

"He's good. Busy with the new job."

"I'll bet he is." Margaret took a sip of coffee. "Is it all the prestige he hoped for?"

"Ian isn't like that."

"Isn't he? I thought that's why he had to leave the city."

Kate took a sip of her tea, hoping the hot liquid would soothe the nervous twisting in her gut. They'd had this discussion before. "You know why we left."

"You were getting better."

"I wasn't."

"And Grace would have gotten over that boy."

"She hasn't."

"Well, you both would in time. That's my point," Margaret insisted, tucking a strand of honey-colored hair behind a perfectly proportioned ear. She was a beautiful woman, but she had yet to find a relationship that satisfied her. "Discriminating" was how Margaret described her attitude toward men, but Kate suspected that deep down she was really afraid of compromise.

"We're not that far from the city," Kate said.

"Then why haven't I seen you?"

"I'm trying to work. I'm overdue with that portrait I told you about."

"You work too hard," Margaret said. She'd gone to art school, too, but after three years of struggling had steered her career into the safer, shallower waters of advertising. "Starving isn't really my color," she'd said at the time. She finished off her bagel with one large bite and dabbed her mouth daintily with a napkin. "C'mon, show me your new studio."

"Sure." Kate tried to sound casual, but her stomach twisted again, the knot of anxiety tighter. She locked the kitchen door behind them and turned to see Margaret staring at her.

"I thought it was supposed to be safe up here."

Kate flushed. "It is."

"Then why are you locking the door?"

"Just habit, I guess." Kate avoided her eyes, moving past her to unlock the studio.

It was obvious that she hadn't been doing much painting. The portrait of the banker had barely changed, but Margaret just looked at it for a moment without saying anything, before examining the rest of the room.

"It's got lots of natural light," she said, stepping over to the window. As she stood there, a screen door slapped and Kate saw Terrence Simnic coming down his back steps with a large, black garbage bag.

"Who's your neighbor?" Margaret asked watching as he hauled it into one of the metal garbage cans neatly lined up on the other side of the storm cellar.

"Terrence Simnic."

"He seems"—Margaret seemed to be searching for a word—"colorful."

Kate laughed, relieved to have something to laugh about. "Yeah, he's kind of strange." She told Margaret about the doll collection.

"How creepy!" Margaret said. "Very Norman Bates.

Are you sure he doesn't have his mother stored some-where in that house?"

"I wasn't about to stick around and find out."

"That's a big bag of trash for one man." Margaret stepped away from the window and moved over to the shelves Kate had filled with paints and palettes and other supplies. She ran a hand over the brushes and flipped the pages of a drawing pad before looking Kate square in the eye. "How are you really doing?

Her question took Kate by surprise. "I'm fine," she said, but she felt as if she were lying.

"You don't look fine."

"I'm not sleeping well."

"Are you taking anything?"

"No!" At Margaret's surprised look, Kate lowered her voice. "And I don't want to. I've just got to get used to being in such a quiet place."

"How are things with you and Ian?"

"Fine," Kate said again, but Margaret just looked at her and Kate cracked.

"Okay, they're not fine. We're still not doing it. I can't do it. We haven't done it in over eight months. Happy?" Tears burned in her eyes, but Kate blinked them back.

There was silence for a moment, and then Margaret gave her a slight smile and said, "Honey, you're not in high school anymore. You're allowed to say sex."

It made Kate laugh, the tears spilling over as she did, and she brushed them away, feeling the knot in her stomach easing a little. "It's been hard," she said. "Ian doesn't understand. It's not like I want to be this way."

"Are you seeing anyone?"

"You sound like him now." Kate turned away from her friend, struggling to regain her composure. "I don't want to see anyone again. It's so boring. Talk, talk, talk.

All the talk in the world isn't going to change what happened."

"But it might help you get over it."

Kate could feel tears threatening again, and Margaret let it go, the way a good friend does, by steering the conversation onto mutual friends. They left Kate's studio and went back to the house, spending a happy few hours gossiping about everything that had happened in the city since Kate had gone.

When her friend finally left, Kate was sorry to see her go. Margaret was laughing at a final joke as she headed for the shiny Lexus parked at the curb, but she paused and turned back to look at Kate, her face suddenly serious.

"I know you've been through hell in the past year, but you can't make it better by shutting yourself off from the world," she said. "Promise me you'll take care of yourself."

"I promise," Kate said, and she managed to smile as if that comment didn't hurt. She stood and stared down the street long after Margaret's car was gone.

As she walked slowly back up to her house, Terrence Simnic came down his front steps lugging two shopping bags. He set them down to open the door of the brown sedan parked in the driveway. As he shoved one bag in the backseat, the second toppled over and clothes spilled out onto the asphalt. Women's clothes. Kate stared at the bra and panties tangled up with some sweaters. Terrence Simnic scooped them up, muttering under his breath. As he shoved them back in the bag, he looked over and caught her staring. Kate tensed, locking eyes with his, her body prickling with apprehension. He shoved the second bag into the back of the car, still staring at her, and then, maintaining eye contact, he walked slowly around to the driver's side.

Kate broke eye contact and ran into the house slamming and locking the door. She stood there, trembling, until she heard the roar of the car engine. When she peered out the front window, his car had disappeared down the street beneath a canopy of trees.

Chapter Seven

Grace lingered when the bell for second period rang, glancing out the windows that overlooked the front of Wickfield High and then up at the big, round, industrial clock fixed on the wall in the long hallway.

A teacher shooing latecomers into her class paused with her hand on the door to stare at her, and Grace turned swiftly, messenger bag banging against her hip, hurrying away before the woman could ask where she was supposed to be. Spanish class, but that was in the opposite direction, and it didn't really matter because she wasn't going.

Damien was coming. He'd promised. "Going to drive on up and get you," he'd said when she talked to him the day before, calling him from a borrowed cell phone. She couldn't call him from her own phone. That wasn't allowed, hadn't been allowed once her parents knew about him.

"He's twenty!" Her mother had said, repeating the number as if that meant anything.

"So what?"

"So he's too old for you!"

"Dad's five years older than you!"

Her father was quick to answer that. "The difference between fifteen and twenty is much greater than the distance between twenty and twenty-five."

They'd met Damien exactly once, one time when she stupidly asked him to meet her out front of their building to go to the movies and her parents happened to arrive home together just as he pulled up to the curb in his dark brown Mercedes. They'd been polite, she couldn't fault them for that, but her father had immediately asked Damien how old he was and her mother had said that Grace wasn't old enough to date.

Even though they hadn't had a problem when she went to the eighth-grade dance with Matt Glick.

"Wasn't that a date?" she'd demanded in the hours-long argument that followed her parents forbidding her to go out with Damien, but her mother hadn't been moved.

"Matt was your age, Grace. And you weren't really dating."

Which showed how little they knew, because she'd kissed Matt Glick in the closet at Emily Neeson's party, though the quick, wet imprint of his lips against hers had all the romance of a postage stamp. They'd been playing spin the bottle in the family room, all giggling and hush-hush with Emily's clueless parents just steps away, and someone nudged the bottle after Matt spun it so that it pointed at Grace.

Kid stuff. She could hardly believe that had been just two years ago. Things were so different since she'd met Damien. Not that it was Damien who made her change. That's what her parents believed, but it wasn't true. She was ready for change, thirsting for it, and maybe that was why the universe sent her Damien. Like he was her destiny.

He liked to talk about things like that, philosophy and stuff. Just because he didn't go to college didn't mean he wasn't smart. Damien was really, really smart. She'd seen his acceptance letter to Princeton, so she knew it was true that he'd gotten in, and so what if once he got there he realized it wasn't the place for him. Conformists, he'd told her. Conformists and wannabes, all of the students he'd met and most of the professors. "There wasn't an original idea in the place."

She'd told her parents this, thinking that they'd understand, that her mother, of all people, would share that sentiment, but her lips had tightened into a thin line and her father had said, "What a crock of shit."

She hadn't told Damien that, hadn't told about the other words they'd used, like "posturing" and "insecure." It wasn't true, any of it. They didn't understand Damien and they didn't want to.

Grace walked quickly down one hallway, then another, both of them leading to the back of the school and the parking lot adjacent to the playing fields where she'd told Damien she'd meet him. Exiting the school was the easy part. She'd already scoped out the door near the gymnasium that she could use. Second period was good because for some reason no class had gym before third period.

The door to the gym teacher's office stood open. Grace peered through the crack and saw Coach Wally Pembroke looking into the file cabinet, his broad back facing the door. She tiptoed past softly enough that she could hear his wheezing. He was supposed to be some sort of legend at Wickfield High. She'd heard other parents tell hers about how great it was that he was still teaching and how these kids were the third generation he'd taught in the town. Like it was some sort of accomplishment just to hobble about shouting, jowly cheeks turning red from the effort. He should be on an oxygen tank.

At the double doors, Grace shifted her bag and took one last look back down the hall before pressing carefully against the handle and exiting the building. She held the door so it wouldn't slam closed, before walking quickly along the side of the brick building until she came to a corner where, with any luck, nobody looking out a window would be able to see her. She walked feeling as if there were eyes boring into her, half-expecting someone to call her name before she got as far as the parking lot, but nobody did.

She headed for a cluster of cars toward the rear, hunkering down between a dusty red pickup and a blue BMW, which just about summed up the differences in the town's demographics, and slipped off her messenger bag to rest beside her. She wrapped her arms around her legs and tapped the toe of one sneaker against the asphalt. It would take Damien at least an hour and a half to get up here from Manhattan. And that was on a good traffic morning. All you needed was one slowdown and it could turn into a two-hours-plus trip.

The sound of an engine made her pop up, but it wasn't Damien's car pulling into the lot. Some ugly old green car belching out smoke from its exhaust pipe. She slipped back down between the cars, this time lying back, bag wedged under her head like a pillow.

It was a beautiful day. She hummed a cheerful Mozart sonata, playing the notes on the ground until she got caught in a tricky section and couldn't remember the next measure. She looked up at the big puffballs of white clouds moving lazily across a bright blue sky. She shaded her eyes and made out the shapes in the clouds, remembering doing that with her mother when she was little.

They'd been lying on a beach then, up at Cape Cod, with the sand gritty between their toes and the sun like a blanket on top of them. "Do you see the alligator, Gracie?" her mother had said, pointing. "Look at its sharp teeth."

She could remember the feel of the breeze against her skin and the distant caw of seagulls and how her father had been sitting nearby immersed in a book, his dark head bent over its pages. She had her own little yellow bucket and a blue shovel and she laughed as her mother sprinkled water over her head, cooling her off.

"What do you see in the clouds, Gracie?"

Her mother's voice lilting somewhere above her, and she could remember the feel of a warm kiss pressed against the top of her head. What had she seen in the clouds? She couldn't remember. Grace closed her eyes, tired of squinting. She had to have seen something, but all she could remember was her mother describing the things that *she'd* seen. Always the artist, nothing Kate Corbin ever saw was ordinary. Jungle animals, five-layered wedding cakes, an Aladdin's lamp. What had Grace seen?

"I see a dog."

"What kind of dog?"

"I don't know, just a dog."

"Greyhound? Boxer? Terrier?"

She could remember shaking her head, shaking off her mother's insistence as if it were a touch. *"No, no! Just a dog!"*

"Oh, Grace. You need to have more imagination."

Grace frowned at the memory.

"Are you going to sleep all day?"

Her eyes flew open. Damien was standing above her,

leaning casually against the Mercedes, looking hot just like always, tight jeans and cool black T-shirt and those silver aviator glasses that she loved. His blond hair was cut brutally short. A smile played on his lips.

"Hey!" She scrambled to her feet and grabbed her bag. "I didn't know you'd arrived."

"You were in la-la land, baby." He accepted her quick kiss, but when she lifted her lips from his, one of his hands reached out and pinched her right nipple, popping out of her bra and against the thin fabric of her knit shirt.

"Ow!" She pulled back, but his other hand wrapped around to hold her pressed against him.

"You miss me?" He increased the pressure on her nipple, all the while smiling at her.

It hurt, but she liked it, too. She could feel heat flooding her face. "Yes."

"Show me."

She kissed him again then, tentatively pushing with her lips dry against his, and then he let his lips part and her tongue darted forward like a bird dipping into an open flower.

He circled the nipple with his finger and pushed against it as if it were a button. She moaned against his mouth, pressing up against him instinctively. Along with her love for Damien was a bit of fear. Not that she was really afraid of him, not that, but just a little anxiety about what he was going to do next. She knew he was capable of doing anything. Wasn't he proving that now by kissing her in this lot and touching her so intimately out here in plain sight where anybody could see them?

She wriggled out of his grasp, and this time he let her go. "We have to leave before someone sees us," she said.

She hurried around the side of the Mercedes, notic-

ing that the panels were coated with dust and the wheel
wells and tires were rimed with dirt. Damien took his
time getting into the car and adjusting the side mirrors
before he pulled out of the lot.

"You're going to get me suspended," Grace said as he
sped out of the parking lot and out onto the road.
Damien drove fast, weaving in and out of traffic and
slipping through traffic lights in that split second between yellow and red.

"You afraid?" His gaze jumped back and forth from
road to rearview mirror. She knew he was keeping an
eye out for police.

"I don't want to get in trouble."

"Then don't come with me." It was said matter-of-
factly, but Damien suddenly spun the wheel and the car
sped over onto the side of the road, tires crunching
through leaves, before jerking to a stop. He looked at
her coolly, his face set. She could see her own face reflected in his sunglasses.

She tried not to squirm in her seat. "What?"

"Either you're coming with me or you're not. I don't
have time for this shit, so decide." The voice was cool
and disdainful. She'd heard him use that voice before,
but never with her.

"I'm coming with you," she mumbled.

Without a word he spun the wheel again and jerked
the Mercedes back into traffic. She wondered what he
would have done if she'd said she'd changed her mind.
Would he have left her on the side of the road?

"Why's the car dirty?" she asked, trying to change the
subject.

"Had a little detour," Damien said. He didn't explain
what that had been, and she didn't ask, but a little smile
played on his lips again. The squirmy feeling in Grace's
stomach eased.

"Where are we going?" she asked when they'd driven
another few miles. Damien had turned on the radio
and was tapping his hand along to the pulsing beat. She
hoped it was back to the city. Maybe they could go to
Bleecker Street Records. That's where they'd met. She'd
gone there with Campbell, the two of them having fun
looking for some new music, but not so much fun that
they hadn't noticed Damien and his friend. Nobody
could overlook Damien; he was too good-looking. She'd
been aware of him the way you're aware of light, a sudden presence in the store, and she'd looked up and seen
him walking toward her, his hands reaching out to trail
lightly across the racks of CDs.

She was sure he didn't notice her, though she'd
stolen glances at him, giggling with Campbell when she
mouthed the word "hottie." At some point Damien and
his friend left and Grace could remember feeling a little bit let down, but then when she and Campbell left
about ten minutes later, they found Damien and his
friend smoking outside, and then Damien offered her a
cigarette.

"You smoke?"

Those had been his first words to her. There wasn't
anything sexy about that, except that it was Damien
who'd said them, his gray eyes cool and appraising,
dirty blond hair falling forward over a chiseled face, a
cigarette stuck between his own pouty lips.

And even though she'd never smoked, she nodded
and took one from the outstretched pack, and then
nudged Campbell, who took one, too. Later, when he
kissed her for the first time, she'd tasted the smoke on
his tongue.

Despite what her parents thought, they hadn't slept
together. As in intercourse. She'd done other things
with him, gotten as far as what Campbell still stupidly

called third base, but she couldn't go for home. She was scared of it. She'd heard it could hurt the first time, but mostly she had this overwhelming fear that protection would fail and she'd be toting Grace Junior along with her to geometry class.

Damien didn't pressure her much, which just showed he was straight up, not that her parents would ever listen. He'd taken to calling her virgin queen, but he said it with a smile so she didn't really care.

She cared more about the other girl she'd seen him kissing. It was just two days before she'd been forced to leave the only home she'd ever known, and the piano movers had already been and gone so she couldn't vent her feelings like she usually did through her music. She'd skipped out on the packing and taken the train uptown to surprise Damien. It had been a really hot day and the subway was a steam bath. By the time she'd walked the final blocks to his building on the Upper East Side, she felt like the ice sculpture she'd seen melting at an outdoor wedding, all shabby and unrecognizable as it dissolved into a puddle of nothing.

Just as she turned the corner up to his place, she saw Damien come out of his building. The timing seemed like a sign. For one happy second she'd thought they must be psychically linked. Only then he swung toward her, and she saw that his arm was around some blond-haired girl. She was model-pretty, tall and super-skinny, and wearing a tiny white eyelet dress and these impossibly high sandals with ribbons that wound around her ankles.

As Grace stood there, stunned, Vogue Girl had leaned into Damien and kissed him with her full red lips. Worse, he'd kissed her back, not some polite little kiss either, but a full scene-stopper. Grace fled before it was over.

She still met him later, keeping their regular rendezvous at a school playground near Campbell's building because Grace could always get permission to visit her friend. When he'd asked why she was being such a bitch, she'd confronted him about seeing Vogue Girl and he'd gotten mad, telling her that she couldn't claim exclusivity if she wasn't going to meet his needs.

Just thinking about it brought back the anger. It had ripped through her, bringing tears in a hot rush, and she ran away from him, dashing half-blind across the park. It might have ended there, but he'd chased her, yanking so hard on her arm that afterward she had a bruise. He told her that he loved her, told her that she could get to him like nobody else, told her that she was his true love. She noticed that he didn't promise to stay away from Vogue Girl, but when he literally kissed the tears that ran down her cheeks, she'd been willing to forgive him anything.

He probably still saw other girls, but she didn't ask. It wasn't like she could complain anyway, since she was the one who had to sneak around just to see him at all. It had been easier when she lived in the city, easiest after her mother had been attacked. There'd been several weeks when her mom barely got out of bed, and Grace had taken advantage of that to escape and see Damien.

It wasn't like that in Wickfield. Her mother was still acting weird, but it wasn't like before. She didn't hide in bed, she was just super-security-conscious. She'd gotten freaked out about some missing college girl, and now she was insisting on watching Grace walk to the bus stop. It was embarrassing, and it also made it hard to slip away and head for the train station instead.

She hated Wickfield. Besides Damien, Campbell and all of her other friends were back in the city. She knew her parents wanted her to make new friends. She could feel the pressure in all their questions. How was your day? How was school today?

"You look ugly when you frown." Damien glanced over at her, then back at the road. "What's your problem?"

"No problem." She turned up the radio and closed her eyes, letting the music drown her thoughts. "No problem at all now that I'm with you."

Chapter Eight

In the man's arms was an offering, wrapped in a shroud and carried through the woods and out along the rocks to the water's edge. He'd chosen the spot with care some months before, driving along remote roads and hiking deep into the forest rising up on either side, following the clear, rushing sound of water until the trees suddenly gave way to a strip of pebbled inlet and he found the creek.

The silence of a church surrounded him as he walked, breathing heavily under the weight in his arms, the wind rocking the branches of hemlock and pine, rustling the leaves of maples and oak that were just starting to turn. The dogwood had been in bloom when he was last here.

The bodies after the miner's were a blur in his memory. Dozens of men and women, most of them elderly or at least middle-aged, victims of cancer or car accidents, their nakedness at once interesting and usual to the boy, who sometimes assisted his father and Poe, holding the hose they used to sluice out the body's fluids, or sorting through jars of face crème to find the perfect skin match.

His mother thought it was morbid. She wanted to forbid him to go down there, but his father wouldn't allow it, yelled at her to leave the boy alone, and wasn't it natural that a boy should follow in his father's footsteps, and was she ashamed of the work that put the food on her table and the clothes on her back?

He'd been eight then, scrawny and short still, a towheaded chicken of a boy, but old enough to see and understand the expression that flitted across his mother's face: the flash in the hazel eyes, the mouth opening to speak before it closed abruptly, her lips pressing against one another until they were nothing but a line across her face. She *was* ashamed.

He noticed other things after that. The way his mother turned her face from his father's kiss so that it landed on her cheek, not her lips, and the small pile of pillow and sheets folded on the edge of the couch in his father's office, and the way his mother's lips pursed whenever his father talked about his work over dinner.

He saw the girl when he was ten, old enough to understand the death, old enough to hold onto the details like small treasures, carrying them around like marbles in a sack, pulling them out to play with one by one in his mind.

It was a rainy spring that year. Thunder showers all through April and most of May. He could remember his mother clucking over the daffodils drooping on the front lawn, and how he'd stood at the window and watched rain overflowing the cupped petals of tulips.

Flood warnings interrupted the music on the radio in the basement. They were working on an old man that afternoon. Ninety-some years of age, so old that the skin seemed to separate from the bones, like chicken boiled too long. Poe wrinkled his nose and said the man smelled sour. The rain had raised the dust in the basement, it mixed in the air with the smell of decay, and the boy wrinkled his own nose and left.

He slipped on his yellow slicker and went to send leaf boats to capsize in the current coursing along the gutters. Sheets of water pounded the asphalt, pushing the dust to the edges, so that the water he stirred with a stick was like silt in the river. He raced along the curb beside it, watching the new green leaves he'd torn from the chinaberry tree get sucked into the storm drain.

The roar of the water overpowered the police siren. He didn't hear its high-pitched wail until the car was less than six feet away, and then it came rushing past him, splashing the water up and over the boy's slicker as it turned hard into the driveway. A dirty white van pulled in behind it.

She was already on the table by the time the boy made it to the basement, the black rubber body bag she'd been brought in being carried, dripping, out the door by a young police officer who looked green.

The floor was damp and there were bits of grass and new leaves tramped in by police. The body was wet, too, which surprised the boy. Poe pressed his polished wingtip against the chrome lever that tilted the table and water spilled from the holes and circled the drain in the center of the floor.

"Jesus," the man murmured, and the boy saw a mixture of horror and sorrow on the thin face that he'd never witnessed before.

His father stood on the other side of the table, blocking most of the body from view, but then he moved and the boy could see all of her. It stopped him in the doorway, his hand reaching out to grip the doorjamb to stop from trembling.

All these years later he could still remember what it was like to see a young female body laid upon that table, small breasts poking at the bodice of her soaking-wet dress. Later he would find out that she was fourteen. All he knew then was that she was young, her body newly developed.

"Barrett girl," his father said. "They live down by the creek and the girl thought it would be fun to see how high it was rising."

He sounded annoyed, and the boy would hear him mutter, "Stupid waste," under his breath over the next two days. It was his way of dealing with grief, his own and the overwhelming grief of the Barrett family.

The girl's skin was the color of his mother's bone china, watery white, and traced haphazardly with the fine blue lines of veins. Her brown eyes were open, staring at the basement ceiling as if she could hear the heavy footsteps and loud weeping that was taking place overhead.

"I've got to get up there," the boy's father said to Poe, shaking his head, his mouth set in a grim line. He moved to the corner sink to wash his hands, and the boy stepped closer to the white porcelain table and noticed a twig in the girl's long, wet hair. A piece of moss curled around the instep of her right foot.

"Tell them she'll be pretty," Poe said. "Tell them they'll know her."

The boy watched, his tongue heavy in his mouth, as Poe took the scissors and cut through the thin white cotton of the dress. She wore tiny panties underneath, no bra. Poe cut away the underwear, too, little scraps of fabric parting to reveal a triangle of peach fuzz.

There was clattering on the steps, and the boy's mother suddenly appeared. Poe looked up in surprise and the scissors slipped, nicking his hand.

"Why did you let him in here?" His mother's voice was cold and hard. She didn't wait for an answer, but grabbed his hand, jerking him after her up the stairs.

The house was filled with strangers, more were coming in the front door, and the boy's mother frowned and pushed him toward the stairs to the second floor. "Go play," she said. "You shouldn't be seeing this."

And something about her face made him loath to argue. Though as he turned, she suddenly pulled him back, crushing him against her in a fierce hug.

Later, much later, when he'd watched her pull away in their old Buick to go to the grocery store, he crept back down to the basement.

His father was dealing with the family in the upstairs office; as he'd crept past he'd heard the murmur of voices and the soft sound of a woman crying. Poe was alone with the body, searching along the shelves for face crème and makeup, and the boy didn't speak, content to stand in the doorway and stare at the girl.

She was clean now, washed inside and out, flushed of the river and all impurity. Her white skin seemed to glow, and he remembered the word "alabaster" from a Sunday School lesson and how the teacher had tried to explain what it meant. He understood now. This girl was alabaster.

The excitement he felt was so overpowering that he had to touch her. He moved without realizing it, standing next to the table and placing his warm hand against the cool skin of her arm.

He shuddered with the force of the contact, the sensation of connection almost overpowering, electrical signals racing from his head to his feet and jolting his testicles on the way.

"Stop," Poe barked, and the boy's hand jerked from

the body. He panted, surprised to feel sweat prickling his forehead and the back of his neck.

"Your mother said you weren't supposed to be down here," Poe said.

"You've always let me before," the boy argued because it was Poe and not his mother.

"This is different. You shouldn't see this, your mother was right." Poe nodded at the door. "Go on now, get out of here, and don't come back or I'll tell your mama on you."

The boy ran then, hammering up the stairs in his sneakers, going until he'd reached the safety of his room. He flung himself facedown on the narrow bed and clenched the quilt with his fists, grinding his hips against the mattress. He had to hold onto the girl, to relive the sensation of his skin touching hers. He squeezed his eyes shut and whispered, "Alabaster."

The man's feet crunched quietly along the pebbled bank until he found the place where the water ran unobstructed, and he placed his burden down along the bank and unrolled the shroud. The water lapped softly against the strip of sand as he worked. When he was ready, he waded into its coolness with the offering once again in his arms.

A trio of crows, disturbed by the noise, rose like an omen, cawing and clutching at the sky.

Chapter Nine

Ronald Haupt liked the beginning of hunting season. He hiked along a trail in the hills high above Wickfield, Remington cradled in the crook of his left arm, right hand playing with the little pouch of extra bullets in the pocket of his flame-orange vest. He hadn't bothered to shave before heading out this morning, and his hand stole up every once in a while to rub at the salt-and-pepper stubble across his chin.

More than forty years he'd been coming up here. First climbing the hills with his father and uncle, then with his hunting buddies, and now mainly by himself. He'd found he liked the solitude. It gave a man time to think, really think, without the constant chatter of every-day life.

The woods weren't silent, but the noise of nature was soothing—bird calls, the rustle of small animals in the leaves, the sound of a branch cracking under his foot. He could handle the noise in the woods, all right; it was the noise of the office he needed to escape.

A CPA in a busy firm, he'd welcomed the relief of

being somewhere that nobody could reach him. Just recently, though, he'd started carrying a cell phone when he went hunting. He didn't like it, feeling the weight of it in his pocket like a constant reminder of financial responsibilities, but he carried it. Seeing Howard Sherman almost lose a leg last year had convinced him.

It was an accidental shooting, that's how the local paper played it, though everybody knew that Howard and his hunting party had been drunk. Howard stumbled over a log and his rifle discharged into his leg. In the time it had taken for his hunting buddies to reach a phone, Howard's makeshift tourniquet had slipped and he'd lost so much blood that it soaked through the stretcher they loaded him onto, leaving quarter-sized splashes of crimson along the trail and the asphalt parking lot where Ron arrived in time to see Howard being medevaced to the local emergency room. Ron couldn't forget all that blood, or the sight of Howard himself, vomit splashed over his flannel shirt and eyes rolled back in their sockets.

Some people (like his wife, Janet) thought that since Ron was a hunter, he shouldn't be disturbed by the evidence of a gunshot wound, but seeing an animal shot cleanly was different than that mess of Howard's leg. It made Ron glad for the first time that a heart murmur had left him stateside during Vietnam. And it had been just the incentive Janet was looking for to convince him that he needed to carry a cell phone.

However, he kept it turned off. Otherwise, he'd have Janet calling every twenty minutes to ask him something trivial. She didn't do this when he was at the office, he couldn't complain about that, but she sure as hell thought it was okay to do it when he was hunting no matter how often he explained to her that a loud, shrilling sound scared away the deer.

"What if I need you?" she demanded, just like she'd been demanding for all the long years of their thirty-year marriage. She was a worrier by nature, predicting doom when their three kids trotted one by one off to nursery school, and making the same predictions years later when they fled the nest for colleges and jobs far away from home. She was a little black rain cloud; he'd sometimes called her that in the early years of their marriage when he saw her negativity as an amusing quirk and not a dominant and relentless force.

Janet was convinced that bad luck lurked around every corner where Ron always saw opportunity. People always said that opposites attract, but after thirty years he knew that opposites could drive each other away. Not that he'd consider divorce. He was offended by the very idea. Getting divorced wasn't simply accepting defeat, it showed a fundamental flaw in character. He'd made a promise thirty years ago and by gum he would keep that promise, even if most days he wanted nothing more than to be left entirely alone.

He'd wished hard for that this morning while he got his gear together and Janet hovered around him quoting some morning TV news story about accidental shootings the first week of hunting season. Like he'd needed any reminder of Howard Sherman before breakfast.

He'd taken off without eating, carrying some foil-wrapped jelly toast she thrust into his hand along with a thermos of coffee. He'd kissed her because that was his job as a husband, and she'd pulled back from it complaining of being scratched by his beard, and then he'd pulled away in the Buick, waiting until the speck of her waving in the doorway vanished completely.

He drove from their comfortable split-level out to old Highway 87 feeling tense, and then his shoulders started to relax and his stomach unknotted as he took the turnoff for Sterling Forest, driving slowly up a long stretch of narrow paved roads until he'd found the lot where he always parked, the soaring forest spread around him like a playground.

It was coming on 12:45 and the toast was long gone, the foil a tight ball in his pocket. Ron's stomach grumbled and he paused for a moment, thinking. He hadn't take a shot yet, though he'd had his bead on a buck, his finger pulling back ever so gently on the trigger when a clattering of acorns spooked the creature.

The buck leapt high, white tail like a flag, and disappeared like a distance runner before Ron could do more than release the trigger.

Still, it wasn't all about the success of the hunt and he figured he'd earned his lunch. He thought it would be nice to sit down by the river that ran from up in the mountains and down through Wickfield before connecting with the Hudson and joining the ocean.

Ten minutes of walking brought him to a spot above its bank, and there he spent another five minutes unloading his gear before he could sit down on a boulder, rifle at the ready, and unwrap the sandwiches he'd packed for himself the night before.

He took a bite of gummy ham and cheese and munched contentedly as he looked down at the silvery water spilling over brown rocks. It was a pretty sound, that rushing water, and he watched the colored leaves carried like little boats along it, some of them whisking abruptly out of sight, others caught in eddies around the rocks, spinning helplessly.

Once in a while something bigger, like a fallen branch, came by, and Ron liked to imagine how it had ended up in the water, either falling from a tree or being tossed there by somebody.

He finished half a sandwich, and was just starting on the second half when something new caught his eye. Something large and pale bobbed slowly down the sweep of silver, and came to rest against the rounded boulder further up on the far side. Ron squinted, but he couldn't tell what it was. He dropped his sandwich and got up to take a better look, shading his eyes and stepping close to the edge.

The sun kept peeking in and out of the trees, and it was too far for him to get a clear look. Something white. Could it be a deer carcass? Who the hell would throw that in the river? Unless it had drowned in flooding and was just now being carried down from wherever it had decomposed.

Yet something about the shape wasn't right for a deer. Too big to be any other animal and the wrong color for bear. What the hell was it?

Ron stepped back from the ledge and went to fetch his binoculars. They'd been a gift for Father's Day this year from his son, who'd made sure to tell him all about the many features—fully coated, image stabilization. Ron was delighted to have a chance to really use them. He imagined the conversation they'd have about it as he stepped back to the edge, his boot slipping a little and sending a shower of flaky stone and pebbles raining down on the wildflowers growing in the shallow, sandy soil far below.

The binoculars had 10 x 50 magnification, and he twisted the knobs impatiently, zeroing in first on that huge boulder and then moving down, down, and there! That was it! It was still out of focus and all he could see was something large and pale, so he twisted the knob again. Worked beautifully, everything becoming sharp and clear, he'd sure have to tell Jim about that, and then he saw it clearly for the first time.

"Sweet Jesus!" It wasn't the body of a deer, but it was a carcass.

The naked body of a young woman bobbed against the far side of the boulder. She was on her back, arms floating at her sides, legs almost straight. She could have been out for a swim, except her head seemed strangely bent on her neck and bits of bark and green algae had traced lacy patterns across her waxy skin and were caught in the long strands of dark blond hair streaming behind her.

Ron stared at the gently bobbing breasts and the dark triangle of hair further down, and looked away, ashamed. There was nothing grisly here, no dripping blood or gaping wounds, yet he retched in the dirt, splashing the stone with the force of his revulsion.

He scrambled for the phone while he was still retching, and he knew, even as he tapped 911 with a shaking hand, that he would never, ever come into these woods to hunt again.

October

Chapter Ten

The discovery of Lily Slocum's body was all anybody could talk about at the university president's party the Friday night two weeks after the body was found. Even with that gap of time, there'd been talk of canceling it. Ian had been pulled into an emergency faculty meeting when the police officially identified the body pulled from the river. After much squabbling, the decision was made to proceed as normal with all classes and campus activities, but with the understanding that for the remainder of the semester every official university function would observe a minute of silence in Lily Slocum's memory.

"She wasn't an especially memorable student," an aging professor of philosophy confided to Kate as soon as the minute was up.

They were standing on the back lawn of the president's house, a pillared Greek Revival monstrosity that some of the faculty privately and mockingly referred to as "Tara."

"A bright enough girl," the old man said, "but not brilliant, not an original thinker."

Kate twirled the olive in her martini and glanced over his balding head, contemplating an escape route. What was the man's point? That Lily Slocum's death wasn't a great loss? That only original thinkers deserved to live?

Despite the drought in the summer and an equally dry fall, the president's manicured lawn was still lush and green. She was surprised some student environmental group wasn't protesting the overuse of water. Japanese lanterns hung in the trees, and young men and women wearing plain black uniforms circulated among the colorfully dressed crowd bearing trays of drinks and various canapés. It was all very pretty, very tasteful, and she very much wanted to leave.

"Did you have her as a student?" the professor asked, and Kate pulled her attention back to his froglike face.

"No, I didn't know her. I don't teach at Wickfield."

He blinked in surprise, and she excused herself to go in search of Ian. She couldn't spot him, and it was hard to navigate through the crowd. She jumped when someone laughed loudly near her, blushing when her nervous reaction caught another's attention. Turning abruptly, she narrowly missed colliding with a rosebush as she tried to bypass a crowd loudly discussing evidence found at the crime scene.

She shouldn't have come. It wasn't as if Ian had asked, at least not in words, but she knew that he wanted her with him, knew that it was expected that a spouse would make an appearance at these events.

"It'll be outside," he'd said when he told her about the party, and she'd heard what he was really saying, that she should be able to handle a crowd outside.

Only she couldn't. She struggled across the lawn, her heels sinking into the overwatered sod, her drink clutched in one hand, purse in the other, as she searched the crowd for her husband.

A large man hurrying the other way bumped into her and Kate lost her balance, falling forward. Martini and glass flew in a wide arc while her purse dropped like a stone, and in that split second between realizing she was going to fall and trying to brace herself, Kate was suddenly jerked upright.

"Steady there!" a man's voice said, and Kate recognized Jerry Virgoli. His eyes widened in surprise when he realized whom he'd rescued. "Well, hello!"

"Hi." Kate stooped down to retrieve her purse, brushing the last of her martini off her slacks. "Thanks for the save."

"No problem." Virgoli plucked her glass off the lawn and deposited it on a passing tray. "I was hoping I'd see you here."

"Oh?"

"Yes, I wondered if you'd given any thought to my proposal."

Kate's head ached. What was he talking about? "I'm sorry?"

"For a show. Size to be determined by you, of course, but given the limited space, I thought a small selection of paintings might be best."

"A show?" Kate repeated dumbly. She felt as if she were back in the assisted-living community where her parents had spent the last years of their lives, only this time she was the one suffering from dementia.

"Didn't Ian tell you?" An expression of anger flashed across Virgoli's face, a flicker that passed so fast that Kate thought she must have imagined it. It startled her when he laughed. "I guess he's just so busy."

"What didn't Ian tell me?"

"We'd like you to do a show at the gallery. It's a small space, but we've had some nice shows and I'm sure we'd get a good response—"

For a minute Kate felt the desire, that familiar hum of interest in what she'd choose to hang and where. It was only a moment. Like a flashlight with dying batteries, the light burned bright for a few seconds before fading away to nothing.

"I'm not doing shows right now," she said.

Jerry Virgoli nodded as if he agreed. "Of course, under the circumstances I completely understand. Ian explained that, but I wanted you to know that the possibility exists, that we do have a nice gallery in Wickfield."

Kate nodded, forcing a smile, but she wondered what exactly Ian had told this man. It sounded as if he knew about what had happened to her. Did everybody know about it? What had Ian said about her? Did everybody know about the assault? Did he discuss it with other people?

Suddenly, the voices in the conversation next to theirs rose and she heard a man say, "They're very hush-hush about the sexual-assault aspect, but we all know that's what happened."

Were they talking about her? Blood rushed to her face. She felt flushed and her head thumped like a metronome. She looked at Virgoli's moving lips, but the only thing she could hear was the conversation nearby. "You can understand the need for discretion," a woman said. "It's not as if they've caught somebody."

No, no, it wasn't her. They were discussing Lily Slocum. Sound rushed back and Kate could hear Virgoli say, "In the future, of course, we'd like to have an expanded Fine Arts wing complete with a larger, university-funded gallery space, but that will require a consensus of faculty—"

He prattled on, and she could follow enough to know that he wanted something that Ian somehow had the power to provide, but she couldn't concentrate on it, her mind flashing to the paint mixing on the floor of her studio and the scent of blood. The crowd seemed to press in on her and the thudding in her head grew stronger.

"So what do you think?" Jerry Virgoli was looking at her, demanding an answer.

"I'm sorry," Kate said. "I've got to go."

She stumbled across the lawn, shying away from people who stepped in her path and hating herself for doing it. She thought she might cry and how stupid was that? This was all so stupid. It was over, a thing of the past, just a few minutes of a life, so why did she have to keep thinking about it?

She felt again the slam against the table, could hear the repeated thud of his body slamming against hers and smell the blood, feel the blood between her legs. She didn't want to think about that anymore. She pressed a hand against her temple, pushing, as if she could push all those thoughts away.

Where in the hell was Ian? At that moment the crowd blocking her view suddenly shifted and she caught sight of her husband. He was at the opposite corner of the lawn talking to a willowy-looking woman with bobbed blond hair, and she could see the woman nodding enthusiastically at whatever Ian said.

As she got closer, she heard him say, "The support you've generated for the center is truly amazing."

"Oh, it's a collaborative effort and of course it means so much to us in Drama."

Kate was close enough to see that the other woman was lightly tanned, her skin carrying the creamy glow of youth and vibrant health. She moved her arms when she spoke, an intricately woven silver bracelet riding up one thin wrist as she gestured, disappearing into the folds of a lacy white blouse. Long, tanned legs shifted beneath a slim blue cotton skirt.

Ian was smiling, and then suddenly he saw Kate. "Oh, hi!"

"Hi." Kate lowered the hand pushing against her temple and moved to Ian's side. She waited for his arm to slide around her waist or his hand to reach for hers, but it didn't happen.

"This is Kate Corbin. Kate, this is Bethany Forrester. She's a professor in the drama department."

Bethany Forrester smiled. She had blue eyes that matched her skirt. "It's such an honor to meet you," she said, extending a hand that Kate numbly shook. "I just love your work. You were one of the first artists whose work really inspired me."

Kate felt suddenly old. Old and fat. And too pale next to this woman. "Thank you," she said. Yeah, thanks for making me feel my age.

"Ian speaks so highly of your work."

"Does he?"

"Oh, yes, and you know that painting he's got in his office? The landscape of the field? It's just beautiful. Ian's always telling people it's your work."

"We're each other's biggest fans," Kate said with a slight smile. She felt Ian's eyes on her, but didn't look at him. It was an old joke between them. Something they'd heard a couple say once on TV, a smarmy thing that they'd adopted years ago because it was so absurd.

"That's so great," Bethany Forrester said, not picking up on the irony. "I think that sort of creative, collaborative relationship is very rare."

"You're not married?" Kate asked, hand creeping up to press at her temple.

Bethany laughed. "No. Not attached at all." She lifted

a thin-stemmed wineglass to her mouth and the silver bracelet vanished up her arm again. A demure swallow and she lowered the glass, patting her full lips with a cocktail napkin. "I'm not averse to it, just haven't found the right person."

"Someone to collaborate with?"

The younger woman nodded. "Exactly. I mean, it's not as if there aren't plenty of people out there—"

"Of course." Kate imagined that Bethany Forrester had probably had her pick of plenty of men. A string of broken hearts from here to Poughkeepsie.

"—but finding the right person just takes so much work."

Kate nodded as if she understood, but the truth was that she'd been so young when she met Ian that it was hard to remember what it had been like to be single. Being part of a couple for so long meant that her fantasy wasn't of meeting someone new, but of being alone.

"I've devoted more time to my career. Between performing and teaching, I don't really have much time," Bethany said, adding to Ian, "And of course there's fund-raising."

"And the academic community appreciates that." Ian's had a dopey grin on his face.

Bethany laughed. "You mean the money."

"Not just that. I've heard all about your contributions to the drama department."

Trying not to roll her eyes, Kate stepped closer to Ian and took his arm. "We really need to get home to Grace."

"But she's spending—" Ian stopped short, and Kate knew he'd remembered. It was a code they'd invented when Grace was a baby, a way of politely signaling to one another that they wanted to leave whatever social event was boring them. It had been a long time since either of them had used it.

"Yeah, okay." Ian said. He hid his annoyance from Bethany, but Kate could feel it. Twenty minutes later, they'd made the rounds of thank you and good-bye and were in the car heading toward home. Ian drove fast, with sharp, jerky turns that broadcast his mood as clearly as if he'd yelled at Kate. She hugged the passenger seat and pressed her aching head against the cool glass of the window.

"You didn't have to do that," he said finally.

"What?"

"Act so superior to Bethany Forrester."

"I thought I was nice to her."

"Bullshit. You didn't like her. Why? Because she liked you?"

"She likes you, Ian, not me."

He laughed, but it was a hollow sound. "If you were so determined not to enjoy yourself, why did you bother to come?"

"I thought you wanted me there."

"I want you there if you want to be there, not if you're going to have a miserable time."

Kate shifted her head to stare at him. The movement intensified the thudding, and she had to blink it back. Did he really think she willed herself to be unhappy? "I did want to be there," she said. "I wasn't feeling bad, not at first. I ran into Jerry Virgoli."

Ian made an exasperated sound. "That's enough to give anyone a miserable night. What did he want?"

"Something about having an exhibit. He said he'd told you about it."

"He's part owner of a rinky-dink art gallery in town and acts as if he's curator at the Met. It's very small and not at all prestigious despite his delusions of grandeur. I didn't think you'd be interested."

Kate felt her stomach unknot a little. So it wasn't that

he'd hidden it from her because he thought she couldn't handle the pressure.

"Everyone seemed to be talking about Lily Slocum."

"I heard that, too. I guess it's natural, people are always curious about things like that. Is that what upset you?" He glanced at her and reached out a hand to cup hers and give it a reassuring squeeze. "Sorry about that."

"It's horrible."

"Yes it is. Poor girl. Everyone's worried that the publicity is going to be bad for the campus. You don't want parents to think they can't send their kids here."

He turned onto their street and she was struck, as always, by how quiet and dark it was at night, so unlike the city. "Wickfield's a safe community," he said. "What happened to Lily Slocum is awful, but that's one homicide in what, a hundred years? It's not like there's a pattern here."

It was unusually quiet in the house. Grace was sleeping over at a friend's. A year ago that would have meant uncharacteristic freedom with sex. They could do it in the living room if they wanted to, in front of the fireplace like a bad romance.

In the way that he seemed to have of reading her thoughts, Ian tugged at Kate's hand, pulling her into an embrace. "I was checking you out at the party," he murmured in her ear, stroking her hair. "You're looking pretty hot, woman."

He kissed her neck, a small butterfly kiss that she shivered under but didn't pull away from. His lips moved upward to her jawline, then her mouth.

She let her lips part and took him in, willing herself to taste only him. They moved together into the room, though she didn't know until he pushed her back that they'd reached the sofa. She landed among its cushions and he came with her, his hands unbuttoning her blouse, his lips coming back to rest on hers and then parting again to plant rapid kisses along her collarbone, and then dipping lower to the triangle of flesh between her breasts.

When it changed she didn't know, just that it became not Ian above her, but the stranger, and that the couch was the hard edge of her studio table. She didn't stop him, she couldn't find the words, but something must have changed, something must have signaled her distaste to him, and he pulled back.

"What's wrong?"

"Nothing." But she couldn't meet his eyes.

"I'm not him. I'm not the guy who attacked you."

"I know that."

But when he moved to kiss her again, she couldn't help her involuntary flinch. Ian reeled back and clambered off the sofa, rubbing at his face.

"Wait." Kate sat up, reached for him, but he pulled away. "I'm sorry."

He stood with his back to her, breathing hard, and she watched him press a hand against his head in a gesture reminiscent of her own.

"I didn't mean—" she began, but he cut her off.

"It's okay." He sighed, a long, shaky sound, and then he turned to her. "I know, Kate, it's okay." He sank down on the sofa next to her and reached for her hand. "Maybe it's time to get some help."

She pulled her hand away. "I've already done therapy."

"Maybe another therapist—somebody different, somebody you'd like better."

"No! It's not like it didn't help, Ian, it just doesn't change overnight."

"Maybe medication then—"

"I'm not going back on the pills! They make me

dopey. I couldn't paint, I could barely stay awake. I'm not going through that again!"

"Well you need to do something!" he shouted. Fists clenched, face red, Ian looked capable of violence, and for one awful moment Kate thought he was going to hit her. Her hands flew up to block his fists, and Ian's face drained of color.

"Oh, God." He backed away, hands falling loose at his sides. "I wouldn't hurt you. You know that, right? I'd never hurt you."

"I know, I know." She stood up and reached for him, to show him that measure of trust, to reassure the man that she'd held and loved for so many years that it was all going to be okay. Only she couldn't tell him that because she didn't know if that was the truth anymore.

They were cautious around each other getting ready for bed, like strangers in their courtesy, deferring to each other near the closet and in the bathroom. She caught him watching her several times as she hung up her clothes and brushed her teeth, but whatever he was thinking remained locked inside him.

They lay next to each other in the vast bed, the sheet a weight on this hot night, but she pulled it up anyway, covering the lower half of her body. She didn't want to think anymore about sex and the lack thereof in their marriage.

They read instead, clutching their books like life-lines, until it was past midnight, when by unspoken agreement they set their books aside and turned off the lights. Ian fell asleep quickly as he always did. Stress never seemed to follow him into sleep and Kate envied that.

Tired but overwhelmed by what he'd said, she lay awake thinking about what she could do. She'd done therapy, as much of it as she could bear—the stupid concerned look on the woman's face and the special, muted tone adopted for talking to people in crisis. She couldn't stand it.

Maybe it was her Yankee forebearers, but she had a deep and instinctive dislike of discussing her personal problems. She'd always poured those feelings into her art, and now she didn't have that; all that had been taken away in twenty minutes. Twenty horrible, time-dragging minutes, but still just twenty of them. It was such a blip and yet it had taken over everything.

So she'd sat through hours of therapy divided into fifty-minute chunks. It was all so strange, to sit there and pour her heart out to a stranger. She had no idea if Dr. Bennett was married or in a relationship or had children or grandchildren. She knew she'd graduated from Boston University because of the diploma hanging on the wall. Otherwise, the office was curiously devoid of personal effects. And despite the cozy setup of couch and armchairs and warm rug, strangely sterile.

For fifty minutes every Tuesday, she sat and talked to Dr. Bennett, who listened and took notes on a legal pad and occasionally asked how she felt about whatever it was she'd just said.

What had she learned? That her pain was normal, that the only way past grief was through it, that it would take time for the nervousness to go away. That medication could help the agoraphobia.

So she'd dutifully started a course of the recommended medication because at that point she was desperate about painting again and anything that promised to restore her art was a positive.

Only it didn't work, not entirely. It had helped somewhat with the anxiety. She hadn't flinched at doors slamming or jumped when Ian or Grace came into a room suddenly. But it made her tired and it didn't help her paint, and once she'd had an embarrassing crying jag in the coffee shop closest to their apartment because she'd forced herself to make the trip only to discover that they were out of her favorite blend. That was the day she decided to go off the medication—it wasn't worth it.

Not long after that, she stopped seeing the therapist, too. She'd gathered all the information she could on how to survive life after assault, and now it was just a matter of time. Only, Ian didn't understand that. He thought therapy and medication were magic bullets that would fix his wife.

Not that she blamed him for that. She'd certainly hoped for that result, too, but it didn't work that way. It was like smoking pot in college, how you could get a nice little buzz going but the paranoia came later to bite you in the ass. Everything came at a cost. What she resented was how he didn't care that the cost was her sense of self, as long as she wasn't freaking out. What she resented was how he expected it all to be gone by now because on his timetable eight months was long enough to deal with having been sexually assaulted. And then he acted as if she somehow wanted to be agoraphobic.

At some point in her worrying, she drifted off.

She was in her studio again, hearing the clang of the battered metal door closing behind her, moving toward her work and registering too slowly that she'd left the blinds open and now they were closed. She thinks, that's odd, and then suddenly he's there, a silhouette in black stepping from the shadows, the silver glint of his knife. She screams and he shoves a dirty rag in her mouth to stifle her. She chokes on the taste of linseed oil as he slams her back against the table, his hands tearing at her clothes.

Brutal, efficient, he strips her bare like ripping leaves from a tree. His voice crawls over her skin, a vicious whisper, promises of what he'll do with the knife if she looks at him. She struggles anyway and he hits her, a gloved fist against her face. Stars explode in her eyes, she swallows blood. He pries her legs apart and forces his way in, ripping against the dryness. The fast, painful thud of his body slamming against hers. Thud, thud, thud, and she can smell blood, feel its trickle down her legs. She turns her head and sees Lily Slocum spread out on the chaise surrounded by flowers. Lily's eyes pop open and she smiles.

Kate woke in a sweat with the sheet knotted around her leg. Ian stirred and mumbled something, but he didn't wake up. She sat up and untangled the sheet, hands trembling and heart pounding in time with her head.

She needed Advil, but there was none in the bath-room cabinet. She padded down the stairs to the kitchen to get a glass of milk and some pain relievers. Glancing out the kitchen window, she was surprised to see that the light was on in Terrence Simnic's basement. The clock on her stove said that it was almost three a.m. Weird.

Standing at the window and sipping her milk, she watched for any sign of odd Mr. Simnic, but other than a moment when she thought she saw a dark shadow, there was no movement of any kind.

Kate noticed that all the windows in the house were covered. Had it always been that way? She had a sudden vision of hulking Mr. Simnic hunched over a workbench in the basement, his large hands cradling the head of an empty-eyed porcelain doll.

A sudden chime startled Kate. Milk splashed from her glass onto the counter as the sound came again. She steadied her hands and took a deep breath. It was only the clock in the living room.

During the day she was barely aware of the noise, but at night it seemed very loud. Everything seemed heightened at night. When she looked back at Terrence Simnic's house, the lights suddenly went out.

Chapter Eleven

The reverb from the sound system followed Elizabeth Hirsh out of the party and onto the back porch of the old house on Hampton. A couple deep in an embrace stood in a corner, pressing hard against the wooden railing.

The slap of the screen door behind her startled the guy, who pulled back, detaching with a sound like a suction cup from the mouth of the girl. He frowned at Elizabeth, but the girl merely glanced around at her, giggling, and then tugging at his hand, led him down the cracked concrete steps and into the darkness of the garden below. The sound of her giggling faded away.

Elizabeth leaned against the railing and drank in air free of the smell of cigarettes, beer, and sweat. It was still warm outside, but cooler than the crowded house. Her head ached. She didn't know why she came to these things. It wasn't like she could have any conversation, not with the mammoth speakers someone always set up, and it wasn't a lot of fun for people like her who didn't smoke and could nurse the same beer for an hour or more.

She picked at the chipping paint on the rail and thought about what she could be doing instead. It wasn't as if she had a boyfriend, not anymore. A year ago she might have enjoyed snuggling up with Joel on one of the saggy couches, content to watch him play beer pong with his buddies.

Not anymore. They'd broken up in May and she hadn't even heard from him over the summer. Until tonight, when he waltzed in with Stacy Levy in tow, both of them all dressed up as if they'd come from somewhere far more interesting. And then he had the audacity to come up, all smiley and happy, and talk to her as if there was no shared history.

Elizabeth felt like leaving after that, but she'd come with Brooke, who was clearly having a good time. When Elizabeth had gone looking for her, she'd found her sitting on the stairs deep in conversation with two guys who definitely looked like engineering or science majors. They were probably all discussing the latest news on global warming. Brooke had woken her up just that morning to see if she wanted to watch some show on PBS about it.

All Elizabeth wanted to do was eat her Cocoa Krispies in peace without having to listen to any talk about the state of the planet, refined sugar, and why the milk she was pouring on her cereal was bound to kill her.

Still, Brooke could be sweet when she wasn't all crunchy granola, and she was the ideal roommate in one respect: reliable. She paid her rent on time, she cleaned her dishes, she didn't run up the phone bill. Unlike Stacy Levy, who had been the heavy partying slut, come home and vomit in the trashcan, and pull all-nighters even if you share a small dorm with someone sleeping less than four feet away type of roommate.

Elizabeth knew what Joel saw in Stacy. Hell, what Stacy had to offer was readily apparent to anybody who looked at her. A walking, talking little Barbie wannabe in clothes too tight and too short, with a pert little nose, perky boobs, and floss-blond hair. Watching her hang on Joel was sickening. Elizabeth had fought the desire to walk up to them, point at Stacy's various parts, and say, "Bobbed, implanted, bleached."

Not that Joel was any great shakes. His hairline was already creeping back and he had the beginnings of a beer gut. He thought he was hot shit, with all his talk of going to Harvard or Stanford for law. Give him ten, maybe fifteen, years and he'd be just like his father: a fat, balding ambulance-chaser kicking back in a Barcalounger in some suburban rec room, watching all the sports he never had the talent to play.

The screen door whined and Elizabeth turned around. It was another couple, two guys this time, one of them with his hands stuck in the other guy's jean pockets. They pulled apart when they saw her, one of them blushing, and the three exchanged nods before the two guys vanished down the steps in the same direction as the first couple.

Elizabeth sighed. Who was she kidding? She missed Joel, missed being part of a couple, missed the cachet of being able to show publicly that at least one person on the planet found her desirable. And hadn't she come here tonight hoping that she'd find someone new?

Suddenly, all the posing she'd done in the mirror before leaving seemed ridiculous. She wanted to go home and peel off these jeans that made her butt look great but were sticking to her, rip off the dual T-shirts she'd taken such care to layer casually, and kick off the stupid platform sandals. They gave her much-needed height and the soles were cork, but they might as well have been made of lead, her feet hurt so much.

She stepped back into the noise of the house, walking quickly back through the sticky kitchen, past the crowd in the living room, and toward the front door. She caught sight of Brooke still on the steps, but couldn't catch her eye. No problem. Brooke was a big girl; she'd find her way home. Joel and Stacy were intertwined on the couch, and she was batting at one of his hands that was creeping up under her shirt. They were both laughing.

Looking the other way, Elizabeth pushed past some students swaying to the thud, thud, thud coming from the speakers, and then she was out the front door and alone again.

It wasn't until she was half a block away, and the music had faded to a distant heartbeat, that Elizabeth realized just how late it was and how many blocks she had to walk, alone, to get back to her apartment.

The streetlights seemed spaced too far apart. There was more than half a block between each one, and that left long stretches of shadowed sidewalk between small circles of light.

She looked back once, but there was no way she could return to that house and let Joel see her. It would be okay. She hurried along, trying not to notice the sound of her own rapid breathing and the way the slightest thing, the distant slam of a car door or the lonely meow of a cat, made her jump.

As she passed beneath the branches of an old oak tree, something fluttered above her head, and she looked up in time to see a cluster of small bats rise into the sky, flapping wildly away.

Her heels clopped loudly on the sidewalk. She had

to watch to make sure she didn't get a toe caught in the many dips and cracks in the cement. The houses sat back in the shadows, most of them dark, a few with lights on somewhere inside, the windows glowing orange like jack-o'-lanterns in the blackness.

A car came screaming around the corner, the sudden loud noise making her jerk and knocking her off balance. She caught herself against a lamppost, hands smacking hard against the metal pole, heart racing. The group of guys crowded into the car screamed something unintelligible at her out the window.

They vanished in a cloud of exhaust and then she was alone again. Clop, clop, clop. She hated these sandals. There was a blister forming on one ankle near the strap; every step rubbed against it, a little sore that would grow in pain. If it hadn't been so dark, she might have taken them off, but then she could cut herself on something unseen. She just had to keep going.

At least six, maybe seven, more blocks to go. It had seemed so much shorter when she and Brooke walked it. She wished she'd stayed with Brooke. Fuck Joel and Stacy. Who cared what they thought of her? She almost turned back, pausing to think about it and rest her feet for a second, but it was a long way back and what if Brooke had gotten a ride with one of her geeky friends and was, at this moment, opening the door to their apartment and wondering what had happened to Elizabeth.

The sound of another car startled her. This one was moving slower, purring along somewhere behind her. Elizabeth started walking again, glancing back once to see the glow of headlights coming toward her. There was no point in turning back, she just had to keep going. Lily Slocum popped into her head and her stomach took an uneasy dip. Hadn't Lily been walking alone when she vanished? And that hadn't even been at night. Elizabeth picked up her pace, ignoring the pain in her ankle.

A four-door sedan, brown or black, drove slowly past. She looked over but couldn't see who was driving. Whoever he or she was, they braked at a stop sign up ahead and Elizabeth watched the rear brake light click on and off, on and off, a fiery red glow.

The car didn't move. Elizabeth's steps faltered, then slowed. Why didn't the car turn? Fear acted like a ratchet, tightening every muscle in her body until she was sure she could feel each individual vertebra. Her steps became mincing, childlike. Move, car, move. Click, click, click, she could hear the noise of the light and the soft rumble of the engine. Waiting. Was the driver watching her?

When Elizabeth was very little, she'd had a habit of clutching her crotch when she was frightened, cupping her vagina with both hands as if that somehow protected her. It had been embarrassing, but involuntary, like the time at Larry Gable's birthday party when he showed the kids the dead rat floating in a corner of his family's pool. She'd been frightened then, clutching so hard that she wrinkled the skirt of her party dress, so that the kids stopped pointing at the rat and pointed at her instead. They'd laughed and made rude noises until the parents came running, and she could still remember the look of horror on her mother's face and how hard she'd tugged at her arms, hissing, "Stop it, Elizabeth! Stop it!"

Even now, her hands were inching forward. She jammed them in her pockets to stop herself and bumped against something, fingers skittering away before she realized it was just her cell phone. Phone! She'd forgotten all about her phone!

She pulled it free of her pocket, and just then the engine gave a soft roar and the car glided around the corner and vanished.

Elizabeth stared after it, feeling foolish, but she kept the phone in her hand, turning it over and over like it was a yin-yang ball, her palm sweaty around it.

She walked faster, crossing the street where the car had been, shooting a fast glance down that long empty street before stepping up on the curb of the next block. Her feet ached, the spot on her right ankle stung, but she didn't slow down.

The next block marked the perimeter of a neighborhood park. When Elizabeth and Brooke had been on their way to the party, kids had been climbing on the jungle gym, their parents lounging on benches nearby. It was dark now, deserted.

As she neared the swings, Elizabeth could hear them creaking, but it was only a breeze. That was a shadow on the last swing, not someone sitting there swaying back and forth, waiting for her.

Sweat pricked along her hairline and trickled into her cleavage. The raw spot on her ankle was actively bleeding now, she could feel the squish of it under her heel, but she didn't stop.

Her skin crawled with the sensation of being watched, and she turned back at the edge of the playground, but there was no one there.

Except a car.

It was back at the beginning of the park. Sitting there along the curb. She hadn't noticed a parked car. Definitely not. She would remember if she'd seen one.

As she stared, the car pulled slowly away from the curb and headed toward her with a familiar purring sound. Jesus, was it the same car?

Elizabeth broke into a run. It was more of a trot, really,

full step with her left foot and half step with her right. Hobbling forward as fast as she could go. The car was coming. The engine noise grew stronger, she imagined she could feel the heat of the motor. It approached in darkness, no headlights.

No longer caring how it would look, Elizabeth punched in 911 on her cell phone and continued to run while holding it against her ear. Only it didn't ring. She looked at the screen and saw zero coverage. She was in a dead zone.

The car rumbled closer. The edge of the park was coming. All she had to do was get past it and there'd probably be reception. Elizabeth counted as she took the steps past the edge of the baseball diamond.

The car was at her back, then it pulled alongside her, moving so slowly that she knew the driver wanted her to know that she was being watched. She kept her focus ahead of her, blinking back tears and clutching the phone like a lifeline.

The car moved past, pausing at the corner before turning left and slipping away into the night. A half block. A quarter. The perimeter of the park was a stand of soaring pine trees. All she had to do was get past them and she'd have coverage. But getting past them meant arriving at the street where the car had turned.

Something was wrong with the streetlight on that corner. It flickered on and off, on and off. As she approached it, the light went out again. She glanced at her phone. No coverage yet.

She didn't see the gloved hand come out of the darkness until it settled on her wrist. The phone dropped, forgotten, onto the street. She screamed once before the other hand closed over her mouth.

Chapter Twelve

Kate was gone when Ian woke on Saturday morning and when he stretched his hand out to her side of the bed, the sheet was cool. He felt groggy, as if he'd had too much to drink the night before, and was surprised to see that the clock read nine-fifteen.

Under the hot spray of the shower, he struggled to clear his head, thinking about the conversation he needed to have with Kate. He would offer to do the work of finding another therapist. Hell, he'd go and do therapy with her if that's what she wanted, but this wasn't something they could deal with alone. It needed professional help.

Steeling himself for an unpleasant conversation, he wasn't prepared to find Kate sitting on the kitchen floor in her pajamas surrounded by papers. As he stood there, stunned, she dug through the pile of papers in the wicker basket they used for recycling. As she pulled out another one, she looked up and saw him.

"Oh, hi. I didn't hear you get up." She didn't sound

as if anything was wrong, which made it stranger. She nodded at the counter. "I made coffee."

He saw her own mug sitting next to her on the floor and looked at the half-full in the coffee maker. Just how many cups had she had? He poured himself a cup and took a badly needed swallow. "Bad night?"

"Yeah, but weird, too." Talking rapidly, she described seeing lights on in their neighbor's basement and how he'd carried out women's clothing to his car and how even Margaret had commented on the enormous bag of trash he'd been carrying.

"Whoa, wait, I'm confused." He held up his hand to stop her, trying to make sense of what she'd said. "Our neighbor had the lights on in the middle of the night—"

"His *basement* lights."

"His *basement* lights on in the middle of the night and because of that you think he's up to something?"

"Yeah, and because of other things. Lots of things. Look at this." Kate stood up, thrusting a paper at him. She looked like a little kid in an oversized striped pajama top that hung almost to her knees, the baggy sleeves making her own skinny arms look even smaller. It was his, she was always appropriating his shirts, though they were way too big for her. He felt a surge of affection, and reached out a hand to push one of her curls back from her face, ridiculously pleased when she didn't shy from his touch.

"Look," she insisted, tapping the page. It was the front-page story about the photo of Lily Slocum being found.

"Okay, I'm looking. What is it?"

"Flowers." She tapped the slightly fuzzy reproduction of the photo of Lily Slocum lying on a chaise lounge surrounded by flowers.

"What about them?"

"They look real, don't they? Who do we know that has access to lots of fresh flowers?"

The laughter bubbled out of Ian before he could stop it. Kate's mouth dropped open in surprise and then she frowned. "I'm serious, Ian."

"I'm sorry, I can't help it." He tried to stop, but dissolved in laughter again. When he caught his breath, he said, "Oh, c'mon, it's absurd. You think our neighbor is a killer." He'd used a spooky voice, but she didn't smile.

"I'm glad you find it so amusing."

"Kate."

She folded the paper with short, sharp movements. "I told you about his weird doll collection. She's posed just like one of his dolls." She didn't look at him.

Ian sighed and swiped tears of laughter from his eyes. "I'm sorry I laughed, but this is just crazy."

She looked up then, eyes blazing. "Crazy like I'm crazy?"

"I didn't say that!"

"But you meant it."

Christ, he didn't know how he ended up in these conversations. He paused, burying himself in his coffee for a moment, struggling with how to proceed. "About last night," he said after a minute.

She looked up at him from under her eyebrows with a glint in her eyes. "Yes?"

"I'm sorry for how I acted, reacted, but I think we need to take a good hard look at what's going on and realize we could use some help."

"We?" Her voice was cold. She stood up and held onto her own mug, her knuckles white. "Don't you mean me?"

"No, not just you. It's me, too. We've all been affected by what happened."

"Rape. I was raped, Ian."

His temper frayed. "I know! Jesus Christ, Kate, do

you think I don't know that? I can say the word—it's you who doesn't like to say the word!"

She reacted as if he'd slapped her, taking a step back, tears flooding her blue eyes. She let her coffee cup drop on the table and walked out of the room. Ian followed her. "Kate, wait."

"Leave me alone!"

"No!"

She ran up the stairs and he ran after her, slowing to a walk when he realized this was like a scene in a bad movie. The slam of their bedroom door made him wince. He paced the hall for a minute, taking deep breaths and resisting the urge to throttle her and her artistic temperament.

She was overreacting because she was tired, tired because she didn't sleep, didn't sleep because she had bad dreams, and had bad dreams because she needed to talk with someone about what had happened. It all made perfect sense, but knowing this didn't make it any easier to deal with nor did it mean she would accept the logic of it.

When he finally opened the bedroom door, it was to find her lying on the bed staring up at the ceiling. She sat up, swinging her legs over the side of the bed, and he braced himself for more anger, but instead she said quietly, "I'm sorry."

Knocked off balance, as he always seemed to be by her despite eighteen years together, he managed to say, "Me, too."

They talked about other things then, the ability to let an argument go part of the glue that held a marriage together. She showered and dressed and he took off to run some errands, and neither of them spoke about what she'd seen at Terrence Simnic's house.

She folded up the old papers she'd scattered across

the kitchen floor and tossed them back in the recycling basket, adding the one with Lily Slocum's picture last, pausing to look at it again and then out the window at Terrence Simnic's house.

The curtains were still drawn, but the van wasn't in the driveway. He'd probably gone to work; florist shops were open on Saturday. Maybe Ian was right and it was crazy to suspect her next-door neighbor, but there'd been so many cases where the mild-mannered guy living next door turned out to be a cold-blooded killer. It always happened, so why not here? She knew better than anybody that nobody was immune.

The thud of her backpack hitting the porch signaled Grace's arrival home. Kate hurried to the door to let her in, hand already raised in anticipation of a thank-you wave to Haley Chin's parents, but their car was nowhere to be seen. The street was empty.

"Hi, sweetie." Kate folded Grace into a hug that her daughter endured for all of three seconds before pulling away. "Where's Haley? Didn't her parents drop you off?"

"Yeah. Her dad was in a hurry."

That didn't sound like Dr. and Dr. Chin. He was a meticulous anesthesiologist. She was a researcher. Something to do with cancer cells. Both of them were serious, smart, and mousy, just like their daughter. Kate felt annoyed that they hadn't lingered long enough to see that their daughter's friend made it safely into her house.

"Did you have a nice time?" Kate asked, picking up the jacket Grace discarded in the hall.

Her daughter shrugged. "It was okay."

"What did you girls do?"

"Nothing much. I'm hungry—can you make pancakes?" She walked toward the kitchen and Kate trailed after her.

"Didn't you eat breakfast?"

"Yeah. Hours ago. It's almost eleven, you know."

"I can tell time, you know," Kate said, imitating Grace's tone and stance, but her daughter only rolled her eyes. "Fine, I'll make pancakes, though I think the word you're looking for is please."

Her daughter trailed her to the kitchen. "I said please."

"No, you didn't."

"Whatever. Will you please make pancakes, Mother?" Grace's proper British accent made them both laugh.

Kate made the pancakes, knowing she was doing so because this, at least, was a need she could meet.

"So, what did you and Haley do? Watch a movie?"

"No."

"I thought you were going to the mall to see a movie?"

Grace pulled a carton of orange juice out of the fridge and poured a glass. "We changed our minds."

"So what did you do instead?"

Grace took a sip. "Stuff."

"Like what? Games? Video games?"

"Like just stuff, okay? Jesus, Mom, what's with the third degree?"

Kate wanted to smack her with the spatula, could actually feel her hand twitch with desire, but she took a deep breath instead. "It isn't a third degree, Grace, it's called parenting. What did you do?"

"We played video games."

"At the arcade in the mall?"

"Yeah." Grace took a sip of orange juice, and then held out a plate for the pancakes Kate neatly flipped onto it.

Grace sat down at the table and picked up the latest *Wickfield Gazette*, the only one Kate had left on the table. So like her father, she thought, watching her daughter absently twirl a strand of long, dark hair through her fingers. She ate quickly, just like Ian, as if the food was going to be taken from her. Kate had always assumed that came from his childhood, but now, watching Grace shoveling food into her mouth, she wasn't so sure.

She sat down in the seat opposite. "How's it going?"

Grace's eyes darted up to hers and then back down at the newspaper. She took a long time chewing her bite of pancakes, as if willing her mother to go away. Kate sat.

"How's what going?" Grace said at last.

"With you—with life, school, all of it." Kate worked hard to sound nonchalant and took a sip of coffee to hide her interest.

"Life is going fine." Grace shoved another bite of pancake into her mouth.

Kate flashed back to her own teenage years, wondering if she'd been like this with her parents. Had they worried about her in the same way she worried about Grace? And had she been this snotty? She couldn't remember much of anything from that time, which was shocking. When had she gotten so old?

"I know this move has been an adjustment," she said after serving Grace more pancakes. "But now that we've settled in, how do you like Wickfield?"

"It's okay."

"And your new school?"

Grace shrugged. "It's school."

"Do you like it more than your old school? Less?"

Grace actually seemed to be considering this as she reached for the syrup bottle and poured it slowly over her pancakes, back and forth, around and around. It reminded Kate of Spirograph. She resisted the impulse to tell Grace to stop, hoping to avoid seeing that shuttered look fall on her face.

"Well, I don't have to wear a uniform." Grace righted the syrup bottle and licked the excess slowly off her fingers.

Use a napkin, Kate thought. Stop slouching and sit up straight. Hold your fork like a fork, not like a club. She thought it all and sipped her coffee to keep from saying any of it. "Anything else?"

"The food isn't as good." Grace cut a wedge of pancake with the side of her fork. "But we can go outside for gym."

"Do you like your teachers?"

"They're okay."

Okay. Fine. Good. The words used to shut her mother up and out. Kate remembered the days when Grace would tell her everything, rushing into her mother's arms at the end of the day, pressing her body against Kate's so hard that at times Kate wished for the intensity of her love to be less. She hadn't felt worthy of this outpouring of affection or able to successfully navigate the tricky emotional waters of elementary school relationships and the clubs and cliques that consumed Grace's thoughts.

There had been many times when she'd wished that Grace had less to say, would just stop talking so that Kate could have a moment's peace and quiet. Now she had her wish and the silence threatened to engulf her.

Grace was reading the latest story on Lily Slocum. Kate looked across at the photo of a cluster of police officers standing on the bank of a creek or river. It was in black and white and the river looked black in it, a roiling black ribbon. She thought about that ribbon wrapping itself around a body and shuddered.

There was a second, smaller photo below, of a group of police vehicles, including a van marked with CORONER on the side, heading down a mountainside. A grim caravan.

"Have you noticed anything odd about our next-door neighbor?" Kate asked.

Grace stared at her mother, fork suspended in midair. "Why did you bring that up?"

"I've just noticed some strange things over there—"

"That's so weird, Mom." Grace shoveled in her last few bites of food.

"Why is it weird?"

"C'mon, Mom, spying on our neighbor? That's the definition of weird." Grace got up and carried her plate to the sink.

"I wasn't spying, I just happened to see some things."

"Whatever." Grace headed out of the kitchen, and this time it was Kate who followed.

"So you haven't seen anything?" She pressed as Grace sat down at the piano.

"No, Mom, I have a life." She sifted through sheet music ignoring her mother.

Her parents' generation would have slapped a kid for a remark like that. Kate settled for closing the piano lid, narrowly missing Grace's fingers. "You have homework to do first."

"I know." The bad seed drew the word out as if only an idiot would have stated something so obvious. She stomped into the front hall, retrieving her backpack from where she'd flung it. Kate followed her. She caught Grace's arm as her daughter started up the stairs.

"Why are you so unhappy?" As soon as Kate asked the question, she knew it was the wrong thing to say.

Grace stiffened at her touch, but she didn't yell as Kate expected. She just gave her mother a nasty smile and said, "I don't know, Mom. Why are *you*?"

Kate didn't know how to answer. She let go and Grace ran up the stairs. The slam of her bedroom door was followed a minute later by the muffled sound of some indie rock band.

Kate retreated to the kitchen to clean up. How did she end up like this with Grace? Somehow, every question she asked circled around to trap her. When had the innocence vanished? Was it her imagination, or had everything changed for Grace, too, when Kate was assaulted? Raped. Ian was right; she didn't like the word and still stumbled over it. For months it had been like a scar she was unable to look at squarely.

Her old therapist would have said she was taking too much responsibility for Grace's behavior. Grace was going through puberty, that's what was wrong with her, and maybe it had hit a little harder last year after what happened to her mother, but Kate was back on track now. She would be observant, would watch her daughter and protect her.

She poured a fresh mug of coffee and sat down to read one more time the article that accompanied the photos. The general tone was that things like this just didn't happen in Wickfield. There was also the suggestion that since Lily Slocum came from outside of Wickfield, maybe an outsider had committed the crime.

The story continued on page three with lots of filler about community reaction complete with quotes from "outraged" townspeople. It reminded Kate of the coverage of sporting events where reporters asked sweaty athletes very predictable questions about how it felt to win the championship game, eliciting standard responses like "unbelievable." It wasn't much of a surprise to discover that people felt outraged about a murder in their community. She skimmed over this part and slowed again when she got to a section about the victim.

A painting was taking shape in her head. It had been a long time since that had happened. She saw the interplay of colors, white against black. A pale expanse of naked skin, swathed in an undulating black ribbon. It would be Lily Slocum, but more than Lily. All women. All victims.

She could feel the desire again, the need to feel the texture of paint on canvas. She mentally selected the brushes she'd use, bristle to start with and sable for the details.

As she tossed the paper onto the recycling bin, she saw the paper underneath with the photo of Lily reclining on the chaise lounge. It was a beautiful picture, the figure seeming to float within the clusters of delicate flowers arranged about her, but the way she was dressed, in that high-necked white gown, looked so eerily similar to Terrence Simnic's dolls.

She stared at it for several minutes before jotting down the antique store's name. She wanted to see the real photo, not a fuzzy reproduction, but the police probably wouldn't allow that. Talking to someone who'd seen the actual photo was the next best thing. Was it open on Saturdays? Kate thought she'd find out.

Terrence Simnic was mowing his backyard, wearing an overly large gray T-shirt and a pair of navy blue Bermuda shorts. Sweat stains circled the armpits of the shirt. He was using a push mower, snaking it slowly back and forth across the dead-looking grass with his long, hairy arms.

She thought of his dining room filled with waxy, vacant-eyed dolls, and wanted to ask him what he'd been doing in his basement at three in the morning. He suddenly stopped mowing and looked across at Kate. It was as if he could tell what she was thinking. Kate hurried to her car, avoiding his gaze.

As she drove toward the center of town, Kate called home on her cell phone. After four rings, Grace answered the phone with a sulky "Hello?"

"It's Mom. Listen, double-check that the doors are locked, okay."

The put-upon sigh was particularly breathy through the phone. "I'm sure you already triple-checked."

"Just do it, Grace. I'll hold on."

Kate heard the squeak of bed springs, and then the sound of Grace clomping down the stairs.

"The front door's locked, big surprise."

"Good, go check the back."

Grace mumbled under her breath what might have been a curse, but Kate chose to ignore it. Clomp, clomp, clomp down the hall to the kitchen.

Suddenly Grace screamed, "Help! He's here!"

Kate slammed on the brakes and the car behind her slammed on its horn. "What? Grace!"

Silence. Kate jerked the car over to the side of the road amidst a squeal of brakes and horns. "Grace? Grace!"

A sudden peal of laughter left her confused, and then filled with rage. "That's not funny, Grace!"

"C'mon, Mom, I was just kidding!"

"Not funny at all."

The antique store was open for business, but there wasn't any. The owner—Kate recognized her from the paper—perched on a stool behind the counter, flipping through what looked like a pile of receipts. She wore a turquoise and white caftan that looked several sizes too large, oversized turquoise bangles and hoop earrings, and a pair of huge white-framed glasses. The effect was of a child dressed up in her mother's clothes, only judging by the look of this woman, her mother, if alive, would be well over a hundred.

"Good morning." Her voice was low and melodious and at odds with her appearance. She hopped lightly down from the stool and came around the counter with a big smile. The ends of a turquoise scarf tied around her beehive of shiny black hair trailed behind her like small sails. "I'm Abigail Thorney. Welcome to Thorney Antiques Emporium. May I help you find something?"

"Yes, actually, I'm looking for this." Kate held out the newspaper and pointed to the photo of Lily Slocum.

Abigail Thorney jerked back as if the paper could bite. "I don't have it anymore, the police do."

"But you found it in your store?"

The older woman played nervously with her glasses. "An unfortunate mistake."

"Do you have any idea how it came to be here?"

Mrs. Thorney's rheumy-looking eyes narrowed. "Are you a detective?"

"No, I'm not, I'm just interested—" Kate didn't know whether to explain why she wanted to see the photo.

"I already told the police everything I know, but do you think they accept that? They've come back twice to ask questions. I think they think I took that photo." Her voice rose on the end of that as if the very idea were outrageous. "If you're not with the police, who are you?"

"I'm Kate Corbin."

"The artist?"

It was Kate's turn to veer back, surprised. "Yes, that's right. How did you—"

But the old woman was waving a hand. "Wait right there. Just a minute." She disappeared behind the counter, and Kate heard clattering and muttering as things were moved.

A minute later, Mrs. Thorney emerged, turquoise scarf askew, patting her hair with one hand, though it didn't look as if a single strand had moved. In her other hand she waved a brochure.

"Here, see." She thrust it under Kate's nose. It was

from a show held more than three years ago. Kate's work had been featured alongside two other friends, all artists from the city, at a gallery in Tribeca.

"You look different," Mrs. Thorney said, jerking the corner of the brochure down to compare Kate with the glossy and glamorous headshot.

Kate blushed. "Well, I'm sure it's airbrushed."

Mrs. Thorney shook her head. "No, I mean you look thinner."

Kate laughed. "You're my new best friend."

"That was a good show. I love your work and so did my late husband."

"Thank you, that's very kind."

The old woman tucked the brochure under her arm. "So why do you want to see that photo?"

It was easier to explain now. Kate talked about seeing the article, about the inspiration for the painting.

"Was the picture really of Lily Slocum?"

"So the police said. Her friend could tell right away. I didn't know. I still don't know how it ended up in the window."

"How do you get the antiques?"

"Some things I buy in lots, others are donated. Some people sell to me directly."

"But you don't remember where you got the photo?" Kate kept seeing Terrence Simnic fussing over the doll. It wasn't a stretch to imagine him with a camera in his hand.

Mrs. Thorney shook her head. "I don't even know when it came in."

"So the police have the photo?"

"Yes, but you could probably get a look at it. I'm sure if you explain that you're an artist and why you want to see it, they'd probably let you take a look at it."

Yeah, that would probably go over really well. Kate

thanked her and headed for the door, Mrs. Thorney
following.

"Are you going to have another show soon?"

Kate thought of Jerry Virgoli. "Possibly at the gallery
in town."

"Oh, that would be wonderful!" Mrs. Thorney's small
hands clapped together with a surprisingly strong sound.
A spray of artificial flowers hanging over the door reminded Kate of her neighbor.

"Do you know a man named Terrence Simnic?"

"The owner of Bouquet? Of course. Why do you ask?"

"No reason, he's my neighbor."

Mrs. Thorney smiled. "This is a small town, Ms. Corbin."

"Kate, please."

The old woman inclined her head. "Kate. This is a
small town, everybody knows everybody."

"Really? Do you know him well?"

"No, not well at all. He's what I think one would call
a loner. Keeps to himself and always has done."

"Does he shop here?"

Mrs. Thorney considered. "Yes, but not very often.
He collects dolls—his mother did, I think, and he kept
it up—and I don't have a large collection of those, but
sometimes I get clothes and things from that period."

"Has he come in recently?"

"Actually, he was here just a few weeks back. Why do
you ask?"

The Wickfield police station didn't look at all like Kate
pictured. She'd assumed that it would be in some historic
stone building, much like the old courthouse with its
Doric columns that sat in the center of the town square,
or the even older bank, with its elaborately carved pilasters

that took up the space of two storefronts on Penton. But the Wickfield Police had a new, practically brand-new, several-story brick building that sat at the end of Aiken Avenue and wrapped around onto Poplar Street. While it lacked the grandeur of the other buildings, it was still intimidating.

Kate parked across the street, but didn't get out of the car. What could she do? Go in there and accuse her neighbor of murder? With what evidence? I'd like to accuse my neighbor of murder because he collects dolls that look like a photo of the victim, he shops at the antique shop where the victim's photo was found, he owns a flower shop and the photo had lots of flowers in it, I saw him with women's clothing but he lives alone, and he was doing something in his basement at three in the morning.

Ian had laughed when she'd told him. Could the police possibly have a different reaction? Kate couldn't get out of the car. Even if they didn't laugh, she didn't think she could face being back in a station. It brought back too many memories of the hours she'd spent in the station in Brooklyn. They'd been kind, but the scrutiny had been unpleasant. What time had she gotten to her studio? Did she walk the same way every day? Was she sure she'd locked the door when she left? Even with Ian at her side, it had been unpleasant, and she was afraid of reliving it just by walking through the doors of Wickfield's headquarters.

At the end of the newspaper article was a number for a hotline the Wickfield police had set up for any information about the crime. A hotline was anonymous. Kate pulled out her cell phone and dialed.

"Wickfield Police Hotline." The female voice sounded bored. Kate hadn't expected that.

"I have a name. I don't know if you've checked this guy, but I think maybe he had something to do with Lily Slocum's murder."

"What's the name, ma'am?"

"I'm not sure he's the one—"

"I understand that, but we need the name."

"Terrence Simnic."

The woman checked the spelling and that was it. Kate hung up feeling strangely let down. That was all. A name added to the list. Probably nothing would happen with it.

Kate drove home wondering if the police would do anything at all. How many names did they have on that list? How long would it take them to get to Terrence Simnic and what could he get up to in the meantime?

Ian might be right about Lily Slocum's death. It might just be a single crime and nothing like this would happen in Wickfield again. Only what if he wasn't and what if it would happen again and again because no one could stop it?

Chapter Thirteen

The room where he kept her was dark and very cold. The Snake (this was how Elizabeth thought of the man because he hissed like one when he talked to her) kept the space pitch black much of the time, cool all of the time.

She didn't know why and the Snake, who rarely spoke, wouldn't have explained that he kept it cold because he liked to see her nipples perpetually erect.

Most of the time, she was chained in one corner like a dog. There was a U-bolt buried deep in the juncture of what felt like concrete block walls, and it wouldn't give no matter how hard she pulled on it. In those first night-marish hours, she'd tugged on it so hard that she'd rubbed her ankle raw. He'd rubbed salve all over it with a curiously light touch, and then he'd beaten her for damaging his property.

Her food was served to her in a dog bowl and so was her water. He liked to watch her bend over to lap at it. After a time, she no longer felt the humiliation of the request.

She did not know how long she'd been there. She didn't know where she was except that she was underground, and she only knew this because she could hear his footsteps coming down a staircase. The light from upstairs would illuminate the last two steps so that the first thing she'd seen of him was his thick soled black workman's boots.

The first lesson she'd learned was that she was to present her naked body whenever he came in the room. Waking up bare, chained to a wall, she'd pulled up the thin mattress where she slept and tried to hide behind it as his measured footsteps crossed the cement floor.

The harsh beam of a flashlight focused on her and he'd yelled, "No!" before dragging the mattress away and hitting her with the short whip he liked to carry.

After, he'd kissed the marks, lingering over the redness on her shoulders and across her buttocks, stinging them anew with the roughness of his tongue until she'd pulled away in discomfort. He'd stopped abruptly, pushing her face down into the stained mattress and holding her there while he wielded the whip again, criss-crossing her legs this time with biting strokes. That had been lesson number two: Don't pull away.

The bed was in another section of the chamber. A huge four-poster in curved and twisted iron, it had a thick, soft mattress covered with pristine white bed linens that the Snake made her change every time it was used. He brought the folded sheets to her in a basket, and she had to strip off the old ones and put on the new ones while he watched, tapping the whip against his gloved hand.

He taught her how the first time, following behind her as she tucked in the sheets with trembling hands and then checking her work. The first time, he found a wrinkle in the sheets and beat her for it. The second time she was careful, oh, so careful, for there to be nothing wrong with it at all, and he smiled when he was done checking it, his lips curving upward. Then he had her get on all fours in the center of the bed and whipped her anyway. That was lesson number three: He didn't need a reason to beat her.

When he played with her on the bed, he dressed her first, and it was perversely true that she'd come to welcome these sessions simply because it was the only time she was truly warm. He made her raise her arms to accept a long, white cotton nightgown edged in lace at the collar and cuffs. There was a placket in the front with a row of buttons that he did up himself, and then he turned her toward the corner of the space where the bed sat, pulling back the thick comforter and tucking her in as if she were a child or a virginal bride.

The first few sessions in the bed, he got in next to her fully dressed, posing and fondling her as if she were a plaything, but it was a welcome change to being treated literally like a dog and she thought it wasn't so bad.

Then things escalated. The first change was that he undressed. Every time he visited he wore the same clothes: dark pants, dark shirt, and a thin black mask that covered most of his face. When he removed the trousers, she saw that he was wearing innocuous white cotton briefs.

It was the briefs that made it all ridiculous; then he slipped those off and she could see he was just like any other white man, all pale-skinned and hairy, with his erect penis bobbing in the air like a skinny, salmon pink balloon. It surprised her to realize he was human, not a reptile after all, and she'd laughed a little, a nervous laugh, but he'd stopped at once, stripping the covers off her, then the gown, and manacling her spread-eagle to the four corners of the bed before he beat her breasts with his whip. She didn't laugh again.

"Let me go!" she screamed at first, and sometimes, "Why are you keeping me here?" After a time, she stopped talking to him, taught by his whip and his indifference that her words didn't affect him. He talked often, sometimes over her screams, telling her in sibilant whispers exactly what he wanted her to do.

Sometimes he turned the lights on—and she'd been surprised to discover that there were lights embedded in the drop ceiling—but mostly he preferred things lit only by a few tall, sputtering candles mounted on ornate iron stands.

Elizabeth liked candles, had many of them scattered about her apartment, and enjoyed the scented ones best. She'd once lined her entire bedroom with them, especially for Joel. All those tiny flickering lights had been very romantic. That was before. She didn't think she could ever look at another candle without seeing these fat, yellow-white pillars.

She stared at the candles while he raped her. Watched the steady drip, drip of the greasy wax rolling down the sides. She'd fought him the first time. Fought him hard enough to feel the satisfying thud of connection with his pelvis, but while he'd dropped her arms to cup his injured genitals, she'd barely scrambled off the bed before he was on her, a hand snaking out from the bed to snatch one slender ankle and bring her down.

The punishment for fighting was the worst. He'd stripped off the nightgown and hung her by her wrists from a hook in the ceiling, suspending her so that just her toes grazed the cold floor, and then he'd doused every candle and left.

She didn't know how long she hung there. An hour? A day? She had lost her sense of time already; the subterranean darkness had seen to that. She couldn't accurately judge by the pain. Within moments the juncture where arms met shoulders felt sore, then hot, then the feeling spread throughout her body, an inferno of pain as her joints strained at their sockets.

She cried, indulging in it since the Snake wasn't there to witness her tears. "You fucking bastard, let me go!" she screamed, but he was gone. Later, she cried, "Help! Please help!" but there was no one there to hear her cries. The walls swallowed them up. She dozed, only to jerk awake when her head tipped too far forward and upset the balance.

She thought longingly of her mother, with whom she had a difficult relationship, and of her younger sister, whom she'd always disliked, and of how much she wanted to see them, hear them, touch them.

She thought that no painting she'd seen of Hell had come close to this because, at least in the Hieronymous Bosch paintings she'd seen, no one was alone in their suffering. There was some comfort in suffering along with someone else.

When he finally came back, when she saw the sliver of light illuminate the steps and heard his heavy footsteps coming down, she felt awash in relief and then ashamed to be glad to see him. He walked silently toward her, dressed in black as usual, whip in hand.

"Have you learned your lesson?"

It was his usual, paternalistic speech. She nodded, it took an effort to move her head. He slapped her face with his gloved hand and she answered correctly, "Yes, Master."

This had been lesson number five: He was to be addressed as Master. He would address her as slave. Sometimes, when he played in bed, she was "little one." She wasn't sure which made her skin crawl more.

"Are you sorry, slave?"

"Yes, Master." Sorry I can't rip off your balls, you bastard. "Sorry, so sorry."

A slight smile touched his lips. He stepped toward her, already reaching up to release her hands from the cuffs, and then he stopped. Stepped back. The smile vanished and his nose wrinkled in revulsion. "You soiled yourself, slave."

The urine had long since dried on her legs. She'd forgotten about it. "What else could I do?"

His gloved hand moved so fast that she saw its flash a split second before the slap blazed across her cheek.

"Master!" he screamed. "You call me Master!"

He turned from her, striding back the way he'd come, and she panicked. "I'm sorry, Master! Please, Master, don't leave me here!"

He didn't respond, but he didn't climb the stairs. Instead he was fiddling with something in a corner, and then he came back dragging a long hose with water dribbling out the front. Without speaking, he aimed the hose at her and turned the nozzle. Cold water sprayed her stomach, then her pelvis. His whip lashed her thigh.

"Spread your legs, slave!"

The spray was so sharp it felt like it was cutting her. She tried to turn to avoid it and the whip lashed her arm. "Stand still, slave!"

He hosed her thoroughly, inside and out, and then he took her down and threw a towel on top of her.

"Dry off!"

She dried hurriedly, watching as he coiled the hose away. When he returned, the smile was back in place.

"Let's get you into your nightgown, little one."

If he saw the tears in her eyes, he gave no sign. He hummed a little as he slipped the nightgown carefully over her head and gently smoothed it down her body. "That's better. Ready to try again?"

"Yes, Master."

She let him lead her to the bed and tuck her under the covers. When he forced himself inside her, she bit hard on her lip and stared at the flickering candles.

Chapter Fourteen

Sunlight streamed across Ian's desk, but it was the
knock on his office door that caused him to look up
from his paperwork. He was amazed to see that it was
after four. Had he really been working straight for more
than three hours?

"Come in!" he called, and Mildred Wooden stepped
in the door. She wore hot pink today, an incongruous
choice for fall except that the suit was in tweed. She
tugged at the glasses strung around her neck and gave
him a maternal smile.

"I have to leave early today, Dean, remember? Is there
anything I can get you before I go?"

"No, thank you, but I've got some donor letters to go
out." Ian handed over a large stack of signed papers.

"Great, I'll just pop those in the mail tomorrow morning."

She took them with a smile, waving good-bye over her
shoulder, and Ian wondered, for the thousandth time, at
her ability to channel everything into something positive.

He sighed as he sat back down at his desk. He wished

he had that ability. Take the disappearance of Elizabeth
Hirsh, for instance. Mildred could probably spin that as
a student taking off for a romantic getaway. That's how
she'd spun Lily Slocum's disappearance initially. And
when the body had been found? Mildred squared her
shoulders, tsk-tsking under her breath about the unfortunate girl and her unfortunate family, but then she'd
brightly suggested that at least it was a chance for the
university to tighten security.

Where was Elizabeth Hirsh? Last seen at an off-campus
party, she'd been missing two weeks. Officially, the university was working with police, but unofficially, there
was quite a lot of tension between the administration
and the police force.

The University's president, Hugh Slater, had held
three emergency meetings since the news of Elizabeth
Hirsh's disappearance. She was the second student to
go missing in less than six months. This was not good
for the school, and Slater was keenly aware of how it
would look to alumni and all other possible donors.

Sixty and silver-haired, he'd come from Stanford, a
large, ruddy man with the charm of Cary Grant but the
bearish good looks of a boxer, which he was rumored to
have been in his student days.

"If public perception is that Wickfield has become
unsafe, we won't be selecting from the top of the barrel
for next year's freshman class," he'd said at a meeting
earlier that day. "We'll be lucky if we get those from the
middle of the crop."

Someone from the English department groaned
under his breath. Slater was fond of clichés and mixed
metaphors, but he'd been brought in to raise the profile of Wickfield, and that he'd done in the five years
he'd been at the helm. The board of trustees loved him—
well, at least its female members.

He'd pulled Ian aside at the end of the meeting to ask if he'd sit in at a meeting with Elizabeth Hirsh's parents. They'd insisted on meeting with the president, but as Slater said to Ian, "She's in Humanities, Corbin, that's your department."

All of these meetings were taking up time that Ian didn't have. The latest thing he'd had to deal with was whether or not to be present at a candlelight vigil for Lily Slocum and Elizabeth Hirsh being held at the non-denominational university chapel later that evening.

Certainly, a vigil was something positive, to paraphrase Mildred Wooden, but it was tricky. By linking both girls were the organizers essentially saying that they thought Elizabeth Hirsh was a victim, too? If so, then it could be a problem for the University. Or could it just be viewed as support for a community in distress? For it definitely was in distress.

The counseling wing of the health office had seen a forty-percent increase in drop-ins since Lily Slocum's body had been found and there'd been a protest march, though what exactly they were protesting, Ian couldn't have said. Maybe it was just a change from chanting about war or the latest embargo against tyrants in developing nations. Hey, hey, ho, ho, this murder thing has got to go. Even without a clear agenda, the protest had attracted a motley crowd of about a hundred students and at least one faculty member, though he was adjunct and viewed, by and large, as a weirdo.

"Nothing like this has happened at Wickfield," a professor emeritus in psychology told Ian gleefully at the end of one of Slater's meetings. "I guess it was just your luck that it happened on your watch."

They'd been standing in front of the coffee and cookies, and Ian surreptitiously scanned the crowd, wondering which professor would be most likely to carry a flask of something to make the dreadful coffee, and these long, boring meetings, more palatable.

"Yeah, just my luck," he muttered, taking a big bite of a stale sugar cookie to avoid saying more. It had been a relief when Dr. Beetleman hailed him from across the room.

"I've heard from the architect and he's got some preliminary drawings," the older man said when he got close enough. "Do you have a minute?"

"Yes, definitely." He took Dr. Beetleman's arm and steered him out of the conference room and away from the throng. "It will be a relief to talk about something other than this latest disappearance."

Dr. Beetleman's lips pursed in a moue of distaste. "Yes, I think some of the people coming to these meetings are attracted by the hope of hearing something salacious."

"It certainly isn't for the coffee."

Laurence Beetleman laughed, eyes crinkling at the corners, and his shock of white hair bobbing. "How true!"

He told Ian about the architect's plans for the Performing Arts Center, and Ian soaked it in. This was what he wanted to think about; the bigger, creative projects that were the real attraction of becoming dean.

They'd been standing in the atrium of Ludlum Hall. It was a large monstrosity of a building, late nineteenth century, and with all the pomp and circumstance and manifest destiny inherent in some of the design of that period. He found himself comparing its heavy lines with what he hoped would be the exact opposite feel of the new arts center. Light, airy, appearing to stay up in the air through sleight of hand—that's what he wanted.

There would be walls of windows and studios laid with bamboo floors, and of course the acoustics would be far superior to anything now on campus.

Talking with Laurence Beetleman about the plans had been one of the few times in this hectic week when he'd had the chance to think about anything besides the murder.

Ian picked up the next set of grant applications and settled back in his chair, trying to summon enthusiasm for another hour's worth of work.

Another knock on the door surprised him. Wondering what Mildred had forgotten, Ian called out, "Come in!" just as he turned his chair to look at the sun setting over campus.

"It's beautiful isn't it," he said without looking around.

"Yes." The voice wasn't Mildred's. Ian swiveled around and saw Bethany Forrester standing in the doorway with a paper in one hand and a briefcase in the other. "You've got the best view," she said, walking forward.

Ian stood up. "Come in, come in—I thought you were my secretary."

"Oh, dear." Bethany gave him a look of mock dismay, and Ian laughed. She couldn't be further from Mildred Wooden. Silhouetted in the light from the window, she looked long, lean, and beautiful. She walked slowly across the room toward him, swaying slightly on high heels, the silver of her bracelet glinting in the sunlight, and a soft shushing sound accompanying each step as her charcoal silk slacks rubbed.

"It's such a spectacular view," she said, looking past him out the window where the sun was giving a terra-cotta glow to gray stone facades and setting every tree alight.

"Yes." He was looking at her. She wore a fuzzy, black V-necked sweater, and he had a sudden longing to place

a hand against that V of pale flesh. Ian hastily averted
his eyes.

"I've finished the letter to some of our Drama alumni
and thought you might like to take a look before I send
it out."

He didn't need to look at it; with anybody else he
would have declined. "Sure. Let me see."

She held it out to him, and whether he contrived or
she contrived he didn't know, only that somehow their
fingers touched. They paused. She looked at him then,
staring directly into his eyes. The sunset made hers look
like amber, pools of transparent brown flecked with
gold.

A sharp, buzzing noise made Ian jump and jerk his
hand back from Bethany's. The phone on his desk rang
again, a shrill rebuke. "Hello?"

"Ian Corbin?" A woman's stern voice. He'd been
seen. Ian felt heat crawling along the back of his shirt
collar and creeping up his neck.

"Yes?"

"I'm calling from Wickfield High School about your
daughter, Grace."

"Grace? Is something wrong? Did something happen?"

"No, Mr. Corbin, at least not that we're aware of.
Grace hasn't been in school all day and since this is her
fourth unexcused absence we were concerned . . ."

Bethany put the letter on the edge of his desk and
waved. She mouthed, "Catch you later," and walked out
of his office as he watched the sway of her hips and the
curve of her ass in her slacks.

". . . need you to come in and have a meeting with
our school counselor, Harold Trowle."

"Yes, of course." He couldn't concentrate. The office
door quietly clicked. She was gone. He felt rock hard
and shifted in his chair.

The woman said something about dates and Ian scrolled through his online calendar. "Yes, okay, and yes, I'll be sure to tell my wife, too."

When he'd hung up the phone, Ian sat back in his office chair and exhaled loudly. Had that really happened? There was a certain dreamlike quality to it that made it feel like a fantasy, but no, there was the letter just where she'd left it.

For a moment, Ian just looked at it. He had the feeling that it could hurt him, and then he realized how ridiculous he was being and plucked it from the edge of his desk. Without thinking about it, he slipped it in his briefcase.

Damien Rattle pulled the ends of the rope tighter around her foot and Grace couldn't help it, she made a faint noise of pain and fear.

"Quiet," he snapped, letting go of her foot and looking at her. "You have to be quiet or it spoils the mood."

"Sorry."

"Are you going to be quiet or not?"

She nodded and he smiled, that perfect smile that she'd come to crave.

They were in his bedroom in his parents' apartment in Manhattan. When they'd met and he told Grace he lived in an apartment on the Upper East Side, she'd pictured a place like her own—small in square footage but nicely decorated with cool furniture and art.

It had the cool furniture and art, all right, but it was anything but small. It was a huge place, four bedrooms, each one of them the size of the living room in her house, each with its own mammoth attached bath. The sunken living room had a spectacular view of the park. There was a doorman downstairs, and a maid upstairs.

The wooden floors were inlaid on the edges and polished to a high shine. The place smelled of furniture polish and fresh flowers, which adorned large porcelain vases on spindly-legged tables in the hall.

Damien's room had an enormous iron bed frame, and he'd grinned when she'd admired it.

"It's French," he said. "Mother found it when we were in Brittany last year. Doesn't it look like something belonging to the Marquis de Sade? I don't think she had that in mind, but we can christen it in high style."

That's what they were doing, christening the bed. He'd produced the rope, a tightly wrapped coil of black nylon, after picking her up from school.

"It looks painful," she'd said, but he only laughed.

"You'll love it."

Only she didn't. She didn't love it at all. First, he'd wanted her undressed. She didn't want to get naked in front of him. So far, she'd been naked in pieces with him, allowing him to touch her under her shirt, to slip his hand down into her pants, to feel her and see her in pieces, but never whole. Somehow, it was more real whole.

"It doesn't work if you're dressed," he'd said. "C'mon, it's much more fun if you're naked."

And he'd smiled at her, the smile she loved, and she'd stood between his legs while he sat on the bed and began the slow undressing of her, taking his time.

That part had been okay, that part she'd even liked a little, her nervousness fading away as he muttered "Perfect" as each part of her body was revealed. She'd glowed from the praise, stood up a little straighter, even admired the way her breasts hung like small apples when he removed her bra.

Then he'd had her lie down on the center of the bed and he'd climbed on top of her, straddling her torso, his jeans scraping the tender skin of her waist. She'd told him it hurt, and that's when he'd first said to be quiet. He'd taken her hands and raised them to curve around the bar of the iron headboard above her.

"Stay that way," he whispered, and then he slowly, ever so slowly, inched out the rope and wound it about both her wrists and tied them to the headboard.

That hadn't been too bad. Exciting, even, with Damien watching her, but then it changed. He'd turned, for starters, taking his eyes off hers and focusing on her feet. He'd jerked them a little too hard toward the foot of the bed, and now he was tying them, one by one, just as he had with her hands. She didn't like it. It felt like she was stretched too far, and she remembered the chapter from her history book on the Inquisition and the illustration that showed a screaming figure stretched on the rack.

"I don't like it," she whispered, hoping that if she spoke quietly he wouldn't be annoyed. He ignored her, finishing with her right foot. He clambered off the bed and stared down at her, moving about the room to view her from different angles.

"Perfect," he said again, and he smiled as he reached out a hand to snake along her leg, moving up and up toward her crotch. She tried to pull away, but couldn't.

"Damien, stop! It tickles!" She spoke without meaning to, her voice a whine, but he only laughed.

"Wait here." He laughed at his own joke. As if Grace could go anywhere. She turned her head, lifting it from the pillow with an effort, but all she saw was his back as he left the room.

Her head flopped back on the pillow and she stared up at the high ceiling, tracing the molding with her eyes and trying to count the fine hairline cracks in the cream-colored plaster.

It struck her as weird that Damien had nothing really personal in the room, but he'd told her that his family also had homes in Connecticut and the Hamptons, so perhaps he didn't stay here much.

Besides the bed, there was a heavy-looking, dark wood dresser adorned with a few family photos in silver frames—Damien, his mother and stepfather—and a mirror suspended above it. To the left was a wrought-iron candle stand with a large, unlit pillar on it. Directly across from the bed was a wooden bookcase filled with a collection of what looked like old law books and a few other things—a white conch shell, a plaster bust of some Roman-looking guy, a silver paperweight. Three photos framed in black hung to the left of the bed. They were black-and-white shots of what looked like water running over rocks.

Not that she could tell from the bed. She'd looked at them earlier, when he'd first shown her the room. From her current position, all she could see were gray blobs and squiggles.

She felt an itch far down her right leg and there was nothing she could do to scratch it. Pressing her leg against the sheets and twisting back and forth didn't work. Another itch appeared on her right shoulder. The top of her head tickled. She could relieve none of them, could do nothing but twist in the rope, helpless. She wanted to call out to Damien, but he'd told her to be quiet.

Somewhere in the apartment, she heard the sound of a door closing. Panic set in. What would happen if the maid came back? He'd said it was her afternoon off, but what if she'd returned? Grace knew the door to this room stood open. What if the woman walked in and saw her?

She tugged futilely at the knots binding her wrists

and tried to pull her legs up, rubbing her ankles raw against the rope in her attempt to get free, but nothing worked.

There were footsteps in the hall. She could hear them approaching, but couldn't tell who they belonged to. What if it wasn't the maid? What if it was one of his parents? He'd said they were in the Hamptons, but what if they'd returned early?

Grace couldn't help the low keen that escaped from her. She wished she hadn't come, wished she hadn't agreed to this stupid idea. What was he thinking leaving her like this?

The footsteps were louder, slow and deliberate and coming toward her over that shiny wooden floor.

"Damien!" It burst from her, she couldn't stop it. "Damien! Is that you?"

The footsteps sped up, and suddenly there was movement in the doorway and Damien came running in, and she was relieved, so relieved. Only, he glared at her and then his hand flashed forward, the slap coming so suddenly that she had no time to anticipate, and her head bounced to the side with the force of the blow.

She cried out and he yelled, "Shut up!"

Tears flooded her eyes and her cheek burned. Grace tugged at her hands, trying to get them free, and stared up at Damien, who looked wobbly.

"I did tell you to be quiet, Grace," he said in a regretful voice. He reached out his hand and she flinched, but he merely stroked the cheek he'd struck, rubbing out the sting. "I told you, but you wouldn't listen."

"Untie me." Her voice came out as a whimper, and he shook his head at her.

"You're still talking, Grace."

"I don't want to do this."

She saw the second slap coming, and moved her

head so it was deflected and his fingers slid from her face to the pillow.

"Stop," he said. "Stop right now."

She was afraid suddenly, really afraid. There was no one in the apartment, only them. His parents were at their house in the Hamptons and it was the maid's afternoon off. That's why he'd done this, because nobody was here to see it.

A sob rose in her and another followed on its heels, and suddenly she couldn't control it, sobbing and sobbing. Damien scrambled off her, untying the ropes with haste, cursing under his breath.

"Okay, okay, you're free."

She pulled her limbs toward each other, curling up in a ball for a moment before rolling to her side and reaching for her clothes.

Damien put a hand on her shoulder, but she shook him off.

"C'mon, Grace, it was just a game." One part defensiveness, two parts coaxing. "C'mon, now, you knew it was a game."

"You hit me." She'd wanted that to come out strong, but instead she sounded pathetic, her nose stuffed, her voice wavering.

"Did I hurt you, baby?" He sounded surprised, regretful.

She ventured a look at him and he smiled at her. A sweet, wide smile that made what had happened seem like a misunderstanding.

"That's right, look at me, it's okay." He stroked her hand and tugged gently on her wrist. She let him pull her to her feet, wrap her in an embrace. "I didn't mean to hurt you," he crooned, holding her naked against him. "It was just a game, baby, just a game."

Chapter Fifteen

Bouquet Florists was on the first floor of an old brick building on Yates Street. Not a fashionable address, two blocks back and several long blocks down from the central business district, and not a fashionable shop, with its faded pink awning and peeling gilt letters on the window.

The store looked like it had been there for many, many years, and Kate wondered how Terrence Simnic kept it going. Perhaps it was just customer loyalty. It looked like the sort of shop that got only certain customers, widows who remembered their husbands bringing them Easter corsages from this shop thirty years ago, or poor college girls who hoped flowers would brighten up their dank apartments and couldn't afford the nicer, bigger shop on Penton.

It could hardly be Terrence drawing customers. As Kate watched from her car across the street, she saw the dirty white van with faded letters pull up out front and her neighbor climb out.

He wore a hangdog expression and a gray cardigan

that stretched across his large, muscular shoulders and hung open in front to reveal a green plaid shirt buttoned to the top.

He trudged up to the front door in his large work boots, looking around in a furtive way that made her slump down in her seat, anxious not to be seen. She'd parked the Volvo in the shade of a massive oak tree and tucked close to the fender of a big red SUV hoping not to be noticed.

He'd been late getting here. Afraid that he would notice her following him, Kate had waited until his van left the driveway before pulling out in the opposite direction, purposely taking a circuitous route to the shop. Not that it had been hard; she'd gotten briefly lost in a warren of back streets.

This was a section of Wickfield that looked like it had fallen on hard times. Slumlord student housing in the form of crumbling duplexes and flimsy-looking apartment buildings. A few single-family homes stood like lone flowers among the weeds, fresh paint and the struggle to keep their yards litter-free making them stand out. There were several cleaner multifamily units, too, obviously rehabbed by developers hoping to flip the neighborhood.

Relief at finding the shop gave way to surprise that the van was nowhere in sight. Where was he? While she'd waited, Kate sketched the shop in a small notebook she carried in her purse. A series of straight lines, except for the awning, which rippled and created shadows. She moved a charcoal pencil deftly over the page, lost in her work.

The sound of an old muffler had brought her out of it in time to see the van come chugging slowly around the corner. It had taken him forever to turn off the van and get out, but maybe it was because she was so nervous about his arrival. She sketched Terrence Simnic standing in front of the building, taking a few tries with the charcoal to get the expression on his face just right. Before she was done, he unlocked the door and disappeared inside.

As she pondered what to do next, a young woman came riding up the street on a bicycle and stopped in front of the shop. From a distance, she looked like she could be Lily Slocum's sister, with her long, blond ponytail and slim build. As she locked the bike to a lamppost, Terrence appeared at the front door, switching the cardboard CLOSED sign over to OPEN.

Kate sketched her quickly as well, just because the young woman was there, and watched her enter the shop. Minutes passed. Kate fully expected to see the girl come out carrying flowers, but eight minutes later the bike was still locked to the lamppost.

Kate tapped her hand against the steering wheel. Come on—where was she? What could be taking that long? The longer she sat, the more certain Kate was that the girl was in danger. What if while she was sitting there, Terrence Simnic had approached the girl, asked her to see some flowers in the back of the shop?

He would tell her they'd just gotten a shipment of roses that she might like and then, while she was looking, he'd wrap one of those simian arms around her neck . . .

Kate got out of the car and started toward the shop. She acted on impulse, surprised to see her feet moving so quickly, but she couldn't let someone else get hurt. She had nothing to defend herself with, much less the girl, only her cell phone and keys. She wrapped the key ring in her fist so the keys jutted out between her fingers.

As she crossed the street, the door to the shop suddenly opened and the girl came out wearing a pink apron and carrying a green bucket stuffed with deep yellow carnations. She set it down along the wall by the front door and went back in the shop, a bell jangling when the door opened.

Kate slowed. The young woman was an employee? That hadn't occurred to her. The bell jangled again and the same girl came back out carrying a large plastic pot of purple mums. She set it down next to the carnations and vanished back inside.

It was too late to turn back. If Terrence could see Kate through these windows, he'd be sure to notice if she suddenly walked away. She kept moving forward, but she tucked her keys casually into the pocket of her black corduroy jacket.

The girl came back out with another pot of purple mums. She arranged the buckets one way, then another, standing back to survey her work with her hands on her hips.

"Hi," she said in a cheerful voice as Kate approached.

"Hello." Kate paused, pretending to admire the flowers. Her heart raced with leftover adrenaline. "How much are the carnations?"

"Four-fifty for a bouquet." The girl plucked a rubber-banded bundle from the bucket and held it out, stems dripping in dots on the dusty concrete. "They're beautiful, aren't they?"

"Yes." Kate took it from her and feigned interest in it, touching the soft petals, the weight of the woody stems heavy in her hands. "Have you worked here long?"

"Just a couple of weeks." The girl shifted one pot of mums out of the shadow of the awning.

"You're a student at Wickfield?"

The girl looked up at Kate. "Yeah, why?"

"No reason." Kate tried a smile, but the girl's eyes narrowed.

"Do you want those?" She nodded at the flowers in Kate's hand.

"Sure."

"You have to pay inside."

Kate approached the door, knowing she was being watched. She'd forgotten the bell, and jumped as it jangled above her head. Feeling like an idiot, she stepped inside and the door closed smoothly behind her.

Color overwhelmed her. Flowers in every imaginable variety and hue filled the shop. They were standing in buckets, arranged in vases, and woven into wreathes. Their perfume was overpowering in the humid air.

Something reminded her of Terrence Simnic's house, and Kate realized it was the gloom. Two old fluorescent light fixtures hung from the ceiling, and one of the bulbs was flickering.

Kate stepped around a jungle of hanging baskets and saw Terrence Simnic standing behind a counter. It was just like she'd pictured, only he was engrossed in arranging roses in a Styrofoam ring. He looked up as she approached, pruning shears in one large hand, a pink rose in the other.

"Hi." She extended the bouquet of carnations.

"Good morning." He met her eyes, but showed no sign of recognition. He moved slowly, setting down the shears and the rose, but when he reached under the counter, Kate panicked.

"I'm your neighbor, Kate Corbin," she said, taking a step back.

"Yep." He held up a piece of green tissue paper and wrapped it around the carnations. It reminded Kate of how she'd swaddled Grace as a baby.

He carried the bundle to the cash register. "That'll be four-fifty."

Was that all he was going to say? She dug in her purse for the money.

"Have you owned this shop a long time?"

"Over thirty years." There was no inflection in his voice. She handed him a five-dollar bill and he rang it up without comment. When his large fingers dropped fifty cents into her palm, she felt revulsion.

"Do you always have college students working for you?"

"Why? Do you want a job?"

"No, um, I was just wondering."

He stepped back over to his project, picking up the rose and pruning shears again. With sure fingers, he neatly snipped the stem off the rose and then cut a section of wire off a spool, inserted one end in the base of the flower, and stuck it into the foam ring.

Up close, Kate could tell it was a funeral wreath. Several more arrangements were propped against a stool behind him. One of them was a half circle of tightly packed white flowers. It looked like the arrangement placed around Lily Slocum's head in the pseudo antique photo.

Kate swallowed and stepped back toward the door. "Well, good-bye." He didn't look up from his work.

Heart pounding, Kate took her flowers and walked swiftly out the door. She listened, feeling as if all her senses were on high alert, but there was silence behind her. Only afterwards did she think how odd it was that he hadn't even offered a "Thank you" or "Come again."

The girl was still outside, crouched alongside a pot of mums, picking off dead heads.

"Did you know Lily Slocum?" Kate asked without preamble. It was no good pretending; she couldn't think of any subtle way to ask.

"No." The girl stood up. "I mean, I knew who she was, but I didn't know her." She tossed the dead flowers in her hand. "Why?"

"Did she work at this store?"

The girl shrugged. "I don't think so, but I've only been here a few weeks." She looked at Kate with frank curiosity. "Are you related to her or something?"

"No."

"So why are you asking about her?"

"I thought she disappeared around here." The lie came to her and she went with it.

"I think it was on the other side of campus," the girl said. "Is that why you were sitting there?" She nodded at Kate's car. "I thought you were waiting for someone."

Kate felt her face flush. If the girl had noticed her, then Terrence probably had, too.

"The owner's my neighbor." At least that was the truth, just not all of it.

"Mr. Simnic?"

Kate nodded and the girl seemed to accept this, though Kate thought it raised more questions. The owner's my neighbor so I thought I'd stalk him. Or better yet, I think my neighbor's a killer.

"Do you like working for him?" she asked. The girl shot her a strange look, and for one moment Kate thought she was going to divulge something.

"He's okay," the girl said instead. "He's a little shy, but he's not a bad guy."

It didn't seem like much of a recommendation, and the girl must have thought so, too, because she added, "I need the money."

The bell jangled and both Kate and the girl flinched. Terrence Simnic stood in the doorway. "I need you inside, Josie," he said to the girl. He stared at Kate without speaking, but held the door for the girl. She shot another look at Kate and scurried inside, sidling past his solid girth. The door closed with another ring of the bell and Kate was alone.

Before she identified as an artist, before Kate knew the word, she'd been adept at identifying patterns. Her parents used to tell the story of how, as a three-year-old, she'd helped her father when he got lost en route to a friend's home by telling him to turn where there were four houses in a row with pointy roofs.

Before she could read, she arranged the cans in the kitchen cupboards by size and color, and could identify different foods by the patterns on their labels.

Beginning drawing classes taught budding artists to look at the world in a way that she'd always viewed it— to see everything reduced to shapes. Square, circle, triangle, oval. Within every portrait of a nude, every still life with fruit, was an arrangement of shapes. Draw the shapes and the portrait emerged from it. Beneath everything was some arrangement, some pattern.

She could see the pattern emerging behind Terrence Simnic and it was dark and disturbing. Only just like her childhood, she was the only one to see it.

Chapter Sixteen

The man was thirteen when his father died. It was a gradual thing, this death that started with a cough that wouldn't go away.

His mother had warned him about his smoking. She'd said that no good would come of that and wasn't it bad enough that he'd had to take care of miners all these years, hadn't he seen enough black lung to teach him anything?

The cancer took him in less than a year, shriveling his body so that at the end the boy could support his weight as he hobbled down the halls of the county hospital.

He'd go there after school, coming in to the dim room to see his father's wan face light up and listen to him ask, as he did every day, "Do you feel like some Jell-O?"

It was the only thing he wanted to eat anymore, and the boy wasn't sure that he could even taste it. The boy's mother clucked her tongue over this when she visited.

"You've got to eat more than that or you'll never get your strength back." Though she'd been right there in the room when the doctor said that there was nothing they could do and it was just a matter of time.

Sometimes, she sent the boy to the hospital alone, claiming that she couldn't bear to see her husband like that, though the boy noticed that she didn't seem overcome with grief.

Through his father's last winter, the boy's mother made him keep up with schoolwork, music lessons, and the deportment classes offered by the only woman more socially conscious than her. On Wednesday evenings, he put on a pressed shirt and his Sunday suit and learned to waltz and speak properly along with fifteen other unhappy children. On other evenings, he sat alone at the piano in the front room while Poe worked alone in the basement beneath him.

His mother drilled good manners into the boy, practicing with him at the scarred Formica table in the kitchen, teaching him the proper placement of silverware and how to hold it. "Don't clutch your spoon like that," she said angrily, adjusting his hand. "If you act like a convict, you'll be treated like one. Manners make the man."

And he knew without her saying it that she didn't like the way his father had sometimes chewed with his mouth open or reached for the bread without asking for it to be passed.

It was June when his father died. His body was brought back to his own funeral home and Poe prepared him for burial.

"Here, take him this suit." His mother thrust his father's Sunday suit, the black wool shiny with wear at the elbows and knees, into the boy's hands.

Poe was washing the body when the boy came down the stairs. His father looked desiccated, his face hollow. The boy was suddenly frightened, but then Poe took the suit from his hands and held out a cloth, and once the boy touched it to his father's skin he was okay. He placed his own hands on the body, the coolness of the skin exciting and centering him, bringing him more fully alive than he ever was without it.

Together, they washed the body. When the boy looked up, Poe was weeping.

Two weeks after the funeral, the boy left the town with his mother. She smiled and laughed, flirting with the taxi driver as he loaded their bags into the trunk of the car she'd hired to take them to the train station.

"This is a new start for us," she said as the whistle blew. The train chugged slowly out of the station, and she squeezed his arm. Her touch repulsed him. She was standing next to him and he was taller now, tall enough to see the vein throbbing against the side of her chicken-like neck.

He felt his hands itch to circle it, to press against her windpipe until she stopped talking. They were passing a vacant lot, and he thought about what it would be like to hurl her from the train, leaving her broken body to rot in a bed of weeds and broken glass.

Chapter Seventeen

There was something depressing about being in a high school on a Friday after school was out. The last of the student cars rushed out of the parking lot as Ian and Kate arrived. Ian parked the Toyota next to a cluster of teachers' cars, all huddled together in one corner as if in defense against the student body.

They found Grace slouched against the wall outside of the principal's office. She affected a look of unconcern and cool, looking hip in her jeans and T-shirt while listening to her iPod with a fierce scowl on her face, but she kept picking at a spot on her jeans and Kate knew that the "who cares" attitude was just a pose.

"I don't like having my workday interrupted for a meeting to discuss your behavior," Ian said in greeting. Grace hunched her shoulders, but didn't respond.

"Why, Gracie?" Kate thought she'd try a gentler tone, but wasn't surprised when that didn't get an answer.

It wasn't the first time they'd been summoned to school to discuss their daughter's misbehavior, but it was a more recent phenomenon. As Kate watched

166
Rebecca Drake

Grace, she remembered an earlier version of her daughter, the elementary school student who'd proudly marched off to school each morning with a neatly arranged backpack, who'd been bursting with news every afternoon, and who'd been traumatized by getting any grades lower than As or Bs.

How fast kids changed. Last year, at the pricey private school where she'd been a scholarship student, multiple meetings had been called to discuss their daughter's "failure to thrive" in the "nurturing environment." It had been humiliating.

At Wickfield High School, things operated a little differently. For starters, there was no secretary to greet them with offers of coffee or tea, nor a tasteful outer office decked out in rich woods and expensive art. There was no hint of Ivy League at Wickfield High and no outer offices.

A broad, puffer fish of a man stood in the front hall wearing jeans and a T-shirt that seemed too young for his age, which was probably mid-fifties. He had close-cropped graying hair and a broad smile that was so smarmy that Kate exchanged looks with Ian.

"Mr. and Mrs. Corbin?" He stuck out a plump, surprisingly strong hand for them to shake. "I'm Harold Trowle. I thought we should meet alone first and then Grace could join us after we've talked."

Grace looked indifferent, and sank onto a bench along the wall as if she'd run a marathon instead of having spent two minutes in the company of her parents. Harold Trowle ushered Kate and Ian through his office, a small space crowded with laminate office furniture including floor-to-ceiling bookshelves overflowing with college catalogs, and into another room that he referred to as the "lounge." This was a large, open room that looked like it had been decorated to establish the guidance counselor's coolness factor with his teenage clientele.

Large beanbag chairs took up one corner. Kate couldn't imagine Harold Trowle settling into one of them. There was a motivational poster of sculls on the river next to a poster of the Ramones.

In the center of the room was a table that reminded Kate of a peanut. "This is where I like to dialogue," Harold said, making Ian wince. The guidance counselor straddled a plastic chair at the top of the peanut, his boots resting on either side of it, and offered Kate and Ian seats around the bottom. He opened a folder resting on the table in front of him.

"As I think we discussed on the phone, Grace has unexcused absences for"—he perused the file, tapping with one broad finger—"six days."

"Six?" Ian sounded aghast. "I thought it was only four. Why weren't we notified?"

"You were, Mr. Corbin."

"When? We hadn't heard from anyone here until I got a call two days ago."

"A letter should have been sent to your home."

"Did you receive a letter?" Ian looked at Kate, who shook her head. She couldn't remember a letter. "We didn't receive any letter."

"Let me see . . ." Mr. Trowle flipped through pages in his folder. "Yes, here it is. Letters were mailed on the tenth of September and the twenty-first."

Ian frowned. "I'm telling you we never got them."

Harold Trowle's mouth quirked in an indulgent smile. "In cases like this, we find that the student has often intercepted the mail."

Kate felt her cheeks flush, and saw that the color was high in Ian's face, too, but before either of them could respond, Harold Trowle filled the silence.

"As you'll see, her grades have slipped." He fiddled with the papers in the folder, extracted a sheet, and slid it across the table with one pudgy finger. Kate got to it first, and Ian immediately pulled his chair closer. It was a computer printout of Grace's classes and her current grades.

"She's getting a D in English?" Ian said. "How is that even possible?"

"If you don't attend class, then it's very easy," Mr. Trowle said. "English is an afternoon class and according to our records two of Grace's absences coincided with exams."

Kate skimmed over the grades once, then read the sheet again, more slowly, feeling shock give way to anger and anxiety. Their cheery straight As eighth-grader had metamorphosed into a surly, below-average tenth-grader. Grace currently had a C in Geometry, a C in Biology, C- in History and another D, this one in Spanish. "Her only decent grade is in Gym," she said.

Harold Trowle nodded. "I'm sure you understand why we're concerned."

Ian's laugh was short and harsh. "*You're* concerned?"

"I don't know why she's doing so poorly," Kate said to Harold Trowle. "She's very bright—you must have seen her test scores."

He held them up and waved them. "Yes, clearly this isn't her best work. Some students find the adjustment to high school very hard."

"She's had over a year to adjust," Ian said. "This has nothing to do with adjusting—it has to do with effort."

"She's new to the school." Kate knew even as she said it that she was making excuses for her daughter, and Ian pounced.

"So what? She was new last year, too, and every kid was new at that school. One of the best schools in the city, a far better education than I ever got, and what does she do with the opportunity?" It was a rhetorical question, but Harold Trowle looked as if he wanted to answer it. Ian didn't give him the chance. "Squandered. All that effort and money—completely squandered."

Kate felt the same anger, but now some of it was directed at Ian. Did he really blame Grace for all of this? "We know why her grades dropped last year. It was that creep."

She couldn't bear to say his name; it felt like dust in her mouth. Ian shifted his scowl from the grades to her face.

"That's been over for some time and look at this." He slapped the paper. "We made this move so she could have a fresh start and she's not doing any work."

Something occurred to Kate. "How is she getting off campus?"

Harold Trowle looked relieved at having Ian's diatribe interrupted. "What was that, Mrs. Corbin?"

"Grace takes the bus to school every day, so when she skips school, how is she getting off campus?"

Wickfield High School was outside of town; there was nothing within walking distance except some suburban homes. Was she just pretending to get on the bus every day? No, because either Kate or Ian had seen her off and sometimes, if everybody was running late, Ian had driven her himself.

Mr. Trowle sifted through the folder again with a slight frown of concentration. "Students are allowed cars on campus, so my guess is that she's leaving with a friend or friends who are also cutting class." His face lightened as he extracted yet another sheet of paper. "Here it is—we had one report of Grace being seen leaving campus in a brown car, but that's all the information we have. Sometimes teens act out because of things happening at home. Are there problems at home? Perhaps between the two of you?"

He folded his hands in front of him on the table, an unpleasantly eager look in his eyes. There was no ring on his left hand. It was at that moment that Kate decided she hated him.

"Things are fine at home," Ian said, though the stiffness of his voice betrayed that as untrue.

Kate added, "All families have problems," and wished she hadn't when Mr. Trowle nodded.

"Yes, yes, of course they do. However, we do find that students with a habit of skipping school have more trouble than most. I know that you recently moved. Perhaps she's going through a transition period?"

Was Grace really so unhappy? Kate thought of the conversations she'd tried to have about school and how Grace had blown them off. Everything was always "fine." She felt a pang of guilt—should she have tried harder, understood that what she'd assumed to be a hormonal teenager's surliness might be unhappiness?

Something the counselor said was niggling at her, though, some small, salient detail that was nevertheless important. What was it? He'd said that she was leaving campus in other friends' cars, that she'd been seen leaving campus . . .

"Mr. Trowle, did you say the car was brown?"

"Yes." He looked down at his notes. "A brown sedan."

Ian looked at Kate. "What?"

"She's seeing him again. He drives a brown Mercedes."

The color fled from Ian's face. "But we told her it was over. She promised us."

It was Kate's turn to laugh. "Yeah, and she gets on the bus every morning with the promise that she's going to school."

*   *   *

Grace had fallen asleep on the bench outside the administration offices. She looked younger somehow, more vulnerable curled up on her side with one cheek resting against her arm and her lips slightly parted. Ian shook her roughly awake.

"What?"

"Get up, right now." He grabbed her arm and Grace jerked away. Ian's lips thinned and he reached out to grab her again, but Kate blocked him.

"Ian, stop."

"Don't tell me to stop! She's been lying to us for weeks!"

"I know, but that isn't going to help—"

"Give me your cell phone!" Ian demanded holding out his hand to Grace. "Right now!"

"It's mine."

"Oh, no, it isn't. We pay the bill for that, it's ours."

Grace dug in her backpack with deliberate slowness. When she emerged with the phone, Ian yanked it from her hand. He flipped open the lid and began punching buttons. Kate knew he was trying to search the call history.

"We know you've been seeing Damien Rattle," she said.

Grace's face went pink, then white. "No, I haven't."

"Don't bother lying about it."

Ian said, "You've told enough lies." He snapped the phone shut. "So he's changed his number, right? That's why I'm not seeing it here? Very clever, but I'm going to find out what it is and see just how many calls you've made to that loser!"

"He's not a loser!" Grace's voice was similar in timbre to her father's and held his entire wrath. Her hands balled in fists. "People don't understand him."

Ian laughed, just as he had at Harold Trowle's comment. An ugly laugh, short and harsh. "Oh, I understand him all right."

"You don't even know him!"

"We know him well enough to know that we don't want you seeing him," Kate said.

"But I love him!"

"You're not old enough to love anybody," Kate said, but she couldn't summon the anger of the other two. Instead, she felt a sick twist in her gut. The prayers of a desperate mother veered between Please let her not be sexually active and Please let them be using condoms. It shocked her to even be having these thoughts. Like most things in parenting, it came before you were ready, before you'd adjusted to the idea that your child would walk, would bike, would run away from you with every means at their disposal.

"I think we all need to take a breath," Mr. Trowle said. He stood outside the circle just a little, his fleshy face looking from Ian to Grace and back again. "Let's try to understand Grace's perspective."

"She doesn't get a perspective. Not on this." Ian's face was red, his fingers tapping against his side in a way that suggested he itched to put them on Grace. Kate looked from him to Harold Trowle, and saw an expression of intensity and anxiety in the counselor's face that suggested someone witnessing child abuse.

Except that Grace wasn't abused, far from it. They'd given her all the love and nurturing any two parents could provide. Until a year ago, Kate had held onto the illusion that if you fed and clothed your children and put them in safe schools and provided them with every opportunity that you could afford, that you'd keep your child safe from the Damien Rattles of the world.

"Let's all just take a deep breath and we can go back inside to talk." Harold Trowle's smarmy smile was in place, but the way he was fiddling with the cell phone attached to his belt made Kate wonder if he had school security on speed dial.

"Ian, he thinks you're going to hurt someone," Kate muttered, tugging on her husband's arm.

Ian blinked, seemed to come out of his pater familias mode and really see the others. Kate linked her right arm through his and then her left through Grace's. She looked at Harold Trowle with a bright, fake smile of her own.

"Yes, let's do that."

A further thirty minutes of humiliation followed, during which Harold Trowle laid out the school policy. Wickfield High would not suspend Grace, not this time, but she would have to serve Saturday detentions for the number of days she'd skipped, during which time she'd make up the class work she'd missed.

Grace barely communicated, giving one-word answers to the questions put to her by Harold Trowle, who dug deeper and deeper into his arsenal of teenage jargon and pop psychology pablum in a futile attempt to reach her. "You've got to give a little to get a lot, are you down with that?" and, "Honoring your feelings is fly, but parents are people, too."

It was hard to sit through, and at the end Kate wasn't sure who she was more annoyed with, her daughter or the counselor. Ian waited until they were all in the car to pronounce sentence, predictably heavy-handedly.

"You're grounded. No cell, no computer. It's school and home for you. Oh, and your lessons with Dr. Beetleman of course."

Hunched over in the backseat, Grace might have

been made of stone. She stared out the window and
didn't reply. Equally predictably, this enraged her father.

"Are you listening to me?"

"I'm not deaf."

"Don't get smart with me, young lady. You really
don't want to push me right now."

No response, but Kate saw the eye roll. She had a
sudden desire to leave them both to fight it out, tired of
listening to their endless arguing. It was one thing to
understand that the reason they butted heads was because they were so alike, but it was quite another to
have to listen to it.

It wasn't that she disagreed with Ian. Something had
to be done. Grace was in trouble and they had to act.
But they'd acted this way almost a year ago and what
had it gotten them? They'd thought that by moving to
Wickfield they could sever the relationship between
Grace and Damien Rattle, but it hadn't worked. And he
was bad news, of that she was convinced.

She'd had his number within minutes of that very first
meeting, seeing that slouching, indolent overgrown boy,
with his expensive car and bad manners, touching her
child. She knew his type, every woman had met at least
one, the bad boy who appealed to some people because
he was dangerous, to others because he was different.

Had they kept Grace too sheltered? Kate thought she
and Ian had been giving their daughter a full but safe
childhood. It had seemed especially important, since they
lived in a huge metropolis, to protect her as much as
possible from the ugliness of life. They'd limited TV viewing, kept careful tabs on her friends and their families,
and placed a premium on art and education so that she
would learn early what to value.

And it had worked. For years it had worked. Grace

had immersed herself in her music and seemed content
moving within the bubble of home, school, and music
lessons. The bubble burst when she met Damien Rattle.

And no amount of telling Grace that this college
dropout was not worthy of her had made a difference.
She'd been hit by first love and hit hard, and maybe
Kate and Ian's desire to protect her had done more
than they intended and kept from her the shrewd ability to recognize fakes.

"After your grounding's over, you can see Damien,"
she said.

"What?" Ian and Grace spoke simultaneously, male
and female versions of the same voice.

"But," Kate said loudly to be heard over them, "and
this is a big but, Grace, you can only see him at our
house."

"I don't want that kid setting foot in our house!"

"He doesn't want to come to our house!"

"Forbidding her to see him hasn't worked," she said
to Ian, and then turned to look at Grace. "You are
much younger than he is, Grace. If he really cares about
you, he'll respect your parents' rules for you. We're not
comfortable with you seeing a boy that age without one
of us being present."

"I'm not comfortable with her seeing that boy at all!"
Ian protested.

"Damien won't agree to that! It's like you don't trust
him!"

"We don't," Kate said.

They'd turned onto their street; home in record
time thanks to Ian's heavy foot on the accelerator. The
Toyota purred, the only one to sound contented, as
they pulled in the driveway.

"How long?" Grace asked as they walked in the house.

"How long what?"

"How long am I grounded?"

"I'm not setting a time," Ian said. "We'll start with a month—"

"A month!"

"—and go from there."

"That's crap!"

"No, Grace, that's called natural consequences! You lied to us, you skipped school, you continued to see a boy we've forbidden you to see—what did you think was going to happen?"

"At least Mom's going to let me see him!"

"At our house," Kate repeated. "Only at our house, only with us present."

"I don't have to put up with this crap!" Grace shouted.

"Oh, yes, you do," Ian said. "As long as you live under our roof you'll follow our rules."

"I'll find somewhere else to live!"

"Until that happens you're grounded."

Angry tears swam in Grace's eyes. "I hate you!" She ran up the stairs, and the slam of her bedroom door echoed through the house.

"Well, that was a fun day," Kate said. "I don't know about you, but I could really use something to drink."

She headed into the kitchen with Ian on her heels. "I can't believe you said that. What the hell were you thinking, suggesting that she see that boy again?"

"It didn't work forbidding her to see him, she did it anyway."

"So you reward that deception by giving her exactly what she wants?"

"It's not exactly what she wants—she has to see him here."

"Do you think you might have consulted me before announcing that?"

Kate slammed the cupboard door. "Yeah, Ian, apparently as much as it occurred to you to consult me about grounding her."

"C'mon, it's not the same thing at all."

"It's not working, Ian. All the threats and punishment are not getting us anywhere."

"It's not surprising, given that you've hardly been present the last year."

Kate choked on her drink. She coughed and set it down, surprised to see that her hands trembled. "What does that mean?"

"Do the math, Kate. When did Grace start having trouble? Right after you were attacked."

Kate's head reeled. Was it really true? She tried to remember when they'd met Damien, what month had that been? What filled her mind instead was the memory of that afternoon, the shock of someone else in her studio, the sound of his voice, the paint dripping onto the floor, the feel of the table hard against her back. She pushed it away.

"And you're blaming me for that?"

"Not for the attack. Of course not."

Kate picked up on what he wasn't saying. "But for Grace? You blame me for her troubles?"

"I'm just saying that if you'd been more present this probably wouldn't have happened."

Dinner was pizza, grabbed individually by unspoken consent. Kate took hers out to her studio, carefully locking herself in like she always did, to sit and stare at the canvas she'd begun. At least it was beginning to work. Lily Slocum's face stared out at her, the only thing she'd fleshed out, the rest of her body and the water rushing about that body outlined in pale charcoal. She chewed her single slice without tasting it, and set it aside without finishing. She perched on a stool, paintbrush clutched in hands held tight in her lap. It wasn't until she felt something wet on her hands that she realized she was crying.

She dreamed she was caught in the river, her pale body being sucked into the dark water's murky depths. Large hands held her down as she struggled to escape. "It's your fault," the owner of the hands said, and she looked up to see Ian above her. He pressed a hand against her head and she was going down, down into the bottom, she couldn't breathe.

She woke in a sweat, her head pressed against the headboard. Ian, as usual, slept on peacefully beside her. She left him breathing deeply on his side of the bed and headed down to the kitchen.

When she was younger, in those few years before she'd met Ian, when she'd shared a small apartment in Brooklyn, sleepless nights had meant more time in her studio. She'd enjoyed walking the streets of New York at night, convinced in her naïveté that she could outrun anyone who gave her trouble, or knee a man in the groin like she'd learned in a college self-defense course. It had never occurred to her that she could be surprised, that a man could so easily overpower her. She'd been invincible in the way that only the young can be invincible.

Later, when she and Ian were settled in their apartment in Manhattan, she'd had the comfort of his body next to hers when she woke up. Sometimes, she snuggled against him and fell back into more pleasant dreams. If sleep still evaded her, she'd take out a sketch pad she kept in a bedside drawer and make drawings until her body relaxed and she drifted off. Sometimes, Ian would wake while she was sketching and would smile sleepily

at her. Sometimes, they'd make love, another nice dis-
traction, his sleep-warm body wrapping around hers,
his skin like a cocoon, slipping into hers with a comforting familiarity.

She took milk out of the refrigerator and poured it
in a saucepan along with a dash of rum. It wasn't good
to drink alone. It was an especially bad habit for an
artist to find solace in alcohol. Kate decided the picture
of Ian and Grace on the fridge counted as company,
and poured a second shot into the saucepan.

Alone at the kitchen table with her spiked milk, she
gave way to the worst of her thoughts, that Grace would
end up pregnant or infected from this creep and that
she and Ian were imploding, their relationship heading
into trouble that she couldn't have anticipated even a
year ago.

It occurred to her that she was probably clinically depressed, and that made her remember her promise to
Ian that she'd find another therapist. The thought of
suffering through yet another meeting with an overly
solicitous person asking, "What do you think of that?"
made her take a drink straight from the bottle of rum.

A sudden flash of yellow light skated across the
breakfast nook, startling her. Kate glanced out the window and saw Terrence Simnic's boxy brown sedan
pulling into the driveway. She ducked down, afraid he'd
see her in the glare of the headlights.

She watched through a gap in the curtains. When the
lights turned out it was hard to see, but she distinctly
heard the sound of a car door slamming and then an
echoing slam a few seconds later. There was someone with Terrence and this late at night? Keeping low,
Kate switched off the small overhead light framing the
table where she sat and pressed her face close against
the window.

It was definitely Terrence, she recognized his hulking profile even in the dark, but it looked like someone shorter was standing just in front of him. She heard footsteps crunching across the driveway, and then silence as the shadows moved up the walk and onto his porch. The jelly-jar porch light was on over the door. The shadows stepped into it. A young woman stood in front of Terrence Simnic, long brown hair pulled back in a ponytail. Kate caught a glimpse of a pale face, and then the girl was stepping inside the house, Terrence Simnic's hand on her shoulder.

Kate's heartbeat rushed like water in her ears. She stood up, pressing her hands against the glass, and watched Terrence Simnic step into the house after the girl. Seconds later, the porch light went out.

"God, oh, God, oh, God," Kate moaned, stepping back from the window. What should she do? Call the cops. She forgot the chair in her way, and knocked it over. It fell backward with a loud thud. Kate scrambled over it and ran for the phone. Only it wasn't in its cradle. Jesus Christ, why was she the only person in the house who ever remembered to put the portable phone back in its cradle? If she pushed the seek button, it would ring on every phone in the house.

She searched the counter blindly with her hands, frantic to find it. The kitchen lights suddenly went on and she screamed.

"Jesus, Kate!" Ian stood in the doorway, hand pressed to his chest. "What the hell are you doing?"

"I need the phone!"

She saw it resting on top of the fridge next to him. Racing over, she reached up to grab it, but he was taller and his hand closed on it first. "It's one o'clock in the morning, you can't call anybody now."

"He's got a girl in there—I've got to call the cops." She grabbed for the phone, but Ian held it out of reach.

"Who has what? Settle down, Kate, you're hysterical!"

"I'm not hysterical, I'm trying to save someone's life. Just give me the damn phone!"

Ian handed it over. "Okay, okay, but just tell me what's happening."

"Just give me a minute." Kate punched 911. The operator sounded less than alert.

"911. What's your emergency?"

"My neighbor has a girl in his house, I'm sure he's going to hurt her, you've got to stop him."

"Ma'am. Please slow down, I can't understand you. You say your neighbor has a girl in his house?"

Kate swallowed, tried to slow down her speech. It didn't help that Ian was staring at her like she'd suddenly sprouted three heads.

"My name is Kate Corbin. I live at 43 Morris Lane. I suspect the man next door, number 45, is involved in the disappearance of Lily Slocum and Elizabeth Hirsh. I've spoken to the police hotline about him—"

"You have?" Ian sounded shocked.

"—it should be on record. I've just seen him take a young woman into his house and I'm afraid—"

"All right, ma'am, I've got a squad car on the way. Please stay in your house. Do not attempt to confront your neighbor—what's his name?"

"Terrence Simnic."

"Okay, I've got it. Don't attempt to confront Mr. Simnic yourself. Stay in your house, do you understand?"

"Yes, yes, I understand."

"The officers should be there in a few minutes. If you don't see a squad car in ten minutes, call back."

"Ten minutes? He could kill her in that time!"

"I understand, Ms. Corbin, but they're on their way."

Kate hung up the phone. Ian was staring at her with his mouth open. "What the hell is going on?"

She explained as quickly as she could. Ian's look of confusion gave way to frustration. "But Kate," he said when she was done speaking, "you have no real evidence that he's done anything wrong."

"It all adds up, Ian. Just look at the total picture."

"I am looking at the total picture. Are you?"

"What's that supposed to mean?"

"It means that there could be perfectly logical explanations for all the supposedly strange things you've seen."

"Sure, you can explain one, maybe two, but this many things together? It just doesn't make sense, Ian."

A squad car came screaming down the street and pulled into the driveway, lights flashing.

Ian shut off the kitchen lights and they got to the window in time to see two cops emerge and march up Terrence Simnic's walk to his porch. Even through the window Kate could hear the rap on her neighbor's door. One of the cops stood slightly behind the other, hand resting on the gun at his side.

Seconds seemed to drag by. The cop rapped for the third time. He turned to look back at his partner and Kate saw boredom on his features. It seemed incongruous for him to look so unconcerned when she was so tense. As if in response to her thoughts, he suddenly straightened up and his partner shifted, both of them with hands on their weapons.

"Police! Open up!"

Ian flinched beside her and Kate's panted breaths steamed the window. They couldn't see the door open, but it must have, for the cop was talking to someone. Then both he and his partner stepped into the house.

"Oh, my God, what if he ambushes them!"

"This isn't the movies, Kate," Ian said, but he sounded just as worried as she did.

Minutes went by with nothing happening. In unspoken agreement, Ian and Kate sank into chairs next to the glass.

"What's taking them so long?" Kate muttered, staring at the empty porch. What if he was holding the cops hostage?

"They've got to question him. Maybe they're searching the house. How old was the girl?"

"I don't know. I didn't get a really good look at her face."

More than ten minutes passed before sudden movement at the porch brought Kate out of her chair. Ian stood behind her. "What's happening?"

"Ssh, they're coming out."

First one officer, then the other stepped back onto the porch. But what was this? They were laughing? Terrence Simnic stepped out on the porch after them and he was smiling. Then they shook his hand.

"What the hell? Where is she? What's going on?" Kate couldn't believe what she was seeing, but the cops were crossing the porch, heading down the walk toward the squad car.

She pushed past Ian and ran for the front door. They were getting in the car when she came running toward them.

"Officers, please wait!" They stopped, and both of them had hands on their guns this time.

One of them held out a hand. "Stop!"

Kate stopped in her tracks. "I'm the one who called in the complaint."

"Okay, ma'am, we'll come to you." They stepped away from the car and walked toward her. "What's going on, ma'am?"

"I'm the one who called. I don't understand—why haven't you arrested him?"

The cops exchanged looks. "What should we arrest him for?"

"Didn't the 911 operator tell you why I called? He's got a girl in the house! She has brown hair pulled back in a ponytail—"

"Ma'am, there's no one there but Terrence Simnic."

"No one else?" Ian's voice startled Kate. She turned to see him standing behind her. He'd thought to put a coat on over his pajamas. She was suddenly aware that she was wearing nothing but a thin cotton nightgown. In the same moment, the cold registered. Her bare feet felt frozen to the concrete walk. Ian had shoes on.

"That's right. He had someone visiting but she's gone home."

Kate crossed her arms over her chest, blocking herself. "How do you know she's gone?"

"He told us so and we looked around."

"Did you check the basement?"

The two exchanged looks again. The older officer, a hawk-faced man with tired eyes, said, "Ma'am, Mr. Simnic was in bed when we arrived. I think you've let your imagination get the best of you."

"But I saw him bring a girl into his house! I saw her! And he's in his basement at three in the morning. Did you look down there? He had women's clothing—I saw him with women's clothing. Explain that." Kate stopped as Ian's hand came to rest on her shoulder, all at once aware that she was babbling.

"Thank you for your time, Officers," Ian said. "I'm sorry we brought you out for nothing."

"No problem. Better safe than sorry, right, ma'am?" The older officer smiled at Kate, and she felt suddenly warm despite the cold.

When they were back inside, Ian stared at her with concern. "I can't believe you just called the cops on our neighbor."

"He's a killer. He might have them fooled, but he's not fooling me." She locked the door and then checked it twice.

"Just because someone's a little eccentric doesn't make them a killer."

"There are too many things connecting him—"

"Except anything tangible."

"How do they know that no one is in his house if they didn't search it? I mean really search it. Why are they relying on his say-so?"

"Maybe because he looks and sounds perfectly reasonable while you're standing out there half-dressed making a fool of yourself in front of the whole neighborhood."

"I saw her, Ian." Kate gestured at her eyes. "Are you going to accuse me of being blind now, too?"

"I'm not accusing you of anything. You're the only one doing the accusing. Jesus, Kate, you really need some help. I hope you'll stop being stubborn and actually get it."

When he went back to bed, she stayed at the kitchen table pretending to sip her milk. It was cold.

Chapter Eighteen

The biweekly dean's meeting with department heads was the least favorite part of Ian's job. When he'd begun in academia years ago, he'd been slow to understand that discussing where the money came from and where it went was an integral part of university life, albeit a despised one. Time had taught him to accept that every meeting would eventually come down to a discussion of funding, but that didn't mean he had to like it.

One of the few positives was that Bethany Forrester, as head of the drama department, always attended the Monday afternoon meeting, and without being conscious of it, Ian began anticipating seeing her. Once he did become conscious of it, he'd reassured himself that his desire to see her was strictly professional. She was a good colleague. Truly collegial, as interested in other people's opinions as well as her own, and without too many of her own personal interests to trumpet. She was easy to work with and a genuine asset.

She was also sexy as hell. There, he'd admitted it to himself. Ian shifted in his seat and tried not to notice the way she was touching the funding proposal, the tips of her fingers tapping lightly against the edge of the paper and straying once in a while to spin the woven silver bracelet on her other wrist. She always wore that bracelet. Was it a special gift from someone?

He found himself unaccountably jealous. It wasn't his business if she was dating someone, but hadn't she said that she had yet to meet anybody worthy of collaborating with on that level?

Focus, Ian, focus. He glanced back down at page four of the report. These were numbers from Jerry Virgoli, head of the visual arts department, who was expounding on them as if everybody didn't have that sheet in front of them. It's a top-tier university, Jerry, the faculty can add and subtract. God, but the man was boring.

Not that Ian could ever express that. Jerry was still sensitive as hell about being passed over for promotion in favor of Ian. It was Ian's unspoken obligation to make him feel like a team player and not the jilted professor. Remembering that, he nodded at some point Jerry was making, trying to look as if he truly cared.

Bethany Forrester yawned discreetly, hiding it behind her hand, and Ian caught her eye across the table. He raised his eyebrows in mock disapproval and she flashed him a quick, guilty smile.

The rush of pleasure he got from such a small gesture surprised him. It was like being back in high school and having the popular girl deign to say hi to him. The last time he'd felt pleasure like this had been in those early days with Kate.

Thinking of Kate reminded him of the incident with the police, and the pleasure he felt was replaced by guilt. Clearly, she was worse off than he'd thought if she'd taken to calling the police on their neighbors. He hadn't been able to look Terrence Simnic in the eye when he saw him on Monday morning.

It was paranoia, obviously fueled by what had happened to her, but he didn't know what to do about it except keep encouraging her to get back into therapy. He'd gone so far as to print out a list of local psychologists that he thought sounded qualified, but he couldn't call them for her.

She seemed insulted whenever he suggested the idea, as if he was saying that getting therapy was tantamount to admitting she was crazy. At this point he didn't care. What if she called the police on someone else and he wasn't there?

"Dean Corbin?"

Jerry Virgoli had finished speaking and sat looking at Ian with an expectant air. It reminded him of a child expecting a pat on the head, but the rest of the faculty members at the long table were watching him, waiting for his wisdom. Ian stifled a sigh.

The curtains were drawn in Terrence Simnic's house. Kate had been watching on and off since Friday night and they'd never been pulled back open. On Saturday night, she'd waited until Ian was asleep before tiptoeing down the steps to look out the side window and verify that the basement lights were on again.

There was no sign of the girl. She was probably tied up in the basement if she was still alive, but no amount of discussing this possibility with Ian had gotten him to believe it.

"This is paranoia, Kate," he'd said when he caught her spying through the kitchen windows on Sunday. "You heard what the police said. If there is any truth in what you say, they would have figured it out by now." A

few hours later, he'd handed her a list of local therapists
culled from the Internet.

"Just call them," he said, his entreaty so heartfelt that
she didn't refuse outright. It was Monday afternoon
and so far she hadn't called one name on the list.

Kate looked away from the window and back to her
easel. The body was fully formed now, a curve of alabaster white trapped in the ribbon of dark water. She
looked from the canvas to the palette balanced in her
left hand, and took another daub of near white and applied it to the female form's left leg. The hair had metamorphosed, transforming from Lily Slocum's blond locks
into something darker, a coffee shade that merged in
and above the dark water swirling around it.

Something was different in the face, too, since she'd
tinkered with it. Was it even Lily Slocum anymore? With
the hair, it looked more like the photo she'd seen in the
paper of the other girl, Elizabeth Hirsch. Was her body,
even now, resting in muddy water?

The slap of a door closing startled her. Kate's head
turned automatically from the canvas to the window, and
she saw Terrence Simnic getting into the dusty white
van.

He was leaving, finally leaving. She'd been waiting
for this for hours. Dumping the palette on the small
table next to the easel, she slipped out of her paint-
daubed shirt and dug in her jeans pocket for the studio
key. It was always there against her. In her old studio,
she'd hung her keys just inside the door on a metal
hook another artist had fashioned from scrap iron into
the shape of a mermaid. The friends who'd cleared her
studio had left it behind, but it didn't matter. She didn't
use a hook anymore. She couldn't feel safe without the
keys physically on her.

She'd thought a lot about the possibilities and only

one had come to mind—she had to get in that house. To that end, she'd spent several fruitful hours researching breaking-and-entering on the Internet. It was true that anything could be found online.

She slipped on her jacket and checked the small pack of tools she'd assembled earlier and tucked in one zippered pocket. Screwdriver, flashlight, old credit card, and a pair of gloves. She put on the gloves and waited an extra five minutes to make sure that Terrence Simnic wasn't just making a quick trip to the store and back, and then she headed out of the studio, locking the door behind her.

She approached the back of his house slowly, carrying a piece of junk mail addressed to Simnic that had come to their house by mistake. If anyone saw her, it would look as if she was just being neighborly.

In case anyone was watching, she knocked on the door first, turning the knob surreptitiously with her gloved hand as she did so. It was locked. Shielding it with the mail, she inserted the screwdriver into the lock and attempted to bump it, following the instructions she'd gotten online. It didn't work. It didn't work the second time either, or the third.

She thought that things like this always looked easier on TV, and then that she would have made a very bad thief. Enough of the screwdriver. She pulled out the credit card and attempted to slip it in the jamb under the lock. Only it wouldn't fit because the door was old and there were multiple layers of paint holding it tight against the frame. All she managed to do was scrape off some flakes of brown paint.

When she'd planned this, Kate had pictured the door giving easily. She hadn't pictured trying for five minutes without a result and feeling every one of those three hundred seconds tick by. The handle grew slippery in

her grasp and a bead of sweat trickled down her forehead and stung her left eye.

It wasn't going to work. She conceded that after one
final try with the screwdriver, and felt, mixed up with
the panicky adrenaline rush, a tiny sense of relief.
She'd tried; she could honestly say that she'd tried.

As she stepped down the back steps, she suddenly
noticed the storm door. It was one of the old tornado
affairs, angled metal doors that led into the cellar of the
house. Brown paint was flaking off them and they
looked like they hadn't been opened in years. Probably
rusted shut. Kate glanced around, saw no one watching,
and tugged quickly on a handle. To her surprise, the
door actually lifted, groaning as it opened to reveal
dusty cement steps leading into the dark chasm of the
cellar.

She really, really didn't want to go in through the cellar. But what if the girl was being held in there? Kate
bounced lightly from one sneakered foot to the other
and then pulled the flashlight from her pocket. With
one last look around, she opened the door all the way,
jumping as it fell back with a bang. A dog barked in the
distance. She swallowed hard and took the first step
down.

A spiderweb caught her in the face as she reached
the third step, and Kate swung her arms madly, brushing away sticky, invisible threads. No one had been this
way in a long time. She held the flashlight in front of
her with her left hand, keeping the right hand free to
sweep the air in front of her. At the bottom of the steps,
her free hand hit wood. Another door. She pushed
against it, and it easily gave way.

"Hello?" Kate's voice seemed to echo back at her,
and she swept the flashlight up from the steps to see a
vast expanse of unfinished basement spread out before

her. The faint light shining through the grimy-looking glass block windows cast shadows over the space, so it looked like shades of charcoal instead of unremitting black. It smelled of dust and mildew and, surprisingly, bleach and some other perfume over it. Laundry detergent. Kate's flashlight revealed an old-fashioned double laundry tub standing between a washer and dryer on the far side of the room. A clothes rack stood beside the dryer, lined neatly with what looked like men's socks and underwear.

Something gurgled to her left and Kate jumped, swinging the flashlight in that direction. It was just a water heater. The big dark lump next to it was an old-fashioned boiler. Something gleamed, and she swung the light back a pace to reveal a shelf filled with rows of dust-covered but neatly labeled canning jars. Tomatoes. Pickles. Beets. They all had their years marked, and the latest were already five years old.

Nobody was down there as far as she could see. There was a hose rolled in a corner and a patch of damp near the drain on the floor. The smell of bleach was stronger there. Had he already killed the girl and cleaned up? Her chest ached from shallow breathing.

Something drew her eye up, and she saw an iron hook screwed tight into a wooden joist from the floor above. The light bounced as her hand trembled. "Sweet Jesus." The words came to her instinctively, though she couldn't remember saying them before. It was something her mother used to say, a prayer as much as an exclamation of shock.

She could almost see a body suspended from here. Was this where he'd killed her? The papers hadn't said how she died, just that her body had been found.

Her light caught a glimpse of a sharp-toothed saw through the gloom. Kate moved toward it, and saw other tools hanging in marked spaces on a Peg-Board running high against a wall. She bumped into a stool she hadn't seen, and its metal legs rasped against the cement floor. Steadying it with her hand, she brought the flashlight waist level and moved its beam across the rough surface of a tool-scarred workbench. An eyeless doll's head grinned at her from the center of the table-top.

Kate suppressed a scream, swallowing it down along with the bile that rose in her throat. For a moment she'd thought it was a real skull, and the relief of it not being one made her legs weak. She swallowed again, steadying herself against the stool before moving the light along the low shelf that ran along the back of the bench behind the head. Rows of little jars, baby-food jars, filled with tiny nails and wire and something blue, green, and glittering that turned out to be dolls' eyes.

So Terrence did work on his dolls down here, just as she'd envisioned. Was that all he worked on? She searched the bench for something more, for evidence that he was working on humans, too. She thought she'd find photography equipment or something belonging to one of the girls, but there was nothing.

In a cupboard near the workbench, she found a cardboard box labeled simply HAIR, but that proved to be synthetic, doll-sized wigs, not human hair.

She left the basement, went upstairs, switching off the flashlight and stowing it in her pocket as she entered a kitchen that smelled faintly of tuna and sour milk from two cracked saucers left on a faded linoleum floor. Terrence's cat was nowhere in sight today. Everything was in order. A dishcloth folded neatly in half was drying over the handle of the kitchen faucet, and a single mug and a bowl were in the dish drainer along with a teaspoon. An old-fashioned clock ticked away above the gas stove; otherwise, there was no noise in the room. There was no sign of anyone either, and no sign that anyone other than Terrence had been here, but then she found the robe.

The sight of it hanging on the back of the kitchen door made Kate's rapid breath catch in her throat. It couldn't belong to Terrence. A woman's robe, white cotton, with lace at the cuffs and collar. Kate's stomach rose again. He was neat, the house so clearly showed that, but he'd forgotten to hide this. She ran gloved hands through the pockets, but they were empty.

The find galvanized her. She moved through the dining room with its curio cabinets stuffed with dolls and into the gloomy front hall, barely pausing to look in the living room with its dark upholstered furniture trapped in time with crocheted antimacassars, and then up the creaking wooden stairs to the second floor. It was even gloomier up there.

"Hello?" she called, though her voice was faint and got swallowed up down the long, dim hall. The walls seemed compressed, but maybe that was the wallpaper with its rows of vertical blue stripes. Prisonlike, with rooms for cells opening on the right and the left, but every room had a closed door. She pictured Terrence carefully closing each one. It seemed that Terrence had a bit of an OCD problem.

Thinking that helped her relax enough to open the door to the right without bracing for some horrific scene.

It was empty. A large painted metal bed covered with a faded chenille spread stood sandwiched between lilac nightstands holding clear acrylic lamps with dusty lilac shades. A matching lilac bureau sat against the opposite wall, a large chip out of a corner.

Something about the bed looked unoccupied and

when Kate pulled back a corner of the white chenille, there were no sheets but a stained mattress underneath. It was depressing.

The bedroom opposite was much smaller and obviously being used, but it was a child's space. Kate looked around, confused. The twin bed had obviously been slept in; while it was neatly made, the faded blue comforter had a slightly rumpled look and there was an indentation in the pillow.

She realized that this must have been Terrence's room, still was Terrence's room, though he was a grown man, closer to fifty than the five-year-old for whom it might have been decorated. The walls were painted baby blue, and a border of matching blue and white sailboats floated around the top of the wall. There were knotted ropes tying back curtains faded from the sun. An equally faded pillow with a stained anchor embroidered on it lay on the windowsill.

A desk in the same dark wood as the bed stood against another wall. There were books in its top slot— Tom Swift, the Hardy Boys, a paperback compendium of true-crime stories. The last tickled the hair on the back of her neck.

A piece of pale blue stationery covered with large, looping cursive lay on the surface of the desk. It was addressed to a local realty company. She read, "Dear Sir, Thank you for your inquiry, but at this time I have no desire to sell the house."

The room was fetid and hot from having a full-sized radiator cranking out heat in such a small space. The old windows were tightly shut, the shades drawn. Through the half-open closet door she could see the sheen on Terrence's polyester-blend easy-care shirts.

It was at once pathetic and grotesque, and suddenly it was too much. Kate backed out the door and pulled it shut, breathing hard. She had to resist the urge to run, screaming, from the house. Only the knowledge of that robe, and of the girl, and of the way his hand had rested on the girl's shoulder, kept her going.

She looked at two other bedrooms, but there was nothing in them. No girl, no weapons, no links to the other two young women who had vanished on the streets of what was supposed to be such a safe town.

"Where are they, Terrence?" she muttered under her breath as she checked a linen closet with neatly folded yet fraying bath towels. Like everything in the house, it was both tidy and caught in a time warp. Terrence was caught in a time warp, a case of arrested development. She wondered just how long ago his mother had died, and then she remembered Margaret's comment about finding his mother, à la *Psycho*, somewhere in the house.

When she glanced at her watch, Kate was shocked to see that she'd been in the house for almost an hour. Terrence could come home soon. Did he eat his lunch at the store or come back here? She could picture him coming back and eating the same lunch his mother had always made him, a tuna sandwich perhaps, sitting alone at the kitchen table, his massive hands wrapped around plain white bread.

She hurriedly opened the next door, which was a bathroom with period fixtures and the original tile floor. A fraying green hand towel hung on the rack next to an old-fashioned sink. There was only one door after this, sitting facing out at the end of the hall. She was about to head there when something on the bathroom floor caught her eye. As she stooped to pick it up, Kate heard a door open downstairs.

Chapter Nineteen

Time stopped. Kate held her breath. The door closed. There were footsteps crossing the floor.

Shit, he was back. She was stuck, on the second floor, alone. She was afraid to walk back into the hallway. There was nowhere else to go but in the tub, hidden behind the shower curtain. It wasn't a safe place to hide. She climbed in anyway, crouching down on the cold, stained porcelain with the white plastic curtain damp against her side. She fished the flashlight quietly out of her pocket. It wasn't much of a weapon, but it was all she had.

She was scared in a way that she hadn't been scared since the moment in her studio when she realized she wasn't alone. Her breath came in shallow bursts and she knew that wasn't helping, could hear the therapist's voice in her head explaining why it was important to breathe deeply so she wouldn't hyperventilate, but she couldn't.

There was no sound for a moment except her own breathing, and then she heard the thud of footsteps, but they were still downstairs. Kate glanced down at what she clutched in her other hand. It was a ponytail elastic, bright pink, something a girl or a young woman would wear, not an older woman and certainly not a man. Here was something tangible, like the robe.

Only it didn't make a damn bit of difference because the footsteps were closer now and then she heard the creak of the stairs. They were coming up, higher and higher. And then she could hear them coming down the hall, thud, thud, thud, the slow, heavy tread that she knew was Terrence Simnic's. The flashlight shook in her hands. The footsteps were louder, closer.

They stopped. Silence in which she heard the muffled gurgle of water in old pipes and farther off, through the old single-pane windows, the distant whine of a leaf blower.

A floorboard squeaked under the weight of heavy shoes. He was outside the door. Afraid of crying out, Kate bit her lip so hard that she tasted the metallic bite of blood. Was he looking into the room? Could he sense her through the shower curtain? Just as she was sure he would enter the room, there was a muffled, high-pitched cry for help.

The footsteps started again, past the bathroom, and then Kate heard the sound of a door opening, the last door, the one she hadn't opened yet, and there were muffled voices, and then very clearly Terrence's voice rose. "Stay there, Beth."

Beth. Elizabeth. It was Elizabeth Hirsh. He had Elizabeth Hirsh in his spare room. She had to get help, had to get the police. Kate scrambled up and out of the tub, shaking so hard that she banged the flashlight against the side. It reverberated loudly with all that tile. Kate froze for a split second. He must have heard the noise. She thought she heard his footsteps again.

Kate burst through the bathroom door, catching a glimpse of Terrence Simnic in the hall just beyond her.

"Stop!" His voice was a guttural roar.

She flew back down the hall toward the stairs, hearing his slower feet behind her. Down the steps, using the banister to jump the rest of them, skidding on the carpet in the front hall, and coming to the front door just as he thundered down the steps.

She turned the knob and pulled at the door, but it wouldn't budge. The door was stuck. She could hear him coming, his breathing loud and wet.

Her hands slipped on the knob. Keening, she twisted again, tugging with all her might. Why wouldn't it open?

A hand fell on her shoulder and she screamed. The door gave way and she jerked free of his grasp, bolting onto the porch just as a squad car, siren blaring, came screaming into the driveway.

"She's in a room upstairs!" she called to the cops who emerged, guns drawn.

"Hands in the air!"

"What?"

"Hands in the air! Now!"

The other officer unclipped a radio from his belt and called for backup. Kate shot her hands in the air. Terrence Simnic was doing the same close by, she could hear his snuffled breathing and see the edge of him in her peripheral vision.

"I'm the home owner," he said. "I'm the one who made the call. She broke in my house."

The officers approached and patted her down. Then they pulled her arms down behind her and cuffed her.

"This is a mistake," Kate said. "He's got Elizabeth Hirsh in an upstairs room. Stop bothering with this and go find her!"

"Ma'am, you need to cooperate with us," the younger cop said. They led her to the squad car just as another car pulled in behind the first. The officers who stepped out of this one looked like the two who'd responded the other night. They conferred in low voices with the police officer who'd cuffed her, all three of them turning to stare at her as she took a seat in the back of the first cruiser.

Another officer had Terrence Simnic in cuffs. He was red in the face and talking loudly. She caught the words "pattern of harassment."

They came out a few minutes later, and she caught a glimpse of a small dark head. She was hauled back out of the squad car by the young cop, his tendons tight on his scrawny neck. He smelled like cheap aftershave.

"Is this the female you saw?" the older officer, the one who'd responded two nights ago, said to Kate.

"Yes," Kate said, "I think so." And then the officer leading the trembling girl brought her closer and Kate could see that she wasn't a girl at all, just a short, slightly stoop-shouldered woman in her thirties with Down syndrome. She looked childlike, with dark hair pulled back in a ponytail and bangs framing her face and matching slacks and a T-shirt.

"Terry," she said. "I want Terry."

"I'm right here, Beth," Terrence Simnic said. His voice was quiet, almost tender as he spoke to her.

"I don't understand," Kate said.

"This is my sister," Terrence Simnic said, and his voice had hardened though he kept his focus on the police, not Kate. "She lives in a group home a few hours from here. I drive up to get her sometimes on the weekend. She's scared of guns, so I couldn't tell you she was there. It would have frightened her."

So that was why he'd been home so late, that was why

he'd had his hand on her shoulder. Kate had been wrong about him, so terribly wrong.

"You lied to the police, Mr. Simnic," one of the officers said. "You could be facing some charges for that."

"She broke into my house," Terrence Simnic said, nodding at Kate. "I want you to charge *her*."

The next thirty minutes were a nightmare. Kate was hustled into the back of the squad car again and driven away while neighbors gawked from their porches. She wanted to shield her face as they drove through Wickfield, but the cuffs wouldn't allow it. They bit into her wrists and every time the car hit a bump she got a nasty jab in the back. The cops up front didn't talk to her, conversing easily with each other about a football game the night before. It was surreal.

At the station, a man came running up to the car with a camera ready, snapping pictures that momentarily blinded her. Only on the last did she manage to turn fully away. She was escorted through the station house with both officers flanking her, and it was easy to see the frank curiosity in the eyes of the desk sergeant and the policewoman who took her fingerprints and lined her up for a mug shot.

She had a sudden memory of college days, when friends of hers would try to impress her with their arrest records for various campus protests. She'd always been proud of not having been arrested. She'd done a few protest marches, she wasn't apolitical, but one of the benefits of being an artist was the ability to see multiple sides of most issues, and the polemic nature of the campus activists was ultimately unappealing. She could remember feeling relieved that she'd never been arrested, mainly because it wasn't something her law-abiding, gentle parents would have understood.

What would they have made of her now? She could feel their shame even if they weren't there to express it. It was hard to hold the block of numbers straight when they took her mug shot. She thought of Ian and Grace and felt hot and cold at once at the humiliation of it all.

After they'd searched her and taken her fingerprints and her picture, she was escorted by the desk sergeant, a kind-looking, stocky older man with thick white hair who smelled faintly of cigars, to sit at a plain metal table in what she assumed was an interrogation room. He left her for a few minutes, and returned with a Styrofoam cup of tasteless but hot coffee.

She warmed her hands around it, wondering when someone would talk to her about what had really happened. Her one phone call had been to Ian's cell phone and she'd had to leave a message.

There was a clock high on the wall encased in a metal cage. She wondered why they bothered to cage it in a room so devoid of furnishing. Had some previous occupant thrown the chair at it?

Thinking about the clock stopped her from thinking about what was happening but just for a minute. How had she found herself arrested for breaking and entering? Oh, Lord, that was a felony. She tried not to think about what could happen, or worse, about what Ian would say.

It was a good thirty minutes before anyone came to talk to her, and when they entered, it was two plainclothes police officers that she'd never seen before, who looked like an advertisement for a muscle-building program, like those old cartoons for Charles Atlas. The shorter, skinnier, "before" version introduced himself as Detective Stilton, and looked at her with a sour expression that might just have been the set of his jaw. The bigger, "after" version said he was Detective Barnaby, and when he reached out to shake her hand, she thought she heard a seam rip in the sports coat straining across his massive shoulders.

"Let's talk about why you broke into your neighbor's house," Barnaby said, swinging a leg over the other chair and dropping into its seat. The metal frame shrieked like a mouse squashed by an elephant. Stilton had brought a folding chair with him. He struggled to open it while Barnaby pretended not to notice.

"I thought he was responsible for the disappearance of Lily Slocum and Elizabeth Hirsh."

"Why did you think that?"

So she explained, and just as with Ian, her rationale for suspecting Terrence Simnic seemed faulty when she verbalized it. When she tried to describe the clues that had led to her conclusion, they seemed paltry. "There were lights on in his basement very late at night," she said, "and then when I saw him going into the house with another woman."

"You thought the woman was at risk?"

"Yes."

Barnaby nodded his big, ruddy head, but Stilton's sour expression just became more pronounced. "Ms. Corbin, why didn't you just call the police?"

"I did! They came to the house, but nothing happened."

"Nothing?"

She swallowed and ran a hand through her hair wondering suddenly if she looked as crazy as this sounded. "They said they'd spoken to Mr. Simnic."

"And he told them there was no one in the house."

She nodded. "He lied! I knew there was someone else in the house."

"But that someone turned out to be his sister, right?"

"Yes."

Barnaby coughed. "People can't just take the law into their own hands every time they suspect someone of something." He spread his large hands flat on the table. A thick white scar cut through the freckles on the left one. "That would be vigilante justice, Ms. Corbin, vigilante justice."

"It's also dangerous, Ms. Corbin," Stilton added. "Think of what could have happened if Mr. Simnic really was a killer and he'd found you in his house."

She nodded, feeling heat in her face and all through her body. It had seemed to make so much sense at the time.

They left her then, and she felt like a child being sent to her room to reflect upon her shortcomings. Twenty more minutes ticked slowly by before someone returned. This time it was Barnaby alone.

"Good news, Ms. Corbin. Upon consideration, your neighbor has decided not to press charges."

"Really?" Kate straightened in her seat. "That's wonderful!"

"You can thank your husband for that," Barnaby said. "Apparently, he talked Mr. Simnic out of it."

She was led back out to the main desk, where Ian and Terrence Simnic stood with Detective Stilton and the police officers that'd arrested her. A gang of disapproving men. Ian had the pinched look he got when he was angry and trying to control his temper. His lips had vanished into a straight line and his face was slightly flushed.

Terrence Simnic, in contrast, was beet red. "You shouldn't have done that!" he said to Kate as she approached, wagging a large finger at her. "You had no right to come into my house!"

"I'm sorry," she said, for there was nothing else to say.

"You scared my sister. She thought you were a burglar."

"I apologize, Mr. Simnic, and I'll tell her I'm sorry, too. I never meant to scare her or hurt anyone. I was trying to help her."

Terrence turned from her to the police officers. "I'll drop the charges, like I said, but she's got to stay off my property."

"She will, Mr. Simnic," Ian said.

"No going anywhere on my property and no going to my store. I don't want her around."

"I won't bother you, Mr. Simnic."

"She's crazy," Simnic said, ignoring her and speaking directly to Ian. "People like her should be locked up."

Kate's hand shook as she signed for her few belongings. Ian stood beside her, his presence looming and vulturelike. She had the feeling he was waiting to feast on whatever skin she had left.

The late afternoon sunshine warmed her briefly and felt good on her face. "This will be all over town before tomorrow," Ian said as he unlocked the car.

"I'm sorry." It seemed to be the only thing that Kate could say.

"What the hell were you thinking?"

"I was thinking that there was a woman in danger and I wanted to help."

"Help someone?" His voice rose. "How about helping me? I could lose my job over this, Kate."

She got into the car, and had to hold onto the side as he pulled, screeching, out of the parking spot. She waited until they'd driven for a minute before answering him. "You're not going to lose your job—"

"Would you care if I did? Do you have any idea how hard I've tried to make things work here? Does my happiness matter to you at all?"

"Look, I'm sorry, I didn't mean—" she began, but he cut her off again.

"You're selfish, Kate. Everything has always been about you, you and your art. And I was happy to keep it that way because I thought we were happy. But we're not happy anymore, Kate. You're not happy anymore.

"What you did today was crazy, Kate. Just plain crazy. Whoever killed Lily Slocum is not living in our neighborhood. A former boyfriend, or someone living far from here, probably killed her. You've let what happened to you infect every area of our lives!"

She couldn't argue with him, not anymore. Her head ached, her body felt as if she'd been beaten, all her muscles tight from tension. She wondered what it would be like to simply curl up in a ball in bed and never get out. Streetlights blinked on as they drove through town, and she watched leaves falling lazily from a tulip tree as they waited at a red light. Had she lost touch with reality because of what had happened to her? Maybe Ian was right and everything she'd seen was nothing more than her imagination playing tricks on her because of what had happened, those fifteen or twenty minutes that had changed everything.

She kept her eyes down when they approached their street, and wouldn't look at Terrence Simnic's house. She felt as if neighbors were watching as she got out of the car. Grace was in the kitchen watching television when they entered the house.

"Mom, you're on the news!" she said, getting up and running to her mother. Kate caught a glimpse of herself, handcuffed, being led out of the police car. It was worse than she thought; a television news crew had somehow managed to get footage. The caption under her photo was "Dean's wife arrested."

"Great," Ian said. "Just great."

Kate hugged Grace, trying not to mind that the only time she'd managed to get her daughter's attention without forcing it was when she was arrested.

She couldn't bear to watch the TV, and left Ian fixated by the coverage. Grace asked a flurry of questions, following Kate into her bedroom and lounging on the bed while her mother changed out of the clothes that smelled like Terrence Simnic's house.

"That's so wild, Mom, I can't believe you did that."

Kate was mildly flattered that her daughter, alone among everybody, hadn't called her a crazy fool, but she thought that was really probably one more reason she should feel ashamed.

She didn't cry until she was alone.

Chapter Twenty

The memories the man cherished were of death in all its completeness. There hadn't been too many over the years. He couldn't afford to do too many. He deliberated over every one, taking his time to observe, to satisfy his desire to look, to savor their coming association the same way that a child anticipates Christmas.

If each event had not lived up to that happy holiday, it wasn't because of any lack on his part. It was just that the actual moment of death was so brief that it could never wholly satisfy. Still, he relived these brief encounters with pleasure, pulling out his photographs to remember the look on each girl's face, the sounds they made when he placed the wire around their necks, such original, soulful music! The exquisite pleasure of marking flesh humming with life and the different, but even more exquisite, pleasure of touching it in death.

He sucked in air through his strong teeth, and looked down on the cool flesh he was arranging on the chaise lounge. It was important that she look like she was sleeping. This was what Poe and the Victorian practitioners of this art had understood.

He arranged a fold in the nightdress to a more flattering position, stepped behind the camera again, and took another look. Still too stiff.

"Now, now, little one, you can't stay that way." He came out from behind the camera and changed the angle of her head. Then the flower wreath she wore needed to be rearranged. He did that, carefully touching the rose petals, and then stepped back again. Yes. Ye-e-s. He stood there enjoying the view.

The camera was mounted on a tripod for precision. Sometimes, in his excitement, his hands shook. His first attempts, before the tripod, had been too blurry to give any verisimilitude. Over time, through trial and error, by trying different cameras and various lights, he'd perfected his technique.

The space where he took the photographs was small, only nine by nine, but it was the second largest of the quadrants in the basement. He'd divided the space himself, installing drywall partitions and insulating the walls and ceiling to soundproof it. As an extra precaution he'd installed an intercom system so he'd hear anything upstairs. It was not a perfect job. There were slight variations in the surface of the walls, but for his purposes none of that mattered. What mattered was the division of space and what that allowed.

In the smallest quadrant, tucked close to the stairs, there was a sink, a commode, and a mattress pad. He installed an eyebolt deep in the cement wall and attached a heavy length of steel chain. The other end of the chain was welded to a metal cuff large enough for a female ankle.

It had taken him time to figure it out. He didn't want

to be inconvenienced by a slave's bathroom needs. His system allowed a slave to move easily between the sleeping pad and the toilet.

The quadrant across from this was slightly larger. Here he had installed four eyebolts in a spread-eagle pattern, two up, two down, and a larger one in the center of the space, installed in a ceiling joist. When that was set up to his satisfaction, and after he'd tested the holding power of each and every bolt, he'd installed a hanging cabinet, oak stained dark brown, with two rows of hooks inside. The cabinet was where he housed his tools.

He'd heard others refer to them as "toys," but this trivialized them. These weren't toys, though he got pleasure from using them. These were tools necessary to mold a slave.

The biggest quadrant was much different from the other rooms. In here was a large, handmade metal bed that he'd specially ordered and assembled. The mattress was thick and plush with a quilted cover, the linens had a high thread count. It was the best bed he'd ever owned and cost far more than the bed he slept in at night. He'd never slept in this one.

Candles on wrought-iron stands flanked either side of the bed so that when they were lit it was cast in a soft glow. He'd painted this room, like all the others, black. It contrasted so nicely with the snowy linens and the gauzy white nightgown with lace trimming its collar and cuffs that was laid neatly across the foot of the bed.

That left the final quadrant, the room the slave never saw, where a chaise lounge covered in creamy white cushions sat in a place of honor surrounded on three sides by klieg lights and screens. In front of it was a very expensive digital camera mounted on an adjustable tripod.

There were always two sets of prints, one for private consumption, one for public. In the private ones, the photos for his own viewing pleasure, the slave would be naked on the lounge. She would have her legs crossed casually, much like Manet's *Olympia*, with her breasts and her bush exposed.

She would look like the whore she was in the first photos, and in the second set, when she was wearing the nightgown, identical to the one in the bedroom except for the Velcro closures up the back, she would look like the angel she became after her transformation.

Behind the chaise, in a corner of the room, was a little table on which rested a pair of secateurs to make his floral arrangements. Under the table were the buckets to hold the flowers. They were always in shades of white and cream or sometimes blush pink. Their scent was powerful, cloying, and it lingered even after the flowers were gone. Sometimes, he could smell their lingering odor while he lay on the bed in the next room, and he wondered if the slave could smell it, too, but it was a fleeting thought and he didn't ask.

There was a danger in caring about what the slave smelled or thought or felt. The only thing of importance was that the slave would serve. That was what the slave was for and that was what the slave would do. Not that the slave would do it willingly. Not at first. Sometimes not at all. One or two of them never stopped fighting their servitude, so they had to visit the room with the chaise lounge sooner than the others.

He enjoyed their photos as much as the others. In death all of them were compliant. If he had any regrets about his work, it was that he hadn't photographed his first death. Not that he'd had such a good system with the second or even the third, but at least he had small Polaroids to remember them by. With the first, he had to rely entirely on his memory to recapture the sweetness.

She was a waitress in a corner restaurant he passed to and from classes. By then he knew the difference between decent food and truly great restaurants, and was used to much better coffee, but sitting in a leatherette booth sipping strong brew from a thick ceramic cup and saucer was pleasant Americana.

He was careful to only enter the restaurant if she was working and to make sure he was always seated in her area. She was beautiful in a small-town way, unaffected, natural-looking, with just a little bit of makeup, which was childishly applied. Once he took the liberty of wiping a trail of lipstick from the corner of her mouth with his napkin, and she'd blushed and thanked him.

She had plump little hands and an endearing, gap-toothed smile. Her name on the plastic lapel pin affixed to her pink polyester uniform was CALLIE.

"That's a pretty name," he'd said when she first served him, and that's when he knew she would be the one. She'd been so thirsty for that compliment, so eager to hear anything nice about herself. He knew then and he'd continued with it, giving her compliments the way other people feed the birds, doling them out in little handfuls, like bread crumbs from a paper sack.

She gobbled up whatever he doled out, happy to swallow every word, eager to believe that at least one person on the planet had recognized her as special.

It was that eagerness, that and a few grammatical lapses, and the way she deferred to him because he was in college. All of it signaled that she was the choice, the one who would be molded by him, and perfected to serve him.

Only she didn't like it. He hadn't anticipated that, hadn't anticipated that she'd give him trouble when, after months of wooing, he'd finally gotten her away from the restaurant and into his small apartment. She'd played coy about going out with him, but it had been just that, play. He'd known she would go with him when he asked; he'd seen the eagerness in her eyes.

Only they hadn't been eager when he suggested she get undressed, when he showed her the bed and told her what he wanted her to do. She hadn't been eager then, standing there in her cheap acrylic sweater, clutching her vinyl purse like he was going to take her envelope of tips away from her.

"You're a beautiful girl, Callie," he'd said, sitting down on the bed that he'd made sure to make that morning, beckoning for her to come to him. But she'd shaken her head.

"No, I can't."

"Why not?"

"It's wrong." Her plump fingers fiddled with the small gold cross around her neck.

A mistake, that. He'd overlooked the necklace and its implications. "Are you saved, Callie?" he'd said then, turning serious just as he'd once been charming, already having developed that chameleonlike ability to be different things for different people.

He let her tell him about Jesus, listening as she talked about the one man she really loved, really served. He'd listened and listened and all the time he'd thought of what it would be like to peel the clothes off that plump little body and devour the flesh.

When she talked, he stroked her hand, then her arm, moving up to her shoulders, and finally taking the cross in his own hand, bouncing its small, warm weight against his palm. Her speech faltered then, she stared into his eyes, and he pulled the cross a little, guiding her closer to him, closer to his lips.

Afterward, she'd chattered, filling a pleasant, post-orgasmic haze with noise. He barely listened, hoping that his silence would quiet her, but she kept talking, non-stop babble about the future. It became clear that she saw the fact that they'd had sex as some sort of commitment. She thought that since she'd offered her plump little body, he would put a diamond chip on her finger and marry her and make her pregnant, so she could swell up like a sow with his child and waddle around some suburban tract home.

Jesus, it was pedestrian! She wasn't the sweet, corn-fed little innocent, but a scheming, stupid bitch trying to scramble up the social ladder.

"Stop talking," he'd said, watching her struggling to get into her clothes. Only she wouldn't stop, her chatter continuing as she fastened her bra and pulled her sweater on.

He hit her as her head emerged from the sweater. A simple backhand, without even thinking about it. She fell sideways on the bed, caught herself against the comforter, and quietly gasped. She stared at him with round eyes, her mouth a perfect little O of fear. She didn't yell at him, she just gave in. And that changed everything.

"Get back up on the bed," he said, and it was his other voice, the voice that he knew he'd had in him, the voice of his father, who'd been suppressed all those years, the voice of Poe, who'd dared to smoke in viola-tion of his mother's wishes.

If she'd argued with him, if she'd simply grabbed her clothes, he would have let her go. Might have. But she didn't argue, didn't try to leave. Ambitious little Callie scrambled back up on the bed like an obedient, eager-to-please dog. He took the sweater off her body and when she whimpered, he hit her again and what blos-somed along with the red mark on her skin was his own manhood.

Along with a sense of power came a deep feeling of
satisfaction. Joy. He felt joy. He held those small hands
above her head with one of his and forced her legs back
open. He thrust inside her, watching her face and feeling his body respond to the fear he saw in her eyes.

She cried some and it made him angry, such a ma-
nipulative trick, tears, and he pulled the chain around
her neck, twisting the cross until she stopped making
those crying sounds, until she made gagging noises instead. He kept twisting until she made no noise, and he
realized that he liked her better that way.

When he was finished, he stripped the clothes from
her body and took the little cross, too, rinsing her skin
and blood from it. He cleaned the scraps of blotchy
makeup off her face, and swaddled her in the sheets
from his bed. He lay with her like that for a long time,
thinking how lovely she looked when she was silent, and
how in death that innocent loveliness that she'd ex-
uded if not really embodied was finally made real.

He had one large piece of luggage, a wheeled Sam-
sonite case in dark green, and he folded her into it,
bending her like an origami crane, to make her body
fit. With the zipper shut and the case upright, he could
see the bulge, but no more than any overpacked bag.

He washed his hands, then made himself a light supper and ate it in front of the TV while the suitcase stood
beside it. They were calling for snow by the weekend.

After midnight, he wheeled the suitcase out to his
car, heaving it with only moderate difficulty into the
trunk, and drove up into the mountains, a trip that took
a couple of hours, near a place where he'd hiked the
year before. He stopped at an emergency pull-off on a
deserted stretch of road framed by forest. The suitcase
bumped along the forest floor and he had to use a flashlight, but it wasn't hard to find a spot.

He left her body in a ravine, nestled among a blanket of golden leaves.

He burned the suitcase and her clothes, but he kept the little cross. It was months before they found her and when they did, she became just another Jane Doe on the police roster because he'd picked someone without ties to other people. Callie was an orphan, Callie had relatives who didn't care about her, Callie lived in a room she rented from an old woman who cared more about her cats than the lonely young woman upstairs and didn't think to report her missing.

Had he always intended to kill her? It occurred to him only after her death, when he thought about how carefully he'd sussed out her living situation, that he had chosen her deliberately. It had not been a random act of violence, but a deliberate conclusion to a relationship he'd cultivated purely so he could end it on his terms.

Now all he had of her was the little cross and sometimes, if he gripped it tight in his palm, he could get a faint picture of the shy face she'd worn when he first smiled at her.

It was easier with the photos and that's why he took his time to get them right. He stepped out from behind the camera for a third time with only a slight sigh of impatience. The slave's left hand had flopped forward, scattering the roses it held onto the floor. He carefully tucked the hand back into place, using a small foam block to hold it there. Then he had to arrange the nightgown to hide the block. Lastly, he gathered up the roses and arranged them in a pleasing fashion within her arms.

He hummed under his breath as his hands moved over her body. "Do you like Mozart, little one? *Eine kleine Nachtmusik* to speed your journey?" He laughed a little at his joke. It was satisfying to enjoy one's work.

December

Chapter Twenty-one

Just as she had watched Terrence Simnic, the neighbors now watched Kate. She could feel their presence behind the twitching curtains and slightly ajar doors of the homes on their block. Walking out to the car for her first, mandatory, appointment with a psychologist, she saw the old woman across the street come out of her house and stare openly.

Kate stared back defiantly until the woman looked away and pretended to be examining the pots of mums flanking her porch steps. Kate averted her gaze from Terrence Simnic's house as she backed the Volvo down the driveway. He seemed to have vanished just like the girls she'd suspected him of taking. The floral van was parked in the driveway, but his other car, the ancient sedan, was gone and she'd seen no sign of it or him since her arrest.

He must have taken his sister with him. Perhaps they'd gone back to the group home where she lived, undoubtedly to escape the local media.

They'd camped out in front of the house for a solid

week. Trucks double-parked along the sidewalk, reporters appearing regularly each morning, clustered
like fungi along the edges of the lawn. They were gone
now. A grisly accident on Highway 87 captured the
short attention span of the reporters, and they abandoned the story of the dean's crazy wife, leaving behind
them a trampled lawn with crushed coffee cups and lip-
stick-stained cigarette butts.

A few days earlier, she'd tried to sneak out the back
door to go to the grocery store, only to hear a high-
pitched voice call, "There she is!" just before a young
woman in a white suit came racing up the driveway, micro-
phone outstretched, like a raptor alighting on prey. A
cameraman lumbered after her. Other reporters jock-
eyed for second place, one man slipping in the dew-wet
grass in his haste to reach her.

"Over here, Mrs. Corbin!"

"Where are you going, Mrs. Corbin?"

Kate couldn't stop flinching at the snapping cameras, but she'd learned to walk to her car. Running just
encouraged them to chase her. They'd reminded her of
a pack of wild dogs.

Images of her arrest were added to the already abun-
dant coverage of the disappearance of both Lily Slocum
and Elizabeth Hirsh. Shots of her being led, handcuffed, into the station were played on every broadcast,
along with a smaller smiling head shot that was at least
three years old and must have been taken from a
gallery brochure.

It was jarring to see images of herself on TV, but
worse to see the footage of Ian, walking briskly toward
his office with his head turned to avoid the camera,
shoulders hunched and briefcase gripped tightly in his
fist.

Even the *Times* ran a piece on it, thankfully small and

buried in the middle of the Metro section, but complete with a bad photo of her hurrying into the police station with her hand blocking her face.

Everyone experienced humiliation at some point. Failed exams, entertaining disasters, a cup of coffee spilled down the front of a freshly starched white shirt while racing for the morning train. Kate could still remember the professor who told her when she was all of nineteen that she'd only ever be middling as an artist. The critique still burned, but his vicious assessment had hardened her determination, and at some point her desire to prove him wrong had become a work ethic that helped her succeed. However, this humiliation was different; there was nothing she could fight against.

She felt angry, the sort of cold anger that kept other feelings, like embarrassment, at bay. Some nights, she'd replay in her mind every single awful detail of her arrest. One of the worst things was that the police clearly thought she was crazy. One of them, the elderly sergeant, had even patted her shoulder when they returned her belongings. It didn't help that Ian had promised mandatory therapy as a condition of the charges against her being dropped.

The psychologist, an older, Germanic-looking woman, had her private practice on the upper floor of a building just off Penton Street. Dr. Greta Schneider had short white hair and a soft face. The office was decorated in peaceful shades of yellow and blue, with comfortable armchairs and a Matisse reproduction on one wall. Yet Kate felt anything but relaxed. There was a chaise lounge available in the intimate grouping, and Kate wondered if anybody really lay down upon it to pour out his or her woes in a prone position. She avoided it, seating herself upright in an armchair and trying not to grip the sides.

"Tell me about yourself," Dr. Schneider said after

she'd asked some general questions, scribbling down the answers on a pad of paper that Kate longed to grab and read. "Problem with authority," it probably read, followed by "exhibiting signs of dementia."

"What do you want to know?"

The doctor shrugged. "Whatever you'd like to tell me."

"Nothing," Kate said, "I'd like to tell you nothing, but I realize that isn't an option." She laughed a little, but Dr. Schneider didn't join in. She just watched Kate, an impassive smile on her face.

The silence was unnerving. Finally, Kate blurted, "Until ten months ago I would have told you that I was a reasonably successful artist with a great marriage and a happy kid."

"But now?"

"Haven't you been watching the news, Doctor? I was top of the hour a few weeks ago."

"And how has that changed things?"

"What, having everyone think I'm crazy? How do you think it's changed things?"

"Who thinks you're crazy?"

"The police. The neighbors. My husband."

The doctor made a note on the pad on her lap. Kate wondered what she was writing down. Was it a confirmation of her craziness? Sweat beaded the back of her knees and dampened her palms. She pressed them against her pants legs and tried to meet the doctor's watchful eyes.

"Do you think you're crazy?"

"No. I mean, I don't know." Did normal people triple-check the locks on their doors? Did normal people break into their neighbor's homes? "I thought I had a good reason to go in his house."

"Whose house?"

"My neighbor's. Terrence Simnic. I had a good reason to go in there. I saw him take a woman in there, but the police wouldn't do anything about it."

"What did you want them to do?"

"Arrest him."

"Why didn't they?"

Kate felt as if she were back in school being asked to dutifully recite what the teacher wanted her to say. "Because she was his sister. I didn't know that."

She stared out the window through the half-open slats of mini-blinds. A small bird alighted on the barren bush outside, bobbing lightly on the thin branch supporting it. It looked as if a breeze could blow it away. So fragile, so vulnerable.

The doctor shifted in her seat and Kate turned back, struggling to explain. "I saw him take a woman into the house. I saw him carrying women's clothes out of his house. He collected dolls that looked like the photo of the missing girl. He worked in his basement at all hours of the night. It all seemed very strange. Doesn't that seem strange to you?"

The doctor made a noncommittal noise in her throat. It might have been a cough. "Let's talk about you, Kate," she said, speaking slowly in a low, melodious voice. "Let's try and take the focus off Terrence Simnic and the death of Lily Slocum for a while."

Greta Schneider's eyes were watchful. They made Kate nervous, but then again she'd always felt nervous in therapy. She wasn't comfortable discussing her life so intently. Her work, yes, but not her life. She could discuss her art and its influences, but she didn't want to discuss her childhood, her marriage, or her parenting and have it all held up to examination.

At the end of the fifty-minute hour, Kate took the stairs down to the exit, passing the dentist office on the first floor. Ironic that both businesses shared the same building. Kate imagined she could hear faint drilling whenever the psychologist asked particularly probing questions.

For the first few days, when the phone calls from reporters were still coming, alternating with repeated knocking on their front door, Kate took to her bed. In this way, her arrest was similar to the first few days after she'd been raped. She pulled the covers over her head and tried to block out the sound.

It wasn't a particularly great coping strategy, but it was a strategy and she hadn't felt like coming up with a better one. She'd expected Ian to try and rally her, just like he had after she was raped, with aphorisms about what didn't kill her making her stronger. However, he didn't say anything, and that's when she first realized that he wasn't talking to her. Not real talking. He'd give her perfunctory greetings, say good night before he turned out his bedside lamp, but there'd been no real conversation since the angry confrontation in the police station when he'd accused her of trying to sabotage his career.

She'd been angry enough herself not to notice at first, but in the days that followed her arrest it became clear that he'd shut down. He was there physically, wasn't keeping different hours, but he'd checked out emotionally and she didn't know if he would ever come back.

It was a strange thing that a couple's happiness could rest on how well they knew each other and what they did with that knowledge. Ian's comments about her selfishness had hurt Kate like few other things in their marriage.

"What do you think about what he said?" Dr. Schneider asked when she'd slowly, painfully recounted the conversation.

"Why didn't he ever tell me this before? If he really

thinks he's denied himself and his career for years because of me, how come we've never had any conversation about it?"

"So you think he's not serious?"

"No, I think he hasn't been honest with me about his
feelings and now it's all suddenly coming out because
he's angry."

As Kate drove the long way home from town, away
from the university and the possible prying eyes of Ian's
colleagues, she turned it over and over in her mind.
Was it selfish to have stayed in New York all those years?
It had certainly been more expensive, but had she really
traded Ian's happiness for her own?

If she had—and that was a big if—it certainly hadn't
been conscious. She had only followed her calling,
pouring everything into her art with the same single-
minded intensity she'd had since childhood. Was that
so wrong? Had Ian felt excluded by that all these years?

She couldn't help but remember the short biogra-
phy that had accompanied her smiling headshot in
gallery brochures. "Kate Corbin maintains a studio in
Williamsburg and resides in Manhattan with her husband and daughter." All the satisfaction contained in
those few words. A full life, a complete life, the kind of
life many people dreamed of having: a successful career, a good marriage, a healthy child. It had seemed
solid, unassailable.

For a year she'd blamed the fractures in her life on
those twenty awful minutes, considering them a demar-
cation between her old life and the new, but now she
questioned whether the cracks had always existed in
her marriage and what happened in the studio had just
completed the job.

Unsettled and unhappy, she retreated to the studio
when she got home, wanting to lose herself in painting,

longing for the creative state where all that mattered was paintbrush and canvas.

She squeezed paint from thin tubes onto her palette and selected a brush to add another layer, dark green, to the river, painting in stripes of color that made it look as if the water were churning. The figure seemed to be struggling now to stay afloat. The face looked muddy, nondescript. Kate sat and stared at it for a while, trying to figure out what face wanted to emerge. Was it Lily Slocum anymore or was it Elizabeth Hirsh?

She couldn't make it work, features emerging with fast brush movements only to be scraped away with a palette knife just as swiftly. It wasn't distressing, she knew with a confidence born from many long hours that it always worked eventually.

It was a sunny, cold day, light moving through the window shades and bathing the wooden floor planks yellow. The soft hum of the electric heater provided a pleasant background lull. The strong, familiar scents of paint and linseed oil filled the air and mixed with the faint aroma of wood-burning fireplaces.

The shift in light alerted Kate to the passage of time. The stripes of color falling across the floor grew longer, now spilllling across the canvas. She switched on the lights and kept working. She came out of a creative fog to look at the clock, shocked to see that it was almost six.

Kate covered her palette and canvas and rushed her brushes into a jar she kept in the sink. Grace should have been home from her piano lesson by now. Why hadn't she come out to say hello?

The kitchen was empty. "Grace?" Kate checked the table and the sink fully expecting to find a used glass and crumb-strewn plate since Grace never remembered to put her dishes in the dishwasher. The kitchen was spotless.

The first hint of anxiety flicked on like a pilot light in Kate's stomach.

"Grace? Where are you?" She walked to the front of the house, hoping to see her daughter at the piano, but the lid was closed. She hurried up the stairs, moving briskly along the hall, already preparing to scold Grace for not telling her mother when she got home.

It was quiet, but Grace was probably plugged into her iPod. Maybe she was actually doing her homework. Kate gave a perfunctory knock on her daughter's door before turning the knob.

The room was empty, the bed still the same heap of covers that Grace had left when she'd been forced out that morning. The flame in Kate's stomach turned up a notch. She looked around, trying to assess from the mess whether Grace had come and gone. Maybe she'd actually gone somewhere with a friend. Only wouldn't she have left her backpack behind? It was nowhere to be found.

It was only as she was hurrying back downstairs that Kate thought to check the answering machine. Grace must have gone home with someone from school. Which she shouldn't do, but if she'd actually found a new friend, Kate was prepared to be delighted and just remind her, gently, that she should call if there was a change in plans.

Only there weren't any messages. Kate picked up the phone to dial Grace's cell and heard it ringing in the hall. It was still in Ian's jacket pocket from when he'd confiscated it.

She was supposed to have taken the bus straight over to campus for her lesson with Dr. Beetleman. Kate found the number in the campus directory on Ian's desk in the upstairs office, but there was no answer when she called. He was probably still teaching and couldn't hear his phone. Grace's lesson should have ended an hour ago.

Ian didn't answer his phone either. It was now ten after six and the sun was going down. Kate hesitated just long enough to scribble a note for Grace and stick it on the refrigerator.

Streetlights switched on as she drove block after block, scanning the sidewalks for a glimpse of a familiar black-haired figure slouching along with a scowl and a backpack. There was no one out; the sidewalks were distressingly empty.

Chapter Twenty-two

Parking was always a hassle on campus. "Why the hell don't they plan for this?" Kate muttered as she circled the same area for the fourth time. "Haven't they ever heard of a parking garage?"

Just as she was about to park illegally, a goateed man came out carrying a cello, which he loaded, taking his time about it, into the back of a small green Ford.

The halls of the music building were flanked with practice rooms, and Kate caught glimpses of violinists and one heavy-bosomed singer before she reached Beetleman's office.

The department secretary, a whey-faced young woman wearing too much perfume, was shutting down for the day.

"I need to see Dr. Beetleman."

The young woman looked up from packing her purse and gave Kate a bored once-over. "He's busy. You'll have to make an appointment for sometime later this week."

"Is he still teaching? I'm looking for my daughter, Grace Corbin?"

The secretary shrugged. "Sounds vaguely familiar, but he's got lots of students. I can't possibly remember all of their names." She turned her attention back to the voluminous purse in which she was trying to stuff a slightly less voluminous lunch satchel.

"Look, this is important. I really need to find my daughter. Now."

The young woman raised her head and sighed as if greatly put upon. "All right. I'll see if I can get him. Just have a seat." She pointed at a small reception area behind Kate.

Perched on the edge of a stiff couch, Kate watched the young woman make a big show of picking up the phone, turning her back to Kate with the phone pressed tight against her ear.

Two long minutes later, the woman turned back and hung up. "You can go on back to his office," she said, waving toward a hallway.

Dr. Beetleman stood up when Kate appeared in his doorway, offering her a large hand to shake and a friendly smile. As always, his shock of rumpled white hair made him look like an aging Beethoven. It was a resemblance he appeared to cultivate.

"I'm looking for Grace. Is she still practicing?"

Dr. Beetleman frowned slightly. "Grace? She hasn't been here today."

It took effort for Kate to keep her voice level. "She was supposed to have a lesson with you."

Dr. Beetleman's frown deepened. "When she didn't show, I assumed something came up. Have you tried her friends?" He gestured toward a chair for her to take a seat.

Kate sank into it, feeling heavy with embarrassment. "What friends? If she has friends, I don't know them."

The professor nodded in a comforting way as if this

were a perfectly natural thing and not a sign that Kate was an inadequate mother.

"She's been having, well—" Kate struggled to find a way to characterize her daughter's metamorphosis into rebellious teen.

"Troubles," Beetleman finished for her. "Yes, Ian's mentioned that."

"Has he?" It was Kate's turn to be surprised. She thought she should probably feel offended that Ian was discussing things with someone else when he wasn't even talking to her, but this man had been like a father figure to Ian. It shouldn't have surprised her.

"Yes. Of course, as I've reminded Ian, I've spent a fair amount of time with Grace."

"Does she talk to you? About her friends, I mean." She sat forward, clutching her hands in her lap.

"Not really. We talk mostly about music, of course. She's a very talented girl, but she needs to work harder."

Kate nodded. "She loves music, but she thinks she also loves this boy."

Dr. Beetleman smiled. "A girl as pretty as Grace has to be careful." He leaned forward and patted her hand and that's when she realized she was clutching the edge of his desk like a lifeline.

"Don't worry. Grace is a sensible girl," the professor said with a smile. "I'm sure by the time you get home she'll be waiting for you."

Wanting to believe this, Kate headed for home, phoning Ian again on the way. He answered on the fourth ring sounding breathless.

"Yes?" He sounded distracted.

"Grace didn't come home."

"What?"

"Grace didn't come home after school, well, after her piano lesson."

"She's probably still in one of the practice rooms. I wouldn't worry about it." He sounded annoyed, and Kate swallowed a desire to scream at him.

"She isn't. I've just come from Beetleman's office. She never showed up for her lesson."

"Have you called her friends?"

"What friends? I don't know any of her friends, I don't even know if she has any."

"Deep breaths, Kate, it was just a question."

"Then answer it yourself. Who are her friends?"

"I don't know, but I'm sure someone does. What about the counselor at school, what's his name—Troll?"

"Trowle. Somebody Trowle."

"So call him. Maybe she got in trouble at school."

"I think they would have called if that were the case."

"Maybe she's joined some club, then. Why don't you just go home and check again. She's probably at home right now raiding the liquor cabinet."

"Jesus, Ian, don't you even care?"

His put-upon sigh was long and drawn out. "What do you want me to do, Kate? Leave work and help you search the streets of Wickfield because our daughter is late getting home? She's a teenager, Kate. That's what teenagers do."

"She's never done it before."

"There's always a first time. Look, I've got to finish up some work here. Call me if anything changes."

The house was ominously silent. Kate walked through the rooms anyway, calling Grace's name. Nothing had been moved; it was obvious Grace hadn't been home.

Kate looked in her daughter's room, trying to tell if anything was missing. Had Grace planned to run away? Had her backpack been unusually full this morning?

With a growing sense of dismay, she realized just how little she knew of her daughter's life. When had that happened? How was it possible that in just a few short years she had gone from what had sometimes been cloying intimacy with Grace, days when Kate couldn't use the bathroom without company and grew so tired of the chatter that her head ached, to this state? Grace might as well have been a stranger.

Kate rifled through her desk drawers searching for anything that would point her toward Grace. A little address book she'd been given as a gift had a few names in it, but they were all old friends from the city.

She knew one girl, though. What was her name? Kate flipped through a pile of textbooks on Grace's desk and finally found a note tucked into the back of a book.

"Where were you?" was written in blue ink.

"Meeting with counselor," followed in black. It went back and forth for several more lines.

"That sucks."

"Yeah. Guy's an idiot."

On the bottom of the page was an ornate H. Kate struggled to remember. Heidi? Harriet? Something like that. If she saw it, she'd be able to pick it out. Suddenly she remembered the school directory. Hadn't they been given one of those when Grace started at Wickfield High?

She raced down the hall to the extra bedroom that Ian used as a home office. It was lined with bookshelves and had an oak filing cabinet. She jerked it open hard enough to make the files jump. Sure enough, there was a hanging file neatly labeled WICKFIELD HIGH SCHOOL.

Kate flipped through the papers it held, school forms and announcements falling like leaves onto the Oriental rug at her feet. C'mon, where was the directory? She had a vague recollection of Grace being given one by the principal of Wickfield with a cheerful prediction of using it to contact "all your new friends." Kate only needed to find one.

It wasn't in there. Feeling desperate, Kate scooped up the papers she'd dropped and stuffed the whole file back in the drawer. And just like that she found it. A slim blue printout in the front of all the other files with the words WICKFIELD HIGH SCHOOL typed on the front page.

Flipping to the Hs, Kate scanned the list of names. Harry, Heidi, Hector—Haley! It was Haley Chin! She remembered now, could picture the shy girl who could barely make eye contact.

The phone rang ten times before it was picked up. A man answered. "Mr. Chin?"

"Yes?"

"This is Kate Corbin, Grace's mother."

"Who?"

She knew then that Grace wasn't with Haley Chin, but she pressed on anyway, asking to speak with Haley.

"She's doing her homework."

"Please, Mr. Chin, it's very important. My daughter is missing."

Haley Chin sounded just as shy over the phone as she did in person. "Yes, Grace was at school, but she didn't come home with me."

"Did you see her get on the bus?"

"No, but I ride a different bus."

"Please, Haley, please try and think back. Where was she at the end of the day?"

"I don't know, Mrs. Corbin. We don't really hang out that much."

Kate could hear the deep rumble of a male voice in the background, and then Haley said. "Maybe she had some club meeting after school."

Leaving behind a hastily scrawled note instructing Grace not to go anywhere, Kate drove to the high school, going in the opposite direction of Wickfield's rush hour, a single stream of cars and vans exiting off the highway heading for home.

Her belief in Haley's suggestion faltered the closer she got to school. Even if Grace had stayed after school, any activity would have to be done by now and wouldn't she have called for a ride home? Keeping an eye out for cops, Kate sped the whole way, missing the entrance and having to screech to a halt and reverse back and cut hard left, rubbing her right front tire against the curb.

There were three cars left in the parking lot, and Harold Trowle happened to be strolling toward one of them. She raced to a stop in front of him, and he took a step back with a startled look, almost dropping the pile of folders he was carrying. He was wearing jeans and a T-shirt again, the strap of an overloaded messenger bag bisecting his chest and raising the hem of his shirt to reveal a slice of white, wobbly stomach.

"Where's the fire?" he said with a broad smile as she hopped out of the car. His false jollity didn't quite mask the annoyance she could see in his eyes. He shifted the pile of folders, bending one of his meaty arms over them to block them from view.

"I'm looking for my daughter. Grace Corbin?"

"Aah, Mrs. Corbin." He shifted the folders again to shake her hand. "Nice to see you. Is something wrong?"

"Grace didn't come home this afternoon. I thought maybe she was still at school."

"No chance of that, I'm afraid. Nobody's left at this time of night but me and Principal Myers. Oh, and the janitors." He checked his watch. "Yep, definitely not at this hour. It's way late." He seemed to recognize the impact of that because he hastily added, "Not that teenagers really keep great track of passing time. Are you sure she hasn't gone over to a friend's?"

Kate shook her head. "But she's not with Haley Chin, that's who she hangs out with the most, so I thought maybe if I came to school . . ." Talking too fast, she forced herself to stop, feeling the anxiety simmering inside burst into full flame. "I don't know where else she could be." Except with Damien Rattle. She didn't say that, didn't suggest it. She didn't want to go down that path. "Do you know any of her other friends?"

A veiled look came over Harold Trowle's face. "My sessions with the kids are confidential," he said. "I can't reveal what they tell me."

"I don't want details about her social life, I just want to know where she might be."

He nodded, that automatic counselor nod that was supposed to convey understanding, but only annoyed her. "Yes, I can see how that would help." He stroked a big palm over his hairless chin. "I'm afraid I don't know anybody other than Haley that she hangs out with."

Her phone rang as she drove home, and she answered it with a breathless "Hello?" The disappointment when it was Ian's voice was so keen that she started to cry.

"What's wrong?" he said at once. "Did you find her? Has something happened to Grace?"

"No, I didn't find her. Jesus, Ian, she's been gone for hours now."

"Okay, calm down, panicking isn't going to help, Kate."

"I'm not panicking!" She was, however, shouting. The emotion had to go somewhere.

"Look, just come by campus and pick me up and we'll go from there."

He was waiting for her on the curb outside Ludlum Hall, his briefcase clutched in one hand, cell phone to his ear with the other. He hung up as she pulled to a stop next to him.

"I've called Campbell's parents, but no one's seen or heard from her," he said as he got in the car.

"Do you think she's with Damien?"

"Probably."

"She was never late home when she skipped school to be with him. Never."

"Because she was busy trying to fool us. Maybe she doesn't care if we know, or she missed the last train out, or she decided to stay in town with that idiot."

The sky was a solid line of black. Neon signs from shop lights seemed to mock Kate's fear. She tried not to think of Grace all alone in the night. "What if he's got her?"

"Who?"

"Whoever took Lily Slocum and Elizabeth Hirsh."

Ian sighed. "Please, Kate."

"I think it's a reasonable thing to ask."

"If you suggest that Terrence Simnic has her—"

Kate cut him off. "I wasn't going to! It was a mistake—I was wrong—please let it go."

They drove in silence for another block. She glanced at her watch. "It's after eight. We have to report her missing."

"No," Ian said immediately. "No way."

"Why not?"

"I don't want to involve the police again if I can help it. Chances are that Grace is at home right now sulking because we're not there to notice her. Let's go home first. If we need to go to the police, we can do it later."

"That's what you thought two hours ago."

"It's still the most plausible hypothesis."

Kate didn't say anything, but her expression must have conveyed what she felt because Ian sighed again.

"What do you want me to do, Kate? Drive straight to the police station and act hysterical because our daugh-

ter is late getting home? They probably have a special
file on us already."

"You mean me."

"I didn't say that."

"You didn't have to."

"Fine. I was trying to include myself in this, but
you're right—you're the one who accused our neighbor of being a serial killer."

"I've apologized, Ian. Many times. I don't know what
you want me to do."

"Nothing, I just want you to stop and think before
jumping to conclusions again."

Houses along their block were studded with welcoming light, while theirs was so dark as to retreat into the
sky around it, shades of charcoal and black, the two
blank windows and shadowed front porch a reproach.

This time it was Ian who went through the house calling Grace's name. Kate didn't follow him, going into
the kitchen instead to find the note she'd left their
daughter exactly where she'd put it. Kate crumpled it in
her hand, thought better of it, and straightened it out
again. They might need it.

When Grace had been small, she'd wandered off
fairly regularly, a child who resisted holding hands, always wanting to be independent, running from their
care from the beginning. She wanted her mother's
company then, but not too close, not hampering her
freedom to wander where she chose. She'd always been
lost in her own little world, absorbed in whatever she
was doing at the moment.

Kate had been the same way as a child, and her
mother had been the one to suggest that they come up
with a system to keep track of Grace in crowds. Either
she or Ian were in charge of keeping Grace in sight at
all times. Ian had little patience with it, forcing Grace to

hold his hand, but she'd make it painful for him, going
red in the face and protesting any infringement on her
personal space.

Kate remembered the anxiety she felt when she was
in a shop and Grace had been standing next to her cart
one minute only to vanish the next. She'd been four or
five then, a small girl with a serious expression that belied her age, her dark hair in two little pigtails on either
side of her round, solemn face.

For years, Kate had relived in nightmares the moment when she'd looked down and discovered Grace
was gone. Cart abandoned, she'd moved rapidly through
the store, calling Grace's name in a level tone first, then
shouting it. People stared and an employee stopped her,
asking what was wrong. He'd called on his walkie-talkie
and they shut the doors of the store and then, just as
Kate was convinced that Grace had been kidnapped,
there she suddenly was, appearing from a far section of
the store with a toy in her hand, holding it up to ask her
mother if she could have it.

The memory of crushing Grace to her chest, holding
her tight, washed over Kate and she felt tears stinging
her eyes. When was the last time she'd held Grace like
that? When was the last time she'd told her daughter
she loved her?

"She's not here and she hasn't been home." Ian
stood in the kitchen doorway looking worried for the
first time. Kate felt a perverse satisfaction that he'd finally been roused to concern.

"We need to go to the police," she said, and this time
he didn't argue.

The desk sergeant on the evening shift was different,
and if he registered their name he gave no indication of

it. They were ushered into the squad room and helped
by a short uniformed policewoman with bobbed brown
hair and freckles who looked barely older than Grace.
Her name badge read L. DOMBROSKI. What did the L
stand for? Kate wondered as she watched her filling out
forms in looping, childlike writing.

"We can file a report now, but there's not much we
can do until she's been missing twenty-four hours," the
policewoman said after listening to them.

"You won't look for her until tomorrow afternoon?"
Kate said. "But anything could happen in that time!"

"All the squad cars will get a copy of her picture,"
Dombroski said in a soothing voice, "and if they happen
to spot her, they'll definitely pick her up. Also, a description will go out."

"Can't you do one of those, what are they called,
Amber alerts?"

"Do you have reason to believe your daughter was abducted, ma'am?"

"Yes, possibly!" Kate said. Ian put a hand on her arm,
more restraint than comfort.

"We don't know what happened to her."

"Has she run away before?"

"No," Kate said. "No, and she wouldn't do that."

"She might." Ian's disagreement was quiet.

Kate turned on him. "What do you mean? You think
she's run away?"

"Maybe." Ian looked grim. "She might have." He
looked from his wife to Officer Dombroski. "She's been
seeing a young man we don't approve of—Damien Rattle." He spelled the name.

The officer wrote this down. "Where does Mr. Rattle
live?"

"Manhattan. I don't know the exact address."

"Upper East Side," Kate said. "Eighty-ninth and Park, I think."

"How do you know that?" Ian asked.

"Don't you remember how Grace tried to impress us with his address?" She looked at the other woman. "She thought we'd accept him if he came from money."

Ian said, "So what happens if she doesn't return home within twenty-four hours?"

"Then we do an organized search and the FBI will be alerted, Mr. Corbin," Officer Dombroski said. "Did you bring a picture of your daughter?"

"Oh, no, I didn't think of it," Kate said, feeling fresh anguish, but Ian reached for his wallet.

"I've got a school one."

He dug it out, laying the small shot carefully on the desk. It was two years old, and it startled Kate to see just how much Grace had changed in that time. Had they also changed so much physically?

Despair washed over Kate as they drove away from the police station. "We can't just sit and wait for twenty-four hours."

"I agree."

"Do you really think she's run away to be with Damien?"

"Yes."

"Then let's go bring her home."

Chapter Twenty-three

They made the long drive into Manhattan mostly in silence, but for the first time in a long time it was com-
panionable. Using Ian's Blackberry and the phone
number Ian had culled from Grace's cell, Kate was able
to locate Damien's address.

"Let's not call him," she said. "If she *is* there, it would
only warn her. I think we're better with the element of
surprise."

"Do you think we should bring the NYPD into this?"
Ian said, and she felt touched that he was actually asking for her advice.

"Not yet. It might just make things harder."

Damien Rattle lived in a prewar apartment building
on the Upper East Side that had Art Deco embellish-
ments and a doorman. Ian had paid a fortune to park
in a lot five blocks away, and Kate felt bedraggled when
they huffed up to the door.

The doorman, a man both broad and tall enough to
have played linebacker, wore a navy blue uniform with
gold braid on the coat sleeves and cap. The effect was of

a dressed bear in some circus, yet he looked them over with narrowed eyes, as if he found them lacking the proper polish, before reluctantly holding the door.

Polished marble floors in the lobby were slippery, and reflected several large upholstered chairs and a round dark wood table topped with an enormous vase of fresh flowers. Their heady perfume contrasted unpleasantly with the smell of grease and cheese. The young Asian guard sitting at the desk had a piece of pizza halfway to his mouth, but put it abruptly down when he spotted them.

"Yes?"

"We're guests of Damien Rattle," Ian said. "He's expecting us."

"I'll just call upstairs and check," the guard said apologetically, hand hesitating over the phone as if waiting for Ian's permission. "Whom should I say is calling please?"

"The Corbins."

He smiled, revealing twisted teeth that seemed incongruous with his neat jacket and tie and gel-slicked black hair. At his request, they sat down in the armchairs and watched his nimble fingers flip through a directory before placing the call. His gold badge said ANAND followed by a surname so long that Kate was still trying to sound it out when he gestured them toward the elevators with another bright smile.

"Twentieth floor, sir, madam."

As the numbers climbed in the elevator, Kate felt her anxiety return in force. What would they do if Grace didn't want to come home? A smaller voice inside was pressing the question of what they'd do if she wasn't here, but Kate suppressed that voice. Think positive, think positive. She wished she'd taken yoga classes last year when a friend suggested it. Now Kate tried to remember what the friend had told her about breath and the importance of breathing in centering herself. She closed her eyes and tried taking long, deep, slow breaths, pushing out with her stomach and then pulling in.

"Are you okay?"

Startled, Kate opened her eyes. Ian was staring at her as if she'd suddenly sprung another head. "Yeah," she said, heat rushing through her face.

There was a slight ping and the elevator doors slid back silently. They stepped out of the silver box onto a dark blue carpet and padded silently toward Number 202, which they could see at the end of the hall.

Just as Ian raised a finger to press the bell, the door suddenly swung open and a woman wearing riding regalia and carrying a glass of what smelled like Kentucky bourbon greeted them with a hearty "Hello!"

Ian took a step back and bumped into Kate, who fought down nervous giggles. The woman's smile faded. She had a mane of white blond hair held back from her face with a tortoiseshell band. The whole thing look shellacked. Plucking a pair of reading glasses from somewhere in the voluminous white shirt she wore tucked into jodhpurs, she slid them on top of a nose not found in nature and surveyed Kate and Ian while shifting in her polished riding boots. After a moment, she whisked the glasses off her nose and said in a surprised tone, "Who are you?"

"We're the Corbins, Ian and Kate." Ian did the introductions and Kate tried to smile. "Are you Mrs. Rattle?"

The woman's confusion changed into a look of distaste. "Rachtel—it's German. My late husband's name. I'm Mrs. Treysmith now." She raised her glass to her mouth and took a quick belt of whiskey, unintentionally flashing a large sparkly wedding set on her left hand. "Have we met?"

"No, but we have met your son," Kate said. "Damien?"

"Yes. I only have one child—Damien was enough for any mother." She laughed, a high-pitched tinkling sound that must have taken a great deal of practice.

"I can imagine," Ian said dryly, and Mrs. Treysmith looked confused.

"Is Damien here?"

"Well, I don't really know. He's a grown man, you know. I can't really mother him anymore as much as I might long to!" Another tinkling laugh.

"Who's at the door then, Joan?" A gruff male voice called in a distinctly working-class British accent.

"Friends of Damien's," she called back. "Isn't that nice?"

"Tell them to bugger off. I'm trying to watch the game."

"Nigel's a huge football fan," Joan confided to the Corbins. "Soccer football, that is. I don't know why they don't just call it soccer. It makes it so confusing when we're talking about sports with friends."

"We're looking for our daughter, Mrs. Treysmith," Kate interrupted. "Grace Corbin. Have you seen her?"

"I don't think so, no." Joan Treysmith didn't look the least bit interested in why they'd be searching for their child. "Sorry I couldn't help." She flashed another bright, dippy smile and started to shut the door.

Ian blocked it with a hand. "We want to see Damien, please."

She frowned, glancing back toward the interior of the apartment and then at them again. "This isn't really a good time," she said.

"Sorry, but we need to talk to him now," Kate said.

Joan Treysmith took another swallow of whiskey. "All right. I suppose you'd better come in while I see if he's even here."

She ushered them into a hallway and called out, "Lola!" A young Filipino woman wearing a shapeless gray maid's uniform that couldn't disguise her beauty appeared in the hall. "See if Mr. Damien's in his room."

The girl nodded and started down the hall. "Chop, chop," Joan called after her. "Don't take all day about it." She turned back to the Corbins and said in a conspiratorial whisper. "I swear, sometimes she moves slowly just to annoy me."

The three of them stood silently in the hall with Joan Treysmith blocking further entry into the apartment. What didn't she want them to see? Kate could hear nothing but the sound of a television in the room beyond her.

"Hum, humhumdehum." Damien's mother hummed some song as she rocked back and forth, the heels of her shiny boots clicking on the floor, which was the same shiny marble as the lobby downstairs.

Her utter calm, childlike in the worst way, transfixed Kate. She stared at her and then forced her gaze away, looking down at her own dusty sneakers, bought on sale at a discount chain.

Was Grace somewhere in this vast apartment? Even now, as they stood here in polite silence, Grace could be doing God knows what with this woman's son.

Three minutes passed like an entire day. Kate could have sworn that the light shifted, moving along the wall with the passage of time. At last the maid reappeared, moving soundlessly on rubber-soled shoes. Tense, Kate sprang forward like a false start off a diving block. The young woman shrank back, fear crossing her otherwise impassive face.

"Is he here?" Kate asked, not waiting for Damien's mother.

Lola shook her head. "He's gone to California." She

vanished down a hall in the opposite direction before anyone could make any more demands of her. Mrs. Treysmith's eyes opened wide and she clapped a hand to her
mouth for a split second, and then waved it in the air.

"That's right, he's gone! I completely forgot!"

"If you're lying to protect your son, I'm going to have
the police down here so fast it'll make your head spin,"
Ian said.

"You can't talk like that to me!" Joan Treysmith looked
deeply offended.

"What the hell is going on out here?" A hulk of a
man with a florid face appeared behind Damien's
mother. In his soccer jersey and track pants, he looked
like a professional wrestler. Perhaps that's what he did
for a living.

"You must be Nigel Treysmith," Kate said.

"Yeah, that's right. What do you lot want?"

"We want our daughter," Ian said, and he stared at
Nigel as if the man weren't twice his size. "I'm going to
ask just one more time, and if I don't get a straight answer I'm calling the police."

At the second mention of police, Mrs. Treysmith's
hands wobbled. "Police? There's no need for that, is
there, dear? Tell them that Damien left."

"That's right, I kicked him out on his lazy arse." Nigel
said. He patted Mrs. Treysmith, whose eyes had clouded
over. "It's the only way he'll learn to do for hisself."

Ian pulled out his cell phone, but Mr. Treysmith shook
his head. "Put that thing away," he said in what was probably supposed to be a placating tone because it was a
slightly softer bark. "I'm telling you the lad ain't here."

"I want to see his room," Ian demanded.

Nigel Treysmith looked at his wife, jerking his head
toward the hall. Joan shook her head, but wobbled
down the hall. Nigel Treysmith swept a meaty hand to-

ward Ian and Kate. They trooped after Joan, and Nigel brought up the rear.

The apartment was much bigger than Kate had imagined, the ceilings high, the rooms large. They passed at least three rooms before arriving at Damien's. She thought of the small place that they'd called home for so long and how they'd had to maximize the space with floor-to-ceiling bookshelves and other space-saving devices.

Damien's room was somehow both ornate and austere, furnished with antiques and empty. Ian strode over to the attached bath and switched on the light. Then he looked inside the wall of closets.

"As you can see, neither Damien nor your daughter is here," Nigel Treysmith said. "Now I'll ask you to please leave."

They were quiet again on the drive home, but this time it was of shattered expectations. "At least we've got a lead we can tell the police," Ian said.

Kate nodded. "They can't have gotten very far."

Neither of them was consoled.

Kate couldn't sleep that night. For the first time in thirteen years she didn't know where her daughter rested, if she rested. Lying in the darkness, she remembered the weeks after Grace had been born when Kate had been afraid to sleep, afraid that Grace would stop breathing. How many times had she reached out a frantic hand to lightly touch the tiny figure in the bassinet? And just as many times had she been reassured by the fierce rise and fall of that thin, newborn chest. Babies seemed to fight for life and teenagers seemed to throw it away.

What if someone had hurt Grace? What if the same person who'd taken Lily Slocum and Elizabeth Hirsh had found her or what if Damien had hurt her, discarding her body like that awful case in Central Park years ago?

And what if his parents had been lying and Grace was tucked away somewhere in that vast apartment, hiding out with him because she didn't want to go home? It was ironic that this was the better option given how hard they'd worked to get Grace away from him.

Wondering where Grace could be alternated with berating herself as a parent. She should have been a better mother. A better mother would have known her child's whereabouts. A more attentive parent would have seen Damien coming, would have helped her ward him off.

"Kate?" Ian's voice in the dark startled her. She'd assumed he was asleep; he was always able to sleep. Never in their married life had she known him to go sleepless even when he'd been up for tenure at NYU, even when Grace was born and every little squawk she'd made had startled her exhausted new mother into consciousness. Ian never missed sleep, yet here he was awake at almost two in the morning.

She reached a hand blindly toward him and found the slight burr of his cheek. He pressed his hand against hers, holding the touch, and she felt warmth flood through her, a familiar response to touch and yet so unfamiliar, too. A place revisited and different this time around.

"I know it's my fault," he said. "I didn't listen to her, I was too quick to get angry with her, and that's why this has happened."

"You think she's run away?"

"Yes. Don't you?"

She hesitated, not sure to share what she really thought, but his hand had left hers and reached across the bed to stroke her hair. It was soothing, hypnotic, and the dark made a good confessional.

"What if he's hurt her," she said.

"Who? Damien?"

"Yes. Or the killer." His hand stopped moving and she spoke fast to ward off any objection. "I know you think that's crazy, but it could have happened. Look what happened to Lily Slocum and Elizabeth Hirsh."

"We don't know what's happened to Elizabeth Hirsh. She could have gone home or somewhere else."

"And never checked in with her parents? Did you read the story in the paper?"

"I skimmed it."

"Her mother said she'd never gone anywhere without telling them."

"Parents always think that. We thought that. Kids change. And if Elizabeth Hirsh has been abducted by some stranger, God forbid, he obviously targets college students."

"Grace isn't that much younger."

"To me it makes a lot more sense that she's run away from home. She's been heading in that direction for the last year, and now she's done it."

She wanted to believe that. She held onto it like a talisman, clutching it along with his hand. "You really think so?"

"Definitely. And she left because of me."

Her turn to comfort. "You can't say that, Ian. It's my fault, too. I've been so wrapped up in my own problems that I barely noticed hers."

"We should have realized there'd be adjustment problems. I guess I just hoped that changing schools, changing neighborhoods would be enough."

His hand was running through her hair again, a hypnotic, soothing gesture. She felt her own hand reciprocating, moving across his jaw and stroking his throat lightly. His skin felt cool under her fingertips, yet charged. She hadn't touched him in almost a year.

He swallowed, and she felt the rise and fall of his Adam's apple. The hand tangled in her hair tightened. His other hand trembled as he placed it lightly against a breast. Her own breath caught and she let her thumb dip into the hollow of his throat and continue down his chest.

He imitated her, moving his hands in unison with her exploration, keeping the touch light.

It was a weird dance, silent and halting, oddly fragile, with fingertips alighting on skin so parched for human contact that just tracing the body, which under ordinary circumstances might hardly qualify as prelude, carried with it extraordinary sensation.

There was an unspoken question everywhere his hands landed, and she answered each by moving her body closer to him and moving her hands in kind. She hesitated only once, when his hand found its way inside and she had a sudden memory of the roughness of that gesture in the studio and for a moment she was back there, slammed back against the table, watching the paints spilling on the floor, smelling the blood.

He stopped at once, pulled back, and she could feel his breathing, hard and warm, against her chest. His willingness to stop refocused her; she came back to the feeling of their bed underneath her, his body warm against hers. She found his hand and guided him forward.

They came in virtual silence; a few muffled "oh's" of exclamation from her and Ian's long exhalation. She tried to hide the tears that came afterward for Grace, but he must have heard the catch in her throat, because he caught them with his hands, smoothing them into her skin like a balm, and then he cradled her just as she'd cradled Grace as a child.

Chapter Twenty-four

Kate forgot Grace was missing when she woke up. Just for a moment, in that weird state between sleep and fully awake, it was as if the last six months hadn't happened and there was nothing more urgent than stretching a hand across the bed to the dark head on the opposite pillow.

Vague memories of a pleasant evening swaddled her, but then Ian rolled over and said, "She's been missing for fourteen hours."

Just like that, the dreamlike state popped like a soap bubble. Kate sat straight up, heart pounding. She looked past Ian at the clock. "It's almost fifteen hours."

Her stomach rose, and she untangled wobbly legs from the bedclothes and lurched to the bathroom to throw up.

"I'm sure she's with Damien," Ian said from the doorway as she rinsed her mouth with water. The face in the mirror was almost unrecognizable, ugly white with large dark circles under the eyes, the hair a tangled mass of red frizz.

"And if she's not?"

He didn't answer her, retreating back to the bed-room. She followed him, surprised to see him laying a suit out on the bed.

"You're not going to work?"

"Of course."

"But what about Grace?"

"I can't sit here all day waiting," Ian said. "She'll come back when she's good and ready and feels like she's punished us enough."

She sank back onto the bed. "I want to go back to the city."

"That's a fool's errand, Kate. They're on their way to California or someplace else."

"We can't just leave her with him!"

"The police will take care of it. Let's let them do their job."

He dressed with his usual calm, knotting his tie with precision in front of the wardrobe mirror, his face that of a Buddha she'd seen in a shop window. His passivity shocked and enraged her.

"We should be doing something!"

"There's nothing we *can* do."

It was an answer she couldn't accept. She trailed him down the stairs to the kitchen, where he made coffee as if it was just a normal day. When he offered her a mug, she waved it away.

"I can't believe you can just go work."

"I have responsibilities—"

"Your responsibility is as a father!"

"—that go beyond this house!"

They were both shouting. Ian turned from her and looked out the window. Any closeness she'd felt toward him had evaporated. Kate's mouth felt dry, her heart a cold, dry stone.

She left the kitchen without saying a word, and climbed back up the stairs to Grace's room. The bed was still rumpled, and she made it as if smoothing the sheets would bring Grace back to it.

Footsteps downstairs, and then Ian called, "Goodbye."

She stood still, wanting to call out, "Stay," but her lips couldn't form the word. The silence stretched on for a full minute, and then the footsteps retreated. When she heard the door shut, she sank onto Grace's bed and started to cry.

Ian drove toward the university on autopilot, heeding the speed limit and stopping at red lights, but feeling anger like a heavy band across his chest. He gripped the steering wheel tighter and tighter with his hands, the only outlet for the rage threatening to overwhelm him. As if he didn't care about what happened. As if he wasn't worried, too. What did she want from him?

It felt like he'd been asking that question all of his married life. Living with Kate was like a damn roller coaster, always had been. Emotional highs and lows were a part of their lives and all because of her artistic temperament.

In the early years of their marriage they'd had long, ridiculous arguments, invariably instigated and dragged on by her and invariably exacerbated by his responses, which were never what she wanted to hear. At a certain point he'd given up trying to interpret her moods, and settled for weathering them the way you waited out a storm.

The less said the better, he'd learned, though it was hard to resist the temptation to humor and encourage her out of these funks. He realized that this was a flaw in himself, this need to see her happy, but he also thought that she should have worked harder at contentment.

A horrible day's painting always resulted in a horrible evening with her. Every emotion had to be taken seriously; every temporary block had the potential to end her career.

What angered him the most, now as well as then, was the assumption that, since he wasn't verbalizing and emoting like she was, he must not care. Of course he cared about Grace! She was his daughter for God's sake! But what good came of sitting around counting down the minutes until the police could actually do something about it?

He pulled into his parking spot, and was walking briskly toward his office when he saw Dr. Beetleman heading toward him. Beetleman smiled broadly, held out a hand in greeting.

"Ian, just the man I'm looking for! We got a set of drawings from the second architect, come have a look."

Ian shook his head. "I'm sorry, Laurence, not today."

Dr. Beetleman nodded. "Of course, another time. Is something wrong?"

"Grace is missing."

"You mean Kate didn't find her?" Dr. Beetleman looked distressed, and Ian filled him in on what had happened. He listened intently and then quietly said, "It's so much stress for you, Ian."

The kindness in his voice crushed Ian. He choked out, "Yes, yes it is."

Dr. Beetleman was from an older generation in which men didn't physically touch each other. He clasped Ian's arm instead, which was as close to an embrace as he got. "If you need anything, anything at all, please ask me or Clara."

"Thank you."

Ian forced himself to keep going to his office. As he turned down his hall, he saw Jerry Virgoli walking toward him. It was too late to turn back. Jerry had seen him.

He nodded at Ian with a small smile. "Dean."

Always the title, never just Ian or even Professor Corbin. It galled Ian, never more so than today, but he just smiled, said, "Jerry," in a friendly sort of fashion, and trooped on. Just like he always did. Just like he always would. The burden of a good husband and father.

Kate drank the coffee that Ian had made, but couldn't eat anything. She wandered through the house, feeling useless, before heading in desperation for the studio. It was impossible not to stare at the painting and see Grace as the figure caught in the dark river, and Kate couldn't bear it. She fled back to the house.

The piano, Grace's piano, was shut, a fine patina of dust covering the lid. Sheet music and books lay scattered across the bench where Grace had left them just yesterday when she grabbed what she needed for that afternoon's lesson. Kate gathered them into a neat stack and when that task was done, she needed another one to keep her hands occupied and went in search of a cloth to dust the piano.

It was hard to imagine Grace existing without a piano. Did Damien have one in that vast apartment? It was hard to remember a time when they hadn't had the piano, and before that a time when Grace, a tiny, twinkling baby Grace, hadn't played the piano—but that had been a different time and looking back on it felt like looking back on someone else's life.

When the wood grain of the upright was gleaming,

Kate sat down on the bench and slid back the lid. She rested her hands lightly on the keys, picturing Grace sitting there, Grace playing. The few notes Kate played echoed loudly in the empty room. She closed the lid.

She was upstairs sorting through Grace's desk when she heard noise at the front door. Kate ran down the steps, heart racing, sure that it was Grace returning. There was a shadow behind the curtained side window. Kate threw open the door, but there was only the mailman retreating down the walk.

Disappointment left a sour taste in her mouth. She stood on the porch watching the mailman walk briskly along his route, and she stayed there, looking up and down the empty street, wanting desperately to believe that at any moment Grace would come.

The weight of the mail in her hand called her out of her reverie. She sorted through it, past credit card offers and the gas bill. Stuck between two shopping circulars was a white envelope with her name and address typewritten in the center. No return address. She turned it over and saw that someone had carefully placed a strip of scotch tape as an extra seal. Kate could feel the weight of something more than a letter.

Curious, she slit it open. Inside were a folded letter and another envelope, small and with a sealed flap. She took out the letter first. Centered on the page was a short, typed paragraph:

An artist should be capable of recognizing genius, yet you told the police that a florist released Lily Slocum. A florist. Is this a joke? I'm not laughing. You think you're smart, but you're not. Here is a riddle for you to solve: What is more precious to you than life itself?

That was all. Kate puzzled over it and then took the smaller envelope out of the first. It opened easily, and a silver necklace slid smoothly out of one corner and onto the porch before she could catch it.

Kate cried out and snatched it up with shaking hands. Dangling from the center of a long chain made of tiny sterling loops was a piano charm. Kate would know it anywhere. It belonged to Grace.

Chapter Twenty-five

There was light, too much light, shining on her face. Eyes burning. Turn it off. She blinked, blinked again, but it didn't go away. She rolled slowly up, sitting, shielding her face.

"Drink," the voice behind the light said. The voice, she knew the voice, but she couldn't see beyond the light. Something hard thrust into her hands. A bottle. "Drink." A hand pushed it to her lips, tilted it, and water wet her throat, spilled from her mouth. She was thirsty. So thirsty. She drank and drank, wiping at her clothes, but there were no clothes. She wiped at skin. Weird.

Her arm hurt. Was she sick? Did the doctor give her a shot? Her head hurt, too. Something heavy on her leg. Blink, blink, blink. "Turn off the light," she tried to say, but it came out funny. The light wouldn't go away. She drank some more and then a gloved hand took the bottle.

"No." She reached for it, but her hand moved very

slowly. The bottle was going away, the light was going away.

"Sleep." The voice said. She was tired, so very tired. Back down. Something soft underneath her. Water tickling her stomach. Why was their water on her stomach? Too tired to think. She slept.

"Wake up." The voice hurt Grace's ears. She tried to put a hand over her head to block it, but then pain shot through her arm as it was wrenched away. "I said wake up!"

Grace opened her eyes, blinking at light, using a slow hand to rub the gunk from them. Something dark swam into focus and then away. Back again. A black boot next to her face. Awareness of her body came next. She was lying on her side on a thin, bare mattress. She was naked. A man stood over her.

Grace scrambled up and back, slamming against a cement block wall. She turned into it, whimpering, drawing her legs up. Something clanked and she looked down to see what was holding her leg. A metal shackle circled her right ankle, a chain of heavy steel links extending from it. She followed it with her eyes and could just make out a bolt jutting out from the concrete wall. She inched one hand down, keeping her other hand over her breasts, feeling the metal and then tugging at it.

"It won't come loose." The voice sounded amused.

She drew the hand back and wrapped it around her body. "What's going on? Where am I?"

"Where you belong, with your Master."

The voice was muffled, weirdly hissing, but there was something familiar about it. She followed the boots up a black pant leg and over a black shirt to a face half-covered by a black mask. His chin was stark white against the black, his lips red and fleshy. His eyes were like wet granite in the mask's open sockets. She whimpered again.

"Who are you?" Her voice trembled. He answered with a gloved hand. Leather landed hard against the side of her face.

She cried out as her head bounced against the cement wall. "Quiet," he said. "I'm your Master."

She heard him clearly this time, the words harsh in her ears, blood sharp in her mouth. Master? It was ridiculous, but it hurt too much to smile. She looked past him, trying to see around the flashlight he gripped in his left hand. Beyond its circle of yellow was darkness.

Where was she?

Somewhere subterranean. A basement? All she could see was bare concrete floor and the twin mattress under her. Paper-thin foam clothed in striped ticking, it was ringed with sweat stains and smelled bad. Very bad. There were some other, darker spots. Were they blood?

She clenched her teeth in a futile attempt to stop them chattering. The room was cold, her skin freckled with goose bumps, but she was shaking with fear as much as from cold. On her right forearm was a red mark. It looked like a puncture. She stared at it, trying to figure out what had happened. Was this a nightmare?

"Focus!" The man accompanied his hissed command with another sharp smack, this one to the opposite cheek. Tears flooded her eyes. She touched her face.

"What do you want?"

She saw his hand coming and ducked down, shrieking. He dropped his light and pulled her hair, grabbing hard so that she had to scramble up to avoid having it yanked out of her scalp. He was bigger than she was, taller and broader, and he held her easily with her hair wrapped around his hand while he beat her with his free one. Thighs and backside, back and forth, a steady, hard barrage as if he were beating a carpet.

She screamed, "No! Stop!" He only hit harder. Single tears became a river. The flashlight rolled around her feet, shining light on other parts of the room, but she couldn't see, could only feel. Pain. Real pain, worse than a skinned knee, worse than a paper cut. Once, when she was little, she'd been thrown from her bike when it hit a stone and had skinned both knees and elbows. The pain was like that, sharp and hot and too much at one time. Where was her mother to comfort her?

Her skin throbbed. She could feel bruises forming and he hit against those, too. "Stop!" He would never stop.

"Please!" One word, whimpered. He stopped.

"Please what?"

She hung there on tiptoe dangling from his hand. The chain links rattled against the floor with her trembling. Pain dulled her thinking. What did he mean?

He hit her again, his fist a cudgel against her thigh. Red flashed in front of her eyes as quickly as it spread across her pale skin. "Please what?" The hiss was louder.

"Please, please—" She scrambled for the right answer. What did he want? What did he mean? She tried to think. "Master! Please, Master!"

In an instant her hair was released. She swayed and a large hand steadied her gently, pressing her body against his while he stroked her hair. "Good, little one. Good."

Her body shook under his touch and he made crooning noises, stroking her as if she were an animal he was trying to gentle.

She could smell him, the odor of sweat and maleness, and she pulled back, but the hand tightened around her shoulders and pushed her face against his chest. "No."

Another bruising blow against her backside. "Don't pull away from me."

Then his hands were moving fast over her body, cupping her breasts, trailing down her stomach. When a gloved finger suddenly entered her, she cried out and he yelled, "Quiet!"

He slid out of her after a minute's exploration and wiped his finger across her thigh. His hands turned her, started down her back with the same intensity. He was a man buying a horse and checking it for flaws. She turned her head to see his face.

"What do you want? If it's money that you want—"

His hand sprang to her head, reaching into her hair and pushing her, slamming her face down onto the pallet. Her nose pressed into the smell of it as she struggled to turn her head. A line of fire streaked across her back.

Grace screamed. Another line of fire, parallel to the first. "Shit!"

"Don't talk," he said, and the third time she heard the sound of a whip slashing the air before it landed across her back. "The slave speaks only with permission from the master."

"I'm not your slave, you bastard!" It was muffled, but he must have heard her. The whip landed again and again. Fast, burning streaks. Pain set off sparklers in her eyes, blinding her with brilliant color. Fire seared through her body. Screams were torn from her with every stroke of the whip until she couldn't distinguish between the shrieking without and within, her body a whistling teakettle of white pain.

She knew he was finished when she heard him panting. She heard his footsteps retreat, but she didn't turn her head. The mattress beneath her face was wet with tears and snot, but she couldn't move. Time passed. She didn't know how much time. She was aware she was still weeping because she could feel wetness on her arms. Then something wet landed on her back. She thought her voice was gone, but the sensation pulled one last hoarse cry from her.

"Ssh. It'll help, little one."

He was rubbing something soothing into her back and she thought it was bizarre, but she didn't say anything. Better not to say anything.

"Are you hungry, little one? There's food for you, but you have to promise to behave."

The tone of voice was singsong, as if he were talking to a puppy that needed to be toilet-trained. She felt acid rise in her throat, but was also aware of the yawning gap in her stomach.

"Can you do that? Can you behave?"

Would he take off her chain? If he took off the chain, she could get away. She nodded. The hand on her back suddenly pressed against the marks. She flinched.

"Answer properly, slave."

"Yes, Master." Fast and low, but he was satisfied. The gentle touch was back.

"Good, little one."

He helped her sit up, but his hands didn't move to the chain around her ankle. Instead he moved away, taking the flashlight with him. Darkness surrounded her like a curtain, but she could hear him moving around.

The beam of light approached. He held a dog bowl in his hand. Stopping just short of her mattress, he squatted to put it down at his feet.

"Eat, slave."

She reached with her hand, but the tip of his boot came down on her knuckles to stop her.

"No. That's not how the slave eats." He nudged her belly with his boot, her skin shrinking from contact with him. "Get on your knees."

New tears of humiliation blurred her sight, but she was hungry. Better to fight him after she'd eaten. She got onto all fours so that her head was down over the bowl and her ass raised.

She sniffed at the bowl. Smelled okay. It was pasta of some sort. She tried to do it delicately, using her lips to try and grab a piece. His hand pushed her head into the bowl. "Eat, slave."

She ate, smearing tomato sauce over her lips and chin, her tears adding salt to the food. When he brought a bowl of water, she didn't have to be told what to do, but obediently got into position and used her tongue to lap it up.

A hand stroked her head as if she were a kitten. The hiss was filled with pride. "I knew you were a fast learner."

Chapter Twenty-six

It took Kate exactly twelve minutes to drive to the police station. A record time accomplished by rolling through stop signs and running lights so red that they'd forgotten yellow existed. Still, it was too slow. Every moment since she'd opened the letter was slow.

She had to concentrate to park the car, so anxious to get into the station that she almost left the Volvo running out front. She caught a glimpse of herself in the rearview mirror as she backed into a parking space, and didn't recognize the wild-eyed woman.

The key stuck in the ignition the way it always did. She had to jiggle to get it loose. "C'mon, c'mon." Her hands shook as she locked the car, pent-up adrenaline that she let loose by running the half block back to the station and up the concrete steps two at a time.

The desk sergeant's bald head crinkled as his eyebrows rose. "I'm surprised to see you, Mrs. Corbin."

"I need to see Detective Barnaby."

"I'm afraid he's not available. What's this about, Mrs. Corbin?"

"Then Detective Stilton." But the sergeant was already shaking his head.

"Sorry, ma'am, but they're both busy. If you'll just tell me what this is about."

"My daughter. It's about my daughter."

"That'll be Officer Dombroski you want to talk to, then." His large fingers pushed the buttons on the phone even as she protested.

The wait for Officer Dombroski was four excruciating minutes. Kate sat on the bench like last time, couldn't stand it, and paced instead. The sergeant watched her from hooded eyes, taking swigs from a can of diet Cherry Coke he'd secreted under the counter.

The young officer who'd taken the missing persons report showed up with a willing smile, but looking distracted.

"Have you heard from your daughter, Mrs. Corbin?"

"No, from her kidnapper."

That got attention. Suddenly the desk sergeant was back on the phone calling the detectives who hadn't been available just minutes before.

Dombroski looked at the letter that Kate thrust out, but didn't touch it. The frown looked funny on her young face, incongruous with her freckles. She escorted Kate through the station, where it looked as if everyone had vanished. A half-eaten sandwich swaddled in greasy paper sat on one desk; partially filled out forms splayed across the surface of another.

Why became clear as Kate followed Dombroski to the back of the squad room. There were uniformed officers and plainclothes detectives, every one with visible guns strapped to the waist or hanging from shoulder holsters, spilling out the door of a large room.

"Hey, Dombroski." A young patrolman wearing too much aftershave glanced their way and stepped out of the door. "You hear they found the Hirsh photo?"

"Yeah, I heard." Dombroski barely glanced at him, but Kate slowed. Hirsh photo? "Did they find a photo of Elizabeth Hirsh?"

"I'm not at liberty to discuss the case with you, ma'am."

Kate was shown into a room with a plain table and chairs that looked like the twin of the one where she'd been held after her arrest, though the big industrial clock hung on a different wall.

Officer Dombroski took a seat across from her, and Kate thrust the letter and necklace across the table. "This came in today's mail."

The policewoman used a pen to hold the note flat without touching it. She read it through in silence and Kate grew impatient.

"He's taken her. The same person who killed Lily Slocum."

The police officer had no expression on her face. She drew the necklace to her with the tip of the pen. "This belongs to your daughter?"

"Yes, yes—it's Grace's necklace. We gave it to her as a gift for her tenth birthday. She never takes it off."

The officer looked at Kate and back down at the necklace. Her slowness infuriated Kate. "This is a waste of time! Shouldn't you be putting this out on the radio? Can't you do something more? What about calling the F.B.I.?"

"When did you say you received this, Mrs. Corbin?"

"Today." Kate looked up at the clock. "Thirty-three minutes ago to be precise." Her leg jigged, and Kate pressed one sweaty palm against it to force it to stop.

Officer Dombroski got up from the table and Kate

sprang to her feet. "We need to find the person who saw her last," she said. "I didn't have much luck the other day, but I'm not the police."

Dombroski held out a hand. "Just wait here, Mrs. Corbin. You need to talk with the other detectives."

"But time is passing! She could be hurt—please."

"I know, Mrs. Corbin." The younger woman gave her an understanding smile. "It'll just be a minute."

It was more than five minutes. Kate watched them tick by as she paced the room. Ten footsteps one way, ten the other. Back and forth. They'd found a photo of Elizabeth Hirsh. That could only mean one thing: Elizabeth Hirsh was dead.

Kate pressed a hand against her mouth forcing back bile. She pressed her hands hard against one wall, feeling the coldness of the concrete press into her palms, and ducked her head, trying to breathe. Images played in her mind—Elizabeth's smiling young face in the paper, and Grace playing the piano, her smooth fingers flying over the keys. Grace as she'd looked the last time Kate saw her, turning at the door, giving that little half wave. The covered stretcher with Lily Slocum's body and the river running behind it, dark and wild.

Kate moaned and pressed a hand against her stomach. Jesus, this monster had taken Grace and it was her fault! If she hadn't seen the first photo, if she hadn't spied on Terrence Simnic, if she'd hadn't gone looking for more evidence. Dear God, please, not her child!

It was important not to panic. Panicking wouldn't help Grace. She had to think, and she couldn't think if she panicked. Kate tried to be rational. Where could he have gotten Grace? Somewhere between school and home. It had to be. Unless she'd cut school again. That was a possibility. Someone had to have seen her, but no one had. She was the new kid, the quiet kid, the kid who could slip in and out unnoticed. That's how she was able to skip school.

Kate paced again. She was in the middle of her fourteenth lap when the door opened. It was Detective Stilton; his face still looked as if he'd bitten into a lemon.

"Mrs. Corbin." He nodded at her, glancing at the wristwatch on his arm and comparing it to the clock on the wall while his other hand jangled something in the pocket of his gray slacks.

She kept her voice steady. "Detective."

He walked over to the table and leaned on it to look down at the note and the necklace. His shirtsleeves were rolled back and she could see tendons knotted in his wiry forearms. "Officer Dombroski says you received these today?"

Jesus, how often was she going to have to repeat this? She sat back down at the table, willed herself to sound calm. "Yes, in today's mail. Forty-five minutes ago."

"Has anyone else seen them?"

"What? No. No one. I brought it straight here."

He nodded, but whether in acknowledgment or approval she couldn't tell. Her leg jigged again, a rhythmic bobbing that this time she didn't bother to suppress.

"Where did you find the photo of Elizabeth Hirsh?" she asked.

He seemed surprised by the question, but it was hard to tell in that face. "At the library."

"Is it the same as Lily Slocum's?"

"Yes."

"So it's the same photographer."

"Mrs. Corbin, I cannot discuss a police investigation with you."

"You can if it involves my daughter!"

"We don't know that."

"What do you mean we don't know? What do you call this?" Kate tapped the letter and necklace.

"Something that we need to look at. Dombroski, bag these." He and Kate watched as the younger officer donned latex gloves before picking up the letter by a corner and slipping it in what looked like a plastic sandwich bag. The necklace got deposited in a second one.

Dombroski carried them out the door as another cop poked his large head around the jamb and spoke to the detective. "Chief needs you in on this."

Stilton headed toward him. "I'm coming."

"What about my daughter?" Kate demanded, springing back up from the chair and blocking his path. "What are you going to do about Grace?" She touched his arm, and the detective looked slowly down at her hand and then up at her face with his flat pale eyes. They reminded her of a shark. She moved her hand.

"We're doing what we can, Mrs. Corbin. Sit tight and I'll get back to you ASAP."

"Sit tight?" Kate snarled, but he'd walked around her and out the door.

Grace had been gone now for more than twenty-four hours. Kate paced again, staring at one concrete wall, then another. Who had chosen this wall color and why? It was a sickly shade of green, like spring grass suddenly kept from the sun. Did they think it would push people into confessing?

She tried not to think about the ticking of the clock, but it seemed to get louder and louder. Her legs were sore. How long had she been walking? She dropped into the chair, but immediately felt the need to get up again. She had to *do* something.

It occurred to her to list everything Grace had done on the day she disappeared. Wasn't that what cops always wanted to know? She had to root around in her purse to find a pen, and then she couldn't find any paper. More rooting around while the clock ticked on and on.

A tube of lipstick rolled out of her bag and across the table. Kate reached out a hand to stop it rolling off the edge, and had a sudden memory of three-year-old Grace wearing a tutu over tights that bagged at the knee, a string of cheap glass beads around her bare little chest, and lipstick smeared across her big, pleased smile. "Pretty, Mommy."

Kate wept, large tears that she couldn't hold back any longer. They trickled down her cheeks, and she found a balled-up Kleenex in her purse to absorb them. She couldn't do it, couldn't just sit there jotting things down as if it were a grocery list. That wasn't going to bring Grace back. She had to go, move, get out of there and find her daughter.

She shoved the lipstick back in her purse along with her pen, and suddenly stopped short. It wasn't just her daughter. Ian. She'd forgotten to call Ian. Kate scrambled for her cell phone, but there was no reception in the room. She opened the door with the cell phone pressed to her ear, and pushed the redial button just as Ian came walking toward her with Officer Dombroski.

"Oh, thank God," she said. "I was just trying to call you." He opened his arms and she fell into them, new tears welling up.

"What's going on?" His arms were strong around her and a small current of relief flowed through her. He'd be able to make them do something.

"He's taken Grace. She didn't run away, she's been taken. It's the same man, the same one who took Lily Slocum and Elizabeth Hirsh."

"Slow down, Kate, I can't understand you."

She felt like shaking him, but that would only waste

more time. She swallowed hard and started again. It took effort not to babble. "A letter came in the mail and Grace's necklace was in it."

"What necklace? And where's the letter?"

Detective Stilton answered, "Right here, Mr. Corbin." He held the baggie aloft and used it to point back at the interrogation room. "Let's talk in here."

Ian took a seat at the table, and Kate reluctantly sat back down next to him. Detective Stilton sat across from them and slid the plastic bag across the table. Ian caught it and began reading.

"The only prints we could find on this letter were your wife's." Stilton said.

"He was probably wearing gloves," Kate said. Stilton didn't look at her.

"You said there was a necklace?" Ian looked from Kate to Stilton.

Officer Dombroski crossed the room and placed the second baggie on the table. Ian picked it up.

"Is this your daughter's necklace, Mr. Corbin?"

"Yes. We gave it to her for her tenth birthday."

"I already told you that," Kate said to Stilton. He barely glanced at her.

"Was she wearing it the last time you saw her?"

Kate said, "Definitely," just as Ian said, "I don't know." She looked at him. "Of course she was wearing it. She always wears it."

"Even in the last year?" Ian said. "Her fashion sense has changed a lot."

"So it's possible that your daughter took this off before she ran away?" Detective Stilton sounded like it was a foregone conclusion.

"No!" Kate's voice rang in the small room. Ian looked away, embarrassed.

"This letter could have been written by anybody," Detective Stilton said. "There's nothing specific in here that points to whoever took Lily Slocum and Elizabeth Hirsh."

"Are you saying this is some kind of joke?" Kate's voice shook with the effort to keep it level.

"Not exactly," Stilton said, and he finally looked at her, a slow, steady gaze from those cold, cold eyes.

It took Kate a minute to figure out what he meant. "You think *I* typed this letter?" Torn between incredulity and anger, Kate gave Ian a look of appeal, waiting for him to refute the allegation. Instead, the look she saw on Ian's face was doubt.

"Oh my God. Not you, too?"

"You've been going through a really hard time." Ian put his hand over hers and Kate jerked away.

"Don't touch me!"

Ian rubbed the hand over his face instead, as if all of this were making him weary. Kate would have laughed, but she was afraid it would turn into a scream. How could they think she would make this up? How could they just sit here? New tears cupped in her eyes, but she held them back. She sure as hell didn't want Stilton to see her cry.

"I swear on everything holy that I did not write this letter." Her voice shook, but at least she didn't scream. "And I didn't take my daughter's necklace. What I told you is the truth. This came in today's mail. I came straight here with it. I didn't even stop to get changed." She indicated her paint-daubed shirt. Something occurred to her and she turned to Ian. "How did you know I was here?"

He flushed, and the mixed look of shame and defensiveness he shot her told her what had happened before Stilton answered for him. "We called him."

They thought she was some crazy woman and they'd

called for her husband to come and get her. "And you just agreed with them and came along to fetch me?" she said to Ian. "Did it even occur to you that I might be telling the truth?"

Again, it was Stilton who spoke before Ian got a chance. "Mrs. Corbin, I'm afraid you're not a credible witness and without your husband's verification that your daughter was, in fact, wearing the necklace—" Stilton paused and looked inquiringly at Ian.

Kate begged, "Ian, please, we've got to find Grace." He wouldn't meet her eyes. A moment's hesitation and then, with a simple shake of his head, he betrayed them both.

Chapter Twenty-seven

There was no sense of day or night. There was only pain and the absence of pain. Grace knew that time had to be passing, but she didn't know what time it was or what day it was, and sometimes, groggy from too much sleep, whether she'd ever existed outside of this blackness.

The sound of the man's footsteps on the stairs terrified her. She pushed back into the corner of the walls, curling up like a snail, not that it did any good. He had the flashlight with him like always and found her easily.

The metal casing rapped the wall. "Up, slave!" She stayed curled in the corner, feigning sleep.

The tip of his boot nudged her ribs. She didn't move. The nudge became a slight kick. If she didn't get up, she knew he would kick her harder until she did. She pushed herself up and stood swaying slightly on the pallet, blinking in the light.

"Closer!"

She stepped off the pallet and onto the cold concrete. It was so cold that she shifted from foot to foot.

"Stand still!"

"Fuck you, I'm cold!"

The blow knocked her to the floor and she tasted blood. For a moment, her head swam and the flashlight's beam became spots of light bouncing around the room.

"Up, slave!"

She rolled to a sitting position, waiting for her eyes to focus before getting even more slowly to her feet. She could feel his eyes sliding over her and then his hands joined in, crawling from her face to her feet. She wondered if he was checking if she were clean or just liked to look at the bruises tattooing her body.

When he moved to unfasten her shackle, Grace panicked. The last time she'd cursed at him, he'd freed her only to drag her into another room with nothing but a brown cabinet on one wall and a set of eyebolts on another. He'd taken leather cuffs with welded links from the cabinet and chained her spread out like a snow angel.

"Slaves need to be trained," he'd said while she hung there. The tip of something had trailed along her skin from her neck down the hollow of her back and then he'd beaten her with it. A stick? A whip? She didn't know. Didn't care. All she cared about was not going back there.

"Please, Master." She jerked her ankle from his grasp.

He grunted and simply grabbed her leg again, his thick fingers digging into the flesh while he unfastened the shackle. It clattered onto the floor, and then he had her by the arm, dragging her along. She pulled back in his grip, trying to break loose.

"I'm sorry, Master, please."

He gave no sign of hearing and his grip didn't slacken. The beam from the flashlight danced on the floor in front of them, and then it swung up and what she saw wasn't that horrible room but a bed.

A large scrolled metal bed frame with a thick comforter. Candelabras stood on either side of the bed, warm light flickering from their wicks. She stopped struggling, staring instead. It looked warm.

"This is for you, little one."

There was a long, white nightgown laid out on the foot of the bed with lace trim at the collar and the cuffs. Something about it seemed familiar. Grace thought about that while she ran a tentative hand over the soft material.

"Dress."

As always, his voice was a command. Relieved that there was no whip in sight, she obeyed his command. She had the gown over her head when why it seemed familiar suddenly clicked.

Uttering a harsh cry, she tore the dress off and threw it back on the bed. He was taken by surprise, she could see it in those granite eyes behind the mask as he loomed over her.

"Put it on."

"No!" It belonged to the girl. Lily Slocum. It was what she'd been wearing in that photo. Grace backed away from the bed, whimpering.

He grabbed her by the hair and dragged her back to the bed. "Dress!"

"No!"

His hands were rough on her arms, trying to force them into the sleeves. She fought him, scratching what she could reach of his skin, kicking back with her legs. She connected with something soft and he cried out and loosened his grip.

Grace pulled away from him, running from the room, but when she slammed her shoulder into the doorjamb, he was on her, his hand in her hair, dragging her back.

He stopped beside the foot of the bed. Placed her hands on the nightgown.

"Dress!"

She shook her head back and forth, not once but several times. "No!"

Slap across the face. "The slave will obey!"

"I'm not your damn slave!"

It was stupid to fight him, stupid to think that she could win, but fear and the kernel of free will that still existed refused to cooperate. She blocked her face in anticipation of another blow, but instead he yanked her by the arm and led her back out of the room. She stumbled along with him, but it wasn't back to the pallet and the ankle shackle. When she saw the brown cabinet she screamed.

He hung her from the eyebolt in the ceiling, admiring the length of thin white flesh displayed like a carcass. It was marred somewhat by her constant talking. In the end, he fixed a ball gag in her mouth and beat her to music from one of his favorite CDs.

When he was winded, he stopped, the fog that came over him lifting slightly so that he could admire the red lines striping her back from neck to knee. They'd fade to purple, another pleasing color on skin so milky.

He fingered her for a moment while she hung there, more as a test of how much fight she had left in her, though he did enjoy the exploration. She didn't resist him, staring at him mutely, the deliciously vague look in her eyes spoiled slightly by drool spilling from a corner of her widely stretched mouth.

Time to remove the ball gag; he didn't want to cut her lips. There was a tear in the rubber where she'd bitten through it. He frowned at that, not liking to see his tools broken.

"You can stay here longer for that," he said, forcing her chin up and dangling the damage in front of her eyes. She stared at him blankly, only moaning a bit as he left the room and switched off the flashlight. He was pleased to see that the restraint had curbed her speech.

Humming a little Mahler, he climbed up the stairs out of one sanctuary and into another, carefully locking the door behind him. The key went into its secret place and then he removed the mask, mopping up the sweat that had formed in it and on his face from the effort of training his slave.

This one was delightful. He'd known she would be. He'd often thought of the challenge before he'd actually taken her, but she was proving to have far more spunk than the others and that was both stimulating and enjoyable.

He changed out of his clothes swiftly, tucking them away, and put back on the bland khakis and yellow polo shirt he'd been wearing earlier in the day. Loafers replaced his boots. He checked himself in a small mirror, struck, as always, by the difference in his face. It was rounder, gentler. He was two halves of a whole person and this affable man was his public self.

The book club was still going on. He could hear the soft rise and fall of conversation interrupted by short bursts of laughter as he came in the back door. He frowned at the pile of dirty dishes, the empty bottles of wine, and the crumbs from a hastily sliced baguette left on the kitchen counter. His wife always tried to impress the other women.

He plucked a grape from a bunch that had been separated with fruit scissors and eavesdropped on their conversation for a moment, just long enough to know he wasn't interested in whatever work they were debating. He could have gone through the other door and up the back stairs to the second floor, but that wasn't his way.

He paused in the doorway to the living room as if he were embarrassed to intrude, just long enough for the women to notice him.

"Well look who's here!" one of the loud ones said, her teeth unnaturally bright. The women were mostly like his wife, plump and middle-aged, showing traces of the beauty they'd once had. A few of them were keeping a tighter hold on youth, working harder at it and resented for their sculpted bodies and revealing clothing. It gave the rest of them something to talk about when they weren't around.

He stepped up behind his wife's chair, and she smiled up at him as he bent to place a gentle kiss on her cheek. His nostrils flared at the smell of wine on her breath. She ordinarily wasn't a drinker. "Enjoying yourselves?" he asked, smiling at the room while he shifted her glass slightly out of reach.

"It's a great book—you should read it," one of the women, a teacher at the local elementary school, said with great earnestness. He perched on the edge of his wife's chair, asking a few questions and pretending to listen, though he was remembering the feel of a slim, young body convulsing under his touch.

After a few minutes he excused himself, saying, "I hope you're not going to leave us all this food," with a nod at his wife's carrot cake while ruefully patting his stomach. Laughter followed after him. "You're so lucky," he heard one of the women say to his wife.

He was reading in bed when he heard his wife close

the door after the last of her guests. He waited a few minutes and when she didn't come upstairs, he went down to find her.

She was standing in the kitchen finishing off the last of the wine.

"Is that your first glass?"

She whirled around, hand to her chest. "Oh, you scared me!"

He crossed the room to her, plucking the stem from her hand. "I thought we'd discussed how much wine you're allowed to have."

She looked at him with big eyes, round brown eyes that had wooed him once upon a time, but had less effect on him today. Sometimes, she reminded him of a milch cow. He reached out a hand to heft her ample breast through her straining blouse and she giggled. He squeezed a nipple and she gasped.

"No more wine," he said. "You know how it affects you."

"Okay."

"I mean it."

She lowered her eyes. "Yes, honey." It was mumbled, but clear enough.

He smiled and smacked her lightly on the bottom. "Good girl. C'mon, it's time for bed."

He made love with her as he did faithfully twice a week, and tolerated her need to cling to him afterward, though he sweated with her weight draped over him.

"All my friends envy me my husband," she murmured in a satisfied tone as she drifted off to sleep. He stroked her head and found his own sleep in dreams of a milky body suspended in darkness.

Chapter Twenty-eight

At no other time in her life had Kate been so utterly alone. She thought she'd known this isolation when years ago, as a young art student, she'd traveled to Italy for the summer. Sometimes, while sipping espresso at a café or falling asleep in a *pensione*, she'd felt the pang of traveling without friends in a country where she didn't speak the language. That had been loneliness, though, a mood capable of being lifted by encounters with other American tourists or Italian art students.

This wasn't loneliness; it was complete and total isolation. To know something, to believe something, and to be totally alone in that belief was a horrible state. Just as bad was the knowledge that the man she'd shared a life with for almost twenty years thought she was crazy.

Two days after the letter had arrived, Ian drove Kate to her meeting with Dr. Schneider, neither of them saying anything while the car wound its way through Wickfield's quiet streets. Kate looked out the window at the placid-looking homes with their neat lawns and leafy trees and felt nothing but bitterness. Such a safe place, everyone had said. Such a good place for kids, aren't you glad you came here and left the city.

When he pulled up in front of the building, Kate got out without saying good-bye. She felt a moment's regret when she saw the hangdog expression on Ian's face as she closed the passenger door, but the chill that had settled on her heart at the police station reasserted itself. She walked without looking back into the lobby of the building and stood leaning against the wall, ignoring the curious looks of people who passed on their way into the dentist's.

She waited until Ian had pulled away, until she was sure that he'd made it past the traffic light and turned left to head to the university, before venturing back out onto the street.

It was two long blocks to the cab company. She walked briskly, passing by Thorney Antiques Emporium without stopping to see if the owner was in the window. It was an easy thing to get a cab to take her back home. During the ten-minute drive, she stared out at the sunshine fighting through the clouds before she was dropped off at her front door.

She was in the Volvo minutes later and zipping along the back roads to Wickfield High.

During the night, staring at the ceiling while Ian slept, she'd replayed that frantic afternoon three days earlier when she'd searched for Grace. She kept coming back to seeing Harold Trowle in the parking lot at the high school.

Why had he seemed startled when he saw her? And he'd been evasive when she asked about Grace. Could he be the one who'd abducted her? In the middle of the night, feverish from anxiety and sleeplessness, it had all made sense.

Now she wasn't so sure. He was certainly an odd

man, but she'd already made that mistake with Terrence Simnic. She couldn't assume anything, nor could she count on police support. If she wanted to find out anything about Harold Trowle, she'd have to go see him in person.

The security guard at the front of Wickfield High's main building was snoozing. She walked past him and into the same hallway where Grace had fallen asleep while she and Ian had been talking with the smarmy guidance counselor.

Relying on memory, she turned down the hallway that she thought led to his office, her shoes clicking loudly on the shiny linoleum floor. Where were all the students? The doors of the classrooms were all shut, but it seemed strange that there was no one walking in the halls and she couldn't hear the murmur of classroom conversation.

"Excuse me!" The nasal bark came from behind. Kate whirled around. There was sunlight streaming through the windows, and for just a second Kate thought the figure she saw was a ghost. Then the figure moved and she realized it was a woman. All of her appeared as shades of gray—the hair, the skin, the clothes. Drab and dour, she pursed her blue-gray lips and looked at Kate as if she'd committed a huge security breach.

"Can I help you?" she said, but her expression and tone belied the offer.

"Yes, I need to speak with Harold Trowle."

"He's not here. They're all at an assembly." The look on her face suggested Kate should have known this.

"I'll just wait for him in his office."

The gray woman shook her head. "You can't do that. You can't be anywhere here without a pass from the office."

She turned without waiting to see if Kate would follow, and they moved in tandem back to the main office. When she stepped behind the center desk, Kate remembered her. The gray woman was the main secretary, the woman in charge of doling out late slips and scheduling appointments with the principal. The nameplate on her desk seemed more like an ironic comment on her personality: MRS. JOY.

"Name?" she said as she filled out a visitor's badge with a gray hand. Even the wedding ring set on her left hand seemed colorless, the diamond flat instead of sparkling.

"Kate Corbin." Was it her imagination or did Mrs. Joy give her a funny look? She'd probably seen Kate on the local news.

"You'll have to wait to see Mr. Trowle." The secretary indicated a stiff-looking couch sitting opposite the desk. Kate dutifully took a seat feeling the woman's eyes on her while she idly flipped through old issues of the Wickfield High yearbook.

When she saw a familiar-looking smiling face, she stopped, startled. Ann Henke, one of the girls who'd disappeared eight years ago. Kate hadn't realized she'd been a student at the school. Her heart beat a little faster.

The book was ten years old and Ann Henke had been a senior. There were multiple photos of her throughout the book. She flipped back through the pages and there were the pictures of faculty and staff. She spotted Mrs. Joy right away, as whey-faced then as now, but she couldn't find any photo or mention of Harold Trowle.

She carried the book to the desk. Mrs. Joy looked up from her perusal of the computer screen.

"How long has Mr. Trowle been at Wickfield High?"

"I don't know."

"I don't see his picture here."

Mrs. Joy gave a put-upon sigh and took the yearbook from Kate's hands. She scanned the open page and then flipped to the front, frowning. "He probably wasn't here back then."

"But he could have been?"

"Maybe." Mrs. Joy sounded doubtful. She handed the book back to Kate. "Why do want to know?"

"I wondered if he knew Ann Henke."

The secretary gave a distinctly unjoyful sniff. "Everybody knew Ann Henke, or at least they claimed they did once she went missing. Suddenly, everybody was her best friend. Nothing like being murdered to make you a celebrity."

"Did you know her?"

"About as well as any kid at the school. I get to know the ones that get into trouble. Who do you suppose gets to look after them when they're sent here? Me. I've told the vice principal many times—I wasn't hired to be a babysitter, I've got my own work to do."

Kate made a sympathetic noise and a little color came to Mrs. Joy's gray cheeks. She sat, forward in her seat and leaned her elbows on the desk, suddenly relishing the conversation. "And don't get me started on Harold Trowle. The man thinks that there's no such thing as a bad kid. He thinks they're just misunderstood." She snorted. "I can't stand that do-gooder sort. It's no wonder, though—he's from California. The whole state's full of weirdos."

Kate laughed despite herself, and Mrs. Joy's lips curved upward in what could almost be called a smile. "Wait a sec—I can tell you when he came." She pulled open a drawer in a file cabinet behind her. "Let's see. Thomas, Tipton, Trowle. Here it is." She pulled out a file and flipped through it. "Yep, that's what I thought. He was hired in 2003."

So he couldn't have killed Ann Henke or those other young women in the past. Or Lily Slocum. Not if it was the same killer. The police said it was the same person, the clues were the same, but weren't there copycats? If it was the same person, why had he waited so long between killings?

Anxiety and despair washed over Kate in equal measure. She put the yearbook back with the others and made a show of checking her watch. "I think I'll come back another day when there isn't an assembly."

"Suit yourself." Mrs. Joy turned back to her computer. "You should call first, you know, and actually make an appointment."

"Thanks, I'll do that." Kate was at the door when she thought of something else. "Do you know if the Henke family still lives in Wickfield?"

"I heard the marriage fell apart after what happened. They say that lots of marriages can't sustain the loss of a child."

The house where Ann Henke had lived was on the opposite side of Wickfield on a street similar to the Corbins' with its old homes and mature oak and sycamore trees stretching enormous boughs across to touch their neighbors.

Kate checked the slip of paper on which she'd scribbled the address given by Mrs. Joy, and saw that the house she wanted was the last one on the block. She parked, the slam of the car door echoing slightly.

There was no one around. She had the sudden feeling that it was as if time stopped when Ann Henke disappeared and like some aberrant version of *Sleeping Beauty,* everything and everybody on this street had died with her.

The concrete walkway was crumbling in places, and the lawn looked patchy and colorless even for December. The brick of the house needed to be repointed. One of the black shutters hung askew. Two stone urns flanked the front door, empty except for a scrim of dust.

Kate rang the bell, shivering in the cold and waiting in silence so complete that she could hear the drone of a lone holdout fly. When no one responded, she pulled open the creaking screen door and used the brass knocker.

The face of the woman who opened the door was an older version of the smiling photo from the yearbook.

"Are you Beth Henke?"

"Yes?" The woman held onto the door as if she were using it for support. She was pretty, like her daughter had been, with the same dark hair, though hers was graying and her face looked prematurely worn.

"I'm Kate Corbin. My daughter is missing and I think she was taken by the same person who took your daughter—"

"I don't want to talk about it." The woman's face crumpled and the door started to swing closed. Kate stopped it with her foot and a hand.

"Please, Mrs. Henke, I need your help."

"I can't, I'm sorry." Mrs. Henke pushed against the door, but Kate held on, pushing back.

"If you could just tell me a little about Ann," she said, speaking rapidly. "Please. I'm begging you, Mrs. Henke."

The woman hesitated, pinching the bridge of her nose with thin fingers that trembled. "All right," she said after a moment. "I don't know what I could possibly tell you, it's been so many years. Ten minutes— that's all I'll give you."

She showed Kate into a hallway with a dusty console

table. The mirror hanging above it also had a film.
Heaped on the table were a woman's handbag, a nondescript jacket, and a pile of mail. "I just got home from
work, I only work part-time most days," Mrs. Henke
said, one hand straying to the mail before moving away
to twist a button on her blouse instead. It was plain cotton, as were the black slacks she wore. They hung on
her thin frame. She stared at Kate with a look torn between pity and confusion. "I suppose we could sit down."

The living room didn't appear to be used by the living. A stiff brown sofa and two patterned armchairs
faced each other in front of an empty fireplace. It might
have been very pretty, probably once was, but time and
neglect had changed things. Dust lay on all the surfaces
and a fern on a corner plant stand shriveled from want
of water and sunlight. Huge floor-to-ceiling curtains
were drawn across the windows, muffling light and sound.

Kate's heels sank in plush carpet that looked like
dingy cream. She took a seat in one of the armchairs
and tried not to sneeze.

"I used to keep this place spotless." Beth Henke's
voice was flat as she switched on a lamp before sitting
down on the sofa. "I guess I got busy."

Her hand strayed to her blouse again. "Are you Elizabeth Hirsh's mother?"

"No, my daughter is Grace Corbin. She's been gone
for three days." Four hours, twenty-five minutes, Kate
added mentally.

As if she could read her mind, Beth Henke said, "I'm
sure you're counting the time."

"Yes."

"I did that, too." Grief had cut deep lines on either
side of Beth Henke's mouth. She twisted the button on
her blouse until she noticed what she was doing, and
folded her hands in her lap instead. "I must have

missed your story on the news. I don't like to watch much; it's too depressing."

Kate didn't correct her, unsure if the woman would believe her.

"I don't know how I can help you," Beth Henke said. "Ann's been gone a long time."

"I hoped that maybe there was some overlap some-where—that maybe the girls knew the same person, or had met someone on campus."

"That seems unlikely after such a long period of time."

"What was she studying?"

"History." Beth Henke smiled a little. "Her father said she'd never do anything with that degree. He wanted her to major in business or computer science or something like that."

Kate couldn't think of anybody in the history depart-ment. "I read that she disappeared on the way home?"

"Back to her dorm," Beth Henke said. "Even though we lived in town, she wanted her independence. Both her father and I thought it was important to let her have the typical college experience." The stricken look on her face made it clear that she regretted this deci-sion.

In a voice that dropped the farther in to the story she got, Beth Henke described the call she'd taken from the police and the frantic efforts of the family to find Ann.

"We did everything they suggested. Are you going to do a TV appeal?"

"I don't know." Kate hedged.

"We thought it would be a good idea—a personal ap-peal could work, they told us—but it didn't help." Beth Henke looked down and her hand moved back to the button, twisting and twisting.

"Did the police have any suspects?"

The other mother shook her head. "Of course they thought it was her boyfriend at first. We all did. But he wasn't involved at all."

Kate asked for his name anyway, but it meant nothing to her. "The police ruled him out as a suspect?"

Mrs. Henke nodded. "Airtight alibi. He was visiting his father in the hospital when Ann disappeared. Massive heart attack the night before she went missing—Ann called to tell us about it."

"But you still suspected him?"

She nodded. "You know how it is—when your child disappears, all you think about is finding her. You're not interested in other people's feelings."

Thinking she was guilty of doing the same thing, Kate asked, "Did you ever hear from the person who took her?"

"You mean aside from the awful photo?" Beth Henke's chin trembled and she covered her face with her hands. For a few moments, the only sound in the room was her loud weeping. Kate spotted a box of tissues on an end table and fetched them for her. The woman went through several before she looked up again, red-eyed.

"I'm sorry to ask," Kate said, "but yes, I was wondering if you'd gotten anything else. Any letters?"

A single hard shake. Beth Henke stood up, tissues balled in her hand. "Please, I've told you all I can. I don't want to talk about it anymore."

Kate stood up as well, but she made no move toward the door. She hadn't learned anything new; she had to find something that could help her. "I know this is an imposition, I know I have no right to ask, but I feel if I could just see some of Ann's things I might find some clue. Do you have an address book or photos of friends I could see?"

The woman looked at her for a long moment, but then she nodded. Kate followed her back to the front hall and up a wide flight of stairs to the second floor and a closed door at the end of a softly carpeted hall.

Beth Henke opened the door and Kate stepped into a little girl's paradise. The walls were a pale pink, the carpet fluffy white, the canopied four-poster bed piled high with lacy pillows and stuffed animals.

It was the sort of room that Grace would have loved as a little girl, but firmly rejected once she became a teenager. Too pink, too girlish, too young. It seemed an odd room for a young adult, but Ann had definitely lived here. There was proof of the different stages of her life in the photos on the walls and the shelf above the white desk and chair: riding a pony as a toddler, poised to dive into a pool, smiling with a grade-school soccer team, preening in a bikini on a beach.

It took Kate a moment to realize that it was the only room in the house that appeared to be clean. Everything was dusted, everything carefully arranged. It was a shrine.

Kate didn't know what, exactly, she was looking for, but she examined the photos and then the two pretty memo boards covered with ticket stubs and yellowing concert programs and ribbons earned at long ago sporting events. No other faces looked familiar, none of the scenes jogged a memory. There was no connection to Grace of any kind and Kate felt desperate.

Aware of Beth Henke standing like a silent sentinel in the doorway, Kate looked at the textbooks neatly stacked on the desk. She found a sketchbook among them.

"Ann took a drawing class?"

"Yes, it was an elective for her."

Kate turned the pages. Charcoal studies progressing

from shapes to still lives of fruit to some rudimentary nudes. She'd had some talent, though her line was a little heavy. Kate flipped back, and noticed that Ann had printed her name and the title of the class in neat writing inside the front cover. It was the name underneath, though, that made Kate's breath catch in her throat.

In the same neat printing, Ann had written: "Professor J. Virgoli."

Chapter Twenty-nine

It started to snow as Kate drove toward the university, a hard driving fall of flakes so tiny that they looked identical. They melted against the windshield, but froze on patches of road. The Volvo's tires slipped in spots, but she didn't slow down, just kept pressing the accelerator while her hands kept a tight grip on the wheel.

What if the police pulled her over? Would they listen to her this time? Probably not, they'd probably just slap her with a big ticket. It didn't matter, none of it mattered, except getting to the university. She didn't know where Jerry Virgoli lived, but she could find out. She had to talk to Ian. Surely he would listen now, surely if he was presented with direct evidence he couldn't ignore it.

She had the heat on full blast, but was still shaking. What if it wasn't Jerry Virgoli? So what that he'd taught drawing to Ann Henke. He must have taught hundreds of students over the years.

Yet she couldn't help remembering that party back in September. It felt like a lifetime ago, standing on the lawn in the warmth of a late summer evening. She could still hear him complimenting her on having a "daughter as lovely as yourself."

Had he talked to Grace at any other time? She couldn't remember, but Grace had been on campus often enough, he had to have seen her. He was an odd man, Ian had said so himself, and he'd wanted Ian's job. It made perfect sense, but still she could hear Ian's voice accusing her of wanting to get him fired.

She pulled into the parking lot on campus closest to Ian's building and switched off the motor, but she didn't get out of the car. There had to be something more, some other piece of evidence compelling enough to make Ian and the police listen.

She stared blankly at the snowflakes gathering on the windshield. The sun had completely gone; the sky was low and thick with gray clouds that suggested heavy snow. She thought of Grace and prayed that she wasn't cold, that she was alive and warm and could wait, just a little longer, for her mother to find her.

The snowflakes formed patterns on the windshield, the wind blowing them about. Little circles of white, they reminded her of blossoms. Suddenly, she thought of the flowers in the photos. Every victim had been surrounded by flowers. They had to have come from somewhere. Hadn't she argued as much to the police? It had been one of the main reasons that she'd suspected Terrence Simnic, but it wasn't him, it was someone else. Someone who had to purchase the flowers.

She started the motor with trembling hands and drove off campus and toward the center of town. She knew of three florist shops in Wickfield including Terrence Simnic's. She started with the one in a strip mall at the edge of town.

All the traffic in the parking lot was huddled near the grocery store. No one was thinking of flowers in December snow. The front window was partially steamed over and the pots of sparkle-dusted poinsettias looked garish. Some of their leaves were brown at the tips and curling inward.

There was no one in the small store besides a young man in a green rubber apron working behind the counter. He barely looked up from his work, giving Kate a quick once-over before grabbing a sheet of red tissue paper to wrap around a scrawny bouquet of daisies.

"Do you keep a customer list?" Kate asked, stepping past buckets filled with roses to get to the counter.

"Nope—we just fill orders as they come in." The young man kept his eyes on his work.

"But don't you get repeat orders?" Kate pressed. "Surely you keep a list of repeat customers?"

He looked up for a moment. "I don't know anything about that."

"Well, is your manager in?"

The man shook his head. He couldn't be more than twenty-five, but he had a taciturn expression suited for someone who'd faced a lifetime of disappointments. With nicotine-stained fingers, he reached for a piece of ribbon from a spool behind him.

"When will your manager be in?"

"Tuesday."

"She never comes in the shop otherwise?"

He shook his head, tongue coming out of his mouth as he concentrated on tying the ribbon around the bundle. "Only Tuesdays."

In the second store, the most upscale one in Wickfield, the front window had a tasteful Christmas scene complete with real fir trees and golden decorations. The manager was behind the counter, directing a young woman in how to properly arrange cut flowers in a crystal vase.

When Kate said that she was with the art department and needed to check the customer log to find out what they'd ordered in the past for a big show, the woman was only too happy to let Kate look at the customer list, kept in a big black ledger that she pulled out from under the desk.

The book was easy to read, a list of names and next to them the flowers they'd ordered. Kate scanned it eagerly, sure she would find Jerry Virgoli, but his name wasn't there. She read over it three times, but there was no Virgoli and no familiar names at all.

Walking back to her car through a half inch of snow, Kate felt despair settle over her. There was only one store left and she'd agreed, on pain of being prosecuted, not to set foot in it. But she had to see the list, she had to know and she had to know now.

For a moment, she considered calling Ian, turning her cell phone over and over in her hand, but ultimately she slipped it back in her pocket. She couldn't convince him because she was barely convinced herself.

The roads were worse. It wasn't yet two, but the snow was falling so fast that the plows and salt trucks had to race to catch up. The side streets were becoming ice slicks, and she had to crawl to avoid spinning out.

What if she was wrong? What if this hunt was nothing but a wild-goose chase and it wasn't Jerry Virgoli at all? Doubt plagued her through the last few streets, and only the thought of finding Grace kept her going.

She parked a block away from Bouquet just like she had before, only then it had been warmer and now snow lashed her face. Jerking the hood of her coat over her head, she walked as quickly as she could toward the shop, slipping and sliding on ice-covered spots.

There was no sign of Terrence Simnic's van. He liked to make deliveries himself, but maybe he'd sent somebody else today. When she came abreast of the window, she slowed her steps and while pretending to look at the display, tried to peer behind it and see who was in the shop.

No sign of Terrence Simnic, though he could be in the back room. If she went in and out quickly, he wouldn't see her. All she needed was the list.

A bell jangled softly as she opened the door, but it sounded loud in her ears. It was warm in the shop, humid. The young woman behind the counter wasn't Josie. She looked up from trimming long-stemmed red roses and gave Kate a smile.

"Can I help you?"

"Yes." Kate wove through buckets of bright-colored roses and lilies, past long, leafy ferns, and around a display of pansies to the counter. "I'm with the art department at the university and we're hosting a big exhibit and I just need to check your customer list to see what we've ordered in the past."

The young woman frowned. She pushed a strand of shoe-polish-black hair behind an ear studded with small metal spikes and shook her head. "That list is like, confidential, you know?" She stripped leaves from the roses; one hand had a small heart tattoo on the back.

"I like your ink," Kate said, trying to sound calm, relaxed, as if it was no big deal.

"Thanks. I just got this one." The girl smiled. Across the bust of her too-tight black T-shirt, big red letters said, "What Are You Looking At?"

"My daughter wants a tattoo."

"Are you going to let her get one?"

Not on your sweet life. "I will if I can find her."

"Where's she gone?"

"My daughter's missing," Kate said in a low voice, thinking that this girl couldn't be much older than Grace.

"Wow!" The girl's mouth dropped open, and Kate caught a glimpse of silver tongue stud. "For real?"

"Yeah." Kate glanced around the shop. Still no sign of Terrence Simnic and there was no one else to overhear her. "She's been abducted. I think she was taken by the same person who took Lily Slocum."

"That really sucks," the girl said. "I'd be, like, just wiped or something if anything happened to Brady." She tapped a picture taped behind the counter of a smiling dumpling of a baby with a big bow apparently glued to her bald head.

"Is that your sister?"

"No." The girl laughed. "She's my daughter."

Babies having babies. Not long ago, this had been one of Kate's worries for Grace, a mother's nighttime fear when she thought of her teenage daughter. It seemed like a different life, the memory was so distant.

"That's why I really need to see the customer list," Kate continued in the same low voice. "I need to check if there's a particular name on it."

The girl nodded. "Okay, yeah, I understand. I think that would be considered, like, extraordinary circumstances, but I think I've got to ask my boss first." She reached for the phone.

"No!" Kate grabbed her hand, and the young woman looked afraid. "No," Kate said more calmly. "I'm really not supposed to tell people—the fewer people that know the better. It's a police investigation, so everything's hush-hush."

"Right." The young woman spoke in a whisper, her face solemn. She searched the counter and then under the counter, but came up empty-handed. "It's not here. I guess it got moved to the back." She walked through a swinging door and left Kate standing at the counter.

It was quiet in the little shop, the only sound the hum of the furnace and the drip from a sink in the corner. She played with the rose leaves on the counter, trying to stay calm. It seemed to take so long. What if the girl had decided to call her boss?

She looked back over her shoulder, but there was no one driving on the snow-covered street. Kate glanced at her watch. It had been just three minutes; it felt like three hours. Surely the girl would come soon. She had to come back out soon. Kate twirled a rose in her hand, watching the blossoms spinning, thinking of the flowers in the photos. They'd found Elizabeth Hirsh's photo. That meant Elizabeth Hirsh was dead. Dear God, please let Grace be alive. Please let her be found.

Another minute. A minute, forty seconds. All the photos were carefully arranged to be aesthetically pleasing. It made perfect sense that it was Jerry Virgoli. Only someone with some knowledge of art could arrange that composition.

Four minutes and thirty seconds. She must have decided to call her boss. Even now she was on the phone with Terrence Simnic, and he was going to have Kate arrested again. There was no guarantee that Jerry Virgoli even got the flowers from this shop. It could just as easily be the first store where she hadn't been able to see a list. Maybe she should go back there and press the stupid man for the manager's number. If she got arrested again, Grace would never be found.

Just as Kate turned to go, the girl came out of the back bearing a computer printout. "Here it is! We've got a notebook thing, but I couldn't find it. I got you a list off the computer. This is the most I could print."

She laid the pages on the counter and Kate eagerly took them, running her finger down the list of names. It wasn't a list of repeat customers, just a record of every transaction over the last two months.

Again, she couldn't find the name of Jerry Virgoli. Kate felt the same rush of disappointment she had at the other shop and the same reluctance to accept it. She scanned the pages again and again, going more slowly each time, sure that she was just skipping over it. But his name wasn't there. The only name that popped out at her again and again was Grace. In every case the customer was Grace Methodist Church.

The name of the church sounded familiar. Someone she knew attended that church, but who? She thought about it as she scanned the list and then, as she handed it back to the young woman, it came to her. The Beetlemans. Wasn't Grace Methodist the name of the church that the Beetlemans attended? She thought she remembered Clara Beetleman commenting on it when she'd met Grace.

"No luck?" The girl looked disappointed.

"No." Kate thought hard. Was there any such thing as a coincidence? She pointed at the name of the church. "They seem to order a lot. Who pays for them?"

"Yep, every week or so they're here to pick out flowers. Usually it's a couple of women from the church buying them."

"Do you have receipts for that? How do they pay?"

"Sometimes cash, sometimes check or credit card. Why?"

"Would you have those receipts accessible?"

"Yeah, but it'll take me a few minutes to get to them."

While she disappeared into the back a second time,

Kate stood at the counter and tried to make a connection. Jerry Virgoli wasn't anywhere on the list, but maybe he attended the same church as the Beetlemans. It fit his personality that he'd attend a church just so he could get closer to the man he admired. It was possible. Could he be getting flowers from the church?

The receipts were kept in a shoebox. Kate and the girl sifted through them, quickly eliminating anything that wasn't connected with the church. It took several more minutes to find anything. "Here's one," the girl said finally, handing over a signed credit card receipt. The neat signature at the bottom read CLARA BEETLE-MAN.

"That's it," Kate said. "That's what I needed."

"Is that the one who's got your daughter?"

"Someone who can help me, I hope." Kate helped the young woman stuff the slips back into the box. "Thanks for your help."

"No problem. I sure hope you find her."

"Me too."

Just as Kate got to the door, it suddenly opened bringing in a gust of wind and snow and Terrence Simnic.

Chapter Thirty

Terrence Simnic stopped short when he saw Kate, one large hand wrapped around the doorknob, the other holding an empty box. Snow blew in as he stared at Kate, his large, blank face filling with emotion.

"What are you doing in my shop?" His voice was loud, brusque.

"I'm just leaving," Kate said, inching left so she could sneak around him.

"You're not supposed to be in my shop," he said. "I told you! The police told you! You're to stay away from here."

"Yes, I know, I'm sorry. I'll leave now, okay?" Kate tried to sound calm.

"Why did you let her in here?" Terrence Simnic demanded, shifting his gaze toward the girl at the counter. The moment his eyes left hers, Kate bolted, dashing past him, their coat sleeves brushing as she ran out the door.

"Hey, stop!" His bellow was loud enough that Kate flinched, but she didn't stop. She flew down the snow-covered sidewalk, going so fast that wind singed her cheeks and cold air froze her lungs. She slipped on an icy patch, falling forward, snow scalding her palms, soaking through the knees of her jeans. Ignoring the pain, she sprang up and kept going.

When she reached the car, she dared to look back, and through the curtain of snow she could see a dark figure moving toward her. The key jammed in the lock. Frantically jiggling it, she finally yanked hard to the left and the lock gave. She shoved the keys in the ignition and hit the lock button, but the engine wouldn't turn over. She tried again. It coughed and spluttered, but wouldn't start.

"C'mon, c'mon," she muttered, staring out the windshield. It was definitely Terrence Simnic, she could see him clearly now, barreling toward her, his large boots smashing through the snow like hammers.

Her hand shook as she turned the key again and pumped the accelerator. He was closer, closer. She could see his angry face locking eyes with her through the windshield. The engine started with a roar and she yanked the wheel hard to the right, slammed on the accelerator, and leapt forward onto the street just as his hand slapped the driver's window.

Simnic jumped off the curb after her, but the car gathered speed, spraying snow, and she watched him retreat in the rearview mirror.

It was just two o'clock, but the snowstorm had intensified and the light changed. The gray of the sky deepened and the dark, bare trees cast long black shadows across blankets of white.

She drove toward the Beetleman house praying that Clara would be there, that she'd help her. Clara had known Jerry Virgoli for a long time and she didn't like him. She had to help Kate. Maybe she knew where he got the flowers; maybe she knew something about him or could help Kate find out something. She'd help. She had to.

The Beetlemans' house looked just like it had when they'd hosted the party, only now a fresh coating of snow covered the front lawn and the maple tree out front was bare. The front walk had already been shoveled and salted, and the porch furniture was shrouded in plastic covers for the winter. There was a fir wreath hanging on the door.

Clara Beetleman opened the door with her usual welcoming smile. "Kate! Hello!" she said, clearly surprised.

"I need your help, Clara. It's about Grace."

"Of course I'll help, but come on in out of the snow. You must be freezing!" She pulled Kate's sleeve, ushering her inside.

The interior was silent and spotless. The wooden floors and the banisters on the stairs gleamed as if freshly polished. There was a small, decorated tree in the front hall, filled with twinkling white lights. It smelled of pine and furniture polish.

"Let me take your coat, it's soaked!" Clara fussed over Kate, helping her off with her coat and pointing out a rubber mat on one side of the door where she could put her wet shoes. "What's this about Grace?"

"She's missing." Kate bent over to work at the laces of her shoes; they were encrusted with snow. "I think she's been abducted."

"What? Good heavens! Have you told the police?"

"Yes, yes, but they don't believe me." Kate stood up, and suddenly the floor seemed to dip forward and she stumbled.

"Steady there, careful." Clara Beetleman's arm came around her waist, holding Kate up. "Come on, you need to sit down." Clara led her into the living room, where Kate collapsed on a sofa.

"You're as white as a ghost," the older woman said. "You need something to drink and when was the last time you had anything to eat?"

Kate tried to think, but her head ached. "I don't know, I might have had a piece of toast for breakfast?" She had a vague memory of Ian offering her something.

"It's no wonder you're about to pass out." Clara Beetleman patted one of Kate's hands. "You just sit right here and I'll get you something."

She bustled away before Kate could protest. It was quiet in the living room. A larger Christmas tree stood in the corner opposite the piano, its thick branches sparkling with colored lights and fragile glass ornaments.

An antique grandfather clock in an engraved case ticked quietly in the corner. Kate felt the same squeeze of desperation and she couldn't stay seated, but got up, pacing around the room. She paused at the far window, gazing out at the backyard. Between the leafless trees she could see glimpses of Dr. Beetleman's studio.

"Here we are!" Clara Beetleman bustled into the room bearing a heavily laden tray. Kate turned to help her, shifting a pile of books on the dust-free coffee table so the other woman could set it down.

"There's cream and sugar, or lemon if you prefer," Clara Beetleman said, pouring a cup of amber liquid from a fat little ceramic pot into a delicate cup balanced on an equally delicate saucer. She passed it to Kate. "Get some of that into you."

The cup trembled in Kate's hand. She took a sip of scalding tea and then another. "She's been gone for almost four days."

"Oh, Kate, you must be frantic." Clara Beetleman looked reassuringly grandmotherly in a long red corduroy jumper with her short, graying hair tucked behind her ears. No one would ever accuse her of being crazy. "What are the police doing?"

"They don't believe me, no one believes me."

"Why?" Clara Beetleman picked up a plate of cookies and held them out. "Here, they're shortbread, freshly baked. Get some food into you."

Kate dutifully ate a cookie. Clara Beetleman took one, too, eating it with small, fastidious bites. Crumbs dropped onto her jumper and she brushed them away with her small, plump hand. A gold ring on her right hand caught the light, the green stone in its center gleaming. The cookie in Kate's mouth suddenly tasted like sand.

She swallowed. "That's a pretty ring."

Clara Beetleman glanced down at it. "Thank you. Laurence gave it to me for my last birthday."

"Do you know where he got it?" Kate felt as if her voice belonged to another person. She looked at Clara Beetleman, but saw the face of a missing girl smiling out from a photo in the yearbook. She saw Ann Henke, vanished in 2000, her young hands framing a smiling face, on one of them a ring of twisted gold with an emerald stone.

"I think he found it at an antiques store." Clara Beetleman poured more tea. Took a sip. "You were saying that no one believes that Grace has been abducted but you?"

"Yes." Dr. Beetleman had given his wife the ring. Dr. Beetleman said that Grace was a talented girl, but needed to work harder. Dr. Beetleman said that a girl as pretty as Grace had to be careful.

"Actually, I think it would help if I talked to Dr. Beetleman. Is he here?"

His wife shook her head. "He's in his studio, but I'm

under strict orders not to disturb him when he's out there—it's one of his little quirks." She offered a small smile as apology. "I'm afraid you'll have to make do with my help."

"I'm sure he'd want to know that Grace is still missing."

"Oh, so you've already told him?"

"Yes, on the afternoon she disappeared. He didn't tell you about it?" Kate couldn't take her eyes off the ring.

"No, I guess he didn't want to worry me."

Kate stood up abruptly. "I really need to talk to him about Grace. I could just go out there and knock on the door."

Clara Beetleman struggled up, letting her cup drop so that tea splashed over the sides and filled the saucer. "Please don't," she said as Kate walked toward the door. She moved quickly for such an overweight woman, stepping in front of Kate, her ample body blocking the door. "Really, he gets so upset if he's disturbed." Her plump face creased with concern, the cheeks flushed.

"All right." Kate looked down at the ring again, then up at Clara Beetleman's face.

"Maybe you could tell him I need to talk to him?"

Clara Beetleman's face relaxed. "Absolutely, dear. I'll tell him as soon as he comes in for dinner."

"I think I should get going, the snow's getting worse."

Clara Beetleman watched from the front door as Kate trudged through the snow back to her car. She was still standing there when Kate drove away.

There was an alleyway that ran between the Beetlemans' street and the one behind it, and Kate went around the block and waited two minutes before turning down it, driving slowly back toward the Beetlemans' home. She could see the Beetlemans' car through the window in the detached garage, but there was a fence surrounding the yard itself and the back gate was locked. Over the fence she could only make out the studio's snow-covered roof.

Why had Clara Beetleman been so adamant about not disturbing her husband? What was in that studio? He'd given her the ring, the ring he'd taken off one of his victims. But that was impossible! This wasn't like suspecting Terrence Simnic or even Jerry Virgoli. She suspected Dr. Laurence Beetleman, beloved professor and famed composer, a pillar of the community, of taking her child.

Nobody would believe her. If she called the police right now, if she pretended to be someone else and reported a tip to go investigate Dr. Beetleman's studio, she knew exactly what would happen. They'd go and he'd talk to them in his usual, reasonable fashion and they'd go away. And if she told them about the ring? He'd have an answer for the ring, explaining that he'd found it in a store and he'd probably name Mrs. Thorney's shop, and everybody knew that she wasn't too careful with the merchandise she got and it could have been sold to her.

Maybe that was what had happened, but Kate didn't think so. She had to get in that studio, but if she waited until he emerged for dinner it would be too dark. She needed him out of there now and somewhere far enough away so that she had time to find a way inside.

If he wouldn't leave for his wife, what would pull him away? A phone call from Ian would work—he wouldn't ignore a summons from the dean. As soon as Kate thought this, she discounted it. Ian would never agree; he'd probably have her committed. He wasn't in anyway—hadn't he said something this morning about an afternoon meeting off-campus with some important

alumni donors? And then it occurred to her that she
didn't really need Ian. She glanced at her watch. It wasn't
three yet. If she hurried, she might be able to beat him
back to his own office.

It was the final day of exams. Students already finished were leaving for the winter break, wheeling suit-
cases across the snowy quad. The halls of the building
were deserted. Kate's footsteps echoed on the stairs as
she took them two at a time.

Ian's secretary sat typing at her desktop, the sleeves
of her fuchsia suit jacket hitched back and a pair of
rainbow-colored reading glasses perched on her small,
upturned nose. She looked up and blinked at Kate.
"Oh, hello, Mrs. Corbin!"

Kate had given up asking to be called by her first
name. "Hello, Mildred. Is Ian back from his meeting?"

"No, not yet." Mildred checked her own watch. "He's
due back in about thirty minutes."

"I'll just wait for him then."

"Of course." Mildred Wooden popped up from her
chair and came around the desk. "If you'd like I can
bring you something to drink and we have some magazines to read." She indicated the waiting area across
from her desk.

"Oh, thanks, but I think I'll just wait for him in his office." Kate breezed past a blinking Mildred into Ian's office and closed the door. There was Ian's massive desk,
all neat and sparely furnished, his silver desktop waiting. She sat down in his leather chair and opened the
mail program.

It took her ten minutes. Keeping an eye on the door,
she composed an e-mail about an emergency faculty
meeting. Scrolling through his SENT box, she found old

e-mails that helped her with wording, and it was a simple matter to find Dr. Beetleman's address. She hesitated just for a moment over the SEND key, thinking of what had happened with Terrence Simnic. Once she hit SEND, it could not be undone. There was no hope that she could lie about having done it either, not with Mildred Wooden sitting outside. Her only hope lay in the next part of her plan, getting into the studio, and that was much harder.

"In for a penny, in for a pound," she muttered, quoting her father's favorite phrase. He'd been a shy, retiring sort of man, but wouldn't shy away from adventure if it came to him. He'd said this phrase before venturing down the tougher ski slopes with her or agreeing to backpack through Canada one summer when she was twelve. She wondered for a moment what he would have made of what she was doing and then, taking a deep breath, she hit SEND.

Chapter Thirty-one

Kate was actually driving down the road when she passed Laurence Beetleman coming in the other direction. Kate slid down in her seat and he sped by. She didn't think he'd seen her.

She parked on the street that ran perpendicular to the Beetlemans' and headed down the alley on foot. The snow in the drifts was up around her ankles now, and there was no way she'd be able to hide her footprints. She didn't care. All she cared about was Grace, finding Grace, holding Grace. It seemed to her that she'd give up so much else, her reputation, her marriage, even her art, if only she could have her daughter back.

The gate into the Beetlemans' yard was locked from the inside. Kate could see it through a slit in the wood, but she had no way of prying it open even if she could reach it. She'd have to go over the fence. It was approximately six feet high and made of wooden slats flush with each other and ending in squared-off triangle tips.

There were three trash cans standing in a row along

one outside wall of the garage. Two of them were empty. Kate took one and upended it next to the fence and as close to the garage as possible so that Mrs. Beetleman wouldn't see her.

She clambered on top of the can, balancing against the fence with one hand and using the other to haul the second empty can. She steadied herself and looked over the side into the yard. As she'd hoped, this section of fence was almost directly behind the studio and obscured from the house.

Hoisting the second trash can over the fence, Kate leaned over so far that the fence points dug into her stomach, then let the can drop. It sent up a little cloud of snow, rocking back and forth precariously before deciding to stay upended just as she'd planned. She managed to get one leg over the fence without scraping it against the top, before turning and bringing the second one over. Balancing with her gloved hands, she stretched her legs down as far as she could, searching for the safety of the upended can.

There was still a gap of a few inches, but her right toe could just brush the plastic, so she let go of the fence. A split-second free fall and then her right foot landed smack and square on the can, but her left foot hit the edge, couldn't hold, and she toppled back, landing with a thump in the snow.

It knocked the air out of her. She breathed hard for a moment, blinking up at the gray sky, before cautiously wriggling her arms and legs. Everything seemed fine, so she got up, brushing off the snow, and looked around. She was just behind the studio and not visible from the house. She moved the trash can to make sure it was completely hidden, and cautiously peered around the side of the studio toward the house.

There was no movement in any of the windows. The

single set of footprints she'd seen from the Beetlemans'
living room window was filling with snow. Clara Beetleman was somewhere in the house. Did she know her
husband had gone?

Kate walked around the side of the studio closest to
the fence line and the cover of trees, conscious of the
quiet crunch of her footsteps in the snow.

There were curtained French doors on this side of
the studio, and she felt something hard under her feet
and knew that it must be a terrace. In warm weather,
Dr. Beetleman would open these doors and step onto
the terrace, lifting his large head up to the sun. Snow
covered the terrace and piled against the edge of the
closed doors. She tried the handle, but the doors were
locked.

There was no way to gain entry from the front of the
house without attracting attention. Even if Clara Beetleman didn't see her, somebody else might and they'd
probably call the police. No, this was the place where
she had to get in and she didn't know how.

She tried the handle again, tugging on it in a vain attempt to get the doors open. The wooden doors were
flush with one another and she had no way of getting
the latch open. Except by breaking a window.

The glass doors were divided by mullions into small
windowpanes. All she had to do was break one of them.
She searched the ground for something to use, and
found a broken branch under a pine tree. It was thick
enough that it would probably work. Would the noise of
breaking glass be heard by the neighbors or even in the
house? She didn't think so, but just to be sure she took
off her scarf and knotted it several times around the
end of the branch.

She picked a pane closest to the door latch and gave
a few experimental taps before ramming it as hard as

she could against the glass. For a second, it was as if nothing had happened, but then hairline cracks spread out like a spider's legs from the point of impact and the window shattered.

The challenges of fund-raising went on and on. Ian sighed as he sat down in his office chair and began the follow-up letter to the alumni he'd wooed that afternoon. With any luck, at least one of them would make a sizable donation to the arts center. He'd certainly sold the place to them. The public relations office had managed to finish glossy brochures showcasing the future center just in time for the meeting.

He wrote a paragraph laced liberally with phrases like "leaders in today's global marketplace" and "the new philanthropists." There were times when he felt like a complete phony, but if it helped build the center, then he didn't care.

Mildred had told him that Kate stopped by. She'd left without leaving a message. He was ashamed to admit that he'd been relieved she hadn't stayed. She probably wanted to talk with him about Grace again, but what more could they do?

He looked at the framed photo of Kate and his daughter that stood on his desk. Grace was laughing in the picture, Kate had her arms wrapped around her and a big smile on her face. Cape Cod in July, a warm sunny day with a perfect blue sky. It was just a year and a half ago, but it might as well have been a hundred. Had they really been happy then? It seemed that ever since Kate's assault things had gone in a downward trajectory. It was as if they were under some unlucky star, but he knew that he had to admit his own culpability in the matter.

He got up from his desk and went to the window, looking out across campus. The last of the students were leaving for winter break, small clusters trudging through the snow toward cars and buses. He envied them. They got to leave. Back in September, he'd entertained so many fantasies about his family's first Christmas in Wickfield.

He'd heard of a farm where people went to cut their own trees, and he'd envisioned a family outing, all three of them bundled up against the cold, with lots of laughter and good-natured arguing about which tree to pick. Grace always wanted a huge tree, and had tried unsuccessfully for years to convince them that seven-foot monsters could fit into their small apartment in the city. This year, for the first time, they could actually have one, but there was no point in getting one now. Not with Grace gone.

A knock at the door made him turn his head, surprised when it opened and Mildred bustled in followed by Dr. Beetleman.

"I'm sorry, Dean, but Dr. Beetleman insisted on seeing you immediately."

"It's okay, Mildred." Ian crossed the room with his hand outstretched to the other man. "Laurence, how are you?"

Dr. Beetleman ignored his hand. His usually friendly face looked angry. "I thought the meeting was supposed to start at four."

"What meeting?"

"The faculty meeting you scheduled this afternoon. I've been waiting in the conference room for twenty minutes. Did you cancel and forget to e-mail me?"

"I didn't schedule a meeting," Ian said. "I haven't scheduled any meetings between now and Christmas. I assumed we'd have too many no-shows."

"Then why did I receive an e-mail from you this afternoon scheduling an emergency meeting?"

"It couldn't have been from me. I've been schmoozing with deep-pockets alumni all afternoon. I only just got back to campus."

"It came from your e-mail address."

"I'm telling you, Laurence, that I didn't send it. Look I'll show you." He went behind his desk and brought up his mail program and looked at the "sent" column. He was stunned when he saw the message.

"I don't understand, I didn't write this."

"Then your secretary perhaps?"

Mildred denied sending it. "Oh, no, it wasn't me, but maybe—" She stopped short.

"Maybe what?" Ian said.

Mildred fiddled with her glasses chain, looking at Ian and then away. "I'm sure I'm wrong, but I suppose it's possible."

"What's possible?" Ian felt a headache coming on.

"When Mrs. Corbin came, she wanted to wait in your office," Mildred said in a low voice, looking at Ian, but stealing a little glance at Dr. Beetleman.

Ian flushed. "Why on earth would she send out an e-mail about a faculty meeting?"

His secretary nodded. "You're right, of course, I'm sure she wouldn't."

Dr. Beetleman started to say something, but stopped short, his eyes widening for a moment as if he'd had some realization. He said gruffly, "I guess it must have been a mistake."

Relieved, Ian said, "Yes, probably some glitch in the mail program. I'm sorry about that."

"It's okay, not your fault."

"As long as you're here, why don't we discuss the adjustments you've made to the drawings?"

"I can't." Beetleman's smile was strained. "I promised Clara I'd help with some Christmas decorating."

*   *   *

Kate cleared enough glass to get her gloved hand through to unlock the door, but getting it open was a different matter. It was stuck, perhaps warped by the weather, and rattled in its frame before finally, grudgingly, inching open. She kicked it open further and stepped inside, her boots crunching on glass underfoot. She left the door ajar.

It was a large room, much bigger than it looked from the outside, about twenty feet by thirty feet and beautifully furnished. One wall was lined with bookcases, and there was a baby grand piano on one side of the room and a large wooden desk on the other. A long, chocolate leather sofa sat between them, with colorful throw pillows in bright shades that matched the Persian rug on the floor. The free space on the walls near the desk and the piano were hung with black and white photos of woodland scenes. Soaring trees, blankets of leaves, and in one that stopped Kate short, a dark ribbon of water running between rocks.

There were curtained windows on either side of the door that faced Beetleman's house, and Kate was afraid to turn on a light switch for fear that it would be seen by Clara. She had to make do with muted light and she didn't know precisely what to look for.

She started with the desk, moving quickly through each drawer, but there were nothing but files filled with compositions and notes about compositions, and other files filled with plans for the new arts center. Architectural drawings for the arts center were spread over the desk's surface. There was nothing that linked Beetleman to the dead girls. Absolutely nothing.

She searched the entire room, scanning the bookcases and looking at all the small artifacts of a long career that they held—small baskets from Peru, jade from

China, a samovar from Russia. Mementos of every sort, but not the ones she wanted. She even searched the piano and the tiny half bath tucked next to the bookcases. Nothing.

Feeling increasingly desperate, she searched under the sofa before collapsing on it in despair. There was nothing, absolutely nothing. What if she'd been wrong and he really had found the ring at an antiques shop? She stared blankly ahead, overwhelmed at the thought of being wrong, when something struck her as odd.

Sunlight through the open French door caught the faint outline of a footprint near the bookcase. The weird thing was that it was only half a footprint and the foot was pointing the wrong way. It was coming out of the wall.

Kate got off the sofa and walked slowly toward the bookcase. No, she wasn't seeing things. Marked in dust on the hardwood floor was the unmistakable outline of the front half of a man's shoe. It was flush with the bookcase, but how could someone have left a footprint under the bookcase?

Kate looked more closely at the bookcase. They were actually three bookcases mounted side by side. The footprint emerged from the right bookcase. Kate shifted a few books from one of the center shelves, but all she found was the back panel of the bookcase. There was nothing visible when she looked at the open side, but when she ran her fingers behind it, they bumped against something metal. It was thin, cylindrical, and about two inches high and there were three more just like it spaced along the wood. It wasn't until she'd reached the third that she realized what they were: hinges.

Kate took hold of one of the fixed shelves and pulled. Some books fell over onto their sides, but the bookcase didn't budge. She ran her hands over the opposite panel and found a small groove, large enough to be a handhold. She pulled on that, and stumbled backward as the bookcase suddenly swung out into the room.

Behind the bookcase was a door. In the place where a doorknob would be was a flat keyhole. There was no way to get past the door without the key. Kate sprang to the desk and searched all the drawers a second time without luck. She checked the drawers' backs and bottoms. She took Beetleman's silver letter opener and tried to slide it between the door and the jamb. The tip snapped off.

Frantic, she looked elsewhere in the room, even checking the window sills, the bathroom shelf, and behind the photographs, but she got nothing but dust-covered hands for her efforts. Keening with disappointment, she spun in circles, trying to find something that would work. She'd come to the conclusion that he was carrying the key when her eyes fell on the metronome.

It was an obelisk of black marble sitting on the edge of the piano, and she'd passed by it during her first search because it looked solid. Except that she'd forgotten that metronomes had doors of their own that opened to reveal the inner workings of the machine. With trembling hands, she turned the little latch and opened the door. And there, small and shiny, was the key.

Chapter Thirty-two

Laurence Beetleman greeted students on his way back to his car with a jovial smile and a wish of "Happy Holidays." Once he was in the privacy of the brown sedan, the mask fell away. He sped through the streets ignoring the snow, and nearly caused an accident when he slid through a red light at the intersection of Morton and Reed. He didn't slow down.

While he drove he hummed Chopin's *Funeral March*, gripping the steering wheel tighter and tighter while imagining that it was her throat underneath his hands. She thought she could fool him, the bitch, and she would beg for death before he was finished with her. She wanted to ruin him, but he wouldn't let that happen.

"You're a dirty little pig, Laurence." His mother frowned down at him while working a bar of lye soap into a lather with her hands. She smeared it across his face, dug into his skin with a washcloth. "Stop spluttering, you won't die swallowing a little soap. It'll do you good. Do you want to live in filth all your life? Don't you want something better?"

He had made a better life and she couldn't be allowed to disrupt it. None of this would be happening if Ian Corbin had been more of a man. He wasn't a leader at all; he was a follower, following after a woman like every weak man. The man had to be the head of the household; that was the natural order of things. Crazy little redheaded bitch. In another century, they would have burned her at the stake.

There wasn't time to waste on getting the car in the garage. He parked in front of the house and jogged up the walk. As he stepped in the front door, Clara came flying down the stairs, small, plump body hustling.

"Goodness, you gave me a start! I didn't expect you back so soon."

He strode into the living room, the mask falling effortlessly back into place complete with smile, but the room was empty. The ornaments wobbled slightly on the tree. The twinkling lights seemed to mock him. He turned to Clara. "Where is she?"

"Laurence, your boots!"

Snow from his boots puddled on the hardwood floor and seeped into the Persian rug. "Never mind that—where's Kate Corbin?"

"Kate? She was here earlier, but she left."

"When did she leave? Did you let her in my studio?"

"Of course not!"

He brushed past her, heading toward the kitchen in the rear of the house, and she followed, blathering on about the snow. "I can't believe that they called you in for a meeting in this weather. What was the dean thinking? Can't you take off your boots? It won't take a moment."

A teapot and two used cups and saucers were on the

kitchen counter. She'd been here, in his house, drinking tea with his wife. He scanned the backyard, but it was dusk and he had to switch on the outside lights to search for footprints.

"Rob called while you were out. He wanted to know what time we were planning to serve dinner on Christmas. I said we weren't sure and asked why he needed to know, and then it came out that they have to eat with her family, too. Why they couldn't have told us this weeks ago I don't know, but of course I didn't say that—"

"Would you just shut up!" It was a growl.

Clara abruptly stopped talking, her large cow eyes going wide. She wasn't accustomed to him shouting, and shrank back against the kitchen counter. He pressed a hand to his forehead. Wrong voice. Wrong manner. His worlds were colliding; he had to keep things separate.

"I'm sorry." He slipped the smile back on with some effort, patted her plump hand. "What did Kate Corbin want?"

"To talk about her daughter. You didn't tell me their daughter was missing."

"She ran away a few days ago. It has nothing to do with us." He could see something along the fence line. What was it?

"She wanted to talk to you, but I wouldn't let her go out to the studio, not while you were working."

"You told her I was in the studio?" It looked like a trash can, but what was a trash can doing on this side of the fence?

"Yes, because she wanted to talk to you."

"Did you let her in the yard?"

"What? No, why would I do that?" Clara laughed a little, but stopped when he grabbed her arm and yanked her to where he stood looking out the window.

He pointed to the dark spot in the snow. "Then tell

me how one of our trash cans ended up on this side of the fence."

Clara whimpered and tried to pull away. "Laurence, you're hurting me."

"Answer me!"

"I don't know!"

"I've told you about letting people trespass. I've warned you about that time and time again, Clara."

"I didn't, Laurence, I swear!"

He opened a kitchen drawer, searching. "You shouldn't have let Kate Corbin in the house."

"Why not? I thought you liked the Corbins."

"She's a crazy woman, that's why." He shifted dish towels, reaching toward the back of the drawer.

"Why does she want to talk to you?"

"I don't have time for this conversation, Clara. You go on back upstairs."

"But Laurence—"

"I said go upstairs!" His voice thundered and she flinched. His hand closed on the item he wanted, but she was still here, standing as if planted in the doorway, her fat body jiggling with barely suppressed emotion.

"Laurence," she tried again, his name a whine.

"Just go," he said in a softer voice. "I'll take care of things."

He waited until she was gone before he lifted his hand from the drawer and pocketed what he'd been after. He unlocked the back door and headed across the snow to his studio.

The key turned smoothly in the lock and the door opened. Kate saw a flight of wooden steps disappearing into darkness.

"Grace?" Her voice shook, barely louder than a whisper. She could hear nothing beyond the rapid beating of her own heart. She ran her hands along the wall hunting for a light switch, but couldn't find one. One step down, then another. "Grace!" She shouted it this time, but there was no echo and no answering cry. All sound seemed to be swallowed up. At the bottom of the steps, she could see the outline of a light fixture. It took a few seconds of frantic fumbling and standing on tiptoe before finally locating the switch, which had been oddly mounted flush against the ceiling.

Light flooded a corner of the room and she looked around, blinking. There was a long chain attached to the wall and some dog bowls near it. But the metal collar at the end of the chain wouldn't fit around a dog's neck.

"Jesus!" Bile rose in Kate's stomach and her legs felt weak. "Grace!" She screamed her daughter's name, tears running down her cheeks, but there was no response, no sound at all except her own rapid breathing.

She fumbled for her cell phone, she had to call the police, but it wouldn't get a signal underground. She couldn't leave. A scent came faintly to her that grew stronger as she moved farther into the space. It smelled like flowers.

Around a partition was another room that was empty except for a wooden cupboard hanging from one wall. She opened it and retched. It was filled with torture devices, whips and clamps and gags and more of the cuffs like the one in the other room. "You bastard," she muttered. "You sick bastard."

She swiped at her eyes and kept going, following the scent of the flowers and turning on the lights as she went. The next room was dominated by a velvet chaise lounge, and several pieces of expensive-looking photography equipment. In a corner stood a bucket filled with white roses and lilies. Kate pressed a trembling hand to her mouth to hold back the bile. Her whole body shook, she didn't think she'd ever stop shaking.

"Grace, please God, not Grace." Had he already taken her daughter's photo? Had Grace been spread like a feast on this lounge surrounded by flowers?

Suddenly, something clanged behind her. Kate spun around, sure that Beetleman had returned, but then the noise came again. Closer.

There was another room. She hadn't seen it in the dark. She fumbled with the knob and the noise came again. The door wouldn't open. Kate slammed against it and only then realized that there was a dead bolt fastened higher up.

She slid back the bolt and flung open the door. Chained to the four corners of a large iron bed, naked, gagged, and bruised but very much alive, was Grace.

His boots left deep tracks in the thick snow as Laurence crossed the yard. It fell on his shoulders and sleeves, caught in the wool of his coat. "Your father has never aspired to anything more than this cesspool of a town. He actually likes it here." His mother lifted her highball glass and took a long swallow. He ran his car across the living room floor and watched her. She had on her shiny dress. They'd been to dinner out of town and left him with a sitter, and now they were back. His father with his tie pulled loose hid on the sofa behind the newspaper, a thin line of cigarette smoke wafting up toward the crack in the ceiling.

"Isn't that right, John?" she said, her words slurring. "He likes the people here. He thinks people like this are salt of the earth. Poor, illiterate, and ignorant—why, he's king among such men. You're nothing but a small-town undertaker and you always will be."

Bitch. A woman like that would tear a man down. He couldn't let her tear him down. Some women wouldn't listen to reason. Some women had to be taught their place.

The trash can had been used to get over the fence. He followed the footprints leading from it around the side of his studio. When he saw the door ajar, Laurence felt a surge of righteous anger. She'd violated his sanctuary.

Shards of glass were caught in the curtains and scattered across the floor. He stepped quietly over them and into the gloom of the room. He waited, listening, certain that he'd find her hiding in the shadows, but nothing moved. His eyes moved around the room, searching for things that she'd violated. It took him a moment to realize just how much she'd discovered. It wasn't until he'd walked farther into the room that he saw the bookcase pulled out from the wall. And then he heard her voice coming from the basement.

Kate's hands tore at the cloth wrapped tightly across Grace's mouth and all the while her daughter's eyes were on her. Both of them were crying.

"It's okay, I'm here now, it's okay," she crooned, just as she had when an infant Grace had woken in the night crying. She couldn't get the knot undone, but she managed to wriggle the cloth free of Grace's mouth.

"It's Beetleman, he's the killer!" she cried.

"I know. I've got to get you out of these." Kate checked the cuff around Grace's left wrist, but it was bound tight.

"There are keys. He leaves the keys." Grace jerked

her head to the left, nodding frantically in the direction of one of the large candelabras flanking either side of the bed. Kate looked, but couldn't see anything but used pillars and wax drippings.

"I can't find them!"

"Up! Look up!"

High above the candelabra an iron hook jutted out from the wall. Dangling from it was a set of keys. Kate grabbed them.

"Hold on, baby, hold still." There were five keys on the ring and she'd gotten to the fourth before the steel cuff finally sprang open. Grace gave a little cry as her arm fell free.

"Hurry, Mom! He's coming back!"

Kate raced around the bed to the other wrist before releasing both ankles. The shackles clattered against the bed frame. Grace scrambled up, wobbling when she stood on her feet. Kate caught her and Grace clung, her shaking arms holding tight to her mother. Kate drank in the feel of her, stroking her hair, but then she pulled back.

"We've got to get out of here." She unzipped her coat. "Quick, take this." She helped Grace into it and put her arm around her daughter's waist. "Can you walk? As quick as you can, sweetie."

They moved together out of the dark room and down the creepy hallway. Grace hobbled slowly, then faster, seeming to gain strength with every footstep. When they reached the stairs, Kate wrapped her arm more tightly around Grace's waist.

"Here we go, honey, one step at a time."

One, two, three. Each step seemed to take an effort. Four. Five. Kate was watching Grace's feet when her daughter stiffened in her arms.

"Going somewhere?"

The voice was a hiss, inhuman. Grace screamed as Kate looked up in time to see Beetleman coming down the stairs. He raised his arm as she pushed Grace behind her. She swung her fist at him, but he blocked her with his arm and then pressed something hard against her side. Her entire body convulsed with pain, and then she fell backward into darkness.

Chapter Thirty-three

When Dr. Beetleman left, Ian sat back down at his desk and looked more closely at the e-mail. It had to have been sent by Kate. According to Mildred, nobody else had been in all day and the mail had been sent from this computer.

Why on earth had she sent it? He called home first, and when nobody answered dialed her cell phone. It rang and rang. The sun was low in the sky. He could see a silver glint from the river far off in the distance. Ian decided he wasn't going to stay late. The work could wait; he needed to find Kate. He packed his briefcase and grabbed his coat, surprising Mildred in the outer office just as she was looping a long, bright orange scarf multiple times around her neck.

"Good night, Dean Corbin. Have a good evening."

"You too, Mildred. Tell me, did Kate seem, well, okay this afternoon?"

"She seemed her regular self if that's what you mean."

"Yes, that's exactly what I mean. She wasn't agitated?"

"No, not that I noticed."

Not that Mildred was a reliable source. Her desire to look at the bright side blinded her to reality. What did she do when she went home? He knew she was single and that she owned a cat, but nothing else beyond that. Did she sit alone in a small apartment with just the TV and her cat for company? At some point he might have thought that sounded like a lonely existence, but at the moment he envied her. How nice it must be to leave work without having to think about it again until the next day and go home to a quiet place with the assurance of an equally quiet evening.

Snow was still falling as he walked to his car, a silent downpour of small white flakes. The temperature had dropped, and he pulled up the collar of his coat. There were drifts along the sidewalks, and the previously black and barren trees were now outlined in white. His car was one of the last in the lot.

He tried calling Kate again, but both numbers rang and rang and she still didn't answer. He pictured the Volvo spinning out on an icy patch or its engine dying and leaving her stranded. He drove through the dark streets toward home following a salt truck.

The Volvo wasn't in the driveway, and the house was dark. Ian made a vodka tonic and drank it while playing back messages on the answering machine. There were no messages from Kate, but there was an interesting message from Dr. Greta Schneider asking that Kate please call if she wanted to reschedule the meeting she'd missed that morning.

"Damn it all, Kate, where are you?" His words echoed in the empty house. It was in that moment that he realized she'd left him. That would explain why she hadn't gone to her therapy appointment and why she wasn't answering the phone. He climbed the stairs to their bedroom steeling himself to confront an empty closet, but when he slid back the door all her clothes were there. Feeling almost giddy with relief, Ian checked her dresser and found it equally full. She hadn't left. He wasn't a complete failure as a husband then. Not yet.

He wandered through the rest of the rooms, but there was no sign that she'd been home since the morning. His sense of relief that she hadn't packed up and gone gave way to anxiety. Where was she? He called the police and was put on hold for ten minutes. He'd already spoken with Officer Dombroski once that day, checking in as he had every day for any sighting of Damien and Grace, but there'd been nothing new to report.

When Officer Dombroski got on the phone, she started talking before he could ask about Kate. "I planned to call you just as soon as we verified this information, Mr. Corbin, which we hadn't until a few minutes ago."

"What information? Is it something about my wife?"

"Your wife? No, sir. It's about your daughter, or about the man she was supposedly traveling with." He heard papers rustling. "Damien Rattle or Rachtel."

"The police found him?"

"Yes, sir, the police in Los Angeles followed a tip on his whereabouts and located him in a Hollywood hotel earlier today. He denied being with your daughter, but they took him in for questioning while checking out his story. Apparently, he was telling the truth—he was able to provide receipts for single travel out to Los Angeles via Greyhound, and after double-checking with the company, we've verified that no one matching your daughter's description traveled by bus that day."

Ian sank into a chair, his head reeling. "So she isn't with him?"

"No, sir, apparently not."

"But then where is she?"

"I couldn't tell you, sir. We don't know that yet, but as soon as we have any more information we'll definitely call you."

When he hung up, Ian just sat there in the dark room. Memories of Grace overwhelmed him. Grace as an infant being held by a smiling, tired Kate in the hospital room. Five-year-old Grace twirling around with her arms outstretched, sun glinting off her short black hair. Grace swaying slightly as she played the piano, her eyes closed in concentration, her long fingers flying across the keys.

Such a short time, only fifteen years, yet it seemed like she'd been part of them forever, and the thought of losing her caused the breath to catch in Ian's throat and he felt a sudden stabbing pain in his chest.

He'd held onto the belief that she'd run away because it was easier. As awful as it was to know that Grace had run away to be with that stupid boy, at least that way she'd left of her own accord. It was far worse to face the harsh reality that she'd been taken.

Grace wouldn't have gone away on her own, her mother was right about that. She'd been right all along and Ian hadn't listened to her. He'd been so sure that her belief in an abduction was just another manifestation of the stress she'd been under since the assault. What if the letter hadn't been a hoax? What if it was real?

Ian ran back up the stairs in search of the letter. He had to find it. The police would need to take another look at it now that Damien had been exonerated. Ian searched the entire house, but couldn't find it anywhere. He called Kate's cell phone again and again, but there was still no answer and his sense of desperation grew. It finally occurred to him to check her studio, and that's where he found it, tucked next to the easel where there was a disturbing canvas of a female form struggling in dark, flowing water. The face on the figure looked like Grace.

He read the letter once and then again, trying to really analyze it. It had been typed on clean white paper.

An artist should be capable of recognizing genius, yet you told the police that a florist released Lily Slocum. A florist. Is this a joke? I'm not laughing. You think you're smart, but you're not. Here is a riddle for you to solve: What is more precious to you than life itself?

It was plain white paper. Plain typeface. There was no handwriting to identify, and when he held the paper up to the light hoping to find a watermark, there was nothing. It was just cheap, generic printing paper sold in reams at every office discount store in the country. Nothing gave any clue to the identity of the writer but the message. He read it again and then another time, taking it word by word.

Whoever wrote the letter was obviously insulted that Kate had thought Terrence Simnic was the killer. It was Simnic's occupation that the letter writer felt insulted by. He used the word florist twice. It was a class thing, this distinction, and it stirred something in Ian's memory. It flashed through his mind too quickly for him to grasp, like a fish darting through water.

He stood up and walked around the studio trying to distract his brain so that the memory would float back and he could grab it. He saw that Kate had a pile of Grace's practice CDs and put one in the paint-spattered player. A haunting melody filled the room and he could picture Grace playing it, her pretty face frowning in concentration, her fingers slowing a bit as she came to a difficult section. The music went on for a few minutes and then stopped, interrupted by a voice. "No, no! Again, with more feeling. You must bring more emotion into your performance. You must feel the music in your soul. Do you have the soul of a grocer or an artist?"

Ian hit rewind. The words were so familiar. Suddenly, he had hold of the memory. He'd been talking with Dr. Beetleman about the architects submitting their plans to the local committee to secure building permits. "A town full of peasants," Beetleman had scoffed. "We have to convince them that they want an arts center."

It wasn't just the same sentiment as the letter, it was the same tone. Ian headed for the door, moving so fast that his hip caught Kate's worktable and sent paints and brushes clattering to the floor. He ignored them, pausing only to grab the letter, which he clutched in a tight fist as he ran to his car.

Chapter Thirty-four

Kate swam toward consciousness slowly. Her body felt oddly heavy and ached all over, as if she'd done something physically taxing and her muscles were spent. She tried to lift her head, wincing at the fresh pain that erupted with the tiniest movement. Her tongue felt thick in her mouth. She tasted blood, and when she licked her lips, salt.

"Wake up." The voice came from far away. Something tapped against her cheek, a steady beat of small blows. She pulled away from it and someone laughed, and then a hard hand caught her chin and yanked her head up.

Kate opened her eyes and saw Dr. Beetleman in front of her, holding her jaw in one large, leather-gloved hand. She jerked back, only to howl in agony as her arms protested. They were chained above her head, wrists cuffed together and suspended from an iron hook. Her toes were on the floor, but her legs were too weak to hold her.

"Don't worry, it will wear off." Dr. Beetleman spoke

calmly. He waved something small and black in front of her. "A stun gun. Gift from my younger son. I'll admit that I was disappointed when he wanted to go into police work. I'd given him so many opportunities, so many, and yet he chose something so ordinary." He imbued the word with disgust. Then he smiled, his fleshy lips curving upward, but his strange gray eyes unchanging. It was like watching a circling shark. She recoiled and he laughed.

"Where's Grace?"

"Where she belongs."

"If you've hurt her I'll kill you." It was a ludicrous threat, and he ignored it.

"You're a big disappointment to me, Kate."

"Not as big as you are to me."

He laughed again. A harsh sound, like metal beating rock. There was no real humor in it. He stroked the side of her cheek with his gloved hand. "Such a pretty face, but too much talk. Your husband should have curbed your tongue years ago."

"Your wife should have cut out yours."

The blow caught her flat against the side of her face. She swallowed the cry that rose from her throat, but couldn't stop the tears stinging her eyes. They trailed down her cheeks, and through their haze she saw his pleasure at the sight of them.

"Your mouth could be put to such better uses. Did your husband never teach you that? Ian has been so lax." He made a tsk-ing sound. She looked past him, trying to find Grace. Through the doorway she could see the dog bowls and chain. The chain disappeared beyond the doorway. Was Grace attached to it?

"It's a pity we don't have more time. I could train you to put it to better use." He blocked her line of sight. "What are you looking for?"

"The police. They're on the way here right now."

"The police?" He sounded delighted. "Somehow I really doubt that. You see, the police think you're crazy, Kate. Just another out-of-control artist. They probably attribute it to drug use." He imitated someone popping pills.

"How are you going to explain this to your wife?"

Another ringing blow. Kate's teeth scraped the side of her mouth. She tasted more blood.

"Don't you dare talk about my wife!" There was no more affability in Laurence Beetleman's voice. This was raw anger, and for the first time she saw him as a killer.

He said as if he could read her thoughts, "You're going to die, Kate, and it's so unnecessary." He reached out a hand to cup her breast through her sweater, and she flinched. He laughed, squeezed harder. "We'll have some fun before you go, don't worry."

"Let go of me."

In answer, he put both of his massive hands on her sweater and ripped it down the middle exposing her breasts. She pulled away, but he simply hooked one hand into the waistband of her jeans and yanked her back, the other hand scooping her breasts free of her bra. He dandled them as if they were fruit. "Just as lovely as I remembered. It's been a long time since I've seen these."

His words made her as nauseated as his touch. He'd seen her breasts before? When? He looked into her face, and must have seen her confusion because he laughed again and said, "You don't remember? Let me refresh your memory."

He dropped her breasts and walked away. She was shaking. Her arms wouldn't last much longer. Already, it felt as if they'd been pulled too far from their sockets. She tried to see where he'd gone, but he was out of her line of sight and all she could hear were his footsteps. She looked the other way, trying to swing in her bonds, hoping to catch a glimpse of her daughter. Had he hurt her?

As softly as she could, she whispered, "Grace?"

The chain in the doorway moved a little and then Grace came into view, scrambling over the pallet closer to the dog bowls so she could catch a glimpse of her mother. Beetleman had taken off Kate's coat and Grace was naked again, her body looking bluish and bruised in the poor light. New tears clouded Kate's vision. She mouthed, "I love you," but Grace simply stared at her with large, frightened eyes, her long limbs tucked close to her body.

"Do you remember me?"

The sibilant whisper electrified Kate. She swung around and stared, a horrified cry caught in her throat. Her rapist stood in front of her. She'd know him anywhere, the same balaclava, the same dark jacket and pants. Above all, the same voice, that frightening hiss that came to her in her dreams. Her whole body shook as he walked slowly toward her.

"I see you do remember," the snakelike voice said, and then he stood face-to-face with her and she looked into cold gray eyes and knew it was Beetleman.

Ian parked behind Laurence Beetleman's brown sedan and tramped to the front door, snow spilling into his shoes and soaking the bottom two inches of his khakis. He rang the bell and stood shivering on the porch. He'd left the house without a coat, and the V-necked sweater he wore over his button-down shirt wasn't nearly enough protection from a twenty-degree day.

There was no answer. He thought he saw movement

in one of the leaded glass panels flanking the front door, and tried to peer through it. Something dark passed over it, but he couldn't be sure it was a person. He rang the bell again, but no one came.

He glanced back at the street where Beetleman's car was parked, and then up at the house. He walked over to one of the curtained windows, but could see only the glistening lights of a Christmas tree through the lace. Maybe they couldn't hear the bell. Or maybe they didn't want to answer. He hurried back down the walk, flapping his arms against the cold, and tramped across the lawn to the fence that enclosed the backyard.

Snow had accumulated against the fence line, and after he'd reached over to unlatch the gate, Ian had to put his shoulder against the wooden slats to shove the door open far enough to pass through.

In a corner of the yard was a small cottage. Dr. Beetleman's studio. Ian remembered seeing it when he'd been here for the party back in September, but he'd forgotten all about it in the months since. The place looked deserted, but a light from the Beetlemans' deck illuminated the wide expanse of fresh snow, unbroken except for a single set of footprints heading from the house to the studio.

Ian followed them, running through the falling snow as best as he could, his feet sinking into drifts as high as mid-calf.

"Stop right there!" The voice reached him at the same moment as the distinct click. It was the sound of a gun being cocked. Ian spun around. Clara Beetleman stood at the edge of the deck wearing a padded green coat and a pair of high black rubber boots. Her arms were locked in front of her and in her hands was a small, black gun.

"You!" Kate cried, and Beetleman laughed.

"Yes, it's me. Surprise." He grinned, and with the mask his face looked like a death's-head. "The arts center needs support at the very top. That idiot Virgoli doesn't have the skills, other people didn't have the credentials or right frame of mind, but then I found Ian Corbin. He'd spearheaded similar, albeit smaller, projects and was eager to try his hand at something bigger. Eager to get the recognition he deserved. He was the right candidate to champion my project. It was all perfect, except for one little impediment." He tapped Kate lightly on the forehead. "You."

"You hid in my studio?" She was ashamed that her voice shook. She didn't want to show her fear.

"Yes. It was quite easy. There's very little security in those old buildings and such convenient fire escapes. And you were so predictable. It was easy to find out when you'd be there. I just had to wait."

"Why?" The question slipped out before she could stop it. He actually chuckled.

"You were ambivalent about moving to our nice little town, so I needed to give you an incentive."

"You bastard."

A gloved hand whipped up and wrapped around her throat before she could react, and then he squeezed. "Careful, Kate, I might have to bridle you."

He pressed his body against hers, moved his face in close. She could smell his fetid breath and the leather from his gloves. The hiss of his voice circled her, became all the noise in the room, as he choked tighter and tighter. Somewhere, dimly, she was aware of Grace whimpering. His face was disappearing behind constellations. She could feel her consciousness slipping away and she would die here, now, in this basement. He would take her body to the same river where he'd left

Lily Slocum and Elizabeth Hirsh and she would float in that darkness forever.

Her feet brushed the floor, she pushed with them, trying to escape. The feel of him hard against her repulsed her. In desperation she brought her knee up as hard as she could, ramming it into his crotch.

He yelled and released her throat, falling back, his hands cupping the front of his pants. She sucked in air with a deep inhale and kicked him again as hard as she could, aiming for his ribs this time and feeling a satisfying crunch as she connected.

Already off balance, Beetleman crashed to the ground, the keys flying from his hand and skittering across the floor. He was on his side, moaning, and she tried to reach the keys with her feet. Even if she grabbed them, there was no way she could use them. She kicked them instead, stubbing her toes against the concrete before one kick connected and she sent them sailing farther out of the room.

Grace was huddled on the pallet, her hands wrapped around her head. "Grace, the keys! Grab the keys!"

At her mother's voice, she looked up and stared from her mother to the keys. "Can you get them, sweetie?" Kate said. "See if you can get them."

Grace ran out the line of the chain, but she was still too far. "I can't reach them!"

"Try again. You've got to try! Lie down on your stomach and stretch across the floor."

Beetleman rolled onto his knees, pushing himself up. Kate swung forward and kicked him again as hard as she could in the stomach. He collapsed with a loud groan.

Grace stretched out on her stomach and reached across the concrete. The keys were less than two inches away, tantalizingly just out of reach. She strained against the ankle cuff, stretching her body as far as it would go. Kate could see the outline of every vertebra in her spine and every knuckle in her long, white hands. Grace began crying. "I can't do it, Mom! I can't!"

"Yes you can," Kate called. "Try again, Grace, try!"

Blood spilled from the thin skin just above Grace's foot from the heavy shackle digging into her ankle as she pulled as far as she could. Her arms strained against their sockets like her mother's as her hands stretched across the concrete. She grazed the keys and then, miraculously, her middle finger closed over the tip of one.

Ever so slowly, inch by inch, she pulled the keys back toward her. Finally, with a cry of triumph, she clasped them in her hand.

"Good girl!" Kate cried. She glanced down at Beetleman who was moving on the floor. They didn't have long. Grace freed herself and ran, crying to her mother, stepping over Beetleman to get to her side.

"It's too high," Kate said of her own chained hands. "You need something to stand on."

"I don't know if there is anything." Grace leapt over Beetleman and ran from the room, her ankle dripping blood.

Kate could hear her searching. "Can you find a chair?"

Grace came back in the room dragging a large, black case. "It's the only thing I could find—I hope it's high enough." She pushed it next to her mother and clambered on top while Kate tried to steady it with one leg.

Grace's fingers moved over the metal cuffs. "I can't see," she said, struggling to insert the key. All at once it connected, the cuff opened, and one of Kate's arms flopped down. The other cuff followed and Kate dropped. Her fall upset the case and Grace landed on top of her.

"C'mon." Kate used her legs to scramble up and Grace

followed, but Beetleman's hand closed over Grace's injured ankle.

"You're not going anywhere, slave," he hissed.

Grace screamed and Kate swung around. "Hit him!" she yelled.

Grace balled up the fist clutching the keys and clouted Beetleman with all her strength on the side of his head. His eyes rolled back and his hand slid from her ankle as he clunked back onto the floor.

They ran for the stairs, but when they got to the top the door was closed and no amount of pushing would open it. Grace tried all of the keys on the ring, but none of them fit the lock.

"They don't work!"

"Try again! I can't do it." Kate massaged each sore arm with the other, watching as Grace took the keys one by one, but without any luck. The key for this lock wasn't on the ring. "He must be carrying the key for the door. We have to go back."

They backtracked through the narrow corridor, but the only thing in the room where they'd left Beetleman was a spatter of Grace's blood.

"Clara, it's Ian Corbin," Ian called, starting back across the yard toward her.

She waved the gun at him as if he couldn't see it. "Don't move!"

He stopped walking. "I came to see Laurence."

"You're trespassing." Her voice was cold. "Get off my property."

"No one answered the front door." He aimed for a friendly voice. It sounded false and she didn't respond. Instead, she began walking slowly toward the end of the deck without taking her eyes, or the gun, off him.

He said, "I thought I'd try around back."

She came down the steps with the gun still held out in front of her. Her plump body bobbed in the snow, but her arms were steady, the gun fixed on his chest. The rush of fear at seeing the gun increased the closer it got. Ian walked backward, moving away from it.

"Stop or I'll shoot!" Clara yelled, lifting the gun a little and squinting along its length. He stopped immediately, standing where he was in snow that had long since soaked through the lower legs of his trousers and trickled from his wet hair into his collar. She kept walking, not stopping until she was approximately four feet away.

"I need to see Laurence," Ian said, being careful to hold his hands out where she could see them. Up close, he saw that Clara Beetleman was agitated. Her hands were steady on the gun, but under the thick hood her broad face was creased with tension.

"You can't see him. Not today."

"Is he in his studio?"

"He can't be disturbed."

"I think he knows where I can find my daughter. Do you know what's happened to Grace?"

"You need to leave."

"She's vanished, just like the others. Lily Slocum, Elizabeth Hirsh."

"I don't know anything about that."

"Kate's been looking for her. Have you seen Kate?"

She shook her head, but he saw the flicker in her eyes. Kate had been here, was here now.

"She came here looking for Grace, didn't she?"

"I don't know what you're talking about," she said, but she blinked rapidly, and he could see the small white cloud from each rapid breath.

"Are they in his studio? Is that where Laurence is

right now?" He looked back at the studio, then at her, and she was trembling now, her fat legs wobbling in the rubber boots.

"You can't go in there!"

"I need to find my daughter."

"You can shoot trespassers on your property! It's the law."

She knew. She knew all about what went on in the studio, Ian realized, and he felt sick as he thought of all the self-deception necessary to keep believing that her husband wasn't a monster. Of course Beetleman wouldn't have shared the details with her. He had probably lied to her about everything, and all these years she'd accepted the lies with the same sweet little smile so that she could go on being the contented housewife of a famous man.

Kate had been right along—Clara Beetleman *was* a Stepford wife, a fearful mouse of a woman who'd do anything, even kill, to protect the comfortable façade Beetleman had built.

"Okay," he said, "I'll leave." He walked slowly toward her, hands up in surrender.

Beetleman had vanished. Kate's eyes swept the torture chamber as Grace screamed, "Where is he?"

"I don't know!" Kate grabbed her daughter's hand, pulling her out and back toward the stairs. Suddenly, Beetleman stepped out from the darkness to block their path.

"You can't leave yet, the fun's just beginning." He'd taken off the mask and his hair stood out like a silver bush around a large face florid with excitement. He had the stun gun in his right hand and jabbed Kate with it imitating a zapping noise. She flinched and he laughed.

"You'll dance again to its tune, cunt, all in good time."

He grabbed her by the hair, and she cried out as he slammed her back against the concrete wall. "Like that, bitch?" he hissed. She stood by, helplessly, as he grabbed Grace's wrist and yanked her to him.

"I've got a necklace for you," he said to Grace, pulling a noose made of thick silver wire from his pocket. It's piano wire, so I know you'll like it." He grabbed Grace by the hair and forced the wire around her neck. It circled her throat, and he pulled it taut using a little wooden handle attached to one end. The band dug into her flesh turning the milky skin around it an ugly red.

Beetleman held Grace by the noose and pointed the stun gun at Kate. "One move from either of you and I'll give this a little jerk," he said, indicating the garrote. "The slave's neck will snap like a bean."

He forced his thick tongue into Grace's mouth, all the while watching Kate's reaction out of the corner of his eye. He sucked on Grace's tongue while she gagged and his eyes danced at Kate, delighting in her revulsion.

After a minute, he pulled away, casually wiping his mouth as Grace coughed and spit. He looked at Kate. "Strip."

Slowly, Kate began to undress, stripping off the remnants of her sweater. "Please let her go," she said.

"All of your clothes!" Beetleman barked.

She undid her bra and let it drop. As slowly as she could, she undid the button and unzipped her jeans. "You don't have to kill her. You have me. Let her go and I'll stay."

"Keep going," Beetleman urged. "Lovely, just lovely," he murmured as the jeans slipped off her hips and puddled on the floor. She stepped out of them on shaky legs.

"I think you're forgetting something," Beetleman

hissed and he pointed with the stun gun at her panties. She slid them off, her face flaming, and stood naked before him, covering her breasts with one arm and blocking her vagina with the other.

"Hands down!" Beetleman ordered, and she let her hands fall to her sides.

"Please let her go," she begged. "You can kill me. You don't need to kill her."

"How noble of you to sacrifice yourself," Beetleman said. "Really, it's quite charming, but when you beg for something, shouldn't you get down on your knees?"

Kate dropped to her knees, folding her hands in supplication. "Please, Dr. Beetleman." It was an effort to say his name with respect. "Please let Grace go. You don't need to kill her. She's nothing to you. I'm the one you want."

He looked at her for a long moment as if he were really considering what she said, but this tiniest bit of hope was immediately dashed as he laughed and said, "Don't be silly, Kate. Of course I have to kill both of you."

He jerked Grace a little closer by the wire handle. "Don't worry. You'll get to watch her die. The neck snaps with such a satisfying little pop. I think you'll like it." He nudged Kate with the toe of his boot. "Get up."

She thought of lunging forward and sinking her teeth into his balls, but even a small twist of his hand could slice Grace's neck. Her daughter's eyes were shut tight with fear and the artery in her neck pulsed against the wire. Kate struggled to her feet while Beetleman watched with a lascivious smile on his face.

"It's time for a little photography session," he said, running his eyes over Kate's body. Grace's eyes flew open and her nostrils flared. She whimpered, and he glanced at her. "Don't worry, slave. You're going first."

He turned his gaze back on Kate. "And after you're done, then I'll immortalize your mother."

Clara Beetleman walked backward, keeping the gun pointed at Ian. She couldn't move easily in the thick snow, and he shortened the distance between them while being careful not to overtake her.

When he judged the distance to be right, he widened his eyes and pointed behind her. "Laurence?"

"What?" Her gaze flicked away from him and he leapt for the gun, his hands closing over it as he knocked her back into the snow. She cried out as she landed, but she kept hold of the gun with one hand and he wrestled with her, trying to pry it loose from her strong grip.

He forced her arm down into the snow, pounding her hand against the snow-covered ground, but she kept her grip on the gun while she tore at him with her other hand, clawing at his face with strong fingers.

"Let go!" he shouted, his grip slipping as the snow melted from the heat in their hands. She answered by pushing up with a last-ditch surge of energy, forcing his arm back as she brought the gun around to shoot him. He rose on one leg, knocking her left hand from his face as he forced the gun hand back down, bringing his knee down against her upper arm.

She capitulated, he could feel the fight leave her, but as her hand fell back against the snow, she squeezed her finger around the trigger.

The single gunshot was like the crack of a whip. Beetleman's eyes flashed toward the stairs and Kate lunged for the stun gun, pressing it against his side and pushing the button. In the same moment she reached for the handle of the wire noose. A blue flash and Beetleman's large body jerked like a fish on a line. He screamed and his hands splayed wide with shock. The handle of the noose slipped from his fingers into Kate's while the stun gun clattered to the floor. He wavered for a moment before falling, his eyes gaping at her as he sank to the floor.

Kate carefully unwrapped the wire noose and lifted it free of her daughter's neck. "We need the key," Grace said, running her hands over the red band the wire had left around her throat. Kate knelt next to Beetleman and ran reluctant hands over his twitching body until she felt a sharp outline in his pants pocket.

"I've got it!" She yanked it from his clothing and thrust it into Grace's hand, and her daughter ran toward the stairs. As Kate stepped over the twitching body, a hand closed around her ankle.

The roar of the shot deafened Ian. He pulled the gun from Clara Beetleman's limp fingers and looked down at his leg. There was blood all over his pants, but he couldn't find the wound. He rose to his knees, the only noise the ringing in his ears, and saw blood pouring from a small hole in Clara's thigh. She was crying, but he couldn't hear it, large tears running down her fat cheeks as her wounded leg twitched against him.

He struggled up, panting, and left her stranded on her back like a great green bug as he ran across the snow toward the studio.

Kate screamed and Grace turned back. "Run!" Her mother yelled at her, trying to yank free of the viselike grip. "Don't stop! Run!"

Beetleman jerked her ankle again and she fell forward, landing hard on her palms and knees. Beetleman rolled a leg over hers. "You bitch," he said with slurred speech. He was much heavier than she was, and she couldn't shift his deadweight. He moved slowly on top of her, like a huge snake trying to suffocate its prey. She could smell his rank odor as he turned so that his face pressed close to hers, and she could see bloody veins running through the whites of his soulless gray eyes.

Her hands beat frantically at his sides and futilely at his body and then she scratched at the floor in search of escape. "I'm going to kill you," he said in a slow, slurred voice just as her hand closed on the stun gun.

"No, you're not." She pressed it against his neck this time and pushed the button. The blue crackle seemed brighter. She smelled burning hair. His body went rigid for a split second before convulsing like it had before, and she pushed the button again, and then a third time before rolling free of him as he flopped on the ground like a fish.

Grace tugged at the door, screaming, and Kate came behind her and wrapped her own hands around her daughter's. "It's okay," she said, pulling the door open. "I've got you."

Epilogue

Wineglasses held aloft to avoid being jostled by the crowd, Kate and Ian followed a circuitous route to the front of the gallery.

People touched Kate as she passed, clapping hands on her shoulder or patting her arm as they offered congratulations. She managed not to flinch. Jerry Virgoli waved from a corner, looking as pleased as if he'd done the paintings himself. "They're brilliant, absolutely brilliant," a voice said, and Abigail Thorney stepped in front of her, effectively blocking Kate's path.

"Thank you, Mrs. Thorney."

"I can't believe they were all inspired by that first photo."

"Yes."

Kate caught Ian's eye above the crowd, and gave him a helpless shrug as he tapped his watch. He rolled his eyes and made his way back through the crowd to her side. He patted the elderly woman on the shoulder.

"I'm sorry, Mrs. Thorney, but time waits for no

woman." He smiled as he said it and the woman looked flustered, letting them past.

Margaret caught them at the door, helping them get their coats and bussing Kate loudly on both cheeks. "Congratulations! I'm sorry you have to leave so early."

"I'm not," Kate said. "It's too crowded in here."

"There's no such thing as too crowded at an opening." Margaret's eyes sparkled. "I think the entire town is squeezed into this space!" Her laughter followed them out the door.

It was refreshingly cold after the crush in the gallery, and Kate lifted her head to the crisp December air as Ian unlocked the Toyota and held open her door.

She slid into her seat and exhaled as Ian started the car.

"Tired?" he said.

"A little. I think it went well."

Ian laughed. "I think 'well' is an understatement."

She smiled and looked out the window as the car sped along the rain-slicked streets and out onto the back roads toward the high school. It was hard to make this drive without remembering her frantic search for Grace. "It's a year next week."

"I know." Ian didn't have to ask what she was talking about.

"Has Grace mentioned it to you?"

"No. I wasn't going to bring it up unless she did."

"Good." Kate stared out the window, but she remembered the way Laurence Beetleman looked when he was wheeled into court for his arraignment, a drooling, whiskered old man who seemed shrunken inside the baggy pajamas. Being hit repeatedly with the stun gun had triggered a heart attack, which probably contributed to the stroke he suffered barely two weeks later.

He'd pled guilty to all the charges, answering the

judge's questions in low, slurred speech. The court-room had been packed with Wickfield residents eager to hear him admit his crimes. In all, he confessed to eleven murders. The body of Elizabeth Hirsh was pulled from the river two days after his arrest. He told investigators the location of Barbara Lutz's body and the bodies of his other victims, but despite a thorough search of Sterling Forest and Bear Mountain State Park, they still hadn't been found.

Thanks to the skills of a brilliant defense team, Lau-rence Beetleman was deemed unfit to serve his four con-secutive life terms in a regular prison and remanded instead to a high security psychiatric hospital. There'd been some outrage among townspeople over this, and a mixture of outrage and pity directed toward his wife, who was alternately referred to as his accomplice or his twelfth victim.

Kate hadn't cared about any of it. She'd been too ab-sorbed in the preservation of her own family to do more than register what happened to the Beetlemans. Relief came when she'd heard the house had been sold and the studio and its torture chamber razed. It would take longer to erase the memories, but time, and ther-apy, were helping with that.

"Ten minutes to spare," Ian said in a pleased voice as he pulled up in front of Wickfield High School.

Kate hurried in to get their programs as Ian parked the car. A student usher pointed them to the right aisle, and they slipped into their seats toward the front of the crowded auditorium just as the lights dimmed.

"I hope she wasn't searching for us," Kate whispered.

Ian harrumphed. "I'm sure she'll let us know if she was."

The curtains parted to reveal a gleaming black piano sitting at the center of the stage. Grace entered from the left and the audience clapped as she crossed the stage, wobbling slightly on the high heels she was un-used to, and took a seat on the bench.

She'd deigned to wear a dress, black of course, but velvet at least, and cut in a way that was high enough to please her parents while low enough to please Grace. She'd pulled her hair back, and Kate felt a pang of anx-iety at the solemn expression on her face.

The visible bruises had taken weeks to heal. The ones they couldn't see would take much longer. "Chil-dren are resilient," Dr. Schneider reassured them after every session. "Families are resilient."

Kate wanted to believe her. She'd suffered too much to believe that what didn't kill you made you stronger, but perhaps what it could do was make you more aware of what you had to lose and much more likely to hold tight to the things, and the people, that mattered.

The opening notes of Chopin's Prelude in E Minor filled the hall. Ian's hand slipped into Kate's, and she held on, smiling.

In a corner of the second floor common room at Ratston State Hospital was an upright piano. It had started its life with some dignity as an instructional in-strument for a local high school, but after years of being banged on by hundreds of tone-deaf students, it had been donated to the tone-deaf inmates of the high security psychiatric facility.

It had been purchased from the high school and pre-sented with great ceremony by the local women's club, who were thrilled at the thought of telling their friends that they'd been in a prison. They didn't know that the grinning inmate who'd come forward to haltingly play *Chopsticks* had sliced off the top of his wife's skull and scooped out the innards with a spoon, arguing in court that in plenty of countries monkey brains were considered a delicacy.

The twenty-five years since had not been kind to the Baldwin. Her cherrywood case, carefully constructed and polished to a high gloss almost a century before, was now scratched and battered. There were chips in the veneer along her sides, and many of the ivory keys had been torn, like a fingernails, from their beds. The lock that had held the lid was scratched and misshapen, and the key long since vanished into the gullet of an inmate nobody messed with who was known as Sawblade.

Laurence Beetleman shuffled into the room, his large shoulders hunched up by his ears as he passed the mismatched couches crowded with inmates braying along to the canned laughter from a sitcom playing on the TV bolted and caged on the wall.

"You going to play the piano, Larry?" an attendant named Tony asked, moving slowly beside Dr. Beetleman. He was a large man, the muscles in his biceps and quads straining the seams of his white uniform, his hairless forearms and bald head gleaming like polished obsidian. His gentle smile belied the fact that he could subdue even the largest inmate by catching his head in the crook of his arm and cracking his skull like a walnut.

The leonine old man didn't answer, but the shaggy head nodded and the side of his mouth that could still move curved upward in a faint smile, while a thin string of drool, glistening in the light, spilled from the slack corner.

The bench took his weight with the faintest of groans and he lifted the lid with a surprisingly delicate touch, his hands stretching toward the keys like a mother reaching out to her child.

The old piano seemed to know that someone with talent was playing her, for she mellowed under his touch and a haunting melody filled the air.

"What's that you're playing, Larry?" Tony asked, dropping into a chair beside him to listen.

"Chopin. Prelude in E Minor." Beetleman spoke clearly, only the end of some words cut off. He worked with a speech therapist sent by the county every week.

He gazed out the tall window as he played, seeing past the steel mesh and the heavy bars behind it and looking over the farm fields that stretched beyond the guard towers and into the deep forest that rose behind them.

One high note, one low, now he was in the passage marked legato and the notes streamed together, became a river, the water running black and wild below him. The body he carried was so delightfully cold and white as he laid it like a boat in the water and watched the current carry it downstream.

"Shut up, Larry!" A deep voice bellowed and Beetleman's hand slipped and hit a false note.

"Yeah, you dumb fuck, don't you see we're trying to watch TV?"

The spell was broken. Beetleman opened his eyes, but Tony patted his arm. "Don't pay no attention to them, Larry," he said, his voice as calm and melodious as the music. "They're just ignorant fools." He got up from the chair and walked slowly toward the group on the couches. "Ignorant fools," he repeated, his voice louder, his arms folded menacingly across his broad chest.

A skinny ferret of a man giggled in a voice as high-pitched as a girl's and aimed a cross made from two nicotine stained fingers at Tony. "Stay away, Satan!"

He howled along with the other inmates as Tony

turned down the volume on the TV. "You all shut up now so Larry can play the piano," Tony said. "You're getting this little dose of high culture courtesy of the state."

One inmate muttered about where he'd like to stick high culture, but Tony ignored it, moving slowly back to the piano. Beetleman was standing up, hands working in the pockets of his pants, looking ready to shuffle away. Tony put a large hand on his shoulder and pushed him gently back on the bench. "You go ahead and play now."

The large hands moved over the keys again, and Tony sat back down to listen. So beautiful that Chopin. He'd never heard of it before; he'd have to look it up. A skipped note jarred him. A minute later it happened again. Tony looked over at the piano and saw that one of the keys made no sound when it was struck.

Tony stood up. "Hold on a minute, Larry, I think something's gumming up the works." He lifted the lid and looked inside.

"That's funny," he muttered, and Dr. Beetleman's mouth crooked obligingly. "I think a wire's missing."